THE FIRES OF HEPHAESTUS

THE STARSEA CYCLE BOOK SIX

KYLE WEST

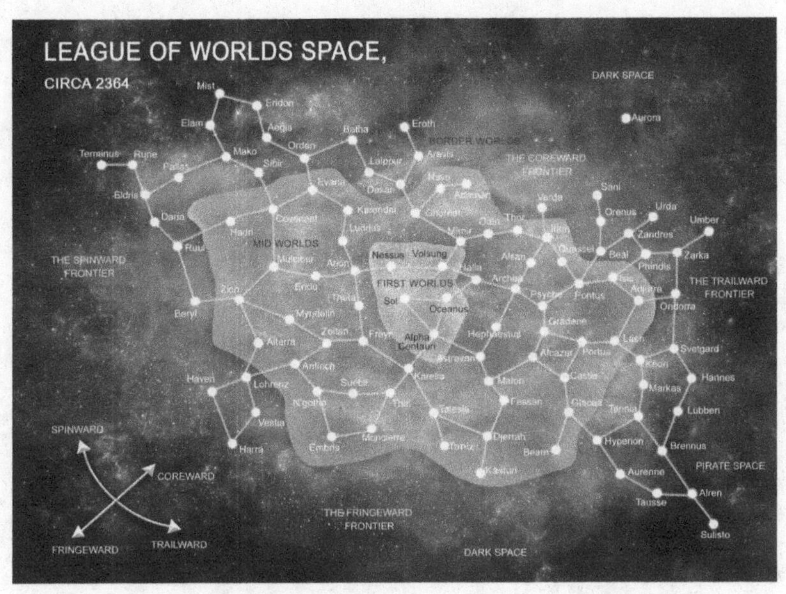

LEAGUE OF WORLDS SPACE,
CIRCA 2364
DARK SPACE
Aurora
Mist
Eridan
Elam
Aegis
Eroth
Batha
BORDER WORLDS
Arevis
THE COREWARD
FRONTIER
Terminus
Rune
Mako
Orden
Lalppur
Sibir
Pallas
Havo
Sani
Evaria
Delan
Orenus
Urda
Eldris
Varda
Umber
Daria
Madri
Covenant
Kavondal
Luddus
Ghorhal
Thor
Oslo
Ilin
Zandres
Ruu
MID WORLDS
Alsan
Quassel
Beal
Zarka
THE SPINWARD
FRONTIER
Mulcibur
Aron
Nessus
Volsung
Mirir
Phindis
Zion
Endu
FIRST WORLDS
Halla
Archia
Isis
THE TRAILWARD
FRONTIER
Beryl
Theta
Sol
Psyche
Pontus
Adjarra
Onboma
Myndelin
Oceanus
Gradene
Zeiten
Alterra
Frayn
Alpha
Centauri
Hephaestus
Alcazur
Portus
Lach
Svetgard
Antioch
Astrevan
Malon
Castia
Keon
Hannes
Haven
Lohrenz
Sueta
Karelia
Markas
N'gonia
Thir
Gisora
Tennal
Lubben
Vestia
Harra
Embria
Monserre
Talesia
Fessan
Djemah
Beam
Hyperion
Brennua
Tanizi
Kasturi
Aurenne
PIRATE SPACE
SPINWARD
Alren
Tausse
COREWARD
THE FRINGEWARD
FRONTIER
Sulisto
FRINGEWARD
TRAILWARD
DARK SPACE

ON THE BRIDGE OF *ETHEREAL*, *Wayfinder's* signal faded from the sensor screen, never to return.

"That's it," Khairu said. "Gone."

Lucian sipped his coffee, watching the empty display. "Well, we knew it would happen at some point."

"We should let the others know. It's time for Plan B."

It had been almost a week since their escape from Nai Elyn, and they'd spent all that time burning toward the Dark Gate, trying in vain to keep up with the faster ship. At least it gave them some much needed time for rest. After Lucian's battle with Xara Mallis, it seemed he could never get enough sleep.

Only now did he feel recovered. And with that, he knew it was time to focus once again on the mission. There were two other Orbs out there, waiting to be found, besides the ones Xara held. And it was up to him, and his crew, to find them.

"We were supposed to meet soon, anyway." Lucian checked his slate. "In a few minutes, in fact. I'm sure they're already gathering."

"Let's go, then."

They headed for the conference room, not far down the main corridor. Within a room on his left, Lucian thought he saw a moving shadow in his peripheral vison. But when he turned to look, nothing was there, only some control panels and an empty chair.

He shook his head and ducked into the conference room on his right.

Over the next few minutes, everyone gathered. Linus and Plato were first to arrive. Though it was early afternoon by now, Linus looked as if he'd just woken up while Plato was sipping from a cup of hot tea. Fergus came in with an instameal that somewhat resembled fettucine alfredo, while Serah and Emma took seats next to each other, each of them absorbed by some sort of game on their slates.

Lucian left them to their own devices for the moment, wondering how best to broach the subject. Telling them Vera and Xara had escaped was easy enough. But sharing the idea he'd been mulling over was another proposition entirely. With the Lost Aspect, he held a power he could have scarcely dreamed of before. A power that would allow him to warp himself, and likely anything around him—perhaps even a spaceship—at a great distance. Silumko had said that would be possible, and in the end, with Xara and Vera gone, it would be necessary. Skipping light-years at a stretch was a potential advantage he couldn't let go to waste.

He cleared his throat, making everyone look up. While Emma set down her slate and watched him attentively, Serah focused even more intensely on her game. She huffed, obviously losing, before swiping the slate off almost violently.

"Sorry. I'm present now."

"You *sure* you don't want to play another round?" Fergus asked sarcastically as he slurped up a particularly long noodle.

"This is Medieval Farming Simulator 7, Fergie. There *are* no rounds, and no second chances. If the turnip crop fails, I'm going to have a lot of disgruntled peasants on my hands, and maybe even lose my queendom. The stakes *literally* couldn't be higher."

Fergus scoffed. "I don't understand the things you waste your time with."

"It's *not* a waste of time," Serah said. "What else am I supposed to do on these long and dreadfully boring trips?"

"Train."

"Well, some of us need a break. I'd go crazy if I trained as much as you and Khairu. Linus has his movies, Plato has his plants and books, and I need my games. And for that matter, maybe even therapy after everything we've gone through."

"In all those games you downloaded on Irion," Plato said, "did one of them happen to be a therapy sim?"

Serah hung her head glumly. "No..."

"Anyway," Lucian said, "I guess you guys probably know why I've called you here. *Wayfinder* has disappeared from our scopes, and we probably have no way of catching it. We need a new approach."

"What do you mean?" Linus asked. "I thought the plan was to chase them to the ends of the galaxy, or something like that."

"In time, maybe, but it might be better to go after the other Orbs first. The ones Xara hasn't found."

"And how can we do that when they're faster than us?" Plato asked.

"That's the thing. I was planning to use the Orb of Space-Time. The Emissary said it was possible to move entire ships with this thing. So, that's our one shot, as I see it."

Everyone just stared at him dumbly. Up to this point, Lucian hadn't hinted this was possible with any of the crew, with the exception of Serah. For her part, she acted as surprised as the rest.

Fergus was the first to speak. "Are you out of your mind? That could rip us all to bloody bits!"

Serah chuckled. "Isn't that a little dramatic?"

"I don't see what's so funny about it. Is it really worth the risk? This isn't just our lives, but every life in the galaxy. We should never, ever forget that."

His somber tone made everyone go quiet. Khairu and Emma were nodding approvingly. Fergus would have fit like a glove at the Volsung Academy.

Serah cleared her throat. "Well, *I* for one won't be spending months and months sitting on this ship when we can just teleport there in one day."

"Well, it doesn't work like that," Lucian said. "I can only warp us somewhere I have a strong memory of. I'm not sure what else goes into it, but memory is an essential component. At least, that's how I found my way back here. I imagined my cabin on this ship, and here I was. After streaming from the Orb of Space-Time, of course. And apparently, the more Orbs I hold, the more powerful the Orb of Space-Time becomes."

"How far do you think you can warp this ship?" Emma asked. "I mean, could you warp us all the way to Archea, if you have a strong enough memory of it? I mean, we were there before, and it's just one Gate away from Hephaestus. We'd have a considerable head start on Xara."

"That's terribly far," Fergus said. "I can understand one person warping across a few thousand kilometers, like what Lucian did when he came back to this ship. But you're talking about an entire ship, its crew, across tens of light-years. It's the difference between a drop of water and an entire ocean."

"Then again," Plato said, "This Silumko fellow seemed to think it was possible. Perhaps there's a critical mass of magic that can be gathered, where if you can stream enough of it, distances simply don't matter anymore." Everyone looked at him. "I mean, if we're talking about space-time, all Lucian would really be doing is folding reality to connect two points. What's the difference between a few meters or a thousand light-years? Both are about the same size when you consider the vast scale of the cosmos."

"All theory," Fergus said. "And you would trust this Silumko? He's a *Swarmer*, for crying out loud. An *Alkasen*."

"And he wants to see me succeed," Lucian said. "From his perspective, I'm the good guy, right? Returning the Orbs to their rightful owners and all."

"Yes," Linus said. "You're a glorified dog playing fetch for the gods."

"Oof," Serah said. "That's harsh."

"No offense meant, Lucian," Linus went on, "but are these Emissaries really the good guys here? They are sort of pulverizing humanity into oblivion right now. And if they aren't the good guys, then who is?"

"Hmm," Plato said. "You're wondering if *we're* the baddies?"

"Not for the first time, mind you. I mean, even if we wanted to take these Orbs and fight the Swarmers, like Xara and Vera want, that would just cause Lucian to mind-meld with this Ancient One. And that sounds like bad news, too. Is there some middle ground, or even some faraway ground that no one has trodden before?"

"I don't think that's proper grammar," Serah said.

"You *dare* question my grammar?"

"Let's get back on track," Emma said. "It seems all this space travel has made some of us . . . loopy."

"That is putting it far too kindly," Fergus said.

"Archea is close to Hephaestus. Just one Gate away. Assuming Lucian can warp the ship there, it certainly makes things easier."

"That's the idea," Lucian said. "My plan was to make a short warp first, to figure out how the process works. Maybe to the Aurora System. Depending on how that goes, I can try a bigger jump next time, maybe to Varda. From there, it's just a few more Gates until Archea itself. I'm not sure how long it'll take the Orb to recharge once being used. We're learning as we go."

"I agree that it's better to test things out," Fergus said. "However, we shouldn't risk everyone on the ship to do so."

"What do you suggest, then?" Emma asked. "We're far from any habitable world, unless you want to go back to Nai Elyn or Nai Shairen. And if Lucian were to test the ship on his own, how would that help us if things went wrong? We'd just be stranded."

Fergus didn't have an answer for that. "Just seems foolhardy to me."

"Emma is right," Khairu said. "We don't have a choice. Nor do we have time to be testing things out like that. *Wayfinder* is faster than us by a great deal. Over the span of star systems, they will be weeks ahead of us getting to Hephaestus, especially if Xara uses the Orb of Atomicism to make fuel for the ship. In theory, they could get their ship going at speeds that should be impossible. That might even be why we fell behind so decisively. During the Mage War, the mages' ships could fly faster and farther than anything the League could put out for this reason. Despite lack of numbers, it almost won them the war. If we don't try this warping thing out, by the time we get back to the League, it might already be too late."

"An excellent point," Plato said. "Makes you wonder if it might be better to use that Orb to go somewhere far, far away from all the action."

"We're not running," Lucian said. "If we did that, the Swarmers would come after us, anyway."

"Actually, Linus raised a good point about them a while back," Emma said. "I know it's a bit simplistic to see things in terms of good and evil, but it seems crazy to think they're the good guys. I'm sure from their perspective, they are."

Khairu shifted in her seat. "From what Lucian has told us, it doesn't seem the Swarmers are actually a *species*, per se.

Silumko mentioned he was of the Preserved, and was once an Ancient. But now, he serves a new master. I'm not sure how it works, but I wouldn't be surprised if it's some form of Psionic control."

"How is he not dead, then?" Plato asked. "I thought the Ancients died out hundreds of thousands of years ago."

"Maybe he's a zombie," Serah said. "A *space* zombie."

Just about everyone rolled their eyes at that one.

"He definitely wasn't a zombie," Lucian said. "But I think Khairu is on the right track. Of course, it's impossible to say. He's the only Swarmer I've seen. And who knows if it's a *he*."

"That begs the question," Emma said. "If Silumko is just a mind-controlled Ancient, could the Swarmers do the same thing to anything else, too?"

That was an uncomfortable thought. The implications were almost too horrifying to consider.

"I *refuse* to believe that," Serah said. "What do they care that we can use magic, anyway? Like it's *our* species' fault that Arian stumbled upon that rotting Orb!"

"Still, the Orbs don't belong here," Emma said. "That fact is immutable. They came from the Light Realm, but they are now in our reality. Nothing will be set to rights if we don't return them to the Heart of Creation. So, if that is our goal, then it makes the most sense to go after the Orb of Thermalism next. According to that vision Lucian had on Psyche, it's on Hephaestus."

Linus cleared his throat. "Well, *technically*, the Orbs of Gravitonics and Atomicism are closest, since Xara is only a few days ahead of us. Since we have the power to warp around willy nilly, why don't we warp right on top of them and blast them to smithereens?"

Serah sighed. "You don't listen, do you? Lucian can't just home in on a particular person or location. It has to be some-place he has a strong memory of. The best we can do is warp to a location they will pass, but how do we know when and where that will happen? Besides, it still requires us having to catch them and launch a torpedo or two. Which, by the way, we don't have."

"Shooting at them would be disastrous, anyway," Khairu said. "Even if we scored a hit, it could blast the Orbs in random directions in space. It would be like trying to find a needle in a haystack."

"*Multiple* needles," Emma said.

"I think it's best to ignore them for now," Lucian said. "If Xara thinks she's still the Chosen, then she'll want to find me, anyway. She's going to have the same idea as us. Find those other Orbs. She doesn't know what we're capable of, so she's going to head straight for Hephaestus. Who knows how long it'll take her to get there, but if Khairu is right, she can get there faster than we think, especially if she makes her own fuel. If I had a way to attack her and get the Orbs, I'd do it in a heartbeat. But chasing them down is impossible. I'd rather grab the Orb of Thermalism, and the Orb of Dynamism, too, that way victory is a sure bet when I face her again."

"You sound confident there," Plato said.

"Why wouldn't I be? I bested Xara with two Orbs, and I'm sure I could do it with six."

At this, Emma's face paled a bit. She still had the Orb of Radiance, and as of yet, Lucian hadn't asked for it back. But due to the way the Orb of Space-Time worked, he'd need all the Orbs. Hopefully asking for it back wasn't going to cause any issues. In the back of his mind, he would always remember what the Oracle, Rhana, had told him on Volsung. Among the Ancients, friends and family had killed each other over a single Orb.

Lucian pushed that thought from his mind. "This is the plan. I'm going to warp this ship to Aurora. While that's just a Gate away from here, it's light-years farther than I've ever warped myself, *and* I'm going to be moving a lot more mass. But since the Emissary said it was possible, I have to believe it is, too."

"He could just be trying to trick you into killing yourself," Linus said. "And thereby, all of us with you."

"That doesn't make sense," Khairu said. "If he wanted to kill Lucian, he would have done it already. Maybe you're just afraid?"

Linus chuckled. "Of *course* I am. I'm sane. Unlike everyone else at this table."

Serah had a laugh at that. "Aren't you the mayor of the Isle of Madness?"

"Yeah. That should tell you something!"

Khairu opened her mouth to speak, but Lucian broke in. "This is what we're doing, end of story. I wasn't going to put it up to a democratic vote. It's just me having the courtesy to tell you how it's going to be. Khairu is right. We don't have time to do much experimentation. We had our first victory in a long time on Nai Elyn, and I won't lose momentum."

"Well," Fergus said, "at least you're admitting your actions could kill us. While I follow you, Lucian, I don't appreciate not having a voice."

Serah's face became indignant. "You've followed Lucian from danger into danger, and somehow, *this* is a bridge too far?"

"Fighting is one thing. At least with an enemy, I can look him in the eyes. This is quite another. What if the ship moves, but all of us stay in the same place? Cold, hard vacuum is a terrible way to go."

"Fergus, I like you, but sometimes you make no rotting sense."

Linus looked from one of them to the other. At last, he breathed a heavy sigh. "I don't like it, but Lucian is the boss. He got me off that rotting island. Now, I can watch movies, play video games, and eat to my heart's content, which is far more preferable. I don't think that debt is due yet, so I have to go with him. Besides, I don't know what everyone is even talking about half the time, so who am I to say he's wrong?"

"Just *half* the time?" Plato asked.

Linus stuck out his tongue.

Emma was staring out the viewport, her expression troubled, but she said nothing. Lucian wondered if she knew what he was going to ask her. Better to do it away from the others.

But she surprised him by bringing it up herself. "I suppose you're going to want your Orb back? You mentioned that each Orb you hold makes the Orb of Space-Time more powerful. You're going to need all the power you can get."

"Unfortunately, I can't risk *not* having it."

She hesitated a moment, then forced a nod. "I understand. Just . . . let me know when you're ready and I can give it back."

"You sound sad about that," Linus said.

"Leave her alone, Linus."

"Just observing."

Lucian shook his head. After months sharing the same vessel, it was hard to keep people from each other's throats sometimes.

"So, when will this monstrosity happen?" Fergus asked, as if their collective suicide was about to take place.

"Soon," Lucian said. "Maybe we can take another day to relax."

"And how would we prepare?" Linus asked.

"I don't know. Maybe you'll want to put on a spacesuit or something, if you believe Fergus's theory is true about the ship moving, but not us."

"It *could* happen," he said, somewhat annoyed.

Serah smiled. "Maybe you have a fear of your head exploding like an overinflated pumpkin."

"Your head doesn't explode in outer space," Fergus said.

"That's only a myth. And for that matter, pumpkins don't explode, either."

"Whatever. You know what I mean."

"Meeting adjourned," Lucian said. "Try to get some rest. It's pretty obvious that you guys are still stressed out."

"I wonder why *that* might be," Plato said sardonically.

Lucian didn't rise to the bait. He remained standing until everyone had vacated the room but him and Serah.

"Tough crowd, huh?" she asked.

"Nothing I'm not used to."

"They're still shaken up. It's a miracle any of us survived. But hey, we bested Xara Mallis. Not just anyone can say that."

Lucian laughed. "It's something."

She grabbed him by the arm. "Come on. I want to talk to you."

She led him out of the conference room and toward their cabin. Only when the door was closed did she speak again.

"Do you think Emma was acting a bit . . . strange?"

"Strange, how?"

"You didn't notice her face when you mentioned giving the Orb back?"

"What about her face?"

"Well, for one, she definitely doesn't want to give the Orb back."

"She agreed to do it. So does it matter?"

Serah just smiled like a teacher explaining a simple concept to a student slow on the uptake. "Lucian, she doesn't want to give that Orb back. Streaming is addictive, as we all know. Streaming a lot of magic is even more addicting. Now that she's had a taste of power, she likes it, whatever she says about walking the Path of Balance. Don't you remember what the Oracle of Binding said?"

Lucian felt himself go cold. "Of course I do. But Emma's my friend. She wouldn't betray me like that."

"I wouldn't think so, either. Then again, there was the part about friends and family betraying the Vigilants. All for the chance to hold an Orb. You should remember that."

"I *have*. You're just assuming the worst."

"I saw what I saw. Emma's a good person, but in the end, she's human. And humans are nothing more than flesh and blood with impulses, good and bad. Take that for what it's worth. Hopefully, you take it, because I want you very much alive for my own selfish reasons."

"That's a relief."

She gave him a light push toward the bed. In the low gravity, it was enough to send him sprawling. Before he could move, she was on top of him. He could easily remove her if he so chose, but having her on top of him was pleasant enough.

Her face remained serious above his. "Just listen, all right? I might be wrong, but you know I have your best interests at heart. You need to be careful about handing off your Orbs to a person, no matter how much you trust them. You're the Chosen, and you earned them. The worst thing that can happen is losing a friend over something like this. People change, Lucian. I know from experience."

Lucian didn't have to pry to know what she meant. She'd grown up in Kiro Village, but even her own father had exiled her when it became clear she was fraying. And just *thinking* of that made him look at her arm. Was it his imagination, or had her wound grown even *larger* since the confrontation on Nai Elyn?

He forced his eyes away. He didn't want to think about it. Instead, he kissed her, and for the moment, they focused on things that weren't Orbs, Swarmers, or the impending death of humanity.

2

THE NEXT MORNING, Emma was conspicuously absent from the crew breakfast. Lucian went to check the bridge, to find that she wasn't with Khairu, who usually ate alone. It would be better to get this over with as soon as possible. Asking for the Orb of Radiance wouldn't get any easier.

He knocked on Emma's door, but didn't get an answer. Pressing the entry button revealed an empty cabin, with nothing out of place. He checked the engine room, also finding it empty. Once he'd checked every room on the main deck, he went down to the cargo hold, the only place she could be.

He opened the hatch in the main entry area, and climbed down a steep set of stairs. The air was colder down here, the ship's ventilation struggling to warm the larger space. The supply crates were fewer since their departure from Irion, allowing him to quickly spy Emma sitting in the far corner, on top of a crate, just steps from the massive loading door. Lucian had the crazy thought she might try to *open* it, especially since the terminal was so close. Not that it was possible to open it while the ship was out in space, but Lucian wondered. She *had* used the Orb of Radiance to upload the ship's orbital path to the Dark Gate, bypassing the ship's quantum encryption.

He still remembered what she'd said after performing that action: *With this, I can do anything.*

"Emma? You okay?"

She gave a small jump before turning to face him. "Lucian. You scared me."

He took up a seat on the crate across from her. "Sorry. I've been looking for you. You weren't at breakfast this morning."

"Yeah. I know. Just wanted some time to think, I guess." She looked down and away. "I suppose you came here for the Orb, right?"

"We can talk about that later. Are you okay?"

"Yeah, I'm fine."

"Well, I'm not sure what this is, but it doesn't seem fine."

She looked down at her hands. "Sorry. I know it might seem like I'm hedging. Well, I probably am. I know I need to give it back to you, especially after everything you've said. It's just . . . harder than I expected."

"Why's that?"

Her cheeks colored a bit. "Well, to be honest . . . I *like* having the Orb. It's a bit uncomfortable to say that, but there it is. I know it's selfish, and I know it's not mine by right. Still, it doesn't change how I feel. Anyway, I was hoping I could work through my thoughts."

"I understand. It wasn't my intent to pressure you."

"I know. It's just . . . I never expected it to make me feel like this."

"Like what?"

"So . . . *powerful*. With the Orb, I can draw as much ether as I want and nothing bad will happen."

Lucian gave a bitter laugh. "Trust me, these things cause more problems than they solve. It seems every time I get an

Orb, my problems multiply. If I could have it any other way, I would."

Emma smiled. "I guess I haven't thought about it like that." She hesitated a moment, seeming to consider her next words carefully. "Well, things haven't been easy since we left Volsung. Not that they were ever easy to begin with. Maybe I've gotten a taste for how sheltered I've been. This whole Path of Balance thing they teach seems like a joke, now. I don't know if I can ever reintegrate with Academy life after everything I've been through. And when you're feeling down, I guess it's natural to cling to anything that makes you feel good, even if it isn't good for you, in the end."

"It's definitely not easy."

"That's what makes giving up the Orb hard. It's been a bright spot, something to help me cope with reality. To think it might go away . . ."

"I just need it to warp the ship. I'm not sure how long that'll take, but I have no problem handing it back once I'm through with it."

"No, I wouldn't ask that of you. You're the Chosen, not me. Just being without it . . . scares me a little." She looked up at him. "I mean, don't you feel the same way? Anytime you push them out of your Focus, don't you feel any reticence?"

Lucian thought about it for a moment. He realized that yes; it *was* a hard thing to do. The longest he'd been without the Orbs was during Vera's training. She wanted him to know what it was like to stream without them. But he always knew he'd get them back in the end. The Orb of Radiance had been easier to release, probably because he hadn't held it for long, so he didn't have the chance to get attached. By now, Emma had held it for about two weeks. Enough time, perhaps, to rely on it.

Lucian didn't know what the effects of losing an Orb could be. It could prove dire, for all he knew. Even fatal.

"The truth is, I'm not sure what's going to happen. I know

for me, I've only been without them for a short time, and I knew I was getting them back. Even so, it wasn't easy."

"That's what scares me. We know ether is addictive. How much more so when it's unadulterated?"

That thought had crossed Lucian's mind before. Ether was so addicting that many mages willingly streamed beyond their capabilities by overdrawing. While overdrawing itself was not the cause of the fraying, it accelerated it. But even if you removed the poisonous aspect of ether, the euphoric effect remained. Even Lucian had to temper his temptation to stream, but he could only hold out for so long before he wanted to stream magic.

"I could try to make the warp without the Orb of Radiance, but I think it's going to be impossible without it."

When Emma's expression suddenly grew angry, all Lucian could do was gape at the sudden change.

"Why don't you just take it, then? That's *clearly* what you want. Why are we even having this conversation? We both know how it ends." Her eyes widened, as if suddenly cognizant of her outburst. She hung her head. "I'm . . . sorry. I'm afraid it's too late to stop what it's doing to me . . ."

"It's not, Emma."

"How do you know that?"

"I guess I really don't. I was just trying to make you feel better."

She suddenly stood, a determined expression on her face. "I . . . need to let it go. Just . . . make it fast, okay?"

It was hard to look at her and not feel terrible. He couldn't help but feel that this was his fault. Giving her the Orb had been his idea, after all. She had found the Dark Gate easily enough, but maybe he could have done the same thing. He'd seen it for a moment after obtaining the Orb for the first time.

"I'm sorry for my part in this. If there's any way I could make it easier, I would."

"How do I give it up?"

"Reach for your Focus and will it into your hands. That's how I do it, anyway."

Emma's eyes seemed distant. Lucian wasn't sure if she had even heard him.

He was about to ask if she'd heard him when she stood, faced him, and thrust out her hands.

Nothing happened at first. But after a moment, green lines traced along her forearms, collecting and coalescing in her hands. The lines swirled until they formed the shape of the Orb of Radiance, which shone like a miniature green star. It bathed the entire cargo hold in its emerald light.

Emma gasped, almost collapsing with the effort. Lucian steadied her as she took a seat, the Orb still cupped in her hands.

"Take it. Before I do something stupid."

Lucian took the Orb, and at once absorbed it. Within seconds, it was gone, flowing along his arms and toward his heart.

Half a minute later, there was no more light. Lucian could feel the Orb thrumming in his Focus, along with a fresh infusion of power. It seemed as if he could move worlds, if he willed it. In contrast, Emma's shoulders sagged dejectedly, as if her soul had been sucked out. Lucian hated to see her like that.

But contrary to her posture, she forced a smile. "Well, how does it feel?"

Lucian couldn't bring himself to lie. "Like I could move the galaxy if I wanted."

"Try to focus on moving this ship first."

Lucian realized that was what he needed to do. "Tell the others we're about to get moving. Don't let anyone in here. I don't know if what I'm doing is dangerous, but it would be safer to act like it is."

"I'll let them know. Be careful, Lucian."

Without another word, she walked out, leaving him alone in the cargo hold.

Still bursting with restrained energy, he sat on the deck and assumed his Focus, clearing his mind of all distractions. That was second-nature by this point. He was surprised at how fast the ether built up, as if the Orbs expected his need. It was too late to hold back now.

Even as magic poured through his Orbs, he directed it toward the center of his Focus, where the Orb of Space-Time stood as the centerpiece. The Orb of Space-Time absorbed three raging rivers of ether, compressing it into a single point of potential. This, Lucian realized, was the power of the Orb. It could contain seemingly *any* amount of magic, allowing for possibilities that should have been unachievable.

What those things were, Lucian couldn't guess. He was experimenting not only with his life, but with the lives of his friends. But if there were any other path, he would have taken it.

With the Orb of Space-Time, it was as if his ether were disappearing into a black hole, adding weight and mass to his Focus. Lucian reveled in the power; it had been too long since he'd felt it. It was like a raging sun about to go supernova, and even as it raged, *more* ether poured into the Orb, making it thrum with potential. Not only from his Orbs, but the other Aspects as well. Their streams were a trickle compared to the torrents flowing from the Orbs, but they added their power all the same, unable to resist the beckoning of the Orb of Space-Time.

At last he stood, clenching his fists and spreading his arms wide. With that action, he streamed a massive Radiant shell around the ship. Through it, he could register the light of ten thousand stars, could find the single point to warp the ship toward. From the Orb of Psionics, he could see possibilities, strange pasts and futures counter to all reason and logic. His own face, older and battle-scarred. His mother, looking into his eyes with surprise, as alive and real as anyone he ever knew. An angular, black reptilian head with fiery red eyes wreathed in a halo of flame . . .

He nearly broke off the stream in shock. Those baleful eyes stared into him, seeming to know him to the core. To challenge and taunt him.

What *was* this?

The Ancient One's voice entered his mind. *Your doom, if you continue to stubbornly refuse my help.*

Lucian formed a Psionic shield around his mind, allowing only his magic within. At once, the vision dissipated, returning him to the cargo hold, where he had yet to stream the ship to the Aurora System. He had enough magic now. All he needed was a memory to attach it to.

But try as he might, he could not imagine Aurora. He could only think of his first sight of Archea. Its surface was arid, more land than ocean, and the massive Archea Station orbited just above its gentle curve. He'd been watching its approach with Serah that day. Serah, who for the first time, was going to step onto a space station, a place other than the world of her birth. She'd been so excited, then. Even he was ready to see it, after spending so long on Psyche.

The vision of the world grew in his mind. It grew so much that it was almost *real*. There was no stopping it. A connection fired between memory and reality. Either the ship would complete the warp, or it wouldn't.

Lucian was yanked forward, as if the gravity were suddenly coming from a different direction. He was streaming all Seven Aspects now, and all those streams were going every which way. He directed them all toward the Orb of Space-Time, and as each stream fed it, reality began to stabilize.

With a final roar of magic, utter silence and darkness followed.

3

WHEN LUCIAN AWOKE, he was in the medical pod. The outcome wasn't exactly what he'd hoped for. Despite his muddled state, he shifted his body and tapped on the interior screen. The machine seemed to take this as a sign that he was alive, because the door hissed open. Various IV's and tubes he hadn't even noticed automatically disengaged from his body, including a catheter. It didn't hurt nearly as much as it should have. If *that* had been inserted, he must have been in here a long time. The stiffness of his muscles was a testament to that.

The lights were red, signifying night hours aboard the ship. He'd begun the stream in the morning, so he must've been in here a long time.

The lights went full spectrum, momentarily blinding Lucian. He stumbled out of the pod and almost made it to the door when it opened to reveal Serah standing there in her space jumpsuit, her blonde hair in disarray.

"Lucian! Rotting hell, you're alive!"

She threw herself on him, as if he had been on the brink of death. For all he knew, he *had* been.

"I'm fine. What the hell is going on?"

"Everything's gone to shit, and *you* need to fix it!"

At that moment, Fergus barged into the clinic. "You're alive? Great. We're in a horrible situation, and I'm not sure we can get out of it."

"What's going on?"

"Pirates. I don't know where they came from, but they're assaulting Archea Station. And a good amount of them are chasing *us*."

"So the warp worked, then? We're in the Archea System?"

"Oh, it worked all right. You got knocked out, so Khairu took charge and put us on a course to Archea Station to resupply. But when we got broadcasts of an all-out siege by pirates, Khairu put us on a course to the outer part of the star system. There must be a hundred Pirate vessels docked up on the station, if not more. Security forces have crumbled entirely. And now, a contingent of those pirate vessels is after *us*."

"What? Why?"

"My guess is they recognize our ship. Remember those pirates in the Pontus System? They were Golden Armada, and so are the ones attacking Archea Station."

"Let's get to the bridge and figure this out," Lucian said, hardly able to believe that this was happening. As they ran up the central corridor, he asked, "How long was I out?"

"You were down in the cargo hold for about fourteen hours," Serah said. "We kept trying to get in, but no one could open the door. I guess you were keeping it closed with your magic. Which pissed me off a great deal, I might add."

"Fourteen *hours*?"

"Captain Chosen One!" Linus bellowed from the direction of the cabins. "By the gods, you're alive!"

Lucian could only manage an acknowledging wave before entering the bridge, revealing Khairu leaning intently over the terminal readout.

"What've we got?" Lucian asked.

She looked him up and down for a moment, electing to focus on business rather than his general state. "Well, at least twenty bogeys on our scopes, all burning full from the direction of the station. Right now, I have us on a course to Argus."

"What's that?"

"Next planet out. A gas giant with a sizeable ring system. Thought we might hide in there. Of course, if they don't torpedo us first. Always a possibility. They're still too far to get a lock on us, though they can pick up our thermal signature easily."

At that moment, Linus and Plato joined them on the bridge.

"Lucian can warp us again," Linus said. "That was one hell of a trip!"

Lucian assumed his Focus, but his concentration immediately collapsed when he tried to reach for the Orb of Space-Time. It was like trying to grab empty air.

"No, I can't. After what I just did, it's going to be a while before we can go anywhere."

"How long's a while?" Khairu asked.

Lucian shrugged. "A while."

Plato crossed his arms. "You seem *far* too nonchalant about this. We're all going to die here!"

"Well, we've got some speed on these ships from the looks of it, but that doesn't guarantee we won't be intercepted farther out," Khairu said. "We can hide out in Argus's rings. We'll get there before them, but they'll have a lock on our drive signature the entire time. We'll have to burn slow through the rings, emit little heat. And hope the ice covers our tracks."

"How likely is this to work?" Fergus asked.

"It's the best I've got."

"That's . . . reassuring."

Emma was the last to slip onto the bridge. She didn't say a

word, and her face was pale and her cheeks hollow, as if she had a nasty case of the flu.

"Let's do that, then," Lucian said.

"Should be there in six hours," Khairu said. She looked at Lucian. "How long before you're ready to warp again?"

"I don't know. Probably more than six hours."

"This is *crazy*," Linus said. "Crazy!"

Lucian had the feeling that things were only going to get crazier.

TWO HOURS LATER, Argus and its broad band of sideways rings were easy to pick out in the forward viewport. The planet was small at first, hardly more than a bright star in the sky. But as the hours passed, it grew with surprising speed, dominating the viewscreen. The scanner showed the pirate vessels behind them keeping pace. Despite its speed, *Ethereal* could not out-fly them, especially considering a potential course correction to the nearest Gate, which led into the Cupid System.

Khairu's attention sharpened upon receiving a new flashing alert.

"Damn. More bogeys coming in hot."

"Where did they come from?" Fergus asked. "How close?"

"I don't know. Their course places them coming in from Beren. That's the next gas giant out."

"What's with pirates and gas giants?" Serah asked. "I feel like I'm detecting a theme."

"Lots of moons," Fergus said. "Practically impossible for the League to wrest them out. Even the Jovian moons weren't fully tamed until the mid-23rd century."

"Thanks for the history lesson."

Khairu's fingers flew on the terminal screen, doing a few

quick calculations. "It's going to be close. I'm already adjusting our deceleration. We're going to have to burn hard."

"And I suppose you'll need me to soften the edge," Serah said.

"You and Linus both," Khairu said. "It'll be as bad as Nai Elyn. Better make it an active stream rather than a ward."

"No worries. I've got it."

Lucian looked at her worriedly, but there was no helping it. No one could stream Gravitonics like Serah.

Within minutes, they were in their crash seats.

"Thirty seconds," Khairu said.

Lucian looked at Serah next to him. "Ready?"

"Not really. Don't have a choice though, do I?"

"That seems to be the theme of everything we've gone through."

"Ain't that the truth?"

"Ten seconds."

Serah closed her eyes and streamed a Gravitonic shield encompassing the bridge. Somewhat begrudgingly, Linus joined her stream. Even after everything he'd been through, the man still detested magic, and wouldn't use it if he had his way.

"Five, four, three, two . . ."

Lucian closed his eyes, assuming his Focus and shutting the rest out. The deceleration force was instant and crushing. Even as his back slammed into the crash seat, his mind floated, inured to outside circumstances. Within the space of a long breath, it seemed it was completely over.

With a gasp, Serah let go of the stream and leaned back in her seat.

"Flipping toward Argus," Khairu said.

The viewscreen swiveled, revealing an arced field of icy debris extending as far as the eye could see. Beyond lay the aquamarine tint of Argus itself, its mass dominating the viewscreen. They'd come startlingly close to slamming into a huge asteroid that had gotten caught up in the ring system.

"Nice work, Talent Khairu," Fergus said.

"Now, for the real fun," she said.

She took manual control of the ship and began picking a path through the millions of floating masses of ice.

Lucian unstrapped himself and went to check on Serah, who was still leaning back in her chair. "You all right?"

His skin went cold when he realized she wasn't moving. Panic welled up in his chest.

"Serah? Talk to me."

Everyone turned to see what was going on. Lucian was already unstrapping her and pulling her into his arms. She was light in the shipboard gravity, and he could feel her pulse thrumming, slowly, from his cheek placed on her neck.

"She overdrew," Linus said. "That deceleration was *worse* than Nai Elyn."

"All of you, stay here," Lucian said. "Khairu, keep us from dying."

"That's the plan."

With that, he ran toward the ship's clinic, his footsteps pounding on the deck. It felt as if he were in a waking nightmare. When he turned into the clinic, he opened the pod and laid her gingerly inside. Her eyes were still closed, but she was breathing. He didn't know what good a medical pod would do for overdrawing, but he couldn't think straight.

"Serah, please wake up . . ."

Fergus entered from behind. "Is she all right?"

The glass door of the pod slid shut. Apparently, the machine had found something wrong with her. Something it wanted to fix.

He placed a hand on the glass, even as the pod's small, adroit pincer arms extended themselves, lifting her and sticking her with various IV's and tubes.

Madly, Lucian scanned the nearby terminal to get the diagnosis, but it seemed not even the medical pod's program knew what was wrong.

He punched the screen. "Work, damn you!"

Fergus placed a hand on his shoulder. "Punching it won't make it work faster. That only works in holos."

Lucian looked at the pod in frustration, where the interior glass had become tinted. Whatever the machine wanted to do, it didn't want him to see.

"Rotting hell," he said. He looked at Fergus desperately. "Do *you* know what's wrong with her? Can you pass out from overdrawing?"

"Yes, it's possible."

"Is it bad?"

Lucian didn't like Fergus's lack of answer.

"Just tell me the truth."

"It could be. She must have taken on a greater load this time. Linus is a decent Gravitist, but nothing compared to Serah. She's better at reverse streams than him. This . . . happens to frays especially. They can get knocked out if they stream too much."

"Then why hasn't this happened before?"

"Well, it can take time to build. There's no rhyme or reason to it. It just is."

"So, she's fraying."

"She's *been* fraying, Lucian. This whole time." His expression softened somewhat. "I'm sorry. That's the truth. I wish I could change it."

The words were like a punch to the gut. After everything they'd gone through, after all the magic she'd streamed, Lucian had counted it a miracle that nothing bad had happened. Not like this, anyway. This was insurmountable proof that something *was* happening. Everything was catching up to her. He'd never felt so powerless. And it hurt even worse just knowing the Orb of Space-Time refused to be used by anyone *other* than him.

"We won't be fast enough," Lucian said, his voice weak. "I always told her we would be, that we could stop this before it was too late. I . . . can't break that promise."

"We *won't*," Fergus said, firmly. "This isn't over. My guess is, given a couple of hours . . ."

At that moment, the tinting of the glass faded, revealing Serah stirring beneath. The door slid open, and the various tubes inserted into her body disengaged. She blinked drearily a few times, her blue eyes finding Lucian's. They were glassy and hazy from some sort of pain medication. There was a moment of confusion before she gave a small smile.

"I'll be up front," Fergus said, ducking out.

"Hey there," Serah said. She looked around, blinking in confusion. "How'd I end up here?"

"You passed out. I didn't know what else to do with you."

"You *never* know what to do with me."

Lucian gave a nervous laugh. "Well, that's true. How are you feeling?"

She didn't answer him for a moment, as if his words didn't register. She looked to be out of it still, but at least she didn't seem to be in pain.

"Thirsty," she said.

"I'll get you some water. Come on. Let's get you to bed."

"What about the pirates? There were pirates, I remember that much. Are we safe?"

"Yes. For now."

She closed her eyes, her smile remaining on her face. "That's good. I *guess* you can carry me. Not really feeling up to walking, to be honest."

"Just relax. I've got you."

He took her in his arms, carrying her out of the clinic and toward the cabin they shared.

"You're so strong," she said, squeezing his arm. "You've been working out, huh?"

"Thanks for noticing."

She giggled. Yes, she was definitely high on something.

He laid her softly on the bed and tucked her in, then returned with a flask of water. She drank a few gulps before settling back. Her eyes found his as she smiled goofily.

"Just take it easy," he said, strapping her in. For all he knew, the gravity could shut off at any time if things got dicey.

"What're you still doing here? Go kill some pirates or something." Her eyes rolled back. "So tired . . ."

"Sleep. I'll be back soon to check on you, okay?"

She tried to say something, but sleep won over.

Lucian stayed for a few minutes to be sure she was okay. He couldn't *not* stay. He hated seeing her so weak and pale. He reached for her forearm, rolling back her shirt sleeve to see her mottled, gray skin beneath. The wound now took up her entire arm, from wrist to well above her biceps. It didn't feel any different from any other part of her skin, but at a glance, her entire arm seemed to be charred.

He gingerly rolled back the shirt sleeve, laying her arm by her side.

He forced himself to leave to check on the situation up front. When he got back to the bridge, he looked out the forward viewport, where Khairu was steering *Ethereal* between two large floating mountains of ice.

"Is she okay?" Linus asked.

"She's asleep. Just shot up with some pain meds." He looked at Khairu. "Status?"

"We're only a couple hundred kilometers into the ring system, so we need to go where the ice is thicker if we hope to lose them."

"Where the ice is *thicker*?" Plato said. "Looks like we could crash any second!"

"It's a risk."

Lucian reached for the Orb of Space-Time, but it was just as difficult to reach as it had been hours ago. At this rate, it would be *days* before he could use it again. But he couldn't use it to go any closer to Hephaestus. He had no memory of that place, and he could only travel to somewhere he'd been before, and only then if he had a strong enough memory to tie him to it.

"Maybe the best option is to find a safe spot to hide out," he said. "Lie low for a week or two, and then come out when they've given up the chase. We can head another direction and circle back to the Hephaestus Gate."

No one made any comment on that plan. All of them were looking at him funny. He tried to ignore that. He knew why they were giving him those pitying looks, as if *he* were the one who had suffered, not Serah.

"She'll be fine," he finally said. "Let's just focus on getting out of this alive."

Lucian looked at Emma, who stared despondently out at the hundreds of floating ice chunks and Argus beyond. It was as if she weren't even here. She had her own affliction to deal with. By now, she'd been without the Orb of Radiance for nearly a full day, and it seemed its lack was taking its toll.

Hours passed, and they were deep enough into the ring system that they had lost contact with every ship giving chase. Lucian had no illusions, though. Their pursuers certainly recognized *Ethereal*, and knew just who was on board. Every pirate under Zheng Yang's banner would want the honor of delivering Fergus to her personally.

"Where would be a good place to hide?" Lucian asked.

Khairu gently navigated around another large chunk of ice. "Ideally, far from where we entered. The more time we're in here, the more impossible we'll be to find."

"Does this world have any moons?" Fergus asked. "Something barren and unsettled."

"Well," Khairu said, "the Archea System is populated enough for Argus to have each of its moons settled. There may not be *many* people, but there are people. A sizeable piece of ice would serve us better."

Lucian couldn't argue with Khairu's logic. Her reasoning was sound.

"I think I'm going to go in the back," Emma said. "Let me know if you need me."

"Is she all right?" Plato asked. "She seems a bit green around the gills."

"I noticed that myself," Linus said. "Perhaps the warping upset her stomach. It certainly has mine."

"*Why* would it do that?" Plato asked.

"It ain't natural."

Fergus was about to respond when his eyes widened. Outside the forward viewscreen, two large, icy asteroids were closing in on them like a pincer. Khairu veered upward, quickly enough that the inertial dampeners couldn't compensate. Lucian nearly fell to the deck.

"Might want to take a seat," Khairu said.

Lucian obliged and strapped himself in.

When Khairu righted the course, they were on the same trajectory as before.

"Maybe it's time we found something," Lucian said. "The longer we fly around, the likelier we are to hit something."

"We need more distance."

Another ice chunk, unseen just seconds before, flew down from above, perilously close to hitting the nose of the ship.

"I accounted for that being there," Khairu said, a bit stubbornly. "I know what I'm doing."

"Now this is *really* starting to make *me* sick," Linus said. "Emma had the right idea. If we're going to die, I'd like to do so in the comfort of my own bed."

As Linus excused himself, Plato shrugged and followed him. "And I from the kitchen."

Fergus sighed. "How can that man think about food at a time like this?"

Neither Lucian nor Khairu answered him. The bridge was quiet with only the three of them.

Lucian watched closely for the next couple of hours as Khairu navigated through Argus's icy rings. He had to restrain himself from telling her what to do. She knew far more about piloting than he did, especially when he didn't know anything at all.

Just as he was about to tell her to find a hiding spot, no arguments, she pointed out a medium-sized piece of ice with an irregular shape.

"There. *That's* what I've been looking for." She angled the ship toward it, flipping the vessel in preparation for slowing down.

"What's so special about it?" Fergus asked.

Khairu's fingers flew across the screen of the pilot's terminal, which was scanning the orbiting body. "Just as I suspected. There appears to be a canyon just wide enough to hide our ship in. We won't stick out like a sore thumb. Plus, the canyon should hide our heat pretty well. It'll take a long time for the ship's exterior to cool off, especially the thrusters."

"Let's go," Lucian said.

Within minutes, Khairu was guiding the ship into the narrow, icy canyon. In the opening above, Argus's rings and the planet beyond were visible, along with closer orbiting debris. It was a beautiful sight that wouldn't have looked out of place on a tourist ad for a space cruise.

As soon as the landing struts clawed into the ice beneath, Khairu shut off the engines, turning the thrusters down to face the ice.

"It'll take some time for the thrusters to cool enough to

make us invisible to thermal scanners," she said. "I could vent them, but that risks destabilizing the ice beneath us, and it could cause surface scarring that will be visible from miles away. We'll just let the laws of physics do their work."

"How long should they take to cool?" Fergus asked.

She shrugged. "An hour, maybe two. Another reason I wanted to gain some distance."

"Well, we've lost contact with those ships. They could fly right above us and not know we're here."

"That's the idea."

"Now what?"

"We wait." She turned to Lucian. "I suggest you get some rest, Talent Lucian. When you wake up, we can decide on our next COA."

Lucian nodded. Though he had passed out during the warp, that most definitely was not sleep. His head was pounding something fierce, and the adrenaline of their escape had long ebbed. He also hadn't had his caffeine fix in over twenty-four hours.

"There'll be time for rest later," he said.

He left the bridge, headed for the galley for a cup of coffee, then went to check on Serah.

4

LUCIAN DRAINED his cup as he headed for his cabin. As soon as he stepped through the open door, he found Serah on her slate, entertaining herself with a game. That was a good sign. She still looked pale and worn, but if she could focus on a game, things were at least getting somewhat back to normal.

"Howdy, captain," she said, not looking up. "We're still alive, I take it?"

"I don't think I remember dying, so yes."

"A little keyed up, huh?"

"Maybe."

She nodded toward his cup. "Are you sure it's not that?"

"No. Coffee is the elixir of life and doesn't produce any adverse side effects."

She snorted. "Addict. So, what's the update?"

"We're parked on a random chunk of ice in Argus's rings now. With luck, it'll stay that way for the foreseeable future."

"I'm sure the view is lovely. So, what's the plan now?"

Lucian shrugged. "I think we're just going to sit tight for a while. At least, until I have the strength to warp us again."

"And I suppose you don't know when that'll be?"

"Unfortunately, no. We'll give it a week and see what happens then."

"This might sound weird, or maybe it's just the drugs, but this is almost kind of . . . cozy."

"Cozy?"

"Yeah. We're safe in this ship, snug on a giant floating piece of ice where no one can find us, and can just take a breather for a few days. Maybe this is for the best."

"That's one way of looking at it, I guess."

"You don't agree?"

Lucian's thoughts went to Emma. He had yet to tell Serah about what had happened to her. He didn't relish telling her she might be right.

"So, Emma might be an issue. Seems she's suffering from withdrawal."

Her eyebrows arched in concern. "You want me to talk to her?"

"No, that's all right. You need to rest. I'm just worried about what's going to happen if I don't give it back. She looked kind of pale earlier, and I don't think it was all the gymnastics Khairu was doing with the ship. Do you think I should give it back?"

"You've got to think about yourself, Lucian. Who's to say *you* won't start suffering the same thing if you go without it?"

Lucian hadn't thought of that. "I guess that's possible. I *could* give it back now, but it'll take longer for the Orb of Space-Time to work again."

"There's your answer. Our lives are all on the line here, and if one Orb is the difference, then it would be irresponsible to give it back. She just needs to work her way through it. You're the Chosen, not her."

"Radiance is not one of my strong suits. Doesn't it make sense to give the Orb to someone who can use it decently?"

"So, you're going to give the Orb of Thermalism to Plato

when you nab it? And the Orb of Dynamism to Khairu? Fergus is a Radiant, too. Shouldn't he also have a claim on the Orb of Radiance?" She smiled victoriously. "See, it all gets rather messy."

"You have a point, there. It took almost all of Emma's willpower to hand it back to me."

"We already know the Orbs might be sentient. They can choose to work, or not work, like with you back on Psyche. We almost died falling in the Darkrift because the Orb of Binding went on holiday. We can extend that logic a bit. An Orb could be powerful enough to affect someone's very emotions, make them form an attachment to it."

"Like a drug."

"Is that crazy? We already know ether is addictive, especially when you draw more than you should. When Emma used the Orb to find the Dark Gate, and to fight Vera and Xara, she was taking on a lot of ether, far more than she could ever use on her own. For the first time in her life, that ether was unadulterated. See where I'm going with this?"

Lucian nodded. "Maybe it's not so much the Orb is addictive. It's more about what the Orb can do. It might be easier for me to give up one, because I still have two other ones. I won't lose the feeling of streaming that much magic by missing one Orb."

"Exactly."

"Then again, having three Orbs makes me more powerful than having two. With the Orb of Space-Time, it seemed I could draw as much as I want. It had a way of compressing that magic. It was . . . strange. Like nothing I've ever experienced. I even drew from the other four Aspects, too, though not as much as from the Orbs. That's seven streams at once, and I could handle all of them. Without the Orb of Space-Time, I don't think I could have managed it."

"Well, I think you have your answer, then."

"What answer?"

Serah nodded sagely. "You're the only one who's qualified to manage the Orbs. Emma had it for a moment, and that was the best for the situation we were in. Now, we know the risks. As the Chosen, you should be the steward of this magic. No one else."

"I can't use Radiance as well as Emma, though," Lucian said.

"You must learn, then."

Lucian knew she had him there. "There's Fergus who can teach me, and Emma too, I suppose."

"Emma will be fine. As soon as I'm up on my feet, I can talk to her."

"That won't be for a while. You need to be careful about streaming, Serah. I don't want to lose you."

"Lose me? Everything would've been lost if I didn't do what I did."

"I know that. Still. We can't mess around with this anymore. We have to fix the fraying first. At the rate I'm going, we should have it all done in a couple of weeks."

She cracked a smile. "A couple of weeks, huh? Well, let's just focus on getting out of here alive before the pirates find us."

"I'm confident I can pull it off."

She pulled him closer. "Well, maybe you can."

From the way she kissed him, Lucian was certain she was feeling better.

"I'm going to go check on things up front," he said. "Be back soon."

"Bring some food with you. Green curry, please."

Lucian left, and after getting the food for Serah, he headed up to the bridge, which was manned by Fergus. He leaned back with a cup of coffee in the copilot's seat, watching the terminal for incoming threats.

"Guard duty, huh?"

"Yes," Fergus said. "Even Talent Khairu needs to sleep, believe it or not."

"I'll believe that when I see it."

Fergus chuckled. "How's Serah holding up? From your mood, I would guess better."

"She's up. Talking, joking around, giving me a slight bit of hell."

"Par for the course, then."

"Pretty much."

Lucian took a sip of his coffee as he gazed out at space, through the crack at the top of the canyon. The ice they were on was rotating slightly, so he could see the stars spinning above rather than the planet. Another few minutes would see them facing Argus again.

"Strangely peaceful," Fergus said. "To think there are potentially hundreds of pirate vessels searching for us right now . . ."

"I thought Zheng Yang's fleet was in the Brennus System, all the way on the other side of the Worlds. How did they get here so fast?"

"This isn't her main fleet. She has smaller flotillas in almost every system on this side of Earth. The further from the core you go, the more you'll find. Zheng doesn't control a lot of her ships directly. She has a lot of captains under her command that give her a share of their spoils. But the fact that they're moving, and apparently all at once, tells me she's up to something big."

"You'd think the League would have taken her out by now."

Fergus chuckled. "I'm surprised you don't understand. Out here, especially beyond Archea, the League is just a name. They're too far away to have much influence. From here, on a typical starship, Earth is three months away, maybe even four. And this is just the Mid-Worlds. The Border Worlds are even farther out, up to a year or more in some places. Sure, the League will have some bases out here, maybe even control some of the larger cities and stations. But the rest is a wilderness. The pirate clans impose some measure of stability, and the Golden Pirates of Brennus are by far the most numerous and powerful. They actually have something of an empire out here, even if it's on the periphery of settled space. They control eleven worlds, either directly or as some form of tributary. And the League can't do a damn thing about it, even in times of peace."

"I see. I guess the League isn't likely to advertise their inability to control the space they claim."

"You've got that right. While the Golden Armada can't match up to the League ship for ship, it's still a force to be reckoned with. Even more so because many smaller pirate captains owe her fealty. Here in Archea, there are several so-called pirate lords. Some even make their home in Argus's rings and moons. We're not as safe here as Khairu would like to think."

"Do we need to get out?"

"Well, if here's not safe, no place is. As soon as we burn hot toward one of the Gates, we can easily get shot down with a stun missile. Or worse." He drained the rest of his mug. "Meaning, our only hope is you and that Orb you found."

"It's not ready yet. Probably won't be for a while."

"That's what I'm afraid of. I'm glad to know the warping itself didn't kill us, but you have to admit, I was right, at least a little. Because we've landed in quite a predicament. I expected to come out near Aurora, and instead, we've found ourselves here."

"It just sort of happened. I didn't have a strong enough memory of Aurora. But I had a strong one of Archea, when Serah and I watched our approach for the first time coming from Psyche. The Orb recognized that and ran with it."

"Maybe," Fergus said. "Either way, we made history. No human has ever done what we did. If the League knew about it, they'd want you to figure out how to make it work for *every* ship. Originally, they had wanted the mages to learn how to *jump* their ships from system to system, but they never figured out a way. Then the Mage War happened, and all that became history."

The spinning of the ice brought Argus and its interior rings into view again. The massive aquamarine gas giant looked so near that it could be touched.

"I just realized something," Lucian said.

"What's that?"

"We've been out of League Space for over a month, and we haven't thought to look at the newsfeeds. Alpha Centauri could be toast, for all we know. There was that failed attack run a few months back, but who's to say there wasn't another, larger one?"

"Well, I doubt AC has been cracked yet. That tends to be where the League fleet musters, at least on this side of the Worlds. But we *might* find out which way the Swarmers are going from the Djerrah System. Did they go to Fessan, Talesia, or perhaps even both?"

Fergus ran a newsfeed app on the terminal. It revealed much of what Lucian had expected; death counts in the millions, panicked citizens, red-faced pundits arguing with each other, criticism of the League Assembly and Hegemon Palmer for doing nothing for anyone but the Solar System, and counter pundits praising Palmer for unapologetically putting the Solar System first. To Lucian's surprise, the Volsung Mages had joined the main League fleet in Alpha Centauri, and from the Fleet's lack of movement, it seemed they didn't plan to move out any time soon.

Panic was already gripping various star systems, including Fessan, Talesia, Karelia, Malon, and Astravan, all of which were under direct threat from the Swarmers. Meanwhile, coreward star systems such as Orenus, Beal, and Pontus were breaking down into anarchy due to the second Swarmer fleet that had laid waste to Sani, but had yet to continue on to Orenus.

Zion in the Spinward Mid-Worlds had completely rebelled from the League authority, ousting all its diplomats while taking over the small League fleet stationed there. The High Prophet Sharo Khalin, the self-christened "Voice of God," was declaring the Swarmers God's punishment on a sinful League, and that all should flock to his protection in order to be saved from the Almighty's wrath. To Lucian's surprise, people were listening. The Oneists' fleet was growing by the day, its numbers bolstered by neighboring systems seeking the protection of their stronger neighbor. By executive order, Hegemon Palmer had ordered Zion's six League Delegates arrested, only to discover they had left the Solar System days previously.

As if *that* were not enough, Zheng Yang's Golden Armada was on the move for the first time since its exodus from the Archea System. From the Border World of Brennus, the mustered fleet was pushing coreward toward the First Worlds to aid in the League's defense. Or so the pundits speculated. Some claimed instead it was to take revenge on the League for forcing her out of the Mid-Worlds.

In short, the hundred or so systems within the League had entered pure pandemonium. The galactic apocalypse was coming far faster than even Lucian would have guessed.

After about an hour of bad news, Lucian closed the app. "I think I've had enough of this."

"The Swarmers might get to Hephaestus before we do, especially if going through this system is a no-go."

Lucian had to wonder. If the Golden Pirate enclaves were rising up on every world trailward of Earth, like Fergus had suggested, then what if they were trapped here for good? There might be no escaping Zheng Yang's net. Surely, she was already being informed of *Ethereal's* presence in the vicinity of Argus.

It was only a matter of time before they were found. The Orb of Space-Time was the only possible way out.

Lucian reached for it again. He seemed to grasp it for a

moment, but his concentration slipped. It wasn't ready to be used, and wouldn't be for a while yet.

"Well," Fergus said, "from the way things are looking, humanity might off itself before the Swarmers have the privilege."

Lucian pulled up a map of League space, projecting it onto the bridge. "Only two possible ways I can see us getting out of this. The first is warping to Halia, and then going there through Oceanus, AC, then Astravan to Hephaestus. The other is the Psyche route, through Psyche, Gradene, Alcazar, Malon, and then Astravan. The first one is shorter, and no doubt safer."

"The League movements in AC might make things complicated," Fergus said. "That said, it's one system shorter, and there won't be pirates to bother us."

Lucian nodded. "That's what we'll do, then. I think it's a no brainer."

"When'll you let the crew know?"

"Don't know. Serah still needs to rest up, and Emma is . . . under the weather."

"Wonder what happened with her."

Lucian kept silent. He felt it wasn't for him to say.

The terminal screen flashed a warning. Two thermal signatures lit up somewhere above them.

"Got company, it seems," Fergus said.

At that moment, Khairu ran onto the bridge. "What's going on?"

"Two bogeys," Lucian said. "From their vectors, doesn't seem like they've seen us."

The ships were too far to be visible to the naked eye, and they only appeared on the screen for a few seconds until all that was left were their heat trails.

"Ten kilometers away," Khairu breathed. "Too damn close."

"Seems this is a good hiding spot."

"I'm just glad most of our heat's vented by now. We've got to stay on low power from now on. Run the engine at minimum capacity."

"That might make it harder to take off if we need to," Fergus said.

"We're past that point. The best thermal scanners can detect trace amounts of heat if we idle. We can't take the risk."

"What will that do to the AG field?" Lucian asked.

"Obviously, gravity will not function. You'll have to rely on your magboots. Or Gravitonic Magic, though I don't recommend it."

"Do it," Lucian said. "Your judgment has saved us so far. Just need to get a message out to the crew."

He sent the message on his slate, informing everyone that the ship was going into low-power mode in ten minutes, and to expect zero-g conditions for the foreseeable future. Thankfully, everyone acknowledged the message. He went back to his cabin to check on Serah and made sure she was still strapped in and safe.

When he returned, Khairu was sitting in the pilot's seat and accessing the terminal. She was at the root power menu, inputting commands. Within a moment, the overhead lights red-shifted, and almost imperceptibly, the vibration in the ship's hull from the fusion engine faded. The vents, which were supposed to run steadily, were barely audible. As soon as the AG field dissipated, Lucian toggled his mag boots. Every part of him felt as if it were floating, though his boots on the deck kept him locked in place.

"Might get chilly," Khairu said. "The thermal shielding on this ship is good, but we can't chance it. Especially around the reactor. We look suspicious if we are anything above one-twenty kelvin. The surface of *Ethereal* is reading one-fifty. A good survey vessel will find that suspicious. And you can bet Zheng Yang has a few of those at her command, and they're probably sniffing above us right now."

"How cold will it get onboard?" Fergus asked.

She shrugged. "Five, ten degrees? No hot water, either."

"Well, we've certainly lived through worse."

"What about the medical pod?" Lucian asked. "Emma and Serah aren't feeling well."

"That can be turned on as needed, since it's power hungry," Khairu said. "Water, oxygen, food. That's all we need to survive. All that's left is to wait this out."

All Lucian could think about was how he was glad Khairu was here. She had invaluable expertise.

"Fergus and I were talking," Lucian said. "When the Orb is ready, we can warp to Halia and wrap around to Hephaestus that way."

Khairu frowned. "That'll be a long trip. Three months at least."

"The other option is Psyche to Astravan. That one's even longer."

"That's true. One has to ask, though. Do we have time for either?"

"I don't see how we have any choice. We're surrounded."

"You're right. There are no good choices. Of course, there's a third option."

"What's that?"

"Warp to Archea Station again. We didn't have our transponder off when we entered this system, which was how they locked onto us. We can try again, this time with no transponder. They shouldn't be able to pick us up as easily. It could give us enough time to make it to the Hephaestus Gate, saving us months on our journey."

It was an idea. "We'll still be close to Archea Station, though. Close enough to be manually detected."

"They won't know who we are immediately. And hopefully by the time they do, we'll be halfway to the Gate."

"It could go wrong," Fergus said. "*Horribly* wrong. And

there's nowhere easy to escape to. Too many ships searching for us." He hesitated a moment. "Of course, there's a fourth option none of us have mentioned."

Lucian already knew where he was going. "No."

"I can turn myself in to Zheng. That's what they want, anyway. You guys will have to learn to get along without me, at least for the next year."

"Nothing will be around a year from now," Lucian said. "We need you with *us*."

"That's a last resort," Khairu agreed. "If Yang wants you, she'll have to pay for it. With blood, if necessary."

"That's her specialty."

"I still like option three," Khairu said. "If we warp back to Archea, we can get some distance to the Gate. It's a pretty sure bet in my book."

"It all depends on them not getting a lock on us," Lucian said. "It's all over if they catch us outside the station. We'd have to turn over Fergus, and who knows what they'd do to the rest of us?"

"Just an idea," Khairu said. "One worth considering, given the state of the Worlds. Travel from Psyche to Astravan will be horribly dangerous, and chaos in the League might complicate the Halia-Astravan route. Whatever the case, we have a lot to think about over the coming days." She leaned back in her seat. "I can take over the watch from here."

"I'll let the crew know."

5

LUCIAN SENT out a message to the group chat, letting them know what to expect from low power mode. Good as Khairu's word, things got chilly fast. The crew's jumpsuits were designed for lower temperatures, but even so, it took some getting used to. And with no hot water, everyone opted not to take showers.

Training was a useful reprieve. Just moving around got the blood flowing, though Lucian was hesitant to stream. He was afraid that any magic would only weaken the Orb of Space-Time. It probably was a useless concern, but it was better to be careful, especially when the stakes were high.

Over the next few days, there were several more alerts, but the ships were never visible on the thermal scanners for longer than a few seconds. Anytime the klaxons blared, it sent a charge of fear down Lucian's spine.

Every few hours, he tested the Orb of Space-Time, but it was much the same as before. It wasn't working. He was beginning to fear that it didn't *want* to work, that like the Orb of Binding on Psyche, it was betraying him. He had to remind himself of what Arian and Silumko had told him. He was the

Chosen of the Manifold. It would work, but only within its limits. He only had three Orbs out of the original Seven. He couldn't expect the Orb of Space-Time to work perfectly until he had them all.

But every time a vessel passed above them, it was a reminder that their days here were numbered.

———

THE WAIL of klaxons woke Lucian from his sleep. Serah woke up next to him, her eyes wide with surprise.

"What's that?"

"Don't know. Stay here. Make sure you're secured." She moved to get out of bed, but Lucian held her back down. "Please stay. You're not ready for action yet."

Her lips pouted a bit, but she nodded. "I suppose you're right. This time."

"Be back soon."

He left Serah and sprinted for the bridge. Everyone else had already gathered there.

"Unmarked survey vessel hovering above us," Khairu said. "What are your orders?"

"Have they detected us?"

"Almost certainly. It's too much of a coincidence they're parked there of all places."

"Are we running hot?"

"Surface of our vessel is one-nineteen Kelvin. They must have a hard visual on us. Probably waiting for reinforcements."

"Wake up the ship," Lucian ordered. "And everyone in their crash chairs."

Khairu inputted some quick commands on the terminal. "Done. It'll take two minutes for the ship to come fully online."

"Be right back," he said. "Get us off this rock as soon as you can and burn as hard as you can through the rings."

"Without killing us," Linus added helpfully.

"She's kept us alive this far," Plato said.

"What about the Orb?" Emma asked. "Is it ready?"

"We'll figure that out in a minute. I need to get Serah up here."

Lucian ran back to the cabin, finding Serah lying in bed.

"What's going on?"

"They've spotted us. We need to get you situated up front."

"Great. And I was just about to fall asleep again."

"Well, we have other priorities."

He unstrapped her and pulled her easily in the low gravity, which was already coming back online. Halfway to the bridge, the AG field suddenly strengthened, but Lucian was holding her tightly enough to keep her secure.

"At least we'll get the heating back," Serah said.

Lucian started running with her in his arms as soon as he'd toggled off his magboots. He placed her in her crash seat, expertly strapping her in.

"Are we set?" he asked.

"The bogey's moving," Khairu said. "Out of sight now."

"Does that mean it's seen us?" Linus asked.

"If he didn't before, he certainly has now," Khairu said.

At that moment, a section of the icy cliff above them exploded with the impact of a projectile.

"Rotting hell!" Linus said. "They're shooting to kill!"

"Trying to flush us out," Khairu said. "But I've got another idea. Hold on to your butts."

Before Lucian could question it, they were blasting forward through the canyon, even as icy shards glanced off the ship's hull. Khairu wasn't angling *Ethereal* up, though, as he thought she would.

She was navigating the canyon itself, twisting and turning through the tight angles with no assistance from the ship's autopilot.

"You're going to get us killed!" Emma said, her face going pale.

Khairu's concentration only deepened. She was deaf to anything and everything that wasn't piloting the ship with maximum attention.

Lucian felt as if he were on a rollercoaster, helpless to do anything but endure the terrifying twists and turns before him. But unlike a rollercoaster, there was a high probability of death, a probability that increased with each passing second.

Khairu made another turn, and before them stood a massive pillar of ice bisecting the canyon. *Ethereal* was going so fast that there was no way she could avoid it.

Lucian reached for the Orbs of Binding and Psionics, drawing ether from both faster than he would have thought possible. In the space of two seconds, he created a dualstream and aimed it for the pillar. The pressure of the stream built until a lattice of blue and violet magic surrounded it.

Then Lucian shattered it. Chunks of ice exploded in all directions, including toward the ship. But Lucian wasn't finished. Streaming even more magic, so much that he was skirting the Ethereal Background itself, he broke the ice up further, until only a thick veil of finely ground ice and snow remained. They burst through the ice cloud, continuing their winding way down the canyon.

"What the hell just happened?" Plato asked. "Did someone shoot that pillar?"

Lucian let go of his Focus. "I did. In a manner of speaking."

It was at that moment that he felt a deep thrumming in his Focus.

The Orb of Space-Time was stirring, perhaps in response to his stream.

"I can start warping, now," Lucian said. "Just get us out of here!"

"Go," Khairu said. "I'll keep us alive until you're done."

"The warp took him *fourteen hours* last time," Linus said. "We're doomed!"

The last thing Lucian saw as he vacated the bridge were four ships, all flying in formation and bearing toward them. Khairu swerved aside so suddenly that Lucian was forced into the bulwark, inertial dampening field or not.

He engaged his magboots for extra safety and made it to the conference room. There, he kneeled and assumed his Focus. The Orb of Space-Time was still there, ready and waiting.

He just had to decide how to use it.

He held the Orb in his Focus, feeding magic from the other three Orbs into it. The Orb of Space-Time pulsed with potential. As all three Orbs fed their ether, fresh streams from the other Aspects opened of their own avail, infusing their power into the Orb. A rainbow of streams surrounded him, all eddying and collecting on his sternum. He existed in a place beyond time, a euphoria of power, magic, and potential.

His thoughts wandered, and he pictured Halia as he remembered it during his first approach aboard *Wayfinder*, its sunward side dappled with white clouds, and a single massive continent surrounding a jagged, interior sea. Despite his intent, he couldn't get the picture to take hold. The Orb was bursting with magic, wanting to be used, but unable to bridge reality with his memory.

The memory wasn't powerful enough to be used. But the magic had to go *somewhere*.

Focus. He had to keep his Focus.

He switched gears, instead remembering seeing Psyche for the first time.

No. *Not* Psyche.

But the image took hold. He was there again, a prisoner aboard the *LPS Worthless*, staring out the viewports at the violet-shrouded surface. After a months-long journey, he'd arrived. The terror of what he'd have to go through lurked in his thoughts like shadows. How could he survive the Mad Moon?

Psyche firmed in his mind. It was too late to backpedal. With each passing second, it grew more powerful, more vivid. More like reality rather than a memory. What would happen when the Wardens detected their vessel? How could they ever hope to escape *that*?

He just wished none of this had ever happened, that he had never tested positive as a mage. If only he were home right now, on Earth, and the Swarmers were nothing more than a distant threat. If only he could go back to the days before he'd left the planet with his mother. He hadn't known anything back then, and he just wanted to experience it once more. Some more time with her before she met her inevitable end.

A homesickness such as he'd never known overtook him. As much as he had seen, all he wanted was to go back, to be with his mother one last time before everything had gone to hell.

But that would never happen. Now, he would never see home again. And he had been through so much that if he ever *did* go home, it wouldn't feel like home anymore.

As these thoughts solidified in his mind, a final burst of magic exploded from the Orbs of Binding, Psionics, and Radiance, flooding into the Orb of Space-Time. Lucian screamed as his consciousness was absorbed by growing darkness.

———

WHEN HE CAME TO, he was still kneeling on the deck. With a groan, he pushed himself up, feeling wobbly. He leaned against the bulwark and guided his way toward the open doorway.

Voices emanated from the bridge. Voices that seemed startled and surprised.

Fergus appeared from the bridge and guided Lucian to the front. "You okay?"

"I'm . . . not sure."

"Let's talk about it up front. Did you get us to Halia?"

Lucian didn't want to admit the truth. "I don't know. We'll see."

With Fergus's help, Lucian walked to the bridge. When he looked out the viewport, he was surprised that all he could see was a panorama of stars. *That* wasn't Psyche, nor was it Halia. Perhaps they were just facing away from the planet.

"Where are we? Did it work?"

"Not sure, yet," Khairu said. "Still trying to pick up on-world broadcasts, but I'm not getting anything."

They *were* on Psyche, then. Nothing would be sent out on any wide-band radio from that moon.

"Wait," she said. "I'm getting something."

The map projected itself from the terminal, showing their location.

Lucian couldn't believe it.

"Rotting hell," Plato said.

Khairu adjusted the angle of the ship with the thrusters, her brown eyes intense.

And sure enough, everyone gasped as Earth slipped into the forward viewscreen, large enough to be about a hundred thousand kilometers away.

"Holy hell," Fergus said. "You took us to *Earth*?"

"I didn't mean to," Lucian said, feeling somewhat faint.

But thinking it through, it made sense. Since he couldn't think of a memory powerful enough to connect him to Halia, his wish to go back home had brought them all here. And what planet did he have a bigger connection to than Earth? But it had escaped them all that Earth would have been the more logical choice from the beginning. Looking at the star map floating before them, it was only three Gates from the Solar System to Hephaestus.

"Our transponder is still off," Khairu said. "If I turn it on now, that'll just make us a target. Some police vessels would chase us down, and I don't think we want that."

"How's the fuel situation?" Fergus asked.

Lucian frowned. "Fuel situation?"

"We took a hit in the rings. Something near the reactor just before you warped us. Most of our He-3 is gone."

"How long did the warp take?"

"About thirty minutes this time."

"Do we have enough fuel to dock somewhere?"

"Well, we have a plethora of choices," Plato said. "Earth only has a hundred orbitals above it."

"Far more than that by now," Lucian said. "Things have changed a bit since you were last here."

"Maybe so."

"L5 is the closest station of any note," Khairu said. She looked at Emma. "Don't your parents live there?"

"Yes," she said, going pale. "I . . . suppose I can make a call."

"Wait, your *parents* live here?" Plato asked.

But she was already working. She opened her slate, and a few inputs later, pressed it to her ear.

"Yeah Dad, it's me. Listen, I'll explain all that later. I need some help, and I need it now . . ."

6

WITHIN HOURS, they were pulling toward L5, the so-called First Wonder of the Galaxy.

Lucian had only seen it as a bright spot passing overhead during his childhood on Earth. Because of its size, it was one of the few orbital objects visible to the naked eye from light-polluted Miami. Long the retreat of the obscenely wealthy, L5 was home to several hundred thousand, all living in several dozen interconnected, rotating cylinders five kilometers long. Those cylinders spun in tandem, providing their own interior gravity, and were connected to a larger, outer ring composed of super-tensile alloys. From a distance, those cylinders looked like shining pearls in a necklace. Another large ring directly next to the first one was under construction, a base upon which to construct even more cylinders. A central spoke connected this ring to the original one. Given time, L5 would be home to millions of people.

The space city was among the oldest in all the Worlds. It had been founded a couple of centuries before even the Mage War, long before the discovery of applied artificial gravity, and decades before the discovery of the Gates. Even in this day and age, new cylinders were added in the same manner as the first ones.

Through the cylinders' clear viewports, Lucian could spy towering skyscrapers shining resplendently, agricultural greenery, and even dazzling lakes and verdant, arboreal parks. The outer ring was a full twenty kilometers in diameter. Even Sol Citadel couldn't match it for scale. Dozens of other habitats had been built since, but none matched L5 in size or beauty.

The space city grew in the forward viewscreen as *Ethereal* burned toward one of its many cylinders. This cylinder was filled with green vistas and parks, along with several tall towers and spacious estates that had been carefully designed to blend in with the scenery. Lucian remembered that Emma had come from a wealthy family, her father being both a shrewd businessman and a prince from Sani. He'd always wondered what her lifestyle had been like.

Well, he was about to find out.

"Is the transponder still off?" Fergus asked.

Khairu nodded. "Turning it on would just make things worse. We're already breaking the law. Might as well break it further."

"We have our own hangar," Emma said. "As long as the ship can receive transmissions, we can dock."

"I have a lock on the signal now," Khairu said. "Says we'll be there in about five minutes."

The ship flew toward the end of the cylinder. Dozens of larger vessels, including passenger liners, interstellar freighters, and local transports, plied the space between *Ethereal* and the cylinder's side. *Ethereal* drew itself even with the lower part of the cylinder, matching its rotation as it burned forward.

A large hangar door slid open, revealing a spacious bay outfitted with two vessels, one looking to be of a similar model to *Ethereal*, while another was a long, narrow pinnace that was basically all engines. From its sleek design, it was obviously built for racing. Lucian knew space racing was a rich person's sport, and the various circuits around Sol got major media coverage every year.

There was room enough for *Ethereal* to touch down next to the passenger vessel, and the hangar doors slid shut behind them. Khairu powered off the ship and checked the fuel gauge.

"Almost clean out. Think we can get this repaired in a reasonable amount of time?"

"I'm certain we can," Emma said.

The vents of the hangar roared to life as air blasted in. It only took a couple of minutes to pressurize.

"What now?" Serah asked.

"We wait," Emma said. "My parents said they'd be here soon."

From her pale complexion, it was clear Emma was nervous about the encounter. She had basically left them behind without warning to join the Volsung Academy. Her father had her life planned out, to keep her powers secret with training from a rogue mage. It made Lucian wonder just how many rogue mages were out there, that a rich person like Emma's father could contract one to teach his daughter.

They didn't have to wait for long. At the end of the hangar, a pair of metal doors slid open, revealing a blonde, middle-aged woman wearing a white dress. Upon seeing her, Emma smiled and left them on the bridge. Was that her mother? Lucian didn't think so. They looked nothing alike.

Within the minute, Emma was rushing across the hangar deck and embracing the older woman tightly.

"Maybe we should go down," Lucian said. "I think we're safe here."

"We should still exercise caution," Khairu said. "Things can turn quickly."

"I agree. Still, seems like we made it in one picce."

They followed him off the ship, walking up to join Emma. She parted from the woman and gestured toward her.

"This is Miranda," she said. "She's been with my family since I was born. She was my au pair, I guess you could say, but as I got older, she stayed with the family. Now, she manages our household."

"How do you do?" Miranda asked, giving a slight bow. She had the same lilting accent as Emma. "The Lady Emma and I were just catching up."

Lucian arched an eyebrow at the title, but said nothing more. If Emma was the daughter of a prince, then he supposed that made her a princess. It was a strange thought, because he'd never thought of her like that. He suddenly felt very out of place.

"This is Lucian Abrantes," Emma put in. "A Talent of the Volsung Academy."

"Nice to meet you." He hoped that didn't sound too informal. Miranda's expression seemed to expect more, so he added, "Ma'am."

Emma introduced the others, and most everyone else was more polished than him. Linus and Plato even bowed graciously, each offering Miranda a kiss on the back of her hand, which seemed to please her.

"You must forgive our sorry state," Linus said. "We've been through many trials and tribulations, so many that it would take days to recount them. My lady, we look forward to the succor and refreshment provided by your house."

Miranda blinked in surprise. "Of course. The Prince regrets not being here in person, along with his lady. Business pressed him, but as soon as he heard the news, he made immediate plans to travel from Luna, and is expected soon. In the meantime, you can take refreshment and enjoy the amenities of the Almaty estate. If you would come with me, I can lead you to your lodgings. Of course, Lady Emma, your room hasn't been touched, except for some nominal cleaning."

"Our ship took some damage from some debris," she said. "Could you get some of the techs to take a look at it? It must be repaired as quickly as possible. Unfortunately, we can't stay long. We have business with the League."

"But of course," Miranda said. "I'm sorry to hear you've been through so much, and that your stay will be short. Your poor parents will grieve at the news! But praise the stars you've come home safe, if only for a short time. You should've seen your father's state when he found out you were gone, and without a word!"

"I'm . . . sorry for that. There was no other way, at least from my point of view. I hope he'll understand my reasons."

"Of course, we learned just *where* you had gone just two months later. I have many questions of my own, but it's your father's and mother's part to hear it first. They should be home soon."

From Emma's drawn expression, Lucian could tell she was nervous at the prospect. "Thank you, Miranda. You can take us to our rooms now. And perhaps it would be a good idea to have the kitchen staff prepare us something. Have it delivered to our doors. We've been living off space food for far too long."

"We shall remedy that soon enough, my lady."

The ease at which Miranda deferred to Emma, and Emma's comfort at taking command, made Lucian see her in a completely new way. Surprise was also written on everyone else's features, and they fell in line almost meekly, none wanting to meet Emma's direct gaze.

Emma seemed to notice this deference, and rolled her eyes. "This is why I don't like to talk about my roots. It makes people act strange. You guys know me. As long as you're in my house, you will be treated as equals."

"This is the fanciest place I've ever seen," Serah said. "Does your dad own this whole tube?"

"No. Our property is situated on about half a kilometer of it. It connects to this hangar directly."

Lucian could scarcely imagine the price tag of such real estate. It ran well into the millions of credits for sure, not to mention the price of maintaining it.

"Please, follow me," Miranda said.

They followed Miranda out of the hangar and into a small lobby with a single elevator. There was plenty of space for all within, and Miranda hit the button that would lead them to the highest floor.

The elevator glided smoothly upward, leading them out of the hangar entirely. Lucian almost gasped as he looked out the clear viewport ahead of him, which overlooked the interior of the cylinder. What he saw was a green, rolling landscape, occupying the lower half of the cylinder, while the upper half was transparent to the stars above. That cylinder extended for about five kilometers, all the way toward the far end, with a winding river running between grass-laden banks below high jagged cliffs, upon which were perched stately mansions and towers. There was even wildlife, birds flying above the trees, and deer foraging by the rushing river below. In the far distance, out of the other end of the cylinder, was a clear view of the silvery moon.

As the elevator came to a stop about halfway up the cylinder, Lucian felt curiously light on his feet. He knew that in space cylinders, the heaviest gravity was along the interior of the rim, and it lessened toward the middle, until there was no gravity at all.

"This way," Miranda said.

Miranda led them down a long corridor that curved upward, a sight that was jarring to behold. On the right side, the viewports looked out onto a vista of Earth, just small enough to be covered by a hand. Nothing but several long freighters impeded their view.

Serah ran up to the viewports. "Holy cow. Just look at it!"

Lucian joined her. It was a view he'd only gotten once in his life, and only for a few minutes at that, on his harried journey to Sol Citadel. It was a memory so strong that the Orb of Space-Time had used it as the bridge to get them here. But now, he had a moment to appreciate it.

"Can you see Miami?" she asked. "You said it was a big city."

"Seems like Asia down there, from the looks of it. We would probably see the lights if it were nighttime."

"I see. I would like to go on the surface one day."

Lucian almost told her she wasn't missing much, until he imagined it from her perspective. As a girl who had grown up in the dangerous rifts of Psyche, never seeing anything more than a small village, at least until she joined him on his adventures, the sight of even a smaller Earth city would probably take her breath away.

"One day, I'll take you."

Emma approached them. "Lucian? I have to wait for my parents. Miranda wants to take you guys to your room."

"Okay, sounds good."

"Is everything okay?" Serah asked.

"Oh, you know. Drama. Nothing I can't handle, though. I'm a Talent of the Volsung Academy, after all. It's rather late, so maybe everyone can try to get some rest. I can get you if I need anything."

"Will we have a planet view from our room?"

"If you'd like. I'll let Miranda know."

The others had already gathered around Miranda, seeming to relax for the first time in weeks. Only Khairu glowered, looking at her luxurious surroundings suspiciously. Lucian was of a similar mind. Maybe it had just been his experience, but no matter how peaceful things seemed, trouble was never far away.

Miranda approached, giving a slight curtsy and flourishing her white dress. "Please, follow me. I think I heard something about a planet view?"

"Yes," Serah said. "Absolutely!"

Lucian wasn't sure why things felt off, but he saw no reason to resist. Maybe he'd been betrayed one too many times. He doubted he could trust anyone again. Much like Khairu had said, he just had to keep his eyes open.

Miranda led them along the interior corridor, which wrapped around the entire cylinder. Out the left viewports was a view of the arcology, where the river wound down the cylinder's length. As they walked, the river turned in relation to them. While it had been down relative to them before, now it was running *sideways*. This place would certainly take getting used to.

"I feel like I'm going to be sick looking out there," Plato said.

"It takes time," Miranda admitted. "I can have someone send up a ginger cordial. It works like a charm."

"That sounds divine."

"This is your room," Miranda said, coming to a stop and looking at Lucian. "I trust it will be to your satisfaction. If you need anything, you can always call for help. Just ask the room's computer for my slate ID."

"Thanks," Lucian said.

She left him and Serah there as she showed the rest to their own rooms. The group continued walking and was lost to the curve of the hallway turning upward.

"This has to be the weirdest place I've ever been," Serah said.

It hadn't been what Lucian had expected either. "Let's get inside."

The door opened automatically, revealing a spacious interior with marble-white floors, a small kitchen and living area with a wall-mounted holo-projector, some minimalist paintings, and a stunning view of Earth.

"Whoa," Serah said, running up ahead. "All this is for *us*?"

As she looked out in wonder, Lucian couldn't help but smile. He was happy that she was doing better. Nothing seemed to hold her down for long.

He went to join her. "Seems like it."

"Is *everyone's* room like this?" Serah asked. "How can one family have so much?"

"That's a question for Emma, though I wouldn't ask her."

"Why not?"

"Well, she's a bit touchy about money. It's kind of a faux pax to mention it. If you're poor, talk about money all you want and no one cares. If you're rich, it's off limits to talk about, at least openly."

"Seriously? Sounds like a rich people rule if I ever heard one."

He laughed. "Maybe so."

They found a bedroom attached to the living area. After taking a shower, they caught up on some sleep. What seemed like a few minutes later, there was a soft chime, what Lucian assumed to be a doorbell. Groggily, he rose, while Serah slept right through it. Checking his slate, eight hours had passed, more time than he had expected. They had left Argus's rings in the early morning, and now it was morning of the next day.

He went to the door to see Emma standing outside, looking a bit distressed. She stepped inside hastily and let the door shut behind her. "Well, my parents arrived last night. My dad gave me the dressing down of the century, so that was fun. You'd think I never moved out at all." She looked inside the living area. "Is Serah around?"

"Right here," she said, standing in the doorway and her hair somewhat frazzled. "Sorry, just woke up. Is everything all right?"

"Well, there's good news and bad news. Which do you want first?"

"Good, obviously," Serah said.

"Well, he's agreed to repair our ship, free of charge. It should be done in a couple of hours. The bad news is, he's being stubborn. He doesn't want me to go when you leave."

"Well, that's hardly his decision," Serah said. "You're a mage, now. You've got other obligations."

"That's what I told him, but he doesn't see it the same way. It's like he's still living in the past."

"I feel for the guy," Lucian said.

"I know, but it's not my fault. I didn't want the future he was setting up for me. I wanted to make my own choices for once."

"Yeah, I get that."

"This isn't up to me, anyway. I'm a Talent of the Volsung Academy. I can't just do what I want. I have to follow orders. And my orders are to help you, at least until I hear otherwise."

"Will your father respect that? I mean, he *has* to at some point."

"I'm not sure. Khairu is checking with Transcend White about what our next move should be. The Volsung mages are in Alpha Centauri now. I almost don't want her to check. Part of me is afraid she's going to recall the both of us. We accomplished our mission and Khairu has been faithfully updating her this entire time. You found the Prophecy of the Seven, and that was our mission. In Khairu's mind, that should be the end. If Transcend White recalls us, then there's nothing we can do about it."

"She wouldn't do that," Serah said. "You're too useful! Without you, we wouldn't have found the Dark Gate. And you lasered the rot out of Vera and Xara!"

"Well, I may have proven my usefulness a bit *too* much.

Unfortunately, Khairu suspects it isn't even up to Transcend White. The Hegemon is overseeing the Alpha Centauri fleet personally. Despite his vitriol against mages, he wants us there to augment the fleet. My father hardly has a voice in that, even if he thinks he does."

"I'm sure he's just trying to protect you," Serah said. "I wish my father was like that."

"I know my problems appear somewhat . . . privileged. To me at least, they're problems. I . . . feel bad for what I did to my parents, for leaving with no warning. But if I had stayed, I would be running part of my parents' business. Even if it all worked out somehow, I'd have to keep my identity as a mage secret. I would have been living a lie."

All Lucian could think was that she could have avoided *everything*. All the pain, all the suffering. And she'd have been set for life to boot. That was, assuming the Swarmers didn't reduce humanity to dust.

"I should count myself lucky," he said. "If you'd stayed here, we probably wouldn't be where we are now."

"I just couldn't live a lie. And I was scared with the wreakings I was suffering. I thought the Academy would help me more than whoever my parents had contracted. I have no regrets about the decision I made, but unfortunately, my father doesn't feel the same way." She met his gaze. "He wants to speak with you, Lucian."

"Me? Why?"

"Because you're our leader. I didn't tell him anything about our assignment, only that we had just completed a top secret mission for the Academy. He got nothing out of me, so I wouldn't be surprised if he tries to get something out of you."

"I have a feeling he won't like me very much."

"No. Probably not."

"Anything I should know before talking to him?"

"Well, I *could* give you advice, but it probably wouldn't do you much good. My father is . . . a force. Let's just put it that way."

"I've dealt with Xara Mallis and Vera Desai. How bad could it be?"

"Well, you have confidence, I'll give you that. Are you ready to go?"

"Do I look all right?"

"To be honest, it looks like you just woke up. At least comb your hair. And wear your Talent's robes. You need to remind him of who you are."

Serah nodded sagely.

"All right. I just . . . don't know how to talk to rich people." He felt embarrassed as soon as he realized he was talking to one now. "You know what I mean."

Emma pretended not to notice his slip. "I'll walk you down there in a few minutes. Try not to take too long. If there's anything rich people hate, it's waiting."

7

AFTER FIFTEEN MINUTES, Lucian had washed and changed into his Talent robes. He didn't feel right wearing them, as if he were representing an institution he didn't agree with.

Emma led him along the curved walkway until they reached the elevator. She pressed the "arcology" level and the elevator car went down smoothly, stopping after about a minute. The elevator dinged, and the doors opened to reveal a scene of nature. A stone balcony overlooked a small lake, into which a high waterfall poured. Trees covered both sides of the river, stretching halfway up the curve of the cylinder on either side and coming to a sudden stop to reveal the canopy of space above. Looking up, it looked like the clearest night sky he had ever seen, with apparently nothing separating the cylinder from the vacuum of space beyond.

Emma motioned him on, toward a set of steps leading down to the lakeshore. In the shallows, in a pair of knee high rubber boots with his back facing him, stood a tall, stately man. He was fishing, his line cast just before the rapids.

Lucian almost did a double-take. That someone would *fish*

here was about the strangest thought imaginable. He looked at Emma for confirmation, but she just nodded toward her father. That was him all right. Lucian noticed that there was another pole nearby. Did the man intend to fish with him?

"Go," she said. "He doesn't really like talking face to face."

With that, she left him there, heading back to the balcony above.

Lucian walked forward awkwardly, not really sure what was expected of him. He settled for standing on the lakeshore, just to the side of Emma's father so he could catch a sight of him. He was about to introduce himself when the man's line went taut, and he started reeling hard.

"Get the net," he called over.

Lucian found the net among a stand of rocks. At the end of the man's line, a long, spotted fish with a pink stripe flailed in and out of the dark blue, almost black, water. The thing had to be half a meter long. Lucian hoped that together, they could catch this fish. It might make things go more amenably.

Emma's father reeled it in with ease, and Lucian came into the water, not minding how the cool water soaked his boots and lower robes. He held the net steady while Emma's father pushed in the fish. On the lower, rounded jaw, Lucian noticed a scar from someone who'd formerly caught it.

"She's a beauty," the man said, admiringly. "How about you throw her back in?"

"You aren't going to eat it?"

"No. I don't catch them to eat them. It's more of a pastime, really. A chance to think and unwind."

"I guess that makes sense."

"You fish?"

"My mom took me once when I was seven or eight. I don't really remember it too much."

"Well, it's simple enough. Here, let me show you."

Lucian let him do so, all the while waiting for his stern attitude to show. He skewered a worm on the hook below some eye-catching lure.

"Live bait is best," he said.

Neither said anything as they both cast. Lucian performed the action easily enough, while Emma's father cast in a different direction, toward some reeds downstream.

Lucian was wondering how to broach the silence, or whether he even should. The surrealism of fishing with a prince on a space cylinder made it hard to believe this wasn't all some crazy dream.

"Of all the places I thought I'd be, fishing on L5 was at the bottom of the list."

The man gave an acknowledging grunt. "Life has a way of keeping you guessing."

Lucian nodded, but said nothing to these foreboding words.

"Emma speaks highly of you. The two of you together, or something?"

He shook his head fiercely. "No, sir. We're just friends."

He gave him a hard look that seemed to understand the undercurrents of Lucian's words. "That's what she said, too." The man looked at him fully for the first time, and Lucian saw fierce blue eyes, a dignified gray beard, and a weather-worn face with deep under eye shadows. "You better not be leading her on, son."

Lucian nearly choked. "I'd never dream of it."

"I believe you. My name's Tristan. Tristan Almaty."

"Lucian Abrantes."

No less than ten minutes passed in silence. Lucian wondered what he was doing out here, whether Tristan was waiting for him to speak. There seemed to be nothing good to say, so he said nothing at all.

At last, the prince nodded. "Let's walk."

They set their poles down, and Lucian waited while the older man slipped off his rubber boots, under which he was wearing a good pair of walking shoes. He motioned Lucian to fall in beside him. As they set off on a beaten path through the trees, Lucian tried to ignore the undignified squelching coming from his own footwear.

As soon as they were under the cool, verdant canopy, filled with the chirping of birds, insects, and small mammals, Lucian could hardly believe they were on a space station. The trail could have been any mountain path, and only intermittent breaks in the treetops revealed the stars above, or the powerful multi-spectrum panels beaming light down.

They crested a low hill, which joined with the cliff overlooking the stream below. The prince seemed to think for a moment.

Lucian looked over at the older man. "I have to ask, Tristan. Why did you want to see me?"

The prince raised an eyebrow, making Lucian think that the man wasn't used to being addressed by his own name. It didn't feel awkward for Lucian to do, though. After everything he'd experienced, he reckoned he'd earned that right.

"You're the ringleader of the circus, are you not? You're the reason my daughter is traipsing around the Worlds looking for adventure."

"With all due respect, she'd be doing that without my intervention."

"Well, that might be true enough. At first, I thought you two might have met here and agreed to go to Volsung together. She said you met onboard the ship, but the coincidence seemed to be too much. That doesn't make sense, though. I don't think you've ever been to L5. You talk like an Earther. Specifically, your accent is about as North American as I've ever heard."

Lucian took that to mean he didn't seem posh enough to have ever walked on L5. It was probably an insult, but he didn't take it as one.

"Emma's right that we met on the way to Volsung. She

mentioned you wanted someone of your own choosing to train her. Except she decided to go a different way."

"Listen," Tristan said. "I know it's too late to change the past. Over the years, my anger has dissipated. It's been replaced with a feeling far less welcome." He stared sadly at the passing water below. "Emma is my only child. My pride and joy. Her mother and I . . . we had such high hopes for her. I spared no expense to cure her, to make her happy, to give her the best education and every advantage. I would have given her the Worlds. She was to be our legacy. Of course, fate had other plans. Despite our resources, things haven't been easy. Maybe I'm partly to blame for that."

Lucian didn't understand why this man he barely knew was pouring himself out. He wasn't sure what to say, so he elected silence. He was less likely to say the wrong thing that way.

"I asked you here for a favor."

"What's that?"

"Well, I *was* going to ask you. As we were fishing down there, though, I got to thinking. Her life isn't her own anymore. No mage's life is. She has to follow orders, whatever those orders may be. It's not the life I wanted for her, but it is the life she chose. There's no helping that."

"So you want reassurance." At the man's silence, Lucian nodded. "Well, I can't promise to keep her safe. That would be impossible, but I can promise to do my best. At least following me, she'll have more choice than anywhere else in the Worlds. I understand you want her to be safe, but there's nowhere safe in the Worlds right now. That Swarmer Fleet out of Kasturi is headed straight here."

Tristan's face hardened. "Alpha Centauri won't fall. We'll turn them back, just like we did last time, and the time before."

"This time is different. We *saw* the Swarmers in the coreward frontier. It's nothing short of an invasion to end humanity for good."

"How can you be so sure?"

"It would take too long to explain everything that's happened. But the truth is, if it's Emma you're worried about, you wouldn't want her to be here."

"If what you're saying is true . . ." He shook his head. "How could the Solar System not be safe? We have the fleet, Starbase Centauri, the Forge of Heaven, the Jovian Yards . . ."

"I'm here to tell you that it won't matter, in the end. The Swarmers destroyed the Builders, an empire far stronger than the League. There's only one chance to save the human race, and Emma is helping with that mission. We're not going to fight with the rest of the mages and the League fleet. We have another mission, one that's more important. Emma has already saved my life, and without her, we would not have survived this long. If she stays here, Tristan, it could be devastating. The League needs her. *Humanity* needs her."

"And what about *my* devastation? I see my daughter for the first time in almost three years, and I hardly recognize her. She's not the same girl, that much is true. But what of a father's grief, and her mother's? If what you're saying is true, then I don't think we will ever see her again."

Lucian remained silent, leaving the prince to figure out the rest on his own.

"It's lonely," he went on, taking in the perfectly manicured landscape. "All this . . . is not enough. Only she could fill it. I'd hoped to see grandchildren raised here, and great-grandchildren, and even beyond."

"I'm . . . sorry. Did you talk about this with her? I'm not forcing her to do anything. She was the one who decided this is what she wanted."

Tristan went silent. The man was obviously having some regrets. Lucian didn't know Emma's complete story, but perhaps there was more to it than just wanting to go to the

Academy. Maybe she'd just resented the control her parents held over her life.

Eventually, they headed back to the forward part of the cylinder, near the pristine lake next to the marble stairs leading up to the balcony, where Emma waited above.

Before ascending the steps, Lucian faced Tristan. "Just so you know, if Emma stayed here, I wouldn't stop her. In fact, part of me would prefer that. But she's a mage and has a sense of duty to the Volsung Academy. She won't let anything stand in between that."

Tristan remained silent. When it seemed like he wouldn't say anything more, Lucian got the feeling he had outstayed his welcome.

"If you need me for anything, let me know."

When he turned to leave, Tristan held up a hand.

"Talent Lucian."

"Yes?"

"As soon as your ship is repaired, I think it's best if you left immediately. Having her here, but not her heart here as well . . ."

Lucian nodded, understanding. "Children leave home someday."

"Yes. But not in such a painful way."

"Emma's got a good head on her shoulders. If anyone will turn out all right, it's her."

Tristan nodded, grateful for at least that.

Lucian continued up the steps, finding Emma at the top, looking out at the river.

"How'd it go?"

"Fine. I . . . think you should talk to him. He may not admit it to you, but he's still reeling over you going to the Volsung Academy."

Her look was questioning, but at the seriousness of his expression, she nodded. "Okay. I will. My mother is supposed to be down here anytime. Why don't you go back up to the house? It's rare to have time to relax."

"Will do. As soon as the ship's repaired, we need to be moving on. I'll let you know when it's time."

"Of course."

Lucian headed back to the elevator to return to his room. The entire ride up, he had a dreadful feeling that just couldn't be explained. When the doors opened, he headed down the hallway toward his suite.

He got the feeling that someone was behind him, but when he turned to look, nothing was there. Just an empty corridor curving upward.

He remained for a moment, wondering if he should investigate the room a couple of doors down. He tried to open the door, but the reader didn't seem to work. It was either that, or he didn't have access.

That was when he noticed a shadow under the threshold, but as soon as he noticed it, it was gone.

"Hey, this isn't funny," Lucian said. "Serah, that you?"

He pressed his ear to the door, but there was nothing.

"Just hearing things, I guess."

He walked down the corridor to his room.

8

WHEN LUCIAN RETURNED to his suite, Serah was nowhere to be found. When he reached for his slate and called her, she answered almost immediately.

"Hey. They've got a *spaceball* sphere here!"

He heard Fergus yelling in the background, along with Plato tittering. From the booming echoes, it seemed that they were indeed inside a large space.

Lucian pushed the thought of the shadow out of his mind. "Where at? We need to be heading out soon."

"Come on, have a bit of fun first! I'll send you the location. We need you on our team. We're getting destroyed!"

Lucian wasn't really in the mood for games, but there was nothing better to do while they waited for the ship to be repaired. He'd played the game himself during boarding school. After the development of applied anti-gravity following the Mage War, the sport had exploded in popularity because it was no longer relegated to only space stadiums. Spaceball spheres could be constructed on planets and moons, too, though of course, it wasn't cheap.

He left the suite and followed the map on his slate. He entered the elevator and rose to the center of the cylinder, feeling lighter on his feet the entire journey. By the time the doors opened, only a marginal amount of gravity was pulling him down.

He climbed up a short ladder, at the top of which the gravity was practically gone. He entered a tunnel about ten meters long, at the end of which he could see a wide, open area. Serah flew by the entrance of the tunnel, a large blue ball tucked under her arm, with her blonde hair streaming behind her.

When Lucian reached the end of the tunnel, he entered a large, regulation size sphere, exactly fifty meters in diameter. Linus and Serah seemed to be a team, passing to each other, while Fergus, Plato, and surprisingly even Khairu worked together. The interior surface of the sphere was elastic, both to absorb the impact of players and to give them a needed boost. Two circular goals sat on either end. Normally, there would have been a keeper, but they didn't have enough players.

Khairu passed the large ball to Fergus, who caught it and sent it hurtling toward the goal. He let out a whoop as it nailed the center, causing the buzzer to go off.

As he and Khairu high-fived, Lucian launched himself into the field of play. "Looks like a bit of a mismatch to me."

"Lucian!" Serah pushed off the bottom of the sphere, launching herself into him a bit too roughly. They both went flying back into the side of the sphere, going flat on the surface and grabbing a handhold to keep from flying off. "Looks like you survived the prince."

"Was there any doubt? Emma's down there with him now. What's the score?"

"3-0!" Fergus shouted. "*Our* favor!"

"How much time left?"

"We're playing first to ten," Serah said. "No magic, obviously."

"Well, there goes *my* plan."

She glowered in Fergus's direction, where he was high-fiving Plato. "I want to wipe that stupid smirk off his face."

Linus came up to join them. "All right, what's the plan this time, team? Shall I go center?"

"Yeah, right," Serah said. "We tried that last time, and Fergus tackled you silly and you fumbled the ball."

"I could hardly see him coming from on top of me!"

"Spaceball requires *spatial* awareness," Lucian said. "Keep track of what's going on in every direction. The best strategy is to stick to the sides. You go to the middle, you're a sitting duck. But the middle is the best place to shoot a goal."

"Then go toward the middle at the end of the sphere so you can shoot?" Linus asked.

"Well, that depends. The defenders will expect that, but yes. We should make that the plan."

"Let's go!" Serah said.

"All right. Linus on defense. Serah, you can be midfield. You seem to be pretty accurate with your tackles, and midfielder has to do a lot of tackling."

"I've gotten a lot of practice as a Gravitist," she gushed.

"I'll be forward, obviously. Just get the ball to me and I'll make magic happen."

"You sound mighty confident, boy," Linus said.

"I don't mean to brag, but I used to watch a lot of spaceball growing up. And I played it in boarding school."

"Oh," Serah said. "So victory is assured, then?"

"Absolutely."

They broke and assumed their positions at the bottom of the sphere while Fergus and his team straddled the top with the ball in hand. Fergus launched the ball with all his might, and it sailed across midfield straight toward Lucian.

Lucian got in front of it, hugging the ball to his chest. The idea was not to let it ricochet off, giving the other team the chance to claim possession.

Lucian stuck to his team's side of the sphere. It would have been faster to launch himself across midfield, but it would also make him vulnerable to the opposing team's tackles. On the side, he was safer, but he had a greater distance to traverse and couldn't get up to speed as quickly.

When Khairu dove toward him first, an intense look on her face, Lucian passed to Serah, who was open just ahead of him. As soon as she caught the ball, she launched off the side and flew toward the goal. Fergus was there to break her up, knocking the ball away in the process. It bounced off the side and headed toward the other end of the sphere.

Luckily, Linus was nearby and managed to nab it. However, he had no momentum, so was a sitting duck as Plato launched himself toward him. He passed to Serah, who was already on a trajectory to the upper part of the sphere, which was empty. She caught it smoothly, turning adroitly in the air and bouncing hard off the elastic side right toward the goal, readying her shot all the while.

At this point, Lucian timed his jump to come in from below. Even as Fergus tackled Serah, she passed the ball to Lucian, who was just meters from the goal. He threw it and it slammed into the ring, his blood pumping as the buzzer went off.

"Booyah!" he shouted. "That's how it's done!"

Fergus glowered and stalked off toward the receiving end of the sphere, along with Plato and Khairu.

"That was *amazing!*" Serah said.

"That was a slick catch, my boy," Linus said. "They didn't have this sport when I was your age."

"Thanks. If we keep playing like this, we'll come back for sure."

They tied up the score 3-3, before Fergus's team came back

with four in a row. They traded a series of goals back and forth until Lucian's team tied the score up at 9-9.

Lucian shot what could have been the game-winning goal. It was from halfway across the sphere, but still accurate, flying at great speed. Khairu launched herself desperately, aiming to intercept, but missed. It was going in.

But just a few meters from the goal, a crash resounded through the sphere.

A breach had formed on the opposite end and air roared around him toward the opening. Instantly, everyone was pulled in that direction toward their doom.

Lucian reached for the Orb of Binding, opening two separate streams. He connected one to Linus and the other to Plato, both of whom were the closest to the opening. He pulled them toward the tunnel. He reached for Fergus and Khairu next, and did the same thing. Lucian felt himself being pulled toward the tunnel as well, and was wondering why until he realized Linus was streaming a Gravitonic disc that was counteracting the force of the escaping air, while keeping the others planted in the tunnel.

Lucian bound himself and Serah last of all, even as he sucked in breath after breath, never seeming to fill his lungs.

Together, they pulled their way down the tunnel. As soon as they passed the entrance, Khairu shut the emergency door, stopping the outflow of air.

"What the hell happened?" Fergus asked.

"Looks like we got hit with some space debris," Lucian said.

"*This* close to L5?" Khairu asked.

"We should get downstairs. Link up with Emma."

Warning klaxons sounded. Hopefully, the rest of the cylinder was safe.

The elevator was working at least. It whisked them down to the habitation ring, where alarms were still going off. As they ran down the corridor toward the central elevator,

Lucian reached for the Orb of Psionics, opening a link to Emma.

Emma, you all right?

Yeah. Something hit near the hangar. We're still assessing the damage.

It hit the spaceball sphere, too. We were lucky to get out alive.

Are you serious? Where are you now?

The main ring.

My parents and I are coming up right now. There are several leaks here in the arcology, but someone should plug them quickly. Miranda is off the cylinder, so she should be fine.

Whatever had happened, Lucian was almost positive it wasn't a coincidence. What were the odds that something would hit that close to *their* ship? Large stations and habitats getting hit by space junk was almost unheard of in this day and age. Surveying satellites kept larger objects away, while smaller objects could be shielded against. Advanced trawlers were always on the hunt for orbital debris, no matter how small.

His priority was making sure everyone was safe. So far, everyone was with him and accounted for. Everyone but Emma.

They waited by the central elevator for a couple of minutes before the doors dinged, revealing Emma and her father, along with a middle-aged woman who was the spitting image of Emma, just twenty years older. She wore a long green dress and white blouse, her dark brown hair done in a ponytail.

"We must take shelter," Tristan said. "I have a panic room where we will be safe."

"What's going on?" Serah asked. "Are we under attack or something?"

"I don't know yet. The security sector was hit, too. They're not responding to my calls."

Lucian retrieved his shockspear. "So, it's an attack, then. We should get to the hangar and get somewhere safe. Figure out the rest later. Is the ship repaired yet?"

"The techs should be finished up," Emma said.

"Like hell I'm getting run out of my home," Tristan said.

"Don't be stubborn, Dad," Emma said. "If they tried to take out the hangar, then they might make another pass. If we have no way of getting out—"

At that moment, the entire cylinder shook from another impact. Lucian almost lost his footing while Emma's mother took a tumble to the floor.

"Mom! Are you okay?"

The older woman blinked in surprise. Then, her expression firmed as she looked at her husband challengingly. "We're getting off this death trap, Tristan. I want to get on the ship. *Now*."

"They're trying to flush us out," Tristan said. "I know it doesn't feel like it, but it's safest to stay put and wait for reinforcements."

"*What* reinforcements?" Emma asked. "Our home is under attack in sight of Earth, and the fact it hasn't been put to a stop yet should tell you something!"

At that moment, an explosion blasted through the door of one of the apartments down the curved hallway. Emerging from the resulting cloud of smoke walked a soldier in black-suited power armor with no insignia, bearing a heavy gauss rifle, his suit glowing with a deployed energy shield. Two more soldiers quickly followed, and together, they clomped down the corridor toward them, raising their rifles as even more troops emerged.

Lucian raised a Binding shield just in time to stop the first shots. The powerful shield, about three meters in diameter, shone brilliantly as the slugs were deflected, poking holes in the walls that were powerful enough to punch into space itself. Air began hissing out of the interior corridor. Lucian realized these men didn't care about losing air. They had their own air supply within their suits, which were impervious to the ricocheted bullets.

They *had* to get out of here, especially with almost a dozen soldiers now pouring down the corridor. Where had they *come* from? Who were they?

They had to fight and ask questions later. Khairu was already reacting, raising her hands and collecting a ball of energy that dispersed in chain lightning that connected with the three frontrunning soldiers. Their personal energy shields ate the impact, but with redoubled effort, Khairu let out a greater burst of magic, overloading their shields and connecting with their armor. The electricity sizzled on the metal, emitting smoke and causing the men to go down.

Plato raised his hands and streamed an ice slick on the floor, causing several more to lose their footing and go down in their heavy armor. Linus kept them planted with a gravity disc. But even so, more soldiers were coming, firing yet more shots that Lucian was forced to deflect with his shield.

Lucian reached for the Orb of Radiance, combining its ether to the Binding stream to create a powerful laser that shot from both of his hands. That laser pierced through at least half a dozen of the black-armored soldiers, their armor glowing white-hot at the point of impact. Their shields didn't stand a chance against its strength.

Nor did the corridor beyond, which melted to the laser's extreme energy. A hole the size of a fist formed, through which air was sucked out at incredible speed. This place was done for, anyway, so Lucian had to finish the job as quickly as possible.

More men were pouring into the corridor, so many that Lucian couldn't kill them all before they ran out of air. While their armor and shields couldn't stand up to magical attacks, the soldiers might make up for it with sheer numbers. And of course, the longer this went on, the more likely there would be casualties on his side.

So, he cut off the stream, taking hold of only Radiance to create a blinding sphere of light which floated above the enemy squadron. Fergus, meanwhile, created a reverse Radiant stream that kept the excess light from blinding them.

It was enough of a reprieve for them to pile inside the elevator and head down to the hangar. As soon as Emma mashed the button, the elevator slid down.

"What is happening?" Emma's mother asked, her voice quavering.

"It'll be all right," Emma said. "We'll be out of here soon."

"Who are those men?" Tristan asked.

The only thing Lucian knew was that they were after *him*. Could Vera and Xara, or even Zheng Yang, have sent them? If so, how did they even know he was here?

It was the brand, he realized. Vera could still sense his location, or at least his general direction. But how could she do so from so far away?

They ran into the hangar. Despite a sizeable breach in its exterior, the vents were pumping air fast enough for it to remain breathable. They paused for a moment between *Ethereal* and the other transport. Emma looked from her parents to Lucian.

"Go," her mother said. "You're needed."

"What about you?" she asked.

"We have other places we can stay. Just go."

Tristan's face was tense for a moment before softening. "You heard your mother, Emma. We're . . . proud of you."

She nodded, tears in her eyes. "Stay safe. They're not after you."

The hangar shook again from some sort of impact.

"Everyone, get on board," Lucian said.

There was no time for further goodbyes. They ran onto the

ship, which Khairu, in her foresight, had already started. She must have slipped away while everyone was focusing on Emma and her parents.

As soon as they were strapped in, the hangar doors slid open, revealing outer space beyond. *Ethereal* turned and advanced outward first. There didn't seem to be any obvious threats. The LADAR display only showed normal space traffic.

When Khairu veered the ship around, Emma pointed.

"Over there. That transport is attached to the cylinder."

"There are several of them," Fergus said.

Lucian saw what she meant. They looked to have crashed right into the surface of the metal, stuck like barnacles on a hull. There were at least six of them.

Khairu increased the thrust, not bothering to turn the transponder on. "Those aren't transports. They're boarding pods. Whatever launched them is still around. Somewhere."

"I don't suppose you can warp us out of this predicament?" Linus asked.

"No. The Orb's barely had time to recover."

"We just have to hope the ship that shot those pods is gone," Khairu said.

"Head for the Alpha Centauri Gate," Lucian said. "That's the direction we need to go to reach Hephaestus."

"Good," Plato said. "That gives your Orb time to recharge."

"Who *were* those people, anyway?" Serah asked.

"Some mercenaries hired for a hit would be my guess," Fergus said.

"Vera and Xara?" Serah asked.

"It seems rather . . . strange. I've never known of totally black armor like that, and there were no insignias on it. They were meant to get the kill, whatever the cost."

"Now, though, they're stuck in my house," Emma said. She looked at the LADAR screen. "Looks like my parents are still with us."

"Have them transmit a private beam to our ship code."

"I'll send it to them."

A moment later, they received a voice request on the dash. Khairu hit accept and Tristan's voice poured out of the speaker.

"We're heading to the Sani Embassy on Earth. I doubt they'll be able to sort out this mess, but we'll be safe there. At least until we get our bearings and figure out what the hell is going on."

"Who *were* those people?" her mother asked.

"We don't know," Emma said. "They were after us for some reason. Something to do with our mission, I guess."

"Where are you going now?"

"I won't say, in case there's someone listening in. Right now, it looks like that ship isn't around. It shouldn't be following you if it is, and *Ethereal* is fast. No one would openly torpedo us this close to Earth."

"They attacked *us* openly," Serah said.

"They might write that off as an attempt on my father's life. I mean, it *could* be possible that they're after you, right?"

"I'm not well-liked in some circles, certainly. But assassination? I would have never dreamed that possible."

"Get to the embassy in Geneva. You'll be safe there."

"Never mind that," Tristan said. "What will *you* do?"

"You just have to trust me. We've survived this long. We'll survive longer."

The message cut off, apparently going off speaker mode. Emma picked up her slate. She said little, but whatever was said on the other end brought tears to her eyes.

"I love you, too," she said. "I'll be okay. Just . . . get to a safe spot. Everything will work out."

She left the bridge to continue her conversation.

"It's a terrible thing to lose one's home," Serah said. "And to leave one's family behind."

"At least we're all alive," Fergus said. "I don't know how

many men they sent after us, but there were at least twenty, if not double that."

"They got more than they bargained for, that's for sure," Plato said.

"We're not out of this yet," Khairu said.

"Are we being followed?" Fergus asked.

"Not right now, but I wouldn't be surprised. I'll keep a close eye on it." She flipped on the transponder. "If something is out there hunting us, then having this off won't help. They found us without it, anyway. In a strange way, it might afford some protection. No one will attack a mage ship. Not openly, anyway."

Lucian wasn't as optimistic about that projection. "So, who could they be?"

No one answered, though Khairu stirred in her seat. "I really don't know, but I have some ideas. They could be mercenaries, like Fergus said, but if they were, they'd have to be the most loaded out mercenaries I've ever seen. Every single one of them had power armor and an energy shield."

"Meaning?" Serah asked.

"Whoever hired them had a lot of resources. And of course, there's always the possibility that they aren't mercenaries at all, but highly trained assassins. There have always been rumors about the League's Blackguards, but they've always denied their existence."

Lucian had heard of them before. Apparently, they were spies and assassins, working for League Intelligence, highly capable and never known for failing their mission. Most people didn't believe they exist, but he had to admit, their totally black armor certainly seemed to fit the textbook description for them.

"Well, there are crazier suggestions," Fergus asked. "Of course, that begs the question. Why would such a force be attacking *us*?"

No one answered him as they left L5 behind, and Emma's parents' ship became lost in the traffic of Earth's heavily traversed space lanes. On the newsfeeds, they were already picking up rumblings of a terrorist attack on L5. Apparently, their cylinder wasn't the only one hit. Three others were attacked as well, also high wealth cylinders, though none had been attacked so extensively as theirs. The media was already painting it as terror attack of the poor against the rich. Never mind how poorer people could finance such an expensive operation.

"Those other attacks have to be false flags," Fergus said. "Trying to distract from the true target."

"Maybe," Lucian said.

"What now?" Serah asked. "We're heading to this Alpha Centauri place?"

"That's the plan," Lucian said. "AC, Astravan, and finally, Hephaestus."

She sighed. "How I *love* space travel."

"I'll take space travel over risking my neck any day," Plato said.

"Nonstop, it'll take thirty-two days," Khairu said.

"Why would we stop, anyway?" Serah asked. "What's the point of the rotting Orb of Space-Time if we can't just go wherever we want?"

"Could be a lot worse," Lucian said.

He was grateful for the reprieve. Anytime they were in deep space, there was less of a chance of being attacked. This close to Earth, the odds of getting hit by pirates were practically zero.

Then again, there was *someone* out there looking for them, though *Ethereal* was likely faster than whatever they had. Even knowing that, it made Lucian uneasy.

"Things seem to be under control for now," Khairu said. "If that changes, I can let you know."

9

AS MUCH AS he tried to relax in bed, he couldn't get the attack out of his mind. He knew he shouldn't be bothered about killing men who were out to kill him, or those close to him, but it wasn't an easy thing to get past. He *had* killed, and he had to make peace with that. He'd had no choice. So why was it bothering him so much?

Actually, that wasn't true. What scared him was that it *didn't* bother him. With a simple thought, he could destroy just about anyone he wanted to. And now that he had the Orb of Space-Time, there was no longer any check on his power. It would keep him safe from the fraying entirely. All the Aspects that had been closed to him—Dynamism, Atomicism, Thermalism, and Gravitonics—he could now use with impunity, if not the same strength as the ones he had Orbs for.

Lucian wasn't sure what to do with that. He was reluctant to use Aspects he was unfamiliar with, but he knew that one day, he'd have to learn to use them, especially if he found other Orbs. Would there ever be time to find the proper training? And just *who* would be the one to give that training?

Lucian had no answers. There was no one to order him about, and his mistakes couldn't be blamed on anyone but himself. Control had escaped him entirely, and he wasn't sure how to get it back.

When Serah entered the cabin, he pretended to be asleep, his back to the door and his face close to the bulwark.

"I know you're awake. You're not snoring." As the door shut behind her, she joined him on the bed, placing a hand on his shoulder. "You okay? You've been shut in here all day."

"I don't know. Thoughts."

"I've got just the cure."

"Let me guess. Video games?"

"Of course. Equally fun and emotionally numbing."

Lucian chuckled. "Well, maybe that's what I need."

"Well, you just look pissed-off right now. Of course, I know you're not pissed. That's just your thinking face."

"I don't look pissed off when I think."

Serah smiled. "*Sure* you don't. But maybe talking about it would help?"

Lucian didn't really want to get into it. What was the fun in talking about his emotional burdens? Didn't *he* need to be the strong one?

"There's just a lot to think about. I don't even know where to begin."

"I have a solution for you. Just start from the beginning."

"Wow. Why didn't *I* think of that?"

"I'm being serious. We have thirty-two days until this Hephaestus place. I mean, if I really wanted to, I could list off all the shit we've been through in the last few months, but I'd probably go hoarse. I'm sure talking about what's bothering you won't take that long."

"What do you suggest, then?"

"Well, if you don't want to talk, you can play that game with me. You've been putting me off for weeks."

"What was it called again? *Medieval Farming Simulator Nine Million?*"

"No, silly. *Medieval Farming Simulator 7.* Trust me, there's nothing like role-playing as a medieval peasant sowing the fields to take your mind off things."

"Wow. Is *that* what you actually do in that game?"

"Hey, the title is accurate. It's good marketing, if you ask me. Farming is therapeutic."

"Is that so? In that case . . ."

"Seriously? You'll try it with me?"

"Why not? I can tell it's important to you."

"Aww. You surprise me sometimes, Lucian."

"Maybe wait a couple of days first. We might still get attacked, after all."

"Of course. That's a given."

"There are *other* ways we can relax, too."

She arched an eyebrow. "Oh?"

He leaned in until his lips were close to hers. "Yeah. I think we still have some herbal tea we picked up from Irion. *Very* relaxing and soothing."

She smiled and punched him in the arm. "*That's* not very nice."

He kissed her, and the tension melted away. It was at that moment, when things were getting a little more heated, that Khairu's voice came out of the intercom, killing the mood as surely as a bucket of water on a kindling flame.

"We've got an issue up front."

Lucian got up. "To be continued."

He left the cabin and walked up to the bridge, where Khairu was leaning over the LADAR screen.

"We're being followed. I've been tracking this vessel on our heat trail. It's matching our speed and vector."

"Is it in torpedo range?"

"Maybe. Depends on their equipment. Could be they're trying to catch up, but can't manage it."

"Maybe they're just going to the AC Gate, too. Wouldn't they be on the same trajectory if they left L5?"

"I admit it's possible. They're about four hours behind and, like I said, matching our speed."

"And if they fired off some torpedoes?"

"Probably twenty to thirty minutes to impact, depending on the technology. We're in a heavily trafficked space lane, so the idea that someone would shoot us out here is ludicrous."

"And in AC too, I imagine."

"Yeah. AC, too. If this ship is still tailing us by the time we get to Astravan, then we've got problems."

"What do you suggest?"

"Well, that's what I was going to run by you. The AC Fleet is about eleven days away, outside Starbase Centauri."

"Thinking of contacting Transcend White?"

"It would keep us safe. I've been in contact with her, and she agrees that this is the best move for us right now."

"She's not recalling you and Emma, is she? We need you both. You're our only pilot."

"There are other pilots. And Fergus is also capable. He was telling me he did some piloting under Zheng Yang, though getting him to admit that was like extracting a tooth. Point being, Transcend White wants us to report to her. I'm sure she has questions and concerns of her own."

"So, that's what this is."

"Lucian, we're being followed. Even if she *didn't* want to see us, it's too dangerous to just let this ship follow us. We'll lose it if we get to the fleet."

"And what if it tries to shoot us down before that?"

She watched him closely. "You don't remember last time?"

Lucian remembered, but he hadn't wanted to mention it. Even if he could shield the ship from torpedoes, it might not work if this ship fired off a whole volley of them. There was the Orb of Space-Time, too, but there was the tricky bit of trying to find a new place to warp to. And it was a process that took time.

"As much as I don't like it, I get your point. Set course for the AC fleet."

———

Six days later, they passed into the Alpha Centauri System. Already up to speed, the remaining portion of the journey would only take five days. The ship that had been trailing them fell off their scopes, likely unable to keep up with *Ethereal* properly. Of course, it would have made more sense to keep their speed up and use it to get to Hephaestus faster, but Khairu was adamant about linking up with the Alpha Centauri fleet. It wasn't something Lucian could argue against. She answered to Transcend White, and there was no way she was going to counteract the order of her direct superior.

The system was filled with chatter of the Swarmers' continuing advance. The main bulk of the Swarmer fleet was out of the Djerrah System now, and well on its way to the planet of Fessan, a lightly populated desert world that had been mostly evacuated. Malon, the next world, had millions of inhabitants and would be difficult to rescue.

Meanwhile, Zheng Yang's Golden Armada was making quick progress coreward and spinward, last sighted in the Alcazar System, bearing toward Malon as well. The rumor was that the pirates planned to attack the Swarmers themselves with their Golden Armada, estimated to contain more than a thousand ships. That was almost as sizeable as the League's gathering on Starbase Centauri. Many pundits conjectured that Zheng Yang would become the savior of the League and wanted to stop the Swarmers as much as everyone else for the sake of humanity's survival.

Lucian doubted her motives were that pure, but he had to admit it was a nice thought and probably kept a lot of eyeballs glued to the newsfeeds.

The five days in Alpha Centauri breezed by quickly. Transcend White sent boarding instructions that would lead them to a berth on the *MS Resplendent,* a battlecruiser that had been given over to the mages to keep them segregated from the rest of the fleet.

On the day of their arrival, *Ethereal* slowed as Alpha Centauri's only habitable world, Chiron, came into view, along with its blue oceans and long, snaky continents. Starbase Centauri was like a smaller version of Sol Citadel, orbiting a quarter of a million kilometers from Chiron itself. If the Swarmers wanted to attack the planet directly, they'd have to contend with the starbase, along with its long range missiles, drone fleets, fighters, and bombers, augmented of course by the power of the League fleet itself.

It was possible for the base to be bypassed, especially if it was on the opposite side of the system from the Solar System Gate, but so far, the Swarmers had paused to take every world they had come across. The thinking was the same thing would happen in the Alpha Centauri System. Granted they made it that far. It was likely they would need the resources of the planet to make their final push toward Sol.

But such an eventuality was months away. It seemed impossible that the Swarmers could carry the day here, especially as they approached the massive fleet stationed in orbit around the planet.

Hundreds upon hundreds of ships shone resplendently by the light of the system's two suns. Dozens of battleships and carriers, each a kilometer or more long, stood against the backdrop of landmasses, white clouds, and dark blue oceans. Smaller frigates and cruisers remained in formation around the larger ships. It was impossible to count just how many there were, but Lucian knew it had to be well above a thousand vessels, perhaps as many as fifteen hundred, not counting the fighters and bombers based on each of the carriers.

"The pride of the League of Worlds," Fergus said, at their approach. "Not since the Siege of Isis has there been such a mustering. And the advancement of technology makes this fleet thrice as dangerous."

"Will it be enough to stop the Swarmers, though?" Serah asked.

Her question went unanswered as Khairu piloted *Ethereal* toward one of those many hundreds of vessels, a long, sleek cruiser toward the tail of the procession, well-separated from the rest.

The *Resplendent* was actually larger than it seemed from a distance, especially as they drew in close to the sternward hangar specified for their use. There were only two such bays on the entire ship. The League's Orion class cruisers were built for both speed and firepower, needing to keep up with the fighters and bombers hurled by the larger carriers. That meant not basing more ships than was necessary.

Ethereal's dash lit with an incoming voice request. Khairu hit accept and a male voice escaped the speaker.

"*Ethereal*, you are clear for docking."

Lucian would have recognized that voice anywhere. He had to resist the urge to punch the speaker.

"Thank you, Psion Gaius. We will be landing shortly."

Within moments, they were pulling into the open hangar, which had barely enough room to squeeze in. As soon as the space was pressurized, the blast door into the hangar slid open, revealing Psion Gaius in his white robes.

Serah put a hand on Lucian's shoulder. "It's hard to tell who you hate more: that guy, or Xara Mallis."

Lucian thought the observation apt. "I wonder."

"We have to face him at some point."

"I suppose."

They piled off the ship, and Psion Gaius stood straight, his hands folded inside the sleeves of his white robes. As his cold blue eyes found Lucian's, there seemed to be a slight smirk on his thin lips.

"Welcome aboard *Resplendent*, Talents." His eyes took in Linus and Plato, unsure of where they stood. His gaze went back to Psion Khairu. "Transcend White is currently indisposed, but we have a comfortable place where you can wait for her arrival."

"That would be fine," Khairu said.

"Welcome home, Psion Yellow. This way, if you would."

With a self-important sweep of his robe, he headed out of the hangar without waiting for them to follow. Lucian had to resist the urge to tether his boots together.

They entered a large central corridor, passing other mages on their assigned duties, including a gaggle of fresh-faced, brown-robed Novices who were scurrying on some errand or other. Lucian watched as they passed, getting a surreal feeling that if things had been different, that might have been him. Now, he felt entirely separated from them, even if his age was mostly the same.

Gaius led them into a small waiting room, with several couches bolted to the deck overlooking the spinning surface of the planet below.

"Transcend White will be with you soon."

He left them there, the door sliding shut behind.

"I'm hungry," Plato said. He headed for the fridge in the small kitchenette and opened the door. "Jackpot."

"That's not yours to eat," Khairu said.

He was already unwrapping the packaging of a sandwich. "I don't see anyone's name on it."

Serah went up to join him, seeming to have no qualms herself. Khairu just rolled her eyes.

"What's *taking* them so long?" Linus asked, staring out the wide viewport.

"We've been here all of one minute, and you're already losing patience?" Fergus asked.

"We've traveled very far, survived Isis, Nai Elyn, *and* Xara Mallis. The least they could do is give us more courtesy."

"Have a sandwich," Plato said. "You sound hangry."

"Can you think of anything *other* than food?"

"You already know the answer to that."

Lucian rose from the couch and poured himself a coffee. Emma remained silent, her face pale. She'd been extremely withdrawn since L5, for understandable reasons, and she had ignored Lucian's attempts to draw her out.

They waited another hour. Then two. Lucian was almost thinking about leaving the room when the door slid open, revealing Transcend White standing in the doorway.

10

"TRANSCEND VIOLET," Linus said, sitting up straight. "I mean, err . . . Transcend White."

Transcend White stared at him for a moment. "Hello. Linus Wander, I presume. Former Talent of the Volsung Academy."

He gasped. "She remembers me!"

"Yes. It's . . . a shame what happened to both you and Plato. Psion Khairu has apprised me of the situation."

"And yet," Plato said, "you voted with the rest to send us to that island."

He stared her down across the waiting room. He took a bite of his sandwich, licked his fingers, and smacked his lips, somewhat dampening the effect of his severity.

"I could blame my inexperience and my recent ascension to the mantle of Transcend, and my desire to prove myself, as factors that lent to my decision. But that would be disingenuous. Clearly, I made a mistake. I've made many such mistakes over my long years. I will not ask for forgiveness, because what I did was unforgiveable. Unfortunately, being a Transcend means committing unforgiveable acts far more often than one would like." She nodded, as if to affirm that. "I'm sure I will commit many more, despite the advancement of my years."

She took a few steps forward until she stood in the center of them all.

"There's no need to update me on anything. I received Psion Khairu's message out of the Archea System, along with other updates on your way here. I'm aware of your situation in full. While congratulations are in order for finding the prophecy, much has yet to be accomplished."

"We were well on our way to Hephaestus until you told us to come here," Lucian said. "We're losing time."

"That was as much for your own safety, and you know it," Transcend White said. "Nonetheless, I have things to say. Questions you no doubt would like the answer to."

"Such as?" Serah asked.

"The fate of my sister, for one. She's alive, as the brand on Lucian is still as intractable as ever. I did a scan of your Focus upon entering this room."

Lucian thought as much. He was just trying not to kick himself for not finishing the job. He had Vera on the ropes, and all he had to do was withdraw the shockspear and stab her through the neck. That would've finished her for good. But such was the shock that the thought hadn't occurred to him at the time.

"Do you know where she is?" he asked.

"I do not. It's possible they're both heading to Hephaestus, too, and it will not be difficult for them to guess what your new Orb does, especially after your confrontation with them."

Transcend White really *did* know everything. Khairu had been especially thorough in reporting to her. Lucian supposed he shouldn't have found that surprising.

"Well, we'll get to Hephaestus way before them," Lucian said. "They're likely still in the frontier, months away."

"You must use that to your full advantage. Psion Khairu also told me about how your new Orb will lead the way to the others, though she didn't tell me about the mechanism by which that worked." She regarded him seriously. "If there was ever any doubt about who you are, there is none now. You are the Chosen of the Manifold."

"Serious question," Serah said. "What can they possibly do to us now? Lucian wiped the floor with them."

"You shouldn't be so confident, Talent Serah. They know what to expect now. My sister is not someone to be underestimated."

Lucian had to admit, Transcend White was right. "So, our main chance is to get to Hephaestus and find the Orb before they arrive. Somehow, I can use the Orb of Space-Time to lead us right to it."

"While that may be true, Hephaestus is quite possibly the most inhospitable of the inhabited worlds in the League, colonized only because of its vast mineral wealth. Its only settlement, Anchorpoint, is only accessible by the Elevator of Hephaestus. That said, Hephaestus Station is the real population center of the system, larger even than Archea Station. Its dockyards are famous for their gang wars and violence."

"That's where Ansaldra is from," Lucian said. "I remember her mentioning that."

"Yes, that's true. It goes a long way in explaining her drive to rise to the top, even if that drive landed her on Psyche."

"On Psyche, *she* rose to the top," Serah said.

"We're getting away from my point here. Saying Hephaestus is a harsh world is putting it mildly. Even if you knew exactly where to find the Orb of Thermalism, it wouldn't be easy to extricate. On Hephaestus itself, no one goes outside Anchorpoint or its local mines. The air is too hot, and the concentration of carbon dioxide is too high to breathe for more than a couple of minutes. You must wear an envirosuit at all times when outdoors. Every time you stream, you'll have to make sure the magic doesn't interfere with the suit—for example, streaming directly from your hands could cause complications. You'll have to set your focal point outside your suit, making streaming more difficult."

"That's easy enough," Plato said.

"Yes," Fergus said, "but that causes streams to lose efficiency. Everyone knows the farther you stream from your Focus, the more ether required."

Transcend White nodded. "These are all complications you must deal with."

"I don't understand," Lucian said. "Why all this talk about Anchorpoint and Hephaestus Station? We have our own ship, so I can feel out where the Orb is. We can just go straight there."

"Unfortunately, it won't be that simple. The League has chartered Hephaestus exclusively to Carthago Corporation, much like how Caralis Intergalactic has the rights to Halia. Both have exclusive charters from the League to exploit their respective planets. I'm afraid you will need permission from the corporation to do anything on world. And that won't be easy to get."

"Why can't we just ignore them?" Serah asked. "Fergus can ward us, right? We have the Orb of Radiance, too."

"I want nothing to do with that thing," Fergus said. "Besides, warding a ship for a moment is possible, if difficult. Doing so for days on end could fray me."

"Scratch that idea, then."

"There *has* to be another option," Lucian said. "Do we have any contacts at Carthago that would let us explore the planet?"

"Unfortunately, it's highly unlikely they'll be forthcoming on that. The chief executive of Carthago is based on Hephaestus Station, and the most practical way would be to convince him personally."

Fergus scoffed. "How in the Worlds would we manage that?"

Lucian already saw where she was going with this. "Looks like we're about to dabble in the unethical."

"Meaning?"

"A thought control stream."

Transcend White nodded. "Seems you've figured it out."

Lucian shook his head. "I tricked an old man playing cards, but now you want me to trick someone whose company is valued in the hundreds of billions of credits?"

"How is it any different?"

"The stakes are higher."

"Are they, really? What would have happened if you'd lost all your credits at that casino?"

Lucian had to admit, it would have made things much more complicated.

"I guess it really is no different. Still, I can think of a lot of things that might go wrong."

"You must put the notion out of your head."

"Is there really no other way?"

At her lack of response, Lucian remained silent. From the others' silence, it seemed they had as little hope as him.

"Perhaps another way will open. One we don't know about, sitting where we are. That's for you to discover on your own."

She paced toward the wide viewport, looking at Chiron's nightside. City lights shone brightly around an inland sea.

"My home's down there," Linus said, joining her at the viewport.

Transcend White ignored his comment. "There's something else we must discuss. Having accomplished your mission, we must decide what will happen to Talent Emma and Psion Khairu."

Both women stood, as if ready to receive and act on her

orders, whatever they were. No emotion was betrayed on each of their faces.

"My suggestion is unorthodox, in that even I don't know the proper course. So I'll leave it to the two of you to decide. Both of you have served excellently, beyond my brightest hopes. This is not a denigration of your abilities, but rather speaks to the impossibility of the task I set before you." She watched each of them closely. "However, I cannot in good conscience ask you to risk your lives again in such a manner. Lucian and his team have the freedom to choose whether or not to risk their lives. I would give you the same courtesy."

Emma opened her mouth, but Transcend White raised a quieting hand.

"You need not answer now. Take some time to think it over." She turned to Linus and seemed ready to say something before thinking better of it. "Of course, the deck of *Resplendent* is yours to explore."

She headed for the entrance and stood in the doorway for a moment, a slight stoop in her back.

"One more thing. No doubt, *Ethereal* has served you well. But I sent you out into the galaxy ill-prepared for the dangers you would face. For that reason, I'll be taking back the ship and giving you a new one. One that will hopefully serve you far better, in both speed and defensive capabilities." She looked at Khairu. "Should you elect to continue on, Talent Khairu, the new ship will be outfitted with comprehensive tutorials that will teach you how to use its weapons system."

With that, Transcend White turned and left them in the waiting room.

"Damn," Serah said. "She said all that as if she were talking about the weather. I need details! Will we finally be able to blast all those pesky pirates to smithereens?"

"Violence should always be the last resort," Khairu said. "Any torpedo we use is a torpedo we can't use later. And it's not like you can just buy them on the open market. If the League won't supply them to us, then we have to shop on the black market."

"That sounds fun, actually."

Lucian looked at Khairu. "Any ideas what you want to do?"

"Yes," she said. "I want some space."

With no further words, she left the waiting room.

"Wow," Serah said. "You need some Karealas sap after that burn."

"I could use some air, too," Emma said.

She also stood and left.

After that, everyone left one-by-one, until it was only Lucian and Serah left.

"You want some space, too?" Lucian asked.

"I don't know," she said. "I'm feeling kind of bummed now."

Lucian felt similarly. "Maybe walking around is the right idea. Maybe they have a gym or something."

"What's a gym?"

"A place where you work out."

"Work out?"

A lot of the idioms Lucian had grown up with didn't seem to translate. Even after several months on the outside, Serah hadn't learned everything yet. Besides, on Psyche, there was no need for places like a gym or working out. "Working out" was fleeing from wyverns, or something.

"Never mind. Let's have a look around. Beats staying in here."

They left the waiting room to find themselves in the central corridor once again. It felt strange to have nowhere to go, nothing to do. Eventually, they headed into the mess hall, which had seating for about a hundred people. At this hour in the late morning, it was mostly empty, but it surprised Lucian to see a couple of familiar faces sitting at one of the corner tables.

Rhea and Damian both looked up to see him, their conversation ending while their eyes widened in surprise, as if they were seeing a ghost. To them, Lucian might as well have been dead, though surely they knew he'd returned to the Volsung Academy several months back.

"Lucian," Damian said, cordially. "It's good to see you alive and well."

Serah leaned over to him. "Who's that?"

"Damian and Rhea. We trained together at the Academy."

Rhea just watched him somewhat suspiciously, electing not to say anything.

"Talent Damian, Talent Rhea," Lucian said. "I hope you're both well."

Damian flashed an amiable smile. "For someone who cheated on his trials, it would seem things have worked out splendidly for you."

Lucian smiled back. "Well, I've done my penance. On Psyche, in case you forgot."

Damian forced a chuckle. "Only joking, friend. I'm glad you're safe and whole."

Rhea's face tightened, but she said nothing. Her gray sash denoted her as a disciple of Transcend Gray, while Damian's red sash defined him as a Thermalist.

"This is Serah," Lucian said. "My girlfriend."

"What's up?"

Rhea's eyes widened as her cheeks went pink. She sputtered for a moment before she found her words. "This is . . . unbecoming of a Talent of the Volsung Academy, Lucian Abrantes. To openly state such a thing . . ." Her cheeks reddened further. "Do the Transcends know?"

Lucian shrugged. "Don't know. Don't care."

"Better be careful what you say," Damian said. "If one of the Psions were to hear . . ."

"I'm not too concerned. I guess it is safer to keep such relationships on the down low, right?"

At Lucian's stare, Rhea's cheeks reddened. He'd always been suspicious that something was going on between the two of them, but her embarrassment made him sure.

Damian was no longer smiling. Messing with his own girlfriend seemed a bridge too far.

"Well," Damian said, gathering his tray along with Rhea. "Welcome to *Resplendent*, Talent Lucian." There was a note of irony in his voice, as if Damian was questioning whether he should even call him by that title. "Will you be staying with us long?"

"Hopefully not. There are a lot of troubles out there in the Worlds. Transcend White will want to send her best to deal with them."

This was too much for Rhea. "We have duties to attend to, Damian."

"It was nice catching up."

Once they were out of earshot, Serah leaned over. "I take it there's bad blood there?"

"I'll tell you about it over lunch."

After they grabbed some chow and sat down, Lucian told her all about Damian's competitive nature, along with him accusing Lucian of cheating during the Trials.

"Come on," Serah said. "You cheated *a bit*."

"Err, maybe. During the Binding Trial."

"Binding? Seriously? That's what you're good at!"

"This is before my Orb of Binding days," he said. "I was a sad, sad man."

"You still are. Sometimes. Luckily, you have me."

Once finished, neither had anything to do, and that got Lucian to thinking.

"What do you think Emma and Khairu will decide?"

"Beats me. Khairu will probably want to stay. Emma's more of a wild card."

"Why do you say that?"

"She's changed, especially since L5. She's going through something, that's for sure."

"She just lost her home. I've tried talking to her a few times, with no luck."

"Same." Serah's eyes became distant. "It's like talking to a wall."

"You think it's the Orb of Radiance?"

"Probably. This might sound bad, but maybe it would be better for her to stay behind. It would take her mind off things. Give her some distance."

Lucian didn't like the idea of either her *or* Khairu staying behind. Both had proven themselves invaluable, and the ship would certainly feel emptier without them. Then again, he wanted their voluntary help, not to force them.

"Maybe I should talk to them. Or would that make things worse?"

"If it were me, I'd give them space. You're not me, though. My advice is, if you're going to do it, say nothing stupid."

"Why would I say something stupid?"

"Well, not stupid. That's a little harsh. Just listen more than you talk."

"I guess I should go find them. Catch you later, then."

After bussing his tray, Lucian headed off to explore the ship.

11

AFTER SEARCHING FOR FIFTEEN MINUTES, Lucian thought to look for Khairu on the bridge. He entered a wide space filled mostly with Yellow and Green Talents, busy at their stations. None looked up as Lucian approached the front viewport, where Khairu stood behind a Yellow Talent, a middle-aged man with clean-cut hair, who appeared to be the pilot on call. He nervously stared out the forward viewport, intent on the controls. Lucian didn't blame the guy. Khairu had that effect, even more so when she was your superior.

"Psion Khairu, can I speak to you for a moment?"

Her face tightened before she nodded. Lucian led her away from the viewport, toward a shallow alcove where they would not be overheard.

"You've hardly given me time to think things through, Talent Lucian."

"I won't bother you again after this conversation, so I'll cut to the chase. Losing you would be tough. You're an outstanding pilot, and we need you."

"I must do what's best for the mages. Figuring out where I'm most effective isn't an easy decision."

"I understand. I know you said Fergus has some piloting experience, but he isn't a replacement for you. With you gone, we'd be down the best Dynamist in the League."

She smirked a bit at that. "Flattery, from you? You must be truly desperate. I'm hardly the best. That honor probably belongs to Transcend Yellow."

"Okay, one of the best, then."

"Lucian, I know you *think* you're convincing me, but you're not. I'm well-aware of the pros or cons, and there's nothing you can do to influence things. Just leave me alone for one day. Is that too much to ask?"

Lucian had to admit defeat. "All right, then."

"Try to get some rest yourself. I know being you isn't easy."

"Damn. That's harsh, even for you."

"You know what I mean. Being the Chosen and all that. Go take a nap or something."

She left him to attend to whatever duties she'd picked up. For Khairu, there was no relaxing. Only different kinds of work.

He left the bridge. After his conversation with her, he wondered whether finding Emma was a mistake, too. Then he remembered how withdrawn she had been. She wouldn't react the same way as Khairu to his concern.

He walked down the central corridor toward the engine room, going purely off instinct. Passing through a sliding door, he entered a much quieter part of the ship, a circular walkway encircling the inner fusion engine. Through the interior plexiglass, engineers were busy at their terminals and nothing seemed amiss.

He wrapped around the engine room, finding a short corridor that was completely quiet. It was where he would go if he wanted some space. A sign above pointed to the sternward escape pods.

At the end of the corridor, through a transparent blast door that had to be an airlock, stood Emma, looking outward into the empty void, as if preparing to space herself.

"Emma!"

She didn't turn, seemingly not hearing him through the thick door. He pressed the entrance button. To his relief, it opened.

She jumped at his sudden entrance, turning around and putting a hand on her chest in relief. "Lucian. You scared me."

"You're scaring *me*. What are you doing in here?"

"Just . . . getting some space."

He nodded toward the outer doors. "Hopefully not *that* kind of space."

She looked horrified at the prospect. "No, of course not! It's just so crowded on board. I can't stand the sight of everyone. All the questions. I just want to be left alone."

"Well, can we at least get out of the airlock?"

Her face became indignant. "Lucian, do you *really* think I'm trying to off myself?"

"I don't know *what* to think. Things have been . . . difficult for you since Nai Elyn. Would it be too much to talk about? Let's step out of here first."

To his relief, Emma agreed. They entered the corridor surrounding the engine room. The engineers within were so intent on their work that they hadn't even noticed Emma had almost walked off the spaceship. He doubted they were paying attention now.

"What did you want to talk about?"

"I don't know. You, I guess."

"What about me?"

"Look, I know I'm probably being annoying. I'm worried about you, though."

"Oh. Sorry. I just have a lot on my mind. Ever since . . . well, ever since I handed *it* over, things have been different. It's . . . hard to feel anything at all. I'd hoped it would get better, but for now, it hasn't. And with what happened to my parents, our house . . ."

"Do you want the Orb back?"

"*No*," she said, with surprising vehemence. "I . . . need distance from it, Lucian. And if you gave it to me, you would suffer the same problem. We can't have that. You're the Chosen of the Manifold. Anything that impedes the mission needs to stand aside. Including me."

"What are you saying?"

"Lucian, I can't come with you. I'm going to be staying here."

From the hard look in her brown eyes, Lucian knew she meant it. He opened his mouth to protest, but nothing came out.

"It's what's best for me," she said. "And in the end, it'll be what's best for the mission."

"Emma, we need you."

"Fergus is a Radiant, and he's better than me, anyway. I can't speak for Khairu, but this is where my journey ends. It's too . . . painful to continue."

"Painful? Seriously, if it's about the Orb of Radiance—"

"Don't offer it to me."

Lucian stopped short. He knew he shouldn't say anything more. He just wanted her to stay. She'd been his first friend outside of Earth, one who had helped him through so many things.

But it seemed now she had moved on. And so had he. He just couldn't bring himself to admit it.

"This is it, then."

"It's for the best. If the Manifold wills me to go with you, it'll find a way. But I feel strongly about this. Staying with the fleet is my path. At least, for now. I need to think about myself for once. And I know you're more than capable. You've grown since we first arrived on Volsung. You're stronger, now. You know how to rely on others. I'm sorry I can't be there for you in the same way I used to. Things have changed."

Lucian wanted to tell her that he needed all the help he could get, but she'd already given him her answer, and he needed to respect that.

"Well," he said. "It's been one hell of a trip. This is what's best for you, and that's all that matters."

She gave a small laugh. "I feel . . . relief, strangely. I know you probably don't, but . . . thank you, Lucian."

At that moment, he felt his slate buzz in his pocket. He retrieved it to see a message from Transcend White, of all people. Khairu must have given her his slate ID.

"Transcend White wants to speak with me."

"Seriously?"

"Seems so."

Emma hugged him tightly. "Be safe, Lucian."

He blinked in surprise as she pulled back, gave him a parting smile, and left.

He firmed his face and turned around. He had to trust that he'd see her again someday. He was happy that she would be out of danger. At least in the near-term.

He headed forward, following the map on his slate to Transcend White's cabin.

12

WHEN LUCIAN KNOCKED on the door of Transcend White's stateroom, he remembered doing the same thing on the liner *Burung* almost three years ago, only with her twin. Back then, he'd told Vera he would not train with her. What seemed like such a fraught decision at the time was now so simple in retrospect. Lucian wished he could have that clarity now, when his emotions were difficult to process.

He held his Focus, and his doubts retreated, at least for the moment. He was calm, collected, and in control.

The door slid open, revealing a spacious stateroom that contained an interior sitting area, a desk, and an open door that led to a back cabin. A generous viewport looked at Chiron's daytime surface below. They were over an ocean now, with a single island being the only visible land.

Transcend White herself was sitting on a small sofa, seeming to come out of meditation. Her eyes focused on Lucian's, and he tried to ignore the idea that she was doing more than looking. He held no Psionic ward, though around her, he probably should have as a matter of course.

At last, she broke her gaze and rose from her seat. "Come with me, Talent Lucian. We have an important matter to attend to."

"What matter?"

"The Hegemon has summoned you."

"The Hegemon?"

She brushed past him and into the corridor outside. Lucian fell in beside her as she made for the stern of the ship.

"Wait. What does *he* want with *me*?"

"That remains to be seen. Be silent for now. We don't know who is listening."

As difficult as it was, Lucian held back his questions.

She led him down the ship's central corridor, ignoring all the glances and bows she received from passing mages. Lucian tried to do likewise.

After a few minutes, they took a lift down to the hangar deck. After passing through the hangar's double doors, she led him toward a small skiff, large enough for two people, magnetically locked on the hangar wall. She climbed into one of the two seats with surprising limberness for someone of advanced age. Lucian shook his head and followed.

As soon as they were strapped in, it powered on automatically and lifted off. It seemed to be on a set program, requiring no action on their part. The ship backed out of the hangar, breezing by *Ethereal* and another ship of similar size, though of a more blocky make. Perhaps it was the new one Transcend White intended them to have.

As soon as they were out of *Resplendent's* gravitational field, Lucian lifted against his restraints.

"So, what's going on? Why does Richard Palmer want to talk to me?"

"If I had any choice, you'd remain firmly rooted to *Resplendent*. Somehow, he's gotten wind of you. We must be wary. He's not as stupid as he seems on the newsfeeds."

"I don't know. He sounds pretty stupid to me. How could the League Assembly have ever appointed that blowhard?"

"Unlike every other field, in politics, stupidity is not a liability."

Lucian watched out the forward viewport as they navigated around the hundreds of ships in the fleet. It seemed they were making for the largest vessel, a titan of a ship that dwarfed all the others.

"That's *Volga*," Lucian said. "The largest ship in the League."

"Yes," Transcend White confirmed. "It's where the Hegemon is staying."

"So, you never told me. Why does he want to talk to me? Doesn't he hate mages?"

"He does. At least on the surface. Anything for the idiots back on Earth to vote for him."

"So it's politics."

"*Everything* is politics. And as for why he has singled you out, I have no idea. That's what I intend to discover."

"How did he find out about me?"

From her stony expression, she didn't like that question. "Hell if I know."

Lucian had more questions, but she was still Transcend White. She was a viper who had betrayed him for her own reasons. He needed to remember that.

But Hegemon Palmer was probably even worse. Despite holding his Focus, he felt a churning in his stomach.

"My advice is to keep silent. Answer him if he has a direct question, obviously, but don't say anything you don't have to say. He may guess more than you realize. Obviously, don't tell him anything about your mission."

"That goes without saying."

At that moment, they drew level with the supercarrier, pulling into a hangar on the colossal vessel. There were well over a dozen of these hangars, all deep. Lucian couldn't remember *Volga's* carrying capacity for fighters and bombers, but it was certainly in the high hundreds.

The hangar before them opened to reveal a cavernous space where at least a hundred light and angular ripsaw fighters were docked. Just seeing those ships reminded Lucian of their flight from Psyche. The League Wardens had chased them with a few of those ships, and they had nearly caught up to *Wayfinder*.

Maybe *that* was why he was being summoned. Had they found out he wasn't supposed to be here, that he had escaped Psyche?

Then again, if that were true, the Hegemon wouldn't be talking to him directly. That would've been way below his paygrade.

The skiff touched down, and it surprised Lucian to see a reception waiting for him—a squadron of about twenty blue, power-armored League Rangers, along with their red-armored commander. Their visors were up and their coilgun rifles holstered at their sides, telling him they didn't plan on blasting him into oblivion, at least for the moment. After his confrontation with them on the *Bolivar*, he probably wouldn't ever be comfortable around League soldiers, especially if Khairu's hunch about the Blackguards was true. How much did Transcend White know about that? Lucian had to assume everything, and if that was the case, then this carrier was the last place he needed to be.

Transcend White rose from her seat, the door opening of its own avail. Lucian followed her, trying not to feel like a child tagging along at his parent's heels. From the way she strode purposefully, it was hard to keep up. Her expression was more severe than usual. Clearly, she was trying to convey strength and authority.

Lucian wasn't sure where she stood with the Hegemon. Technically, *he* was her superior, but then again, Transcend

White could rip him apart with a simple streaming of magic. How did that balance out?

The red officer approached, inclining a square-shaped head that reminded Lucian of a block of granite. "Welcome to *Volga*, Transcend White. I'm Captain Andersen."

"Take me to him," she said, somewhat impatiently.

"That . . . was the idea." He regarded her with his icy blue eyes, as if looking for further acknowledgement. But seeing he would not get it, he cleared his throat and spun on his suit's massive magnetic soles. He pointed with a heavily armored gauntlet. "Lead them to the Hegemon, men."

The cacophony of heavy soles on the deck was almost deafening. Transcend White shook her head at the loud display. It had to be some power move on the Hegemon's part, and Transcend White was not impressed.

They entered a large, central corridor, not unlike the one on *Resplendent*, but this one was at least three times as wide, and filled with League sailors in blue flight suits, technicians in slate gray, and droids doing basic maintenance and cleaning tasks. Everyone scurried aside for the Rangers, who didn't slow their pace as they strode forward with purpose, their armor whirring with each movement.

They came to a central lift, and Captain Andersen motioned the other men to stay behind. "As you were, soldiers."

The men remained where they were standing, all but useless. Lucian wondered what it felt like to get into your armor just to fetch two mages who were no threat at all, all for the vanity of one man. Perhaps it was something they were used to by now.

To work the lift console, Andersen allowed his gauntlet to retract, inputting a code that would take them to a "lounge deck." The entire ride up was awkward and silent.

When the doors dinged open, Andersen gestured forward. "The Hegemon awaits."

Lucian and Transcend White took a couple of steps forward, and Andersen went down the lift, leaving them in a luxurious lobby. Lucian wondered what the point of all those guards was. If they really intended to hurt the Hegemon, why would they let him be alone with him? Then again, not everything had to make sense, especially when dealing with an irrational person.

Wide viewports looked upon thousands of stars, with couches facing holo-deck tables lining the periphery. On the lounge's opposite side stood a long bar with a generous assortment of liquor. There was probably space for a hundred people to mingle, but it was all completely empty.

Empty, save for one man, sipping an amber-hued drink from a highball glass. His shock of wild, orange hair, combined with his ruddy face, told Lucian it could be none other than the Hegemon himself. Seeing him in this setting, rather than behind a podium blathering about the mages or the Swarmers, was more than a bit surreal. He was much smaller than Lucian had thought, his shoulders hunched and his bearing puny. It was hard to believe this was the same person adored by billions back on Earth.

The Hegemon put down his glass and picked up his slate, which he stared at between two pudgy hands. The machine was blasting some sort of news channel, the pundits arguing about the coming League Assembly elections. The man sat entranced, apparently not even noticing their entrance. All the pomp and ceremony of their arrival was completely dispelled by this lacking reception.

But maybe that was the point. To show Transcend White she was not as important as news about himself.

Transcend White proceeded forward, as if nothing strange were happening. Only when she stood a few meters away did the Hegemon shrink his slate and pocket it, the newscasts silencing with that action. He turned to regard her, a somewhat superior smirk on his lips, as he watched her with the ugliest, beadiest, rat-like eyes that Lucian had ever seen.

"My dear Vivienne," Palmer said, in a posh English accent that belied his outward appearance. He rose and gave a slight bow, almost looking comical in his pinstripe suit. "I want to thank you for coming on such short notice. I know how busy you mages are with . . . well, whatever you mages do."

Transcend White gave no reaction to him calling her by her proper name. As the Hegemon, it seemed he was trying to show he had access to information about her, even something as personal as her own name. Apparently, the guy was just as much of a blowhard in person, but Lucian was hardly shocked at the revelation.

"You would do well to call me Transcend White in the future, Hegemon Palmer. You vastly overestimate your standing."

"Forgive me, Transcend White. I must admit, I don't have much experience dealing with your kind." Palmer's attention turned to Lucian. "Ah, the star of the show! I've heard quite a bit about your exploits. I can't wait to hear your story over a glass of cognac or brandy."

"How do you know about me?"

"From the Earth Wardens, of course. Your demonstration of stealth is like nothing we've ever seen! We've been trying for *decades* to get the mages to perfect it, to no avail. That little enterprise of you sneaking into the Solar System without *anyone* knowing it, without you even being logged by a Gate since bloody *Varda* . . . it's beyond conception! But somehow, someway, you've cracked the code. Just think of how this can help the war effort. Imagine a mage on almost every ship, cloaking it with the magic you teach them. The Swarmers will be utterly destroyed!"

Lucian wasn't really sure how to respond to all that, so he

just said nothing. It wasn't like he owed this guy an answer, anyway.

"So, how did you manage it, my boy? I need to know if it's replicable. It must be, if someone of your youth and inexperience can manage it."

It only took half a moment to think of a lie that was good enough. "A Radiant shield. One of the mages on our ships is the best when it comes to that. He can make the ship invisible across all spectrums."

"So, it wasn't you?" the Hegemon asked. "The ship is registered to your name, along with several other mages. The only other male mage on board would have been a certain . . . Fergus Madigan, was it? Is that who you mean?"

"Yes," Lucian said, wondering how he had access to this information.

"Can he teach it? I'm not sure if you've noticed, but we're at war, boy. Such knowledge could be the difference between victory and defeat!"

"It's . . . not easily replicable."

"But it *is* replicable? From what little I understand, it's physically impossible for a Radiant mage to make a shield that powerful. Our sensors should have picked you up immediately as soon as his stream weakened. But it seems he's found a way to keep consistent not just for hours, but weeks at a time."

"Fergus is one of a kind."

"He's from the Irion Academy, if I'm remembering my facts correctly. I've already looked into his records. Consigned to Psyche, but miraculously deemed fit for service by the Volsung Academy right before his sentencing, courtesy of High Mage Quentin Vasser, and approved by Transcend White herself."

"That's correct." Lucian wasn't sure of those details, but apparently, Transcend White had been in touch with Vasser after accepting all three of them into the Volsung Academy as Talents. He just had to assume she had her ducks in a row.

The Hegemon had been asking Lucian questions so quickly that Transcend White hadn't had the opportunity to step in. During this first silence, she jumped at the chance.

"I don't see why you're bothering Talent Lucian with this," Transcend White said. "I'm afraid he is quite right. Fergus Madigan is an especially talented Radiant. Though a single lapse of judgment almost consigned him to Psyche, High Mage Vasser and I agreed it would be a waste of his abilities. You can clearly see why. We knew Talent Madigan was skilled, but we didn't know how much so."

"Of course, of course. Still, I would like to get to know Talent Lucian. He's clearly someone of importance, since he *was* the registered captain of *Ethereal*, and not Fergus Madigan, who you agree is one of the most talented mages in the Worlds."

Transcend White hesitated only a moment before responding. "Talent Lucian is an up-and-coming star, with strong leadership potential."

Lucian tried not to betray his surprise. Even if he knew it was all an act, it felt strange to be complimented by Transcend White, even in a roundabout way.

"Still," the Hegemon said, "I'm very much interested in Lucian here. I have a strong sense there's more to him than meets the eye."

Transcend White's eyes narrowed. "Whyever would you have that notion?"

"Whyever." He chuckled at the word. "You really show your age sometimes, Transcend White. Your manner of speech reminds me of a pre-war holo."

"And your speech is crasser than the meanest dockhand on Hephaestus Station."

"Forgive any crassness, Transcend White, but you won't put me off any longer. I wish to speak to Lucian, and nothing will stand in the way of that. I just wanted to do you the courtesy of feeling like you had a choice. You know, to save face."

A burst of Psionic energy pushed Palmer square in his chest. He back flipped maladroitly over the sofa, arms akimbo, while letting out a piggish squeal. Lucian's eyes popped at the sight.

The Hegemon landed on the deck, not too hard because of the low gravity, but the position left him looking very undignified. When he stood, dusting himself off, his face was red, his orange hair even more unkempt than usual.

"I could have you spaced for that."

"Palmer, you're a pathetic, sad prig of a man. That you are the leader of humanity is perhaps the cruelest joke the Manifold could think of."

"Tell me how you *really* feel."

"We owe you nothing. This is mage business, and I won't give you information that you will use to destroy us. If this is what you called us here for, then this has been an utter waste of time." She turned, fuming. "Come, Talent Lucian. This audience is over."

"I'm afraid I must insist. You might push me around with one of your spells, but I'm still League Hegemon. None of your dirty tricks will change that fact. You owe me allegiance and respect." He smiled. "As you're so stupidly forgetting, if I might be so blunt, I can make your life very unpleasant."

Transcend White turned to Lucian, as if weighing him anew. As if wondering if he was up to handling the Hegemon on his own. From what Lucian had seen so far, the man was pretty unimpressive.

"Even you wouldn't be so bold, Palmer," Transcend White said. "I imagine something must have gotten into your head lately. Whatever could that be?"

His eyes widened slightly, though Lucian didn't see why these words should have any effect.

At that moment, Transcend White raised her hand, which became awash with violet Psionic Magic. Palmer's eyes widened in fear.

"Stop at once! I command you."

Palmer's eyes glowed as his face grew apoplectic. But Transcend White ignored him, the magic from her hands forming a stream connecting to the Hegemon's head.

"It's as I feared," Transcend White said.

All of a sudden, the Hegemon's mannerisms changed, and he gave a small, cunning smile, even as Transcend White's own eyes widened in surprise, and perhaps even fear.

"As I thought," she said. "How long have you branded him, Vera?"

13

LUCIAN'S EYES WIDENED. Vera was possessing the *Hegemon*?

"You are about to engage in assassination," Vera said in the Hegemon's voice. "What will happen when the Blackguards come?"

"They will not," Transcend White said, her face showing signs of strain. Her stream could not have been simple to hold.

"Pitiful. You think *you* can overpower me? Even *you* cannot undo my brands, sister. Not even with the full power of the Spectrum. I was always more gifted with magic."

Lucian reached for the Orb of Psionics. "Maybe she can't, but *I* can."

"Lucian," Vera said. "Or shall I say, *Chosen*? Yes, perhaps you have the power. But I'll kill this foolish man before you even have the chance. Imagine how difficult it must be, running from the League, never able to find safe harbor. That is your fate if you try to stop me. You would be the ones who assassinated the Hegemon."

Transcend White snarled, thrusting her hands outward as a thick band of violet magic shot from her fingers. The Hegemon

121

twisted, as if a demon were being exorcised. Lucian realized that wasn't far from the truth.

"How do we stop her?" Lucian asked.

Transcend White's face contorted with effort. "Just watch the lift. Make sure no one comes up."

Lucian nodded, turning his attention to the elevator. He watched nervously, but nothing came out of those doors. It seemed no one had caught on to what was happening. At least, not yet.

At last, there was a startled cry from Transcend White. She fell to her knees, gasping for breath, while Richard Palmer sat slumped on his sofa, his eyes closed.

He went to Transcend White to help her up. "You okay?"

She gave a shaky nod and stood slowly. "I've . . . failed. Vera's brands are sticky. Hard to untangle. And very dangerous. I only survived because I know some of her tricks."

"Is he . . .?"

"No, he's not dead. But I always knew something was off with him. It goes a long way toward explaining his erratic behavior."

"So she's possessing him, like the Sorceress-Queen with Selene."

"It's not the same type of brand. The Hegemon is merely influenced, not outright controlled. Vera can see through his eyes, suggest things, and influence his feelings. Direct control of him cannot be sustained, as we've seen here, and especially across such distance."

"Wait. I thought it was only possible to possess mages. Does that mean . . .?"

Transcend White shook her head. "Wouldn't that be the ultimate irony? However, I do not think Palmer is a mage. I believe there are many things we don't understand about magic, and Vera has long had an affiliation with a darker power.

A power that could very well give her knowledge lost since the time of the Ancients."

"She learned it from the Ancient One?"

"Perhaps. But there is no time to conjecture. This place is no longer safe for you. What Psion Khairu suspected is all but confirmed. Vera was behind the attack on L5, and she could guess your location by using her brand. That she moved so quickly to assassinate you means her influence on the Worlds is far greater than I first imagined."

Lucian immediately saw the implications. He could no longer safely travel within the League. The Blackguards, loyal to the Hegemon until death, would follow him wherever he went. At least, if there was no way to extricate Vera from the Hegemon's mind.

Transcend White sighed. "Who knows how long she's been working at his mind? I don't know how she's managed it, but she has a powerful tool in Richard Palmer."

"We have to drive her out of his mind. I did the same thing with Selene."

"I'm afraid it won't be that easy. The Hegemon is unconscious, which will make it practically impossible to undo Vera's brand. We cannot risk killing him, which is almost certain to happen if you tried to force it."

"So, what? We just let Vera control Palmer? Allow him to try to *murder* me again?"

"The other option is worse. If the Hegemon were to die, we would be blamed. It would be the end of the mages, at least as we know them. It would cause the fleet to fragment, and the Swarmers would doom humanity." She shook her head. "No. We have one chance only. We must continue the charade. Vera will not want to lose Richard Palmer, so she will continue it as well."

"You can't be serious . . ."

"We've spoken of this enough. You can't remain here any

longer, Lucian. He will wake up at some point. It could be minutes or hours. With luck, you'll have enough time to get on board your new ship. Follow my lead."

They went down the elevator, leaving the posh lounge behind. After half a minute, the doors opened, revealing Captain Andersen and a few of his blue-armored soldiers.

"Transcend White," he said, his blue eyes betraying surprise. "I didn't get the signal that the meeting was—"

There was a brief flash of violet light in his eyes, unseen by the other soldiers behind him.

"The Hegemon is not to be disturbed for the next hour. He's had a bit too much to drink."

Captain Andersen's eyes remained glassy, and the violet light was extinguished, replaced by a befuddled look on his face. "An hour he said?"

"That's right. An hour."

One of the other soldiers stepped up. "Sir, this isn't protocol!"

Andersen shot an annoyed look at the Ranger. "Stand down, Ricci. You heard Transcend White."

"But—"

"You want to join the droids on head duty?" At Ricci's silence, he turned back to Transcend White. "You're clear to depart. Can you find your way back?"

"Yes, we're perfectly capable, Captain."

As they walked down the corridor, Lucian felt Captain Andersen's eyes on his back. It seemed at any moment he would command them to stop. It was difficult to act naturally.

They entered the hangar and walked toward the skiff. As soon as they were inside and secured, it lifted of its own avail. Lucian heaved a sigh of relief.

Transcend White's voice entered his mind. *We are still being watched. Take great care in what you say and do.*

I can't believe this is happening . . .

I should have been more cautious. I haven't seen him since arriving with the mages. I grew suspicious when he knew you had arrived, and guessed something of your significance. It was her hubris that made her think I wouldn't catch on to that.

The ship navigated through the various gargantuan ships-of-the line, smaller battleships, and light cruisers, along with swarms of ripsaw fighters and lancer bombers running drills. Besides those, there were dozens upon dozens of hulking fuel freighters designed to keep the engines of the fleet churning. It was hard not to feel like they were surrounded in hostile territory. Perhaps, Lucian realized, that was because they were.

What will happen to you?

I don't know. She won't openly attack me, but she will use others against me in her own way. Ironically, our goals in the near-term may very well align. Vera wants to stop the Swarmers, too. It's what comes after—assuming there is an after—that worries me. I don't know how much of her mind she can devote to influencing the Hegemon, but since we know she is currently in a spaceship, in transit to Hephaestus most likely, she likely has all the time in the Worlds.

Lucian couldn't help but wonder if she could do the same to *him.* Perhaps the Orb of Psionics sheltered him from her direct control, but it also suggested she could have possessed him at any point before that. Or perhaps the brand she'd placed on him was of a different sort, one meant to keep tabs on him rather than control him outright. Lucian wanted to ask Transcend White to clarify, but they were already pulling into the hangar of *Resplendent.* Psion Gaius, along with Fergus and Serah, were waiting near where the skiff was to put down. Had Transcend White told them to wait there?

As soon as Lucian and Transcend White were out of the skiff, Psion Gaius walked up.

"Ready and willing to serve, Transcend White."

"Psion Gaius, I have a task for you. There is no time to question, only to obey."

"I am yours to command, your High Eminence."

"Talents Khairu and Emma have told me privately that they wish to remain with the fleet. I intend to honor that. Talents Fergus and Serah have chosen to continue on with Talent Lucian. Linus and Plato will be readmitted to the Academy, but it's not a decision I can make right now in haste, and the other Transcends are dispersed on other appointments."

"I understand, your High Eminence, but what does that have to do with me?"

"Everything, it would seem. The Manifold works quickly, and if we don't move with its tides, we stand to be splintered in the maelstrom." She nodded toward the ship next to *Ethereal*. "You are to go with Talents Lucian, Serah, and Fergus to Hephaestus, and pilot their ship."

Lucian blinked. *"What?"*

For the first time in his life, Psion Gaius could not hide behind his professional mask. He stared at Transcend White in shock, and perhaps even in offense. "That . . . cannot be, Transcend White. What of my duties here? How will my absence be explained? Frankly, things would fall apart the instant I—"

"Gaius, you dolt. This is an order, not a negotiation. You *will* go, you *will* pilot their ship, and you *will* protect Lucian and his companions with your life. The fate of the Worlds rests upon their shoulders, and by extension, yours." Her eyes narrowed as she leaned forward. "Do I make myself clear?"

Gaius's complexion went ghostly as he swallowed a lump in his throat. "Perfectly, Transcend White."

"Lucian will update you on everything. All those questions you've had about their mission, you will soon learn."

She gave them all a stern look, warning them not to argue about the arrangement. But Lucian couldn't help himself.

"Can't you just message the other Transcends and ask about Linus and Plato?"

"There's no time, and that must be done in person. Get on

that ship and burn as hard as you can for the Astravan Gate. Any moment now, the Hegemon will wake up. He might spare me, but he has already proven he wants you dead. Do you know how many Blackguards are in this fleet, just kilometers away?"

Somehow, Psion Gaius was the first to see reality. "Come on. We've got to go."

"Hold on just a second," Serah said. "This is moving too fast ..."

But Gaius was already heading toward the ship. Fergus looked at Transcend White, and then Lucian and Serah, before following.

"Is this seriously happening?" Lucian asked.

"Good luck," Transcend White said. "Always remember, Lucian, who you are, and the rest will fall into place."

Lucian couldn't even bring himself to respond as Serah started pulling him toward the ship.

"Looks like this is happening. Couldn't even rotting say goodbye to our friends."

Linus and Plato were probably asleep, or in the ship's saloon attached to the officer's wardroom. A goodbye would have been nice, but a message on his slate would have to do.

Gaius led them into a transport that was slightly larger than *Ethereal*, but it couldn't have looked more aesthetically different. It was blocky, especially toward the back. While it was probably capable of atmospheric operations, it was easy to tell by its lack of aerodynamic design that it wouldn't be as nimble as *Ethereal*. Its unassuming form looked like a light cargo ship, the kind used by self-employed traders, small corporations, or perhaps even smugglers and pirates. He'd seen countless like it docked at Archea Station and Volsung Orbital. It would blend right into the questionable ports they planned on visiting.

He ran up the boarding ramp after Serah, entering a central, functional space that seemed to be a hub between other parts of the ship. A round table was built in the wall, with seating for about five. Three different doorways led deeper into the ship, while the deck below them was nothing more than a grate that rattled with each step, with hatchways that led to lower cargo holds.

The ship thrummed as it was powered on, and the overhead lights instantly brightened. Lucian went up front, down a short tunnel toward the bridge. On their way, they passed a sizeable cabin, probably meant for the captain of the vessel due to its proximity to the bridge.

The bridge itself was roomier than *Ethereal's*, owing to its blocky design. Gaius was already taking up the controls. Lucian could only stare at him balefully, unwilling to believe that this was reality now. Since when had he learned to pilot a *ship*? Was it required training of all the Psions, or something?

Gaius seemed to feel Lucian's animosity as he turned toward him. "Believe me, Talent Lucian, this isn't what I want, either. Let's just make this as painless as possible. For some reason I don't understand, the Hegemon is after you. I won't ask questions for now, but I most certainly will later."

Lucian couldn't bring himself to respond. He wanted to tell him to get the hell off his ship, but Gaius was the only pilot they had. At least, until Fergus could familiarize himself with the ship's controls.

Gaius was already piloting the lumbering vessel out of *Resplendent's* hangar. Lucian braced himself, anticipating that the sharp movement would make him lose his feet, even with inertial dampening.

But much to his surprise, his feet barely budged.

Gaius noticed his astonishment. "The best inertial dampening equipment that money can buy. She might not look it, but *Ragnarök* can burn harder than almost any ship in the galaxy. You need good inertial dampening with the acceleration curves she's capable of."

"How fast can she go?" Fergus asked.

"Faster than anything *you've* been on." Gaius manually piloted the ship out of the hangar and into the fleet, touching the terminal before him. "Transponder is off, and ignoring all hails." He gave a smug smile. "In a strange way, I'm somewhat looking forward to this."

"I've never wanted to punch someone so much," Serah said.

"I'd advise against it, Talent Serah. I'm Psion White, your superior. I am not afraid to enforce discipline, should the situation call for it."

"I . . . don't think you know what you're saying."

"Insolent, aren't you?"

"It's one of my best qualities."

"You'll be glad I'm here before long. I'm quite capable."

The ship's dash lit with incoming voice requests from multiple ships: *Nirvana, Avius, Ganges, Alexander, Vindicator,* among others.

"Seems they've finally figured out we're doing something questionable," Gaius said.

"Are they going to attack us?" Lucian asked.

"No. Not yet, anyway."

The terminal displayed a star map, including their flight plan that would take them to Hephaestus. When Lucian saw the time projection, his eyes nearly popped out of his head.

"Seventeen *days*? Are you sure that's accurate? Seems fast."

"I'd sit down if I were you," Psion Gaius said. "It's not only the inertial dampening that's powerful."

Lucian barely had time to strap himself in before the force of two gravities pushed him back into his seat.

"Whoa!"

While there was no discernible change in the stars before him, the rearward view on the terminal showed Chiron shrinking with noticeable speed. Within a couple of minutes, even the largest of ships had disappeared, and the planet was perceptibly smaller, completely fitting within the screen.

Looking at the stats on the screen, the acceleration curve would take them to .08 the speed of light at its highest extent, with an average speed of .04 the entire voyage. He blinked at that. *No* ship he knew could go that fast.

"We must be burning fuel like crazy."

"We'll be almost dry when we arrive," Gaius said. "But from the way Transcend White was behaving, speed is of the essence."

"Will someone tell me what the rotting hell is going on?" Serah asked. "Lucian, why was Transcend White acting like you could die at any second?"

"Probably because I *could* die at any second. For all I know, they might even shoot some missiles after us."

"They won't go that far," Gaius said. "Her High Eminence mentioned the Blackguards. If she fears the Hegemon will use them against you, that's how they plan to kill you. A missile would be too messy. The Blackguards can at least make it look like it was someone *other* than them."

Fergus chuckled darkly. "As if getting your face blasted by a coilgun isn't messy."

"Now, when will you tell *me* just what is going on?" Gaius asked.

"Let's wait until it isn't a struggle to breathe," Lucian said.

"Well," Psion Gaius said, "the flight program is taking us on this curve for another four hours. Until then, there's not much we can do."

"Four *hours*?" Serah asked. "What if I stream a gravity ward?"

"No," Lucian said, thinking of her arm. "No magic."

"It's not your choice."

"Two gravities for four hours won't kill us."

Serah went silent. Lucian resisted the urge to sigh. Now, he'd have to deal with her being mad *and* the gravity. And of course, Psion Gaius. Lucian wasn't sure which of the three was worse.

A thought struck Lucian. He had the Orb of Space-Time, along with its ability to stream any Aspect with impunity. There was no reason *he* couldn't stream the anti-gravity ward. He'd watched Serah do it countless times and she had already given him a few pointers besides. After everything he'd gone through, how hard could it be?

So, he reached for Gravitonics, reversing the stream against the direction of gravity to create a lifting effect. He expanded the ward until the bubble covered the four of them. He increased the speed of the stream, until the extra g-forces were almost completely neutralized. Enough to move around, talk, and breathe.

"Not bad," Serah admitted, grudgingly. "Can you hold it, though?"

"I don't know. We'll see."

Just by feeling, Lucian had used about half his ether to make the ward. As a natural Psionic, Gravitonics shouldn't be too hard for him.

"All right, Talent Lucian," Psion Gaius said. "You have quite a bit of explaining to do."

The last thing Lucian wanted to do was let Gaius in on anything. But it seemed he had no choice.

"What did Transcend White tell you?"

"Nothing. While she lets me into her counsels, she hasn't revealed anything that has to do with you."

From his tone, it was clear he felt betrayed by that. Maybe it would do something to deflate Gaius's self-importance, but Lucian wasn't holding his breath.

"I can't *believe* we took off without giving Linus and Plato a choice," Serah said. "I feel like scum."

"It all happened so fast," Fergus said. "There's nothing we could have done."

"Well?" Gaius asked, haughtily. "Are you just going to keep me in the dark?"

"Can we space him yet?" Serah asked.

Gaius glared. "That's no way to speak to a superior."

"You're *not* my superior."

Gaius stood. Lucian noticed then how tall and physically imposing he was, especially when he lowered his thick, black brows. He towered over Serah, but from the way Serah glowered back, she wasn't intimidated in the least.

"Are you done trying to be a bully?"

"I'm the most senior mage on this vessel. You *will* defer to me. You *must* defer to me."

Serah just smirked.

"We won't follow you because we don't respect you," Fergus said. "We respect Lucian."

"Lucian?" Gaius asked, disgusted. "This bumbling fool of a Novice, exiled for his incompetence, who almost killed himself and others with his carelessness—"

"Actually, I'm a Talent now. And as you said when you took me prisoner, I didn't get exiled for incompetence. The Transcends betrayed me."

"You grossly misrepresent yourself. You overdrew for your Trials. You disrespected your instructors, used dangerous magic that could have seriously hurt or injured other mages, among other infractions. And now, you've been readmitted to the Academy beyond all reason and logic." Gaius sat back down in the pilot's seat, seeming to be at a loss. "Nothing makes sense anymore. I figured you two were transfers from Irion or Mako, but I'm suspecting there's more to it."

"Only *now*?" Serah taunted.

Gaius seemed to ignore her glibness. "On one fact, we can all agree. I'm here, whether you like it or not. You must tell me what's going on. Transcend White ordered as much. Or does your authority supplant hers?"

From his tone, it was clear Gaius thought that was an impossibility. If Lucian insisted it did, it might make Gaius's head explode.

"All right, I'll tell you. But you have to agree to stop trying to boss people around. I'm in charge here, and you're about to find out why. If you doubt anything I say, talk to Transcend White yourself."

"That would not be wise. I would not risk any communication being intercepted, now that I know the Blackguards are after you."

"What about the ship?" Fergus asked. "The transponder needs to log it with traffic control to dock anywhere in the League."

"We have a new transponder. A blank slate. We can name this ship anything once we are sure we are out of range."

"Won't they still be able to get our thermal signature as we pass through the Astravan Gate?"

"Possibly. But the Sol-Malon corridor is among the busiest in the Worlds. Hundreds of ships pass through the Astravan-Centauri Gate every day, and it would be impossible to accost every single one."

"They could ban passing through the Gate," Lucian said.

"That would be highly damaging. Ships carry enough fuel to reach their destinations, and little more. It would consign many crews to death. The Hegemon would have to be highly motivated to kill you to suffer that bad press."

"Well, you just have an answer for everything, don't you?" Serah said.

Gaius ignored the jibe. "Which begs the question. How motivated *is* the Hegemon about killing you?"

Of course, it wasn't the Hegemon who wanted Lucian dead. It was Vera. If she'd gotten the Hegemon to send Blackguards after him, she must have given up all hope that he'd join her side. Lucian supposed stabbing your old mentor in the stomach had the tendency to do that.

From the way everyone was quiet and watching him, he knew it was time to let one more person into his crazy world. But why did it have to be *Gaius*?

Better to get it over with quickly. "This is going to be a long story."

"I'm listening."

Lucian sighed. "It all started the day I found out I was a mage…"

14

HOURS LATER, Lucian was done. He'd let go of the gravity ward as *Ragnarök* shot forward as fast as the inertial dampeners could compensate.

Gaius sat silently, contemplating everything he'd just been told. For someone who had just been told Xara Mallis was still alive, the Orbs of Starsea were real, Arian and his prophecy had been found, and that Lucian had found a new Aspect that manipulated space-time itself, Gaius seemed eerily calm.

At last, he stirred in his seat. "I would not believe any of this, except that Transcend White herself believes it. I always knew she had a twin sister. What I didn't know was that she was still alive. And the fact that she's controlling the Hegemon..."

He trailed off, looking out the front viewport, deep in thought. For once, he seemed humbled. He didn't know what to say or do.

When he looked back at Lucian, his blue eyes were haunted. "And you. Four Orbs..." He shook his head. "It seems impossible."

"That's where we stand."

"And the Orb of Thermalism is on Hephaestus. That will be difficult. If not impossible."

"Nothing is impossible," Serah said. "Didn't you hear what we've been through?"

"Well, we'll have to take Transcend White's suggestions to heart. The new transponder will help, but I fear it's only a matter of time until they know we're on Hephaestus. Vera knows where you're going. Thankfully, Hephaestus Station is quite large. Over a hundred thousand live there, so we might be able to blend in, especially in the Undercity."

"The Undercity?" Lucian asked.

"The slums connected to the dockyards of the Lower Torus. There probably isn't a greater cesspool in all the Worlds, except perhaps Anchorpoint itself. It's hard to say how much time we'll have to explore. No doubt, the Hegemon has agents everywhere."

"The key is finding the Carthago CEO," Lucian said. "How do we do that?"

"Not necessarily the CEO, but someone high enough to authorize our descent from Hephaestus Station," Gaius said. "Of course, the simplest way would be to get hired by them."

"Hired?" Serah asked. "How hard is that?"

"I don't know," Gaius said. "But as mages, we have certain *persuasive* advantages that others don't. What I do know is that their offices are in the Upper Torus, far removed from the squalor of the Lower Torus. However, it's impossible to get there without the proper credentials."

"And how do we get those?" Serah asked.

"You're asking me as if I know everything."

"You certainly *act* as if you do."

"Don't be ridiculous. I certainly know more than anyone here, but even I have my limits."

"If your head were any bigger, it'd go supernova."

"I'm merely stating facts."

"So, what's the plan?" Lucian asked, trying to change the subject. "At this rate, we'll be docking at Hephaestus Station in seventeen days."

"I suggest, if you have any money, to send it to a private account before the League freezes it," Gaius said.

"Khairu held the purse strings," Fergus said. "Do you have anything we can work with?"

"I can authorize sums of up to five hundred credits per year from the Academy's treasury. Anything more needs to be cleared with the Transcends."

"Do it," Lucian said. "I have a wallet you can sync it to."

In a previous life, five hundred credits would have been a life-changing amount of money for Lucian. As it stood, it would probably take ten percent of that just to refuel this ship and dock it for a few days. And who knew what other expenses they might have?

"As long as I can have access, too," Gaius said. "Upon receiving your key, I'll sync the funds."

Gaius would not make this easy. "Don't trust me?"

"I could say the same for you."

"Who cares," Fergus said. "Yes, Gaius, you can have access to the wallet. All of us can tap into it, anyway. Show him the key, Lucian."

He saw there was going to be no way out of this. He drew up the key on his slate and showed it to Gaius.

"Memorize it. I'm only going to show you once."

Psion Gaius took a minute to study it. "Got it, thanks. Thankfully, on Hephaestus Station, most people don't care where funds come from, private or open. They just want to be paid."

Gaius went back to checking the sensors, finding nothing of concern.

"There's nothing on our scopes right now. I'm going to shift course a bit, come into the Gate from a different trajectory so we're not so obvious. Once that's done, we can install the new transponder."

Lucian couldn't argue with that, so he just remained silent.

Within a few minutes, Gaius stood and reached into the pocket of his white cloak, bringing out a tiny data stick. He opened the console ahead of him, retrieving the old transponder data stick and clicking the new one in place.

The terminal screen showed a cursor, requesting a new name for the ship.

"Well?" Gaius asked.

"*Wyvern*," Serah said. "They are known for their speed and deadliness."

"It doesn't sound . . . professional," Gaius said. "Like a pirate's brig."

"Is that a problem? It'd help us blend right in. Last time, I didn't get to name the ship, and look how that worked out for us."

"What are you even talking about?"

"Well, we let Selene name our little air skiff *Vengeance*. We ended up crashing not even a day later."

"So, you want *Wyvern*, then?" Lucian asked. "I'm for it."

"We need something worthy of a true mage ship," Gaius said. "How about *Servant of Light*?"

Serah mimed throwing up.

Fergus shook his head. "Sounding like a mage ship is the last thing we need."

A memory returned to Lucian. He knew not why. Maybe it was thinking of their destination of Hephaestus, who was the Greek God of Fire.

"Our ship is fast, so maybe something to do with that," he said. "How about *Talaria*?"

"What does *that* mean?" Serah asked.

"It was the winged sandals of the Greek God, Hermes. They allowed him to go fast."

"Hmm," Fergus mused. "I like it. Dignified and fitting."

"I must admit, I've heard worse," Gaius said.

Serah crossed her arms. "All right, *fine*. But promise me if we wreck this one, *I* get to name the next one."

Gaius typed in the name and held his hand over the confirmation button. "Once it's entered, there's no going back."

"Do it."

Gaius pressed the button, and the name was confirmed.

"*Talaria* it is."

With that piece of business taken care of, Lucian just wanted to get some space. "I'm going to look around the ship."

He left the bridge. His anger about Gaius coming on board had cooled somewhat, but now he placed the blame on Transcend White. Then again, he didn't know what she could have done. How long was this expected to last? If he just overpowered him with the Orb of Psionics and spaced him, would anyone know or care? Gaius would gladly do it to him, especially if Transcend White gave the word.

He headed toward the stern of the ship, where the power plant was. When he entered the massive anterior room, he could see why the back of the ship was so bulky. It contained a fusion reactor that was twice the size of *Ethereal's*, and three times the size of a typical ship of *Talaria's* specs. He supposed that was where all the juice was coming from. Still, it had to be fuel-inefficient as hell.

The size of the reactor would no doubt come as a surprise to anyone who saw it. *Talaria* looked like a sturdy cargo ship from hull to core, and any outside observer would assume the bulky anterior was for cargo. Combined with the weapons systems, anyone who tried to waylay them would be in for a rude shock.

Lucian took stock of the vessel, finding six cabins, each with two bunks, along with a clinic, galley, wardroom, and a sizeable cargo hold that extended below the entire main deck, accessible via hatchway in the storage room aft. Equipment, such as spacesuits and weapons, was kept in lockers near the main entrance, similar to *Ethereal*. While *Ethereal* had a longer and more narrow design, meant for smooth atmospheric operations, *Talaria* was bulky and designed almost purely for space travel.

The ship was bigger, too, at least twice as much. It almost felt empty as he wandered from room to room.

He bumped into Serah in the main storage room, which was filled with heavy crates and plasteel cylinders.

"You doing okay?" she asked.

Lucian sat on a nearby footlocker. "Honestly, no. I can't believe this is reality ..."

She sat next to him. "We don't have to talk to him. I suppose it's like a job, really. Be professional and shit, but you don't have to be friends."

Lucian smiled. "You act as if you've worked a real job before."

"I've watched holos, so I know how these things work."

"Of course. Still, that I would be friends with that man. That's not happening. Not now, not ever."

"He's a real tool, that's for sure." She looked around the storage room. "It's quiet on this ship. Too quiet. This place feels empty without Linus and Plato clucking at each other like old hens."

"Yeah. I mean, I'm happy they'll be out of harm's way. At least for a while."

"I guess Emma decided not to come, either."

"Maybe it's for the best. For her, I mean. You were right. Giving her the Orb of Radiance was a mistake. I . . . . think it might've broken her."

"Why do you say that?"

"She's not the same anymore. I don't know if it was what

happened on L5, but she was changing before that, anyway." He looked at the deck. "I can't help but feel responsible."

"She found the Dark Gate for us. I don't think anyone else could've done it."

"Maybe. I'm not convinced, though. I saw it for a brief moment."

"When?"

"When I first absorbed it. I'm not sure how, but I saw it. I probably could've found it again if I'd just believed in myself."

"You did the best you could. You shouldn't beat yourself up about it."

It was hard not to do that when Emma wanted the Orb back. Now, Lucian understood what the Oracle of Binding, Rhana, had meant when she said friends and family betrayed each other to gain an Orb. For anyone who wasn't the Chosen, they had a dark hold. So much so that if they held it, they would never want to let it go. That Emma had let go spoke of her inner strength.

Lucian just hoped that she wouldn't have to pay the ultimate price.

"Maybe some distance is good," Serah admitted. She wrung her hands. "And I'm, ah . . . sorry for the way I acted around her. It's embarrassing to admit it, but when I saw her the first time, I thought there was no way you'd choose me over her." She thought for a moment. "I guess I'm more insecure than I let on. I can see why you like her. Why you're worried." She let out a sigh. "I . . . trust you more, now. If you had chosen her, it would've hurt, but I would've understood, too. She's got it all."

Lucian didn't want to have to go through this again. "Well, maybe this is both of our faults."

"What do you mean?"

"Neither of us really believe we're good enough."

She gave a light laugh. "Yeah. You might be right there. Two losers, huh?"

"I'd hardly say that."

"True. You're the rotting Chosen of the Manifold. I'm just a rift rat who's along for the ride."

"Rift rat?"

"That's what Rifters call people who don't have a bed to sleep in at night."

"Damn, that's cruel."

"Psyche's a cruel world."

"You'd expect in a cruel place people would have a bit more decency."

"Not to a fray."

"Well, you have a home now. And friends who have your back."

"Yeah. Just wish the rest of them were here, instead of Mr. Toolhead up front." She stifled a yawn. "I'm pretty beat. It's almost midnight. Maybe I'll read an old book. Not one of those lit-films, but an actual book with actual words. I've downloaded literally thousands of them but haven't read one since *Wayfinder*. Probably Linus's influence. That man likes his holos."

"Sounds like a plan."

"Are you staying up?"

"For a while. I need to think things over."

"All right." She stood and kissed him on the cheek. "See you in bed." She frowned for a moment. "Not sure which one is *our* bed."

"Take the captain's suite before Gaius gets the same idea. If he gives you lip, send him to me."

Serah cracked a smile. "I don't think that'll be necessary, but I'll keep it in mind. Goodnight."

She left him there, and Lucian sat, thinking. Once she was gone, he realized just how cold and lonely this ship was. It was dingy compared to *Ethereal*, and it seemed everything besides the power plant, engine, and inertial dampening were dated.

Maybe that was part of the plan. The ship didn't look as rich a target.

Lucian wondered what would happen now, along with how to deal with Gaius. Even after what had happened with the Hegemon, he didn't trust Transcend White. He didn't trust her Psion. Had she summoned him to the hangar just as they were about to board, so that she could keep a better eye on him? Did she have a reason to separate him from Emma and Khairu, and even Linus and Plato? And what would happen to her, now that she knew her sister was meddling with the Hegemon himself?

They were all questions Lucian didn't have the answers to. All he *could* do was focus on the goal ahead.

Get to Hephaestus and find the Orb of Thermalism.

15

FIVE DAYS PASSED as *Talaria* sped toward the Astravan Gate, leaving the two stars of Alpha Centauri A and B far behind. Always in deep space, far from any planets and even other vessels, Lucian felt most at peace. Here, his troubles seemed far, even if in reality he was speeding closer to new ones every day.

Those troubles were hard to forget, since they dominated the newsfeeds almost every day. There were videos and holos of the destruction unleashed by the Swarmers on Fessan. Likewise, the Swarmers pouring in from the coreward frontier were overwhelming Orenus by now and well on their way to Beal, which was just one Gate away from Pontus, a system they had visited not too long ago.

In the spinward Mid-Worlds, Beryl, Mulciber, Altarra, and Myndelin had sworn fealty to High Prophet Sharo Khalin of the Believers, and his crusade was growing. To what end, no one knew. In the trailward frontier, Zheng Yang's Golden Armada thundered toward the core of the League, bypassing Alcazar and its League base and heading toward Malon, apparently in preparation to defend the system from the Swarmers in

Fessan toward galactic south. Pundits and popular opinion screamed for the Hegemon to join forces and push back the Swarmers, but from what Lucian could tell, nothing had happened on that front.

He was glued to the news, not just to keep up with current events. He was wondering if *he* might be the subject, whether his face might be plastered across everyone's slates and telescreens. All the Hegemon had to do was tell people to capture this very dangerous criminal for a reward of ten thousand credits, and he couldn't set foot on any planet or station in the Worlds. But it never happened, much to Lucian's relief. Whatever Vera's plans were for Lucian, it wasn't to go out like that.

The passage through the Astravan Gate was uneventful. They blasted through at a speed of .07C, paid their Gate toll, and didn't receive any attempted hails. The Gate Wardens probably thought it was impossible for *anyone* from the fleet to travel here so quickly. Or maybe the Hegemon, and by extension, Vera, weren't hunting them as hard as Lucian had originally thought.

It was hard to say exactly what to expect. Perhaps Vera knew exactly where he was going, and felt no need to stop him. It was an uncomfortable thought.

It only took four days to cross the Astravan System and pass through the Hephaestus Gate. They were already decelerating from their top speed of .08C, a process that would play out over the next eight days of their voyage. Lucian kept busy training with Fergus and Serah, and did his best to ignore Gaius's presence. Gaius, for his part, seemed nonplussed at being excluded. Clearly, he was not thrilled about being their pilot.

Lucian would have never guessed it, but he missed having Khairu.

He also did all the research he could on Carthago Corporation. Its CEO, Dante Rocheford, was easily researchable from the data Gaius had downloaded before leaving the AC fleet.

He'd been in his position for greater than thirty years, and under his purview, the company's profits had increased over twenty times than when he'd inherited the business from his father. The company employed millions, with the most upper of the corporate echelons being based out of Upper Torus, at the very top of the elevator.

It was hard to know just what to expect until they got there. As much as Lucian didn't want to admit it, Gaius was right in that the simplest solution was for all of them to become employees of the corporation, in a role that would send them down to Anchorpoint on the surface. He doubted the company suits visited the surface much, but the miners and factory-grunts would by the thousands. Lucian could always discover more information. A drink bought for a friendly bar patron could give him a real feel for things. And failing that, a psychic stream from the Orbs of Binding and Psionics.

There was another option, though. Apparently, the mages had a small, shared embassy on the Middle Torus, which could prove a useful resource in gaining access to the Upper Torus. Then again, that would require trust, and coming up with a reason for why they needed access. Lucian wasn't inclined to trust anybody with the exception of Fergus and Serah, who had more than proven themselves.

Just a day away from docking at Hephaestus Station, they received clearance to park at the cheapest hangar they could find in the Lower Torus. Even so, it was still ten credits a day, and fuel would be fifty to completely top off.

With those details settled, the four of them sat in their seats on the bridge, watching the approach of the fiery planet of Hephaestus. To Lucian at least, it lived up to its name. The continents were black, bereft of life, interspersed with deep fissures that glowed molten red. Massive craters marred its surface, most of which contained lakes of lava in the center. Rough mountain ranges marched along its large landmasses, riven with volcanos, and few clouds spotted its atmosphere. There were only two oceans, or perhaps small seas, that Lucian spied. Each occupied one of the poles, and there was not a trace of ice. The poles contained what few clouds there were, while the rest of the planet seemed tinged with smoke, so much that in many places, it was completely gray and opaque.

In short, it was the most inhospitable place Lucian had ever seen.

"I think we've just found Hell," Fergus said.

Indeed, if there were a hell, Lucian thought it would look something like this.

"Look," Serah said, pointing out the viewport. "Is that the station?"

"It is," Gaius confirmed.

As they approached, Lucian's breath caught. Hephaestus Station consisted of three concentric toruses; a large one on the bottom, a middling one above that, and on top, a smaller one, all sharing the same axis, which shot thousands of kilometers straight down to the surface of the planet below.

"That's the Elevator of Hephaestus, then," Lucian said. "I've always wanted to see it."

"A marvel of engineering, constructed with the help of the mages before the Mage War," Gaius said. "The super-tensile metals it's made from are impossible to create without Atomic Magic, at least at scale. There will never be another like it in all the Worlds. Truly, a relic from the Age of Wonders."

"Mars has an elevator, from what I heard," Serah said. "Luna, too."

"Yes, but their gravity is much less than Hephaestus's, which is greater than even Earth's."

"It must've taken a lot of magic to make," Lucian said.

"Indeed. Many things were done then that are impossible now."

"Seems like a lot was lost."

Gaius gave him a sideways glance. "A dangerous thing to say."

Lucian knew what he meant. It was that logic that led Vera and Xara to start the Starsea Mages. There were some who still believed magic should be unrestricted, that mages should still dare feats like this, fraying or not. Most of those mages had died in the Mage War, or had been consigned to Psyche.

As they approached the station from above, Lucian could see the Upper Torus, like a halo crowning the rest. Extensive parks, lakes, and greenery could be seen within its translucent surface, along with a few business parks with glittering skyscrapers, all built within its curving interior.

The Middle Torus seemed to be a mix of office buildings and mid-rise residential towers, interspersed by narrow streets and small parks. The density was much greater than the Upper Torus, but looked far removed from the squalor Lucian had been told to expect.

But when the Lower Torus came into view, Lucian could see massive industrial buildings through its translucent upper surface, along with towering, blocky tenements. There were so many buildings crammed there that it was a wonder they could all be fitted. It didn't look as if there was room to live and breathe. Unlike the other two toruses, there was no green space, and Lucian could already tell, without stepping onto its streets, it was an urban hell of seediness and misery.

And it was to where *Talaria* was bound, along with most of the shuttles, transports, and freighters coming into the station. The dockyards seemed to encompass most of the Lower Torus, or as Gaius called it, the Undercity, which was located directly beneath the shell where the buildings were placed. Hundreds of ships flew to and from the station, and *Talaria* was just one of many, not likely to be noted. Lucian noticed their ship blended in well with others that were of a similar size and make.

Below, the Elevator shot straight down to the blasted

surface of the planet, on an island surrounded by a lake of lava, which was surrounded by mountains and volcanoes. Lucian could see multiple cable cars zipping up and down the elevator on separate tracks. There seemed to be a central shaft with larger cars, used for raising and lowering bulk materials at a slower pace.

"They call it a space station . . ." Fergus said. "A space station!"

Though L5 might have been larger and more populous, Hephaestus Station was the greater feat of engineering. While L5 was confined to cylinders several kilometers long, the diameter of the largest torus had to be at least ten kilometers, with a circumference over three times that.

They burned toward a small, open hangar, barely fitting inside it before the heavy doors shut behind them. They watched as the hangar's vents powered on, pressurizing the chamber within a few minutes. Clamps closed in around *Talaria's* landing struts, ostensibly to keep it in place in case the unthinkable happened and the torus stopped spinning. Really, though, it was the dockmaster's measure to ensure payment. No payment, no ship.

Two double doors opened, revealing a heavyset man of late middle age with a gray beard and eye patch. He walked toward the ship, along with two toughs on his either side.

"It's time to render payment," Gaius said.

"Ten credits a day, right?" Lucian asked.

"That was the agreed upon sum."

"All right, then. Let's head down. Keep alert."

The others nodded and followed Lucian's lead. Fergus holstered a coilgun to bring with them, but Gaius raised a hand.

"They will not allow that on board the station. Shockspears are fine."

"I can do more damage with a shockspear than a gun,

anyway," Fergus said.

"Projectile weapons are banned. Was I the only one who familiarized myself with Hephaestus Station law?"

"There's law, and what's actually practiced," Lucian said. "There can be a big difference between the two."

"So, are you saying you want Talent Fergus to bring his carbine?"

Lucian ignored his point. "Come on. The dockmaster is waiting for us."

They left the ship, heading down the boarding ramp. The bearded man stood several paces away, his arms folded over his leather jerkin. His puffy arm sleeves and eye patch made him look like he belonged in Zheng Yang's fleet, or perhaps a fleet from eight centuries ago.

"You Sergei Kova?" Lucian asked.

The man gave a single nod. "You're late."

"Our time of arrival said 1:00 local. It's 1:06 right now."

"Look at the contract, kid. There will be an additional five credit charge for being past the arrival window."

Lucian almost wanted to write it off, but he couldn't let this guy push him around. If he gave in easily, he'd make himself a target down the line. "I won't be paying for that."

"Well, tough. Your ship ain't leaving unless you sync over another five credits."

"You *really* going to bust my balls on this, mister?"

The two toughs on his either side cracked their knuckles. Not too long ago, that might have intimidated Lucian. But it was hard to get scared after beating both Xara Mallis and Vera Desai.

Sergei's bushy gray brows went lower. "You talk tough for a little nincompoop. I got more guys back there, but I'd rather talk sense than beat it into you. This ain't my first space race, kid. Cough up the creds, or else your ship's getting impounded."

"It's not worth the trouble," Psion Gaius said. "Five credits won't hurt us either way."

But Lucian actually *had* read the contract, probably while Gaius was familiarizing himself with the station's law that no one actually followed. He knew that this fellow was taking them for a ride. Why show up with those henchmen unless to shake them down? He had no sympathy for the man. It was the principle of the matter, not the credits. Lucian had gone too far and seen too much to be pushed around by the likes of him.

Lucian flexed his fists for a moment. "Let me tell you how it'll be. If you try to get a single sub-cred out of us that isn't due, I'll take it up with the Shippers' Guild. I know this is Hephaestus Station, and everyone's trying to shake down everyone else. I'll let it slide as long as you think carefully about what you say next."

At the mention of the Guild, the dockmaster's eyes went wide. "No need for that, captain. We don't want them sticking their noses in our business. I didn't see the Guild markings on your hull, is all. The paperwork alone will drag this out into infinity."

"Then do the right thing. This isn't my first space race, either."

The dockmaster met his eyes for a moment. The man was so stubborn that Lucian was sure he'd have to influence his decision with a mind influencing dualstream, something he didn't exactly want to do.

At last, the man relented. "*Fine.* Just this once, and count yourself lucky. I don't want any trouble out of you, you hear? I don't need those guildie dogs breathing down my neck."

From the way he said that, Lucian was sure it wouldn't be the first time. "That wasn't hard, was it?" He looked at the others. "Let's go."

As they left the master and his men behind, Lucian couldn't help but flash him a smile.

"Great," Fergus said, once they'd passed through the airlock. "Now they're going to do something to the ship."

"They're welcome to try. If they touch it, the security system will let us know."

"What was all that about the Shippers' Guild?" Serah asked.

"I know they have a presence on this station. They protect shippers from having things like this happen to them."

"Yeah, but you're not a member."

Lucian looked up and down the corridor, which was thankfully empty. "Yeah, but *he* doesn't know that."

"Even so," Gaius said, "it's a needless risk. What if he finds out you're not? It's easily verifiable. Besides, it's better to keep men like him on your good side. If we'd paid the fee, he would have been more amenable to us. He might have given us useful information."

"Rot that," Serah said. "You know what five credits can buy? We could get the same information off a drunk man in a bar with just a drink or two."

Fergus considered. "That . . . might not be a bad idea, actually. We could learn a lot, potentially."

"I say we go straight to the Mage Embassy," Gaius said. "They would get us the resources we need with no muss or fuss."

"Absolutely not," Lucian said. "Who do you think the mages report to?"

"Their respective leaders. But I don't see how that—"

"The Hegemon could've told the embassy to watch out for us. We're safer in the Undercity. At least, until we get our bearings."

They came to the end of the corridor lined with heavy hangar doors. They were just one among dozens.

And, passing through this tunnel, they entered the main part of the torus into the Undercity of Hephaestus Station.

16

THEY FOUND themselves in a claustrophobic alley lined with dark, towering buildings that loomed over either side. Smog hung thickly in the air, a pall through which even the blaring neon signs couldn't fully pierce. Alcohol, casinos, and strip clubs seemed to be the principal products the establishments were advertising.

Fergus hacked. "They haven't replaced the air recyclers in decades, from the smell of it."

Despite the many doors and places of business, Lucian couldn't get over how empty the streets were. There were a couple of men in heavy trench coats skulking near a bar over a vent blasting steam, while a shifty-looking man stood on a corner in the distance, keeping watch. Looking up, Lucian could see a metal surface. At first, he thought it was the top of the cylinder, but he realized it was too low for that, perhaps fifty meters above their heads.

"It's the surface layer," Gaius said. "They built the main city on top. This here is the Undercity. Originally, it was zoned only for industry, but as the generations have passed, slums mixed themselves in."

"Looks shady as hell," Serah said, observing what appeared to be a geometric gang sign spray painted above a passing shop's door.

"Perhaps the night would be better spent on the ship," Fergus said.

"There's a fee for that," Lucian said. "Contract says two credits per person, per night."

Serah huffed. "That's highway robbery."

"I'm sure we can find somewhere here we could stay," Lucian said. "Looks pretty cheap."

"I'd rather sleep in the Fire Rifts," Serah said.

"Well, we could go up to the surface level. At that point, we might as well stay on the ship with the prices we'll pay."

"Eight extra credits a night won't kill us," Fergus said.

Lucian didn't want to talk to Sergei again. No doubt, the sly dockmaster would try to hoodwink them out of more money.

"I'm tired, anyway," Gaius said. "I'm with Talent Fergus on this one. Either the ship, or the Embassy. We would stay there for free, and it's in the Middle Torus, far from this filth."

"What's the good of being here if we're just going to hide in our ship?" Lucian asked. "We're mages. We've been through hell and back, and we're on a mission, and an important one. We're going to find someplace to stay here, and that's final."

Neither of them offered a rebuttal, but Serah stubbornly set her jaw.

"Lead on, then," Gaius said. "I'm sure you know *exactly* what you're doing."

Lucian didn't respond, instead leading them down the narrow street, ignoring the looks he got from the men loitering along the buildings' sides. Looking up, he could see that there were wide, higher walkways, more well-lit than down here. So, he took a spiral staircase up, hoping to get a better sense of the environment. They climbed several flights before exiting onto one of these walkways, a dingy promenade that seemed far busier than the one they'd left behind. From its gentle upward curve, it seemed to wrap around the entirety of the torus, and Lucian could see hundreds of tall tenements and massive factories with smokestacks extending along it, before the ceiling above cut off the rest from view. A particularly large factory hung off to their right, with a billboard declaring that it was owned by "arthago Corporation", with the first "C" sputtering in and out.

"The most advanced space station in the Worlds," Fergus said, "and they couldn't think of a better use for this space than smoke, squalor, and misery?"

Lucian had to admit, something had gone very wrong to create this hell. It had taken root long ago, and over generations, urban rot festered in every nook and cranny. But from the grand, open spaces, long fallen into disrepair, it was clear that the smog-ridden slums spreading before them had not been the original vision of the builders of the Lower Torus. But it was the use humanity had found for it, for reasons Lucian couldn't begin to guess.

At that moment, a large truck roared by, people barely dodging its path in time as its tires screamed on the pavement below them. The back of the truck was filled with armored toughs bearing assault rifles. The logo of Carthago Corp was emblazoned on its side, a small circle resting on an upside down triangle, with two raised arms, resembling a person with hands raised on high.

As soon as the truck was gone, dozens of people filled the area that had cleared, a mix of spacers in jumpsuits and locals wearing dingy, faded apparel. They were mostly men with heavy beards and tattoos, with muscles that told Lucian they were used to heavy work, or at least unhealthy levels of stim treatments. The building entrances on either side led into bars and taverns, and further staircases and alleys created a maze-like lattice of connectivity, clearly designed from the ground-up rather than the vision imposed by the station's builders. Two men were having a fistfight in one of these alleys, with a crowd of onlookers betting on who would win. From the surface level above them, Lucian knew there was even more population density, as yet unseen.

Lucian paused at an intersection, trying to decide which way to go.

"Just admit you don't know where you're going," Gaius said.

"Yes, I do. I'm trying to find a hotel."

"Hotel?" A grubby-looking man came up to them, staring with hollow eyes. "I know a great one. My cousin runs it."

"Get lost," Lucian said.

The man blinked, but said nothing more.

"I found something," Fergus said, looking at his slate. "Supposed to be one of the nicer establishments here. It's run by Carthago corporate, by the Elevator."

"All right. Let's head over."

"Not too far, either. Turn right here."

Lucian nodded and headed that way. More trucks rolled past, almost slamming into them unless they skirted the edge of the buildings. Lucian just wanted to push them off the walkway with a good kinetic wave.

They headed along the width of the torus, in what appeared to be a nicer area where the buildings were more well-maintained and the streets quieter, but the buildings still had high walls that made them impossible to access without credentials. They eventually found the hotel, close to the rim of the torus. The Elevator beyond could be seen through a wide viewport, along with a cable car that connected to it.

The hotel was just before the cable car station. Lucian led them inside the front entrance to the self-service kiosk. The rooms were cheap enough for him to order three, two for Fergus and Gaius, and one for him and Serah.

"Only two credits," he said, scanning his slate. "Not bad. Comes with a free meal, too."

"This is all so unnecessary," Gaius said. "With one call, we could be on our way to the Mage Embassy, comfortable as can be, with a solid base to work from."

"All it takes is one backstabber for us to wind up dead."

"Are you *always* this paranoid?"

Serah leaned over to Gaius. "Well, Lucian has a knack for trusting the wrong people. I, for one, am glad that he seems to have learned his lesson. That said, maybe just this one time we can treat ourselves to something nice."

"What, you too?"

"It's just . . . simpler. What do you say?"

Lucian watched the three of them. He ground his teeth, then canceled the transaction.

"You want the Embassy? Fine. But if something bad happens, I get to tell you *I told you*."

"Sorry, Lucian," Fergus said. "This entire torus is just . . . depressing."

Already Gaius was making a call. "Yes, Psion White here, of the Volsung Academy. We have four mages here on Academy business and we need lodgings for, say, the next week."

Lucian listened as Gaius made the arrangements. He was surprised at how fast it went.

Gaius shrunk his slate and pocketed it. "They're expecting us, now. No one else is in, so we'll have the whole place to ourselves."

"Sweet," Serah said.

"They even sent transit passes to all of our slates. We're free to go wherever we want on the station, even the Upper Torus."

"Let's go, then," Fergus said. "We can rest, get a good breakfast, and hit the ground running."

"Lead the way," Lucian said.

Gaius led them out of the dingy hotel, everyone walking with a bit more pep. Did they *have* to act so excited about it? Lucian had to admit, though, it would be nice to stay where they would have access to resources. The transit passes alone would make things far easier.

Lucian figured they'd be using the Elevator to go up to the Middle Torus, but the navigation on Gaius's slate was leading them toward a shuttle terminal, just a quarter of a kilometer away. They walked down the street, passing a group of drunken men heading back from a night on the town. Once they'd passed, one of them turned around and challenged Lucian.

"You want to have a go, tough guy?"

The others pulled him away, apologizing for his belligerent behavior. Lucian just shook his head.

When they got to the shuttle, they were the only occupants as they scanned their passes. After they'd strapped themselves in, it began piloting itself automatically upward, leaving the Undercity and the Lower Torus behind. Lucian had to admit, it *would* be nice to stay someplace where he didn't have to always look over his shoulder.

As they neared the Middle Torus, a male voice blared out of the speaker. "Next stop, Fountain Park, Middle Torus."

They docked at the station, and the doors slid open, revealing a wide open park with trees and a tall fountain shooting multiple stories into the air. The park was ringed by mid-rise buildings, and above their roofs, Lucian could see yet more buildings and parks situated along the curve of this smaller Torus. The city's cleanliness and well-lit public spaces, despite it being "night," made it an entirely separate entity from the Undercity below them.

"That should be it," Gaius said, pointing to an unassuming building across the park with a stone veneer, about three stories tall.

There was no one else out walking this late, but even so, Lucian couldn't help but scan the area for threats. If it weren't for the curving of the torus, he'd believe he was on a planet. Strangely, the architecture wasn't too far removed from the Undercity. It was as if they had both been constructed in the same way, but different pressures over the decades had forced them to evolve in divergent ways, one into a stately area for the upper middle class, and the other into a poverty-ridden slum.

They entered, the security doors recognizing the credentials on their slates. They passed into an expansive lobby, with a white marble floor and pillars that gave Lucian the sense that this place had once been a hotel. A crystal chandelier hung from the vaulted ceiling, which was lined with frescoes of streaming mages, scenes depicting the construction of the station long ago with the aid of magic.

"Fancy," Serah said.

They approached a middle-aged woman at the reception, who wore a suit-robe hybrid that denoted her as a member of the Irion Academy. Her sharp features regarded them somewhat suspiciously as they approached. Even Psion Gaius wasn't wearing his customary white robes. Even he recognized that in certain settings, it was best not to look like a mage.

"I'm Psion Gaius," he said. "We spoke earlier. You must be Adept Sana?"

Her composure seemed to brighten instantly. "Why yes, Psion Gaius. Forgive me. To be frank, I wasn't sure it was you."

"You'll have to excuse our state. Our business here entails blending in with the local population."

"Oh? The Embassy was not aware of any rogue mages operating in the vicinity."

"Our reasons are our own," Fergus said, his tone suggesting that was the end of the conversation.

"Of course," Adept Sana said. "Well, be welcome to the Hephaestus Mage Embassy. Our resources are at your disposal, and if the place seems rather empty, well, most of the staff here were recalled on account of the war." Her face hardened. "Nasty business, that. I digress. Your rooms are on the top level. Because of your rank, Psion, I have assigned you the penthouse suite."

"My thanks," Gaius said, as if such treatment were to be expected. "I would also like you to plan for us to go down to the surface, if possible."

"The surface? Whatever for? There's nothing down there but Anchorpoint and the mining convoys. Your heart would quail to see it! If you think the Undercity is bad, just wait until you see the poverty there."

"I insist. Certainly, you have channels to get permission from Carthago Corporation?"

"Unfortunately, it's not that easy. The process will take a long time, and even then, there are no guarantees. They won't allow anyone who isn't an employee, or at the very least a mining contractor."

"There's no other way down there?" Fergus asked.

"I'm afraid not."

"How can we become employees of Carthago, then?" Serah asked. "Can't be that hard, right?"

Adept Sana looked horrified at the prospect. "Why would you do that? It is not befitting your rank!"

"I agree," Gaius said. "It could lead to other issues."

They had already shared too much with this random woman none of them knew, so Lucian cut in. "Let's get up to the suite. We can talk about things there."

"Of course," Adept Sana said, looking somewhat disappointed. She was clearly bored and wanted to chat more. "I can lead you straight there."

Lucian doubted they needed help, but he let her, anyway. She was almost giddy as she led them to the elevator.

"Where are all of you coming from?" she asked, as the elevator began moving up.

"Alpha Centauri," Fergus said.

"Ah, of course. How are things with the fleet? I'm sure it's far more exciting than here."

Lucian supposed the Hegemon trying to murder him qualified as exciting. When no one answered, Adept Sana kept quiet.

The elevator dinged open, revealing a small lobby with a pair of double doors. She scanned the doors open, revealing a spacious chamber filled with comfortable furniture, along with floor-to-ceiling windows overlooking the curve of the torus, where down below, a long strip of green parkland with a central stream wrapped upward into the distance. Tall buildings flanked either side of the park, half of which had their windows lit at this late hour.

"I'll let you get situated," Adept Sana said. "If you need anything, just call reception. I'm afraid we're lightly staffed. A couple of employees might come into the office tomorrow, but don't be surprised if you're the only ones here besides some maintenance droids."

To Lucian, that was perfectly fine. Less people meant less possible traitors.

"Thank you," Gaius said.

Adept Sana gave a gracious bow before backing out of the room.

When the doors closed behind her, Serah went to the pristinely white couch and plopped down. There was even a gift basket filled with fruit, nuts, and cheeses, which she dug into immediately. "Now *this* is the life."

"Don't get too comfortable," Fergus said. "We should be on high alert. Though this is an embassy, we're not necessarily safe."

Lucian was glad at least one of them recognized that.

"I had a look into her mind," Psion Gaius said, "and Adept

Sana means no harm. She lacks company, and that's the only reason she was chatty."

"That's dangerous," Lucian said. "What if she'd had a ward set?"

"She didn't," Gaius said. "And even if she did, it wouldn't have mattered."

Was Gaius trying to flex his Psionic abilities? Lucian realized that maybe *he* should be the one setting a ward.

"Either way," Gaius continued, "we learned something valuable. Not even mages can gain access to the Elevator. Which means, obviously, that we must become employees of Carthago Corporation."

"How hard can that be?" Lucian asked. "I had plenty of shit jobs before my mage days."

"Unfortunately, your record is wiped clean the minute you're admitted to the Academy. It works the same for all Academies, as a measure to ensure mages can't find any work outside of the Academies. So, if we apply for jobs, we must do so without any curriculum vitae."

"Curriculum vitae?" Fergus asked with a chuckle. "Are you trying to become an exec or something? Big corporations like Carthago are always looking for fodder for their machine. They'll take anybody with a pulse."

Gaius's cheeks colored slightly. Lucian had to admit, it felt good to see him off-balance.

"No, not an executive. But it would be far better to get *some* form of respectable work. That would give us more flexibility to move around. If we just apply for the lowest-paying, most menial job—"

"You might break a sweat?" Serah finished.

"No. We would have to follow every order of our superior without question, or risk exposure. Besides, do you *really* see me blending into that kind of crowd?"

"What kind of crowd?" Lucian asked.

"You know, the rougher sort. The kind we saw in the Lower Torus."

"Oh," Serah said. "You want to be around people who are more uppity. Where did you say you were from, again?"

"You put it coarsely, but yes. And I hardly see how my origins are relevant."

"You would fit like a glove in Ansaldra's court."

"I beg to differ. All I'm saying is, given the choice, it would be better to be assigned to a more managerial role."

"Whatever you say."

Lucian had to keep himself from laughing. "Well, I'm not sure how you plan to get into a *managerial role* when none of us, as you've said yourself, have curriculum vitae that's verifiable on the GalNet."

"Simple. You and I are Psionics. It's pretty easy to bend someone to our will when the situation calls for it."

"Where does that leave Serah and Fergus? Neither of them can perform mind control streams. Do you expect them just to sit here in the embassy all day?"

"No, of course not."

Everyone waited for Gaius to come up with another suggestion, but he remained silent.

"Look," Lucian said. "Whatever we end up doing, we're doing it together. That means all of us go for the same job. Something that's easy to get, where they won't give a crap about our experience. I don't care if it's surfing on a lava wave down there. We'll get the same job, and at the first opportunity, strike off on our own to find the Orb of Thermalism."

"I don't think that's how surfing works," Serah said.

"What about all the equipment we'll need?" Fergus asked. "We'll need food, water, a heat-resistant tent with an air filter, envirosuits with spare parts . . ."

"I'm sure all that stuff is down in Anchorpoint. We just have to find it."

"That begs the question," Fergus said. "Have you . . . felt anything pointing toward it?"

Lucian hadn't even tried to do so. The Orb of Space-Time, being the Aspect that brought all magic together and made it work properly, could also feel out the other Orbs. The Prophecy of the Seven had led him to that realization. But he hadn't thought to use that ability. Not yet, anyway.

"I don't know. Up here in space, it won't do much good. I need to get closer. Once we're on the surface, I'll at least know which direction to go."

"How does this Orb even work?" Gaius asked. "Have you even tried?"

"No, I haven't. But I trust what Arian said. I trust the Prophecy of the Seven. And as long as you're with us, Gaius, you need to trust it, too."

"*Psion* Gaius."

"I'm going to punch you," Serah said.

"Do you agree? *Gaius*?"

The White Psion looked as if he wanted to murder him.

Fergus cleared his throat. "Perhaps our time would be better spent looking for jobs. I'm sure there are postings on the Hephaestus job boards."

"The most intelligent thing I've heard all evening," Gaius said drolly. "Forgive me."

He left the living area, heading into a back area, which Lucian assumed to be a bedroom.

"He's being a baby," Serah said. "This guy is *seriously* Transcend White's number two?"

"He just can't stand not bossing people around," Lucian said. "I don't know what Transcend White was thinking, putting him with us."

"Regardless of how we feel about him," Fergus said, "we need to be adults and work together."

"I know that. I just really despise him."

"I know. And I'm telling you that you need to set that aside. There's more at stake than ego here, but the way people are acting, you'd think ego was all there was."

"Are you seriously suggesting my ego matches Gaius's?"

"Maybe. You've certainly bruised his."

"That's his problem, not mine. Honestly, it was long overdue."

Fergus leveled his gaze, and it was clear the man was losing patience. And as calm as Fergus always was, Lucian definitely didn't want to see him angry.

"I get it," Fergus went on. "He picked on you. Psion Gaius used his power to put you down. Now, the tables have turned, and you can't help but do it back, knowing there's nothing he can do about it. And not just defend yourself, but completely pulverize him if you wished it. You've got to be the better man. I know leading isn't easy, but you've got to decide what kind of leader you want to be. Someone who *makes* people follow you, or someone who *inspires* people to follow you. It's one or the other, and only rarely can it be both. Gaius will learn that things have changed, given time. Show him a better way."

"The man's head is more bone than brain."

"Show him a better way."

Lucian sighed. "Fine. I'll try."

They sat quietly for the next few minutes, each of them looking up job postings online.

"Ice hauler," Serah said. "Anyone want to work on an ice freighter? Could be interesting. I remember watching a docuseries about it after leaving Volsung. *Ice Route Freighters*, or something like that."

"We need something *on* Hephaestus," Fergus said.

"It was just a joke." Her eyes widened suddenly. "Oh, here's one! Mining laborers desperately needed. Pays three credits a week. Qualifications are basically nothing. It's with an XVA Staffing Professionals."

"Let me search that," Fergus said. "Looks like a staffing agency. They must really be hurting for work."

"Looks like an easy in," Lucian said. "And it goes down to the planet?"

"Mining laborers, it says," Serah said. "Only one problem. Will Gaius go for it? I saw that man's hands. He hasn't touched a rock in years, probably."

"Well," Lucian said. "This is the only one I'm seeing where we can all get the same job. I'm looking at all the listings they have, and this is the only one with no experience required. So they won't care about our CV's. Damn, benefits are next to nothing. It's criminal that they can get away with this."

"We're far from Earth, and H-Station is hardly known for its labor laws," Fergus said. "Carthago got a lot of concessions from the League to develop the planet."

"Makes sense," Lucian said. "Well, should I submit my application? Says we can start as soon as tomorrow."

"What time tomorrow?" Serah asked, stifling a yawn. "It's already two in the morning."

"It would be better to get started sooner rather than later," Fergus said. "Every moment we stand still is a moment for the Blackguards to catch up. A dome surrounds Anchorpoint. Not even the Blackguards can get in unless they go down the Elevator."

Yes, there were always the Blackguards to consider.

"Let's do it, then."

Before he could second-guess himself, Lucian submitted his application. Much to his surprise, a few seconds later, he received a message congratulating him on his acceptance, giving him an address to show up to, and a time.

"They want me there tomorrow at 18:00."

"Same," Serah said. "Wow, that was easy. *Too* easy."

"Well, at least we get to sleep the day away," Fergus said,

standing and stretching. "I think I'm going to bed. Goodnight, everyone. I'm sending Gaius the application link."

Fergus left them there. Serah leaned back on the couch and closed her eyes. She looked as if she could fall asleep right there.

"Come on," Lucian said. "Let's get to bed."

They headed into a back bedroom that wasn't occupied. The bed looked large and comfortable, its white sheets matching the pristinely eggshell walls decorated with prints that depicted scenes of nature from various worlds, including the oceans of Volsung, the mountains of Irion, and what Lucian presumed to be the cloud forests of Mako. The floor-to-ceiling windows looked out onto the curving torus below, where through the upper skylights, the surface of Hephaestus radiated red with heat.

It was hard for Lucian to believe that they would be down there soon.

After they showered, they both settled down to sleep.

17

HE STOOD ALONE on the surface of Hephaestus, on a promontory of black igneous rock above a roiling sea of red lava. Across the fiery surface, half-cloaked by acrid smoke, loomed a massive volcano, belching thick fumes into the dismal sky. Rivers of red bled down its side, joining the lake of fire.

He didn't know what he was doing, or how he had found himself here. All he knew was that he needed to get to that mountain of fire and ash.

The heat was unreal, like nothing he'd ever felt before. His Thermal ward was at maximum strength, and his skin was still baking. Where were the others? There was no sign of civilization out here.

Soon . . .

Lucian had almost forgotten that voice. He hadn't heard it in months, and almost believed that it was gone for good upon his acquisition of the Orb of Space-Time. Arian himself had told him that Orb would heal magic within him. But if that were true, how could he be hearing the voice?

Remember what I told you, Chosen, all those months ago. The more Orbs you gather, the closer the transformation draws nigh. You have four Orbs now, including the Lost Aspect, the one I sought with all my power but never found. It will make a delightful surprise when your mind is mine.

Leave me alone.

Ah, but that cannot be. You are the Chosen of the Manifold. It is your fate to become one with me. To meld with the Ancient One. Don't tell me you forgot that conversation we had on the surface of Psyche. And with the Orb of Thermalism, you might say I will form a majority stake on your Focus. Four Orbs of the original Seven. I could make you do things you would never believe possible.

You're lying.

You think so? We shall see. Perhaps there is enough will for you to resist. But you have felt the Orbs and their power. Imagine what you could do with them if you accept my help. Such power! Do you not feel their pull, their inevitability, even now?

Lucian had to admit, he *could*. It was a tantalizing promise, one that was almost impossible to resist, like water to one dying of thirst. How long could he hold out against feeling unadulterated ether pulsing through him? He could draw from all Seven Aspects, if he wished, because of the Orb of Space-Time. And the more Orbs he held, the more ether he could open himself to.

Such thoughts were dangerous.

Why do I keep hearing your whispers? Why do you even bother trying to trick me?

There is no trickery. Only the truth. I'm preparing you for the transition. It is almost certain that you are the true Chosen. But there is always a sliver of doubt. Even now, Xara Mallis speeds across the stars. But with your progress, we may no longer have any need of her.

We? There is no "we" here.

That's where you're wrong, Chosen. Soon, you and I will be one.

That is an event to be celebrated, not maligned. And with the Lost Aspect, we can heal magic forevermore. It will be up to us how to choose. To make the Ascendant Beings dance upon our strings. The Shadow Realm will prevail!

What are you talking about?

We will take the fight to them. I was there when you spoke to Silumko. He was one of us, an Ancient. But now he is enslaved to his masters in the Light Realm. But with the Orb of Space-Time and the rest of the Aspects, we can do what I never dreamed possible. The Preserved would fight for us. The Alkasen would no longer be a threat to your race.

Was that true? Somehow, deep down, Lucian knew it was. It would require finding the rest of the Orbs. In the days of Starsea, the Seven Orbs did not save the Immortal One and his empire from the *Alkasen*. But what would have happened if he'd had the Lost Aspect at his command?

We have the power to save humanity, Lucian. I can show you how. I have knowledge. For all of Vera Desai's miscalculations, she at least recognized this. You will need both to survive the coming darkness. But you must accept my help. If there is a time you doubt your power, reach out to me. Only I can grant salvation.

Lucian felt a fury such as he had never known. He was tired of the Immortal One violating his mind as if it were his own.

Get out. This is my mind. My thoughts. I won't have you in here manipulating me.

Then fight me. If you can.

With a roar, Lucian clenched his fists and reached for all four of his Orbs. He needed ether, and plenty of it. He didn't care if this was a dream. The voice haunting him was real enough.

It had to end now.

He collected the ether of his three conventional Orbs into his Focus: Psionics, Binding, and Radiance. He also reached for the Orb of Space-Time, compressing the ether, but not sure what to do with it.

You don't know the first thing about what you're doing.

Lucian ignored the voice, creating a Psionic shield, amplifying its power with additional ether from the Orbs of Binding and Radiance.

Pathetic, the Ancient One said. *Is that all you have?*

Lucian focused on the voice inside him, somehow able to detect the presence through the power of the Orb of Radiance. He redirected his streams at that voice, filtered through the Orb of Space-Time.

But before any connection could take place, the Ancient One vanished, leaving Lucian brimming with magic with no outlet. Unbalanced, it seemed as if his Focus would collapse on itself like a neutron star.

By instinct, he reached for the other four primary Aspects: Dynamism, Atomicism, Thermalism, and Gravitonics, knowing they were necessary to at least ballast the current Frankenstein stream he'd created. Those Aspects fused into the master stream, all filtering through the Orb of Space-Time. The stream was now balanced, but the power was still building with no outlet.

Lucian focused on the distant volcano. Not knowing what else to do, he set his anchor point near the mountaintop. With a roar, he unleashed a strange stream, a pillar of black light laced with lightning and fire. The pillar roared across the surface of the lava, which was instantly vaporized upon contact. When the pillar connected with the mountainside, a massive explosion resounded, the mountain collapsing into itself while plumes of smoke and magma issued from the mountain.

The stream came to a sudden end, Lucian collapsing to his knees. The volcano was still tumbling inward, smoke blasting outward across the surface of the lava. Even with a Thermal shield, there was no way Lucian would survive that hot blast of ash and heat.

So, he simply watched and waited.

This was just a dream, but it felt so real. What was the difference between real life and a dream when he could feel the heat baking his skin, the fear induced by the Ancient One's presence, could smell the sulfurous stench of the air?

Was he actually here? How could that be possible?

No. This *couldn't* be real. He closed his eyes, remembering the penthouse and falling asleep next to Serah. It had been a single moment of peace before this nightmare.

And as he closed his eyes, all he could see were a pair of red eyes, staring balefully, like twin coals glowing in a dark room.

There was a moment of intense, searing pain, and then darkness.

———

LUCIAN WOKE UP IN A SWEAT, his heart pounding. He wanted to scream, but he was so paralyzed that he was unable to do so. Serah was still sleeping calmly, and outside, the city had come to life. Pedestrians were filtering in between buildings, electric trams running down central avenues, and ships flying to and from the station through the torus's transparent top.

The day outside was bright, created by massive sun-lamps spaced at regular intervals above. Lucian sat, trying to calm down and collect himself so he could figure out just what the hell had happened and what it meant.

But no amount of thinking seemed to help. The Ancient One was just taunting him, as usual. And the vision was of the surface of Hephaestus, a place Lucian had never seen in his life. And yet, he knew the scene was real, even if he had never experienced it. Where had it come from? What did it mean?

Serah stirred from beside him but remained asleep. He

stepped into the shower, hoping it would calm his nerves somewhat. It was already almost noon. His stomach growled. His last proper meal was before docking on Hephaestus Station.

By the time he finished showering, Serah was up, scanning through her daily notifications. She looked up at him and smiled.

"Hi, handsome. Sleep well?"

He sat on the bed, and his lack of answer made her put down her slate.

"What's wrong?"

"I had this crazy dream. Still can't get it out of my head."

"Really? I had one, too. There was this flying horse out in space, and . . ." She shook her head. "Never mind. I lost it. Was it just a dream, or more like a vision?"

"I don't know. It felt like a vision."

He told her about it, in as few words as possible. She just watched him with concern.

"That *is* crazy. You think it was real?"

"It *felt* real. I . . . don't really want to talk about it. We have a lot to take care of today."

"All right," she said, her tone somewhat worried. "Be out there soon."

When he headed out into the main part of the suite, he found Fergus and Gaius already at work on their slates, with some takeout Chinese food spread out on the glass table before them.

"Figured we'd fill up on something palatable," Fergus said. "Doubt XVA Staffing will feed us good grub."

Lucian filled up a bowl gratefully. "Any updates?"

Gaius remained silent, telling Lucian he wasn't in the mood for talking. Which was fine by him.

"Yeah," Fergus answered. "We're supposed to meet at the local XVA office. It's in the Lower Torus. I've sent the address to your slate."

Lucian looked at the incoming message, which contained the building's location. "Doesn't seem far. And that was at 18:00?"

"That's what it says."

Gaius frowned. "I'm incredulous that you didn't think to consult me before making this important decision."

"You ran off last night. That's on you."

"I'll have you know, Talent Lucian, that I am here to support you, per Transcend White's instructions. Forcing my hand is not something you should be proud of."

Before Lucian could get in his own response, Serah walked into the room, showered and in clean street clothes. She surveyed the food. "What's this?"

"Lunch," Fergus said. "We got Chinese. Dumplings, salted fish, garlic vegetables, fried rice . . ."

She plopped down on the couch and filled a plate. She took a bite of a dumpling, her eyes widening. "Huh. Not bad." She filled her plate and started chowing down. "So, did I miss anything? Other than hearing about how Gaius has descended from on high to join us on the labor force."

Gaius's cheeks reddened, but he offered no comment. Trying to defend himself from every barb must have been like trying to swat flies. Lucian would have felt bad, but the guy deserved it.

"I'll have to see it to believe it," Serah said. "Either way, glad you're still part of the team."

"As if I had any choice in the matter. Now, moving on. We have a lot of work to do. Research, preparation—"

"Wait," Fergus said, his body stiffening.

Lucian's senses went on high alert as he reached for his holstered shockspear. "What is it?"

Fergus faced toward the double doors leading into their suite. Then, his eyes roved along the walls, glowing green with Radiant Magic.

"Thermal signatures. People are out there. We need to move."

"How?" Serah whispered. "That's the only way out."

At that moment, the double-doors blasted open, revealing two Blackguards in power armor raising coilguns in their direction.

Lucian's reaction was instant, a Binding shield going up and deflecting the stream of slugs fired at them. Psion Gaius raised his hands, blasting a powerful kinetic wave that splintered surrounding furniture while slamming into the two men, forcing them into the hallway. Meanwhile, Fergus was bashing the window with his shockspear. The shatter of glass resounded throughout the suite.

"Go, go, go!" he ordered. He sidled onto the ledge outside, skirting it until he was lost to view.

Psion Gaius took shelter behind Lucian's shield as two more men appeared. Gaius, with hands still raised, targeted the head of the rightmost Blackguard with a reverse Psionic stream. The man suddenly raised his coilgun at his compatriot, firing right into his helmet. The man went down, and then he pointed the gun at his own helmet and fired. Their armor powered off as they slunk to the floor.

"Holy shit, that was crazy!" Serah said.

"Just get to the window," Gaius said, cool and collected. "The party's just getting started."

They backed out onto the edge, crunching over broken glass. Fergus was already ten meters down the side of the building, with nowhere left to run. Lucian knew that escape was up to him.

He spied a tall glass tower in the distance, but creating four separate tethers was all but guaranteed to make him delve. After his dream last night with the Ancient One, that was the last thing he wanted.

He remembered his words, that if he ever needed help, to

only reach out to him. Lucian shook his head at the very idea, even as everyone watched him for the next move.

"Gaius first," he said. "Find the closest shuttle port."

"What in the Worlds are you . . . ahh!"

He shot off through the air, toward the building. Even as Gaius was halfway there, a Blackguard poked his head out of the window and aimed his rifle. Serah raised a hand, creating a gravity orb that floated right beside him. Lucian felt himself pulled toward it, but he was far enough away to mostly ignore its effect. The Blackguard, however, was yanked hard toward the force, and careened off the side of the building, firing a few ineffective shots toward the torus's ceiling. Lucian hoped it didn't blow out a panel that was large enough to empty out the entire station.

Once Gaius was safe and sound on a distant balcony, he sent Fergus next, drawing more ether to make him fly faster. He made the passage in half the time as Gaius. As soon as he slowed for the landing, Lucian created two tethers, one for him and one for Serah. He drew more ether from the Orb of Binding, magic streaming from his chest and infusing into his hands.

Serah strained to keep her gravity orb active. Lucian didn't know how much magic it took to do that, but from her struggle, it had to have been a lot. And yet, as long as it remained, they would be safe from further attacks. At least, until a few of the soldiers got the idea to shoot at them from the streets below.

Which was exactly what started happening. There was time enough for one shot to be fired before Lucian gathered the requisite ether. He and Serah flew in tandem above the rooftops and parkland below them. People pointed up at them in awe, even as a few high shrieks from coilgun slugs streaked past them, shattering the glass of the skyscraper ahead.

Lucian and Serah drew up and landed lightly. Within the

window of the building before them sat a bespectacled office worker at his desk, gaping.

"There's a shuttle port down there," Gaius said, pointing. "We've already attracted too much attention."

"We've got a head start," Lucian said. "There's no way we're losing them on this torus. It's too small. We have to get to the Undercity, find a place to lie low . . ."

"Rot that!" Serah said. "Let's just take the ship and get the hell out of here."

Gaius broke the window leading into the office tower. The office worker cowered in the corner. Gaius looked at him. "We were never here."

The man just stared dumbly as the four of them filed past.

"Where are the stairs?" Lucian asked.

The man just pointed with a shaky finger toward his left. Lucian nodded his thanks as they entered the hallway.

They found the staircase easily enough and flew down. They raced across the lobby.

"Stop at once!" came the blare of a nearby security droid.

After a glance, Lucian saw it had no weapon, so he ignored it.

They burst through the front doors and headed left across a busy plaza between tall buildings, above which Lucian could see the transparent surface of the torus ceiling. Beyond the panels loomed the molten surface of the planet. They ran for a few blocks, and Lucian was grateful there weren't many speeding vehicles to impede their progress, just a few auto-delivery vans making rounds. Looking down the streets in the embassy's direction, there was no sign of the Blackguards.

"So . . . tired . . ." Serah panted.

"Almost there," Gaius said, not seeming to break a sweat.

They entered the platform just as the doors of a shuttle were closing. Lucian created a reverse tether, one on each door, which held them in place. The people on board screamed as they cowered toward the other end of the transport.

Lucian and the others slid in, having the whole back space to themselves. The doors closed, and the shuttle continued on its journey. From the way the other passengers were looking at them, about a dozen in all, it was as if they were pointing guns at them.

"We're with the League," Gaius said, trying to calm the crowds. "Stay safe, citizens."

It was the longest three minutes of Lucian's life as the shuttle glided toward the Lower Torus and the Undercity it contained.

As soon as the airlock doors hissed open, the passengers all but scrambled out. Lucian and the others walked out more leisurely, coming out in a different neighborhood than the one they had left yesterday. The people waiting on the platform looked at them curiously, wondering how the four of them could have caused such an uproar. Lucian supposed their appearance was not enough to warrant fear, despite the frightened state of the passengers that had just disembarked.

They were on an elevated street, and though it was noon by now, the lights here were not as bright as the Middle Torus. The tall, dingy buildings lent a decrepit air, and the tinge of smoke was almost enough to make Lucian start hacking. He could see the source, rows upon rows of factories belching smoke as far as the eye could see, casting shadows over shabby tenements and dark alleys.

"Industrial sector," Gaius said. "One of the rougher parts of the station. We should get down to the Undercity. We're more likely to lose them there."

"How far are we from the meeting place?"

"The XVA offices are all the way on the other side of the torus. We'll have to catch a train."

"How long will that take?" Serah asked.

Gaius went off, leading into the crowd milling about the station. It looked as if he knew where he was going, so Lucian followed.

They found a stairwell in a dark alley that led below the main level of the Lower Torus. Soon, the open air was left behind, replaced by a network of wide tunnels with scarred, metal surfaces rife with gang tags. It was just as busy down here as it was up there. Perhaps even more so. They passed shops with barred windows with blazing neon signs: convenience stores, small take out places, food carts, tattoo parlors, brothels.

But it was the people that caught Lucian's attention the most. He noticed two things most of all: an unusual thinness to everyone's physique, probably because of malnutrition, and skin that was almost ghoulish in appearance, despite the race of the person. It was a cacophony of noise, and it seemed fights, arguing, and boisterous laughter all mixed and intermingled as if no excess of emotion were out of place. Hostile eyes stared as they passed. Outsiders rarely came here.

On their left, in a dark alley, Lucian saw what he thought to be a man, smiling. A second later, though, the man was gone, apparently disappearing deeper into the alley.

"This place gives me the creeps."

"Just keep walking," Gaius said.

"You know where we're going?" Serah asked.

"Of course I do. There should be a train up this tunnel."

At that moment, Serah was pushed, two men materializing from an alley and pulling on her arm, each with hungry looks in their eyes.

"Get off me, you freaks!"

Lucian extended his shockspear, branding it with electricity. At the action, the men scampered off into the darkness like rats.

There were no screams, and no one acted as if anything unusual had happened. People continued with their business, and the only difference was that they were afforded a bit more space than usual.

"You okay?"

"Yeah," she said, her voice shaky. "They just came out of nowhere."

"Animals," Gaius growled, disgustedly.

Lucian drew her closer. Though Serah could have wiped the floor with both of them, the last thing they needed to do right now was stream. In a place like this, without magic, they were much more exposed. He just had to hope people thought his shockspear was battery-powered.

As they advanced down the tunnel, the space they'd enjoyed before was eaten away as new people fell in around them.

"Watch out for pickpockets," Gaius said, pushing aside a filthy, scrawny teenager who had gotten too close. The teenager cursed Gaius in a local dialect that was practically unrecognizable, but he didn't press his luck again.

This was easily the roughest place Lucian had been. It made the OLH neighborhood, where he'd grown up, look like the Florida Shoals or even L5.

"There's the station," Fergus said, as if it were a lifeline.

As they ran up to the boarding platform, Lucian noted the heavy barricaded doors, probably to prevent unauthorized access. He had to scan his slate to get in, and was automatically debited twenty sub-creds for access. Despite the paltry sum, it was apparently too much for some people to pay. Lucian noted a group of five lanky youths wearing black clothing and head-bands, standing on each other's shoulders to get over the partition. The ones that reached the top helped pull the others along. When there was only one left, his comrades left him behind, hooting and laughing as they ran into the dirty coach ahead. The boy, a few years younger than the rest, let out a litany of curses that would have made a longshoreman blush.

They entered the coach just in time, which was quite full, except in the area around the rowdy youths. Lucian made his way there, seeing that it was the only spot. The youths smiled mockingly as the train rolled out of the station.

One boy leered at Serah, the other boys seeming to egg him on to do something.

"Hey baby, why don't you come sit over here?"

Serah ignored him, and Lucian just wished he could do something about it without causing too much of a scene. But that was going to be impossible.

"Hey, are you deaf, or just dumb!" He snapped his finger. "I'm talking to you!"

Lucian was over it. Before the boy could say anything else, he frowned in confusion. It seemed he was trying to open his mouth, but simply couldn't. His eyes widened as the others looked at him with a mix of confusion and repressed laughter. The boy grabbed his mouth, trying to pry it open, but of course, an irreverent youth couldn't stand up to the Orb of Binding. He started groaning in panic.

"What's wrong?" Lucian asked. "Cat got your tongue?"

"Beat his ass, Krake!" one of the boys said, large of frame with the build of a sports star. "You just going to *take* that?"

All he could do was groan, and gesture wildly at Lucian.

Serah leaned over. "Leave him be. I think he's learned his lesson."

Lucian released the stream, and the boy started panting wildly, as if he'd been without breath. He looked at Lucian as if he were staring down a viper about to strike.

The train started slowing. Lucian nodded toward the doors. "This is your stop."

The hulking youth who had spoken earlier narrowed his eyes. "No, it ain't, clown. You want to have a go?"

"He's crazy, Roark," Krake said. "I'm out of here."

To Lucian's relief, the boys scampered off the train without causing any more drama, settling for just staring him down. The big guy, Roark, went last, and Lucian couldn't resist tripping him up by binding his feet together as the doors closed behind him.

"Seriously?" Gaius asked, as if bored. "You need to learn to control yourself."

"Why? What's the point if I can't teach someone a lesson who deserves it?"

With a jolt, their window got shouldered by the big guy just as the train started rolling off, cracking the glass. He just *had* to get his shot in to save face. Lucian shook his head. It just wasn't worth it.

"You'd think people would learn by now," he said. "Rotting hell, all of us are wearing shockspears!"

"As I said," Gaius said. "These people are wild animals, making a scene so they can attack at the slightest provocation. Picking a fight here is like picking a fight with a rabid street dog. Sure, you'll probably win, but you could also die foaming at the mouth. Never pick a fight with someone with nothing to lose."

"That's harsh," Serah said. "These are people, Gaius, not dogs. They've had hard lives, and you can't expect everyone to be as educated as you."

"Until they prove anything to the contrary, that's what they are to me. Mongrel dogs. The dregs of society."

Fergus shook his head. "They are the people that society forgot, Gaius. If people are treated like animals, don't be surprised if a few start acting like them." From Fergus's tone, it seemed as if he were speaking from a place of conviction and experience. "No one deserves to live like this."

"Don't take it so personally. It's only my opinion. Souls like theirs are lost, and there's no point in showing them the light."

"That's exactly the problem. Enough people with opinions

like yours is what keeps things like this from ever getting solved. It's classist and perpetuates an unjust society."

"And what of personal responsibility, hmm? Are you arguing that these people are incapable of it? That to me sounds classist." He sighed. "Not that it'll matter in a few months, anyway. This whole place is likely to be blown to smithereens."

A few heads turned his way at that, but then they went back to their normal business, for which Lucian was thankful.

As brutal as Gaius's words were, Lucian knew they were probably true. It was highly likely that in months, if not sooner, this system would become a battleground, and it wasn't clear whether anyone could save it. Just thinking of all these thousands of people, trapped in this carbon alloy ring spinning in space, was almost enough to make him shudder.

The rest of the ride was silent. It took about thirty minutes to get to the other side of the ring, where they stepped off into the area they had been in yesterday, filled with bars, clubs, and casinos. They wandered down dark tunnels toward the center part of the torus, finding a dingy building with the company logo over the entrance.

Lucian paused outside the doorway. "Make sure your shockspears are hidden. I doubt they'll allow us to take them."

Already, they were hiding them under their street clothes. A mage's shockspear could shrink small enough to fit in a pocket, at need, without looking too conspicuous.

"All good?" As heads nodded all around, Lucian pointed them inside. "All right, let's move."

They went through the open entrance, finding a reception desk that was shielded by bulletproof glass. Inside the partition sat a very bored looking middle-aged woman, heavily made up and smoking a cigarette.

"Names?" she asked, drolly.

"Is this XVA Staffing?" Lucian asked.

"Yeah. You have an application with us or something?"

"Really professional," Gaius muttered. "We were told to show up at 18:00."

Her eyes narrowed. "You're early, honey."

"Could we wait here?"

Her eyes went to each of them in tandem, seeming to take in their appearances for the first time. "You sure you're not lost?"

Lucian frowned. "Yeah. Why?"

"You're . . . not the usual suspects, is all." She cleared phlegm from her throat. "You all might want to turn around and enjoy your last couple of hours of freedom. The contract is for three months. You'll be going down the Vator and after that, no turning back. Just want to make sure you understand that."

"It's okay," Serah said. "We can teleport back."

Lucian blinked. What was she doing?

"Are you right in the head, young lady?"

"Just making a joke."

"Anyhow, if you're really set on waiting around, you can go on back. I can't let you out once you go in, though."

"That's fine," Lucian said. He just wanted a safe place to hole up.

"Just sign on the dotted line."

She handed over a beat up slate that had at least two hundred pages of legalese.

"You don't expect us to read this, do you?"

"Well, you've got time. You want to get paid, you sign."

"Fine, then." Lucian signed.

The others followed his example, all except Gaius. His eyes roved the contract line-by-line, his frown deepening with each passing minute.

"You know," he said, soberly. "This contract contains many illegalities that won't hold up in any League court."

"You a lawyer or something?"

"No."

The receptionist gave a saccharine smile. "Welcome to Hephaestus Station, honey."

Gaius sighed. "Why do I even bother?"

Like the rest of them, he signed the contract.

The heavy door leading into the backroom clicked and opened.

"Wait in there. The foreperson will be with you shortly."

18

THEY ENTERED THE OPEN DOOR, finding about a hundred chairs lined up in ten rows, all facing a very antiquated projector screen. The four of them took up seats in the back corner and waited.

Over the next couple of hours, people filed in. Men, mostly, thin and malnourished with the look of the Undercity on them, and others that were healthier with more meat on their bones. In all cases, they avoided eye contact, and picked a seat that was as far from the others as possible. There were only a few women—three, by Lucian's count. One of them gave Serah a strange look as she filed in.

"If I had your looks, I'd be dancing at Candy's."

"Nobody asked you," Serah retorted.

The woman smirked and sat down two rows ahead.

Soon, the room was filled with cigarette smoke, and smoke from other substances besides. Some of the men talked in low voices, men who probably knew each other from previous contracts. But for the most part, it was quiet.

The clock went past 18:00, and still, the foreman hadn't

showed up. He eventually did, about forty minutes late, and his ruddy cheeks, red eyes, and lumbering walk telling Lucian he was three sheets to the wind, or maybe even four sheets. He had a thick walrus mustache, droopy eyes, and a foul disposition. Behind him marched four more men, all wearing black riot gear, face masks, with shock batons on their belts.

"This looks promising," Serah said.

"Who said that?" he barked, his eyes looking for the source of the voice.

Serah looked as if she wanted to say more, but Lucian put a hand on her arm, restraining her.

He stood on the podium and looked at the crowd. He scowled a bit, as if he didn't like what he saw.

"I'm Foreman Holloway, and for the next three months, you are my slaves. I tell you to do something, you do it, or else you'll get a shock from my electro whip." He touched the weapon at his side. "My men have full authorization to use their batons on *anyone* who doesn't follow orders. Mark my words, you'll see us use them before tonight's done. We clear on that?"

From the chorus of "yes sirs," Lucian assumed that was the right answer, so he responded in kind.

Holloway nodded to a tough beside him, who pressed a button on a remote control. Immediately, a corporate movie started playing on the screen as the lights dimmed, projecting the logo of the company.

"XVA Staffing Professionals," came a placid, female voice. "Where staffing is our profession."

Serah snickered, and immediately a guard came to their row and flashed a light in her direction.

"Rotting hell," she said. "Cut that out."

"Step over here, ma'am."

"She meant nothing by it," Lucian said.

"Trying to be a hero, huh? You, over here." The tough was already brandishing his shock baton.

Lucian did *not* want to have to deal with this. But before he could do anything, he noticed a telltale violet blaze in the eyes behind the man's riot mask.

"Err . . . as you were. Try not to let it happen again."

The guard turned away. Lucian looked at Gaius, but from his poker face, it was hard to believe he had done anything.

They continued watching the film, this time without laughter. It had nothing to do with mining or Hephaestus, instead showing a group of young people laughing on the beach, and then a montage of a diverse group orbital diving, and then a proud young woman shaking hands with a guy in a suit.

Serah asked, leaning over. This time, she was quiet enough not to be heard. "What the hell is this shit?"

"Corporate brainwashing."

Gaius shot them a look of warning, so Lucian went quiet.

About five minutes later, the film ended, and Foreman Holloway faced the crowd.

"All right, this is how it'll be. You're to head into that room and dress in the company jumpsuits. Look for the one with your name. Once you're dressed, we're going to walk in an orderly fashion to the company shuttle port. It'll take us to the Elevator. The ride down will take about twenty hours, and we'll have training during that time."

"Twenty *hours*?" Serah asked.

Thankfully, the foreman didn't seem to hear her. One of the guards opened the door to the backroom, with his other hand on his shock baton. The foreman nodded toward the opening.

"Hop to it."

Mumbling, the miners headed that way.

The three men found their gear next to each other, while Serah had to head to a separate changing area for the women. Getting the envirosuits on was easy enough. Keeping their retracted shockspears hidden was more difficult. To keep them out of sight, Lucian, Gaius, and Fergus had to change a little too closely for comfort, using their backs to obscure the weapons. Serah was on her own, but judging from the lack of alarm, no one seemed to notice or care.

Within a few minutes, everyone was dressed in crimson-colored jumpsuits with built-in liquid cooling and helmets. The surface of Hephaestus was far too hot to bear for any length of time, and besides that, the carbon dioxide levels were high enough to be lethal after breathing it for a few minutes.

The four of them gathered in the middle of the room.

"No one told me the ride down would take that long," Serah said.

"Come on, let's go!" one of guards ordered, brandishing his shock baton. For good measure, he used it on the exposed hand of the man closest to him. The man barked a curse, but it got the rest of them moving.

"Treating us like cattle," Gaius said.

"Remember the goal," Lucian said. "If you want nothing overheard, just think it."

Lucian didn't want to tell them to use Psionics with that many people around, but he was sure they would get the message.

As they passed through the open door, two guards were posted, patting everyone down. When it got to be Lucian's turn, he opened a mind control stream.

The next four are good. Let us through.

The man's eyes glazed over for a moment, hesitating. After a moment, he cleared his throat. "You four are good."

The other guard was about to protest, but Lucian opened a second stream to him, implanting the same thought. His mouth instantly closed.

Lucian and the rest slipped through, several of the men around them grumbling. But no one directly challenged him, much to his relief.

They entered a long tunnel, narrow and empty. The heavy

soles of their suits clomped off the metal surface. They walked down that corridor for about ten minutes before it ended at an airlock. The foreman scanned the door open, revealing a long shuttle with seating for about a hundred people.

"Let's move!" he said. "If we miss our elevator car, all of you are getting spaced!"

Lucian doubted he would go so far as that, but the threat had the intended effect. Everyone scurried onto the shuttle in silence, strapping themselves in. Lucian noticed a heavyset fellow with a thick beard and scarred face staring him down in challenge. Lucian met his gaze and saw pure murder in the man's eyes. What was this guy's deal?

Once everyone was strapped in, the shuttle broke away from the station, flying toward the Elevator of Hephaestus in the center of the torus. It was far thicker than Lucian had first guessed, with multiple cables and cars of various sizes zooming up and down. Most were large and blocky, obviously designed for carrying freight, though a few had sleeker designs, along with viewports intended for passengers. The line of the Elevator stretched until it was only the width of a hair, lost to Hephaestus's hazy, red-glowing surface below.

Soon, they were attached to one of the Elevator cars, and the door opened, revealing a space that would be cramped for the fifty of them. When he saw all the lines of seats with shoulder straps, Lucian wondered how they were expected to use the restroom. This elevator car was clearly not designed for comfort, only efficiently conveying a large amount of people to the surface as quickly as possible.

"Strap in," the foreman barked.

"Boss," one man rumbled, "I've got to take a leak."

"Sit down, I said! I've got no time for grunts too dumb to hook up their piss bags."

Two guards came out of nowhere, thrusting their shock batons into the man's side. He squealed in pain. If the man hadn't peed himself before then, he probably had now. Lucian wanted to say something, but he'd have to back up his words with power. That was something he couldn't do right now, especially with the Blackguards coming after him. He needed to get on world, no matter what.

Either way, he was glad they were getting off the station now. Though he wouldn't rest easy until the Lower Torus was left well behind.

Once everyone was strapped in, including the security guards, the foreman stood up front and faced them all. "This is how it'll work. You're not allowed to get up for anything. We'll bring you food and water. Just remember, we're not here for the views. You have a VR helmet under your seat, so you can be trained up by the time we hit the ground. Put it on now."

Lucian reached under his seat, finding the helmet. He placed it over his head, but only found a black screen. The padding on his ears kept sound from entering.

As he felt the elevator car disengage and head down, a video played. He spent the next four hours of his life learning about mining. The terminology of the equipment and spaces he'd be working in, the minerals he'd be looking for, how to use the Ares driller, the personal machine the company used to excavate with. The video presented a rosy picture of what it'd be like working in the mines below, workers smiling and laughing, generous pay, large buffets and rec areas during off hours.

It all smelled like a load of bullshit to Lucian, especially after Foreman Holloway's treatment of them.

A couple of hours later, he felt a rough kick in his shin, just short of causing pain. When Lucian raised his helmet, a blue-armored guard thrust a tray of slop in his direction. Lucian caught it just in time before the guard moved on to Serah next to him. Looking out the viewport, they had come a good way down toward the surface of the planet, but were still high enough above it to be in space.

Serah took off her headset next to him. "I'm over this place already."

The guard turned back, but something in Lucian's gaze must have made him move on to the next in line, Gaius.

Lucian opened a Psionic link to her. *It's all about getting down there. And you have to remember, we always have a way out, if it comes to that.*

Even thinking of using the Orb of Space-Time in that way made him leery. Yes, it could get them back to Hephaestus Station easily, but it would also put him in the path of the Blackguards. And of course, he could warp them to somewhere even *farther* away, but he would need the time to gather the ether to make such a transition. From the way they were being treated like slaves, they might not get a spare moment.

Lucian forced himself to eat and went right back to his VR training. He closed his eyes and fell asleep during it, and it seemed no one was any the wiser. By the time the simulation turned off, the elevator car trembled. He lifted off the helmet to see a reddish haze outside the wide viewports. They had entered Hephaestus's atmosphere. There was no telling just how far they had come down.

In the morning was more virtual training, mostly comprised of following on-screen prompts to learn how to use of the Ares driller. The video closed by telling him he would be rewarded with one full credit for doing his duty and reporting any agitators to an XVA security officer immediately.

With that, there were thankfully no more training videos, just the hazy atmosphere outside. Most everyone in the elevator car was asleep, including Serah, who was snoring softly on his right. As Lucian stared out that window, all he could think about was what the hell he'd gotten everyone into. He had to look for some way to escape so they could go after the Orb of Thermalism, but they couldn't do that until they got to the surface. Lucian just didn't know what to expect. But the last thing he, or any of them, would do was go into the mines to work on an Ares driller for the next three months.

After an identical breakfast to the meal they'd had last night, the haze outside cleared, and Lucian could see the surface below, a hellish wasteland of black rock and lakes and rivers of fire. The air outside roared past as the elevator car shot down toward the ground.

"Looks hot as hell out there," some man nearby said.

He got hit with a shockstick from a nearby guard. "No talking."

"Why not?" he said. "You think that thing can shut me up?"

"You're about to find out, miner scum."

The guard gave a sadistic smile as he zapped the man on his side and kept the baton there for a good five seconds. The man gyrated for a few seconds before going still.

Serah's voice entered his mind. *They enjoy that way too much.*

Just keep a low profile. We'll find a way out of here.

I want to teach him a lesson.

No. We're not here to start a revolution.

She sighed from beside him. *I guess.*

Lucian felt uneasy as the elevator car lowered. The fiery surface outside disappeared, replaced with blocky metal buildings under a clear dome. The air outside was dreary and smoke-tinged from the refineries, smelters, and factories surrounding the elevator.

At last, after twenty long hours, the elevator car came to a halt. The doors slid open, letting in a wave of warm, dry air. Whatever the purpose of the dome above, it obviously didn't keep out all the heat of the surface.

"All right, you sluggards," Foreman Holloway said. "Let's move."

The guards stood on either side of the doorway as the miners stiffly stepped out onto a metallic loading platform below. Outside came the din of ringing metal and the blast of furnaces. The sharp, metallic fumes hanging in the air almost made Lucian choke. Ash floated in the air, eddying about on hot gusts of wind.

It wasn't clear exactly where they were going, but for now, it was down a metal staircase leading them to the rocky surface below. Apparently, this domed settlement was the only livable part of the planet, but somehow, someway, Lucian had to find a way out. And not only that, but to find the Orb of Thermalism in a terribly inhospitable environment.

He didn't even know where to begin.

19

ONCE THEY REACHED THE SURFACE, a bus with thick tires was waiting for them. From its sturdy construction, Lucian could tell it was airtight, designed to operate outside the confines of Anchorpoint and its interior dome. Behind their group marched more groups of miners, so collectively there were hundreds of them. Lucian had to wonder if this was normal, or whether it had something to do with the war kicking into high gear and the need for bodies on the ground.

Serah watched the bus leerily and checked to see if the guards were watching them. "No rotting way I'm getting on that thing."

Fergus and Gaius came to stand nearby. Fergus spoke. "What's the plan?"

They all acted as if he knew what he was doing. "No rotting clue."

"Well, I'm with Talent Serah," Gaius said. "You don't *truly* expect us to fulfill our contract, do you? They are marching all these poor people down to be slaves for life."

That earned him more than a few head turns, but before

anyone could say anything more, the foreman turned his head from where he had been speaking to another foreman.

"This is the plan. All of you are getting on this shuttle here, and it'll take you to the mines. Inside the mines, there'll be an all you can eat buffet, hot showers, and your barracks. You'll start work tomorrow, and you'll get paid at the end of every week." He leveled his gaze at the entire crew. "Questions?"

"Yeah," a burly man said, his thick forearm tattoos exposed by his rolled-up sleeves. It was the same guy who had stared Lucian down earlier. "How do I get off this rock? This shit ain't what I signed up for. Contract said we'd be working out of Anchorpoint, not the fire mines."

"This *is* your contract, miner scum," the foreman said. "We *are* going out of Anchorpoint, and the company operates from here. It's not the company's fault if you don't know how to read." He put a hand on his electro whip. "Unless you have something else to say?"

The man opened his mouth, but two guards stepped forward, apparently eager to have a go at him.

Lucian, at that point, had had enough. He reached for the Orb of Psionics and Binding, creating a psychic dualstream designed to parse the foreman's thoughts. He wanted to find out what this bastard intended for them, and what he could do about it.

Holloway's eyes became hooded, shining with a violet sheen. Lucian just had to hope no one would notice, or at least realize its significance. His first question was where were they *really* going? The answer came to him immediately.

They intended to stuff them onto that bus and run them into some dilapidated mines north of town, a gate closing behind and locking them up. When Lucian questioned *why* they did that, he realized Holloway didn't know himself. He was just getting paid a credit a head, so out of this group of fifty-two, that was a tidy profit for him. He'd already delivered five similar groups in the past four weeks, and he wasn't being paid to ask questions.

Lucian cut off the stream. He'd learned all he cared to figure out, at least for the moment. Clearly, this company was operating an illegal human trafficking operation.

The question was, how to convince everyone standing here of it?

Already, the first few were heading toward the open doors of the bus.

Lucian stepped forward, shouting loud enough for everyone to hear. "Get on that bus, and you'll never see the light of day again."

An old man, who was already holding the handrail, turned back to look at Lucian curiously as Holloway's beady eyes narrowed.

"I've had about enough out of you. Garcia, Kovac, make an example out of him."

Unfazed, Lucian shouted again. "He's going to enslave us! If we don't fight back, *right now*, all of us are as good as dead."

Holloway's face turned a deep shade of crimson only amplified by the reddish light of the planet. "Guards!"

Lucian reached for the Orb of Psionics and made a connection to each member of his group. *Ward Psionics. Now!*

He didn't have time to explain any further. He could only trust them to follow the order. By pure instinct, he created a Psionic ward large enough to cover not only him and his friends, but the rest of the miners in the vicinity. He then streamed Thermalism *forward*, combining the stream with the Psionic ward. Somehow, he knew this would inflame the emotions of everyone under the ward. He set the ward with a Binding shell, allowing it to take effect.

He felt the emotions of the men around him almost as if they were his own. Those emotions were anger, fear, frustration, betrayal, a need to set things to rights, whatever the cost.

And under the effect of the ward, those emotions, a hundred sparks, took flame, kindling a fire that would give these unfortunate men and women the courage to fight back.

A lot of the miners were murmuring now, while the guards were pushing their way toward Lucian.

The burly man looked at Lucian, seeming to see him in a new light. "You're not clowning around, are you, kid? Come to think of it, my buddies who went down in the last few months haven't come back yet . . ."

The miners were now shouting, already pushing forward toward the guards as a unit. Two guards battered their way through the crowd toward Lucian, but he was already unzipping the top part of his jumpsuit, where his shockspear was hidden. The crowd's emotions now boiling over, Lucian let go of his emotion amplification stream.

Just as the guards raised their shock batons, Lucian extended his weapon with a thought. "Stand back, if you know what's good for you."

"Here we go again," Serah said, following his example.

The next moments were chaos. As the two guards cowered, not having anything more than shock batons, the foreman was taking a more violent approach. He drew a handgun and pointed it Lucian's way. The crowd of miners scattered in fear, leaving him open to attack.

There was no point in hiding what they were now, especially with their lives at stake. Lucian raised a Binding shield just as the first shots were fired. The foreman's eyes widened. By now, all four of them had drawn their shockspears, and each was branded with a Dynamistic stream.

"Psychos!" the foreman said. "Shoot them down!"

The man fired a few bullets as the crowd dispersed in all directions. Lucian's companions stayed behind his shield as he approached the foreman, opening a new stream to tether the handgun to him. Released of his weapon, his eyes went wide with terror. He turned tail and ran.

It was at that moment that the other groups started to fight back against their own guards, and all semblance of control was lost. The guards were outnumbered at least twenty to one, so even with shock batons, and the foremen having conventional weapons, they didn't stand a chance. The closest guards were jumped, their shock batons liberated, while the rest were quickly routed down the wide metal ramp leading into Anchorpoint.

Klaxons began to wail, echoing off the metallic walls of nearby factories. An automated female loudspeaker blared off the side of the nearest building.

Code red. Disturbance detected in the Elevator District. All miners are to return to their barracks. Code red. Disturbance detected in the Elevator District. All miners are to return to their barracks . . .

Lucian looked around in shock. Some of the miners were running back to the Elevator, trying to enter empty cars, but even more were fighting back, grabbing the shock batons of downed guards. Gunshots rattled from the foremen who hadn't yet fled, and men screamed and died as the bullets found their marks. Even so, the miners were too numerous, swarming and tackling their oppressors. The bus screeched down the ramp, running down a fleeing guard.

Some of the miners let out a cheer, but with the alarms blaring, Lucian knew the bloodbath was only beginning.

"I thought we *weren't* trying to start a revolution," Serah said.

"Things got away from me."

Lucian noticed many people were collecting around the big guy who had spoken earlier. He was already barking orders, trying to get people organized and prepared to push on. In the distance, Lucian could see more guards pouring out of a nearby building armed with assault rifles.

"Magic Man!" the burly man hollered, pointing at Lucian. "You're with me. Can you clear a path?"

"Sure thing."

A squadron of guards in power armor ran up the ramp, aiming their rifles at the mostly weaponless miners. Lucian streamed a kinetic wave that barreled down the ramp at breakneck speed. The guards screamed as they flew high into the air, landing hard on the ground below. Lucian spied a few of their weapons and tethered them toward him. He handed them to the big guy to dole out as he saw fit.

"You with the League?" he asked. "It's about time they sent someone to clean up this mess."

"Something like that. Look, we need to secure this area. Get everyone off planet. There are thousands of miners just like you who are enslaved underground, unable to escape."

"No shit. You got some advanced intelligence, or something?"

Lucian nodded, deciding not to explain. His eyes were now on a group of miners, running down the ramp with hands raised in surrender. It seemed they were trying to convince the guards that they weren't a part of this. It didn't matter. They were shot down anyway.

It was with that action that every man and woman around him knew where their loyalties were. It was fight or die.

Right now, there were hundreds of miners around them milling about and looking for something to do. Lucian saw that someone would have to lead them. He didn't want to be the face of a revolution, though. All he had wanted was to create a distraction so he could escape and find the Orb of Thermalism.

This had all gone so far beyond him.

"What are we doing, boss?" the burly man asked.

"Taking over Anchorpoint. We've got the element of surprise on our side, and from there, we can figure out how to liberate the mines."

"Shit. I was afraid you'd say something like that . . ."

By now, at least two dozen men had gathered around Lucian, all waiting for orders on what to do.

Fergus leaned close to him. "If we're doing this, we need to find more weapons so they can at least defend themselves. We need to find some sort of transport that we can use to explore the planet. Always remember that the Orb is the actual goal."

"I know that," Lucian said. He pointed to the building from which the power-armored guards had emerged. "There must be some more weapons in there. We need to get everybody here armed to the teeth, and in power armor, if possible. We can't stop until every part of the city is secured. Don't kill civilians, obviously. Only people who point a gun at you."

He didn't know why, but at that point, something Ansaldra had told him entered his head. That it was a leader's part to make decisions by which people lived and died. He hadn't understood what she meant at the time, but she had promised he would, one day.

Perhaps that day had come.

He and his friends ran down the ramp. As if of one organism, the masses followed after.

———

Using a passkey obtained from a fallen guard, they accessed the building. Within thirty minutes, the building, some sort of barracks, had been cleared and its weapons distributed.

The revolution then took on a life of its own. Anchorpoint was not a large settlement, perhaps no more than twenty thousand people living in the close confines of the dome. More people, enslaved in the factories, stepped away from their work and joined the uprising. By the time a couple of hours had passed, the Carthago guards were being completely routed.

They fled to the motor pools, driving off in all-terrain rovers outside the dome.

They left behind empty streets, empty factories, empty barracks, and empty guard towers. Even the Elevator was secured, and for the first time since it was opened nearly a century ago, it ceased operation. Smoke rose not just from the stacks of factories, but from the smoldering fires of security rovers.

Lucian stood in the center of Anchorpoint, a central shopping area where a large amount of the rioters had gathered, looting stores and terrorizing the local population. Things had gotten out of hand hours ago, and there was nothing Lucian could do to curb it. Somehow, without meaning to, he'd been the spark to start a rebellion. Not even he knew if the blaze of revolution would grow, or be squashed underfoot when reinforcements inevitably arrived.

"What now?" Serah asked. "We're free. If being trapped under a dome with no way out can be called free."

Lucian looked up into the sky, where the translucent barrier protected the interior space from the heat of Hephaestus's atmosphere. "We have to find a way out, I guess. Maybe we can find a skycar."

"And by find, you mean *steal*," Fergus said.

"Whatever we have to do."

"Have you felt for the Orb?" Gaius asked.

"Not yet. I've been trying not to die for the last few hours."

"Well, things have calmed down now, if you haven't noticed. The sooner we get moving . . ."

At that moment, Lucian noticed a breaking in the bilious clouds above. Multiple warships were coming down, heading for the city.

"Looks like the cavalry has arrived," Serah said. "*Their* cavalry, that is."

Lucian had to agree, especially as more ships appeared

from above, having the look of transports about them. Already, the revolutionaries around him were breaking and seeking cover.

Lucian himself was at a loss for what to do. There was nowhere to run, and nowhere to hide.

Whatever was coming, they would have to face it.

20

THE SHIPS LANDED SOMEWHERE on the periphery of the dome, where Lucian assumed there was some sort of spaceport. Things grew deathly quiet in the city, though some lingering fires still smoldered. Lucian and the others wandered the narrow alleyways, looking for a place to lie low.

He shouldered his way into a convenience store, where a clerk and his family were cowering behind the counter covered in a sheet of bulletproof glass. The eyes of his two daughters were haunting, each no more than seven, while his wife held both of the girls toward her body protectively.

"Get out!" the man managed, raising an impactor rifle in their direction.

Lucian raised his hands in a gesture of peace, but streamed a Psionic shield just in case. The man's eyes widened at the display.

"We're not here to hurt you. We just need a place to lie low."

The rifle shook in the man's hands, and then, after a moment, he lowered it. "Well, I won't stop you. Just stay away from my family."

"No worries. Thanks."

They found a corner to crouch in, out of sight of the man and his family. Lucian let go of the Psionic shield, judging there to be enough distance. Serah peeked her head above a windowsill to get a view outside.

"Still quiet. I wonder whose ships those are."

"Carthago Corp, who else?" Gaius asked.

The man called from up front. Apparently, voices carried better in here than Lucian had expected.

"You don't know who it is? It's all over the newsfeeds!"

"Who?" Lucian asked.

At that moment, a voice exited the store's PA system, picking up mid broadcast.

". . . it's unknown when the Golden Armada changed course in the Astravan System, but the bulk of their ships have completed the passage into the Hephaestus System. We have reports that the vanguard is already securing Hephaestus Station and the Elevator. We have reports of chaos, both on the station and the surface, and a rebellion is already underway in Anchorpoint itself. Carthago Corporation, who has held the exclusive League contract to exploit the planet for the past three decades, cannot at the moment be reached for comment. There have long been allegations against the company for human rights abuses, complaints which have gone unacknowledged by the League Assembly, the Planets' Courts, and even the Hegemon himself."

"Rotting hell," Serah said. "It's Zheng Yang!"

Lucian could only listen in shock.

"An interesting development," Gaius mused. "One has to wonder whether we were the source of the rebellion at all."

"What do you mean?" Lucian asked.

"We already know Zheng Yang is a fan of subterfuge. It was one of her agents who discovered Talent Fergus on Archea Station. If Yang is here, then clearly she has designs on Hephaestus while the

League is busy fighting for its life. It would not surprise me if she were the one responsible for this minor rebellion, even if you aided it with an emotion amplification ward."

"I suppose we will see," Fergus said. "As convoluted as all that sounds, it's something I could see her doing. She was always a wily one. It's how she rose to her position."

"Well, if *she's* here, where does that leave us?" Serah asked. "She might know you're here!"

"That, I doubt. Not even she is all-knowing."

"Well," Lucian said, "she could find out very soon."

"I suggest finding some resources," Gaius said. "Food, water, whatever we can carry. XVA has already kindly given us enviro-suits. Of course, we could also use a transport that can get us out of town."

"And then?" Serah asked. "You expect us to just *survive* out there?"

"Well, I'm certainly not going to be taken by Yang for questioning."

Fergus watched out the window, looking into the hazy alley. He nodded, as if coming to a decision.

"As Transcend White and her twin often say, the Manifold is always one step ahead of us."

"What is *that* supposed to mean?" Serah asked. "Don't tell me you're going to surrender yourself."

"We need to find a way out of here, Fergus," Lucian said. "With those ships landing, there isn't much time."

He nodded. "You're right. Perhaps we can find something out there in town."

From his voice, though, he didn't seem convinced.

The shopkeeper shouted at them. "If you're taking it, you need to buy it!"

"We were just leaving," Lucian said, heading for the door. "Sorry for the trouble."

They headed into the alley, the acrid-tinged air barely breathable. Lucian led the way, not exactly sure where he was going. They needed some sort of flying vehicle to get out of here, be that a skycar or a spaceship, but neither of those options were looking likely.

Lucian was beginning to think using the Orb of Space-Time was necessary. He stopped, letting the others gather around him.

"Look, I don't think there's any way out of this. Carthago is going to collapse. That much is clear."

"If it hasn't already," Fergus said.

"What are you thinking?" Serah asked.

"We have the Orb of Space-Time. I can warp us back on board *Talaria*. From there, we can escape the station and head down to the surface. Carthago won't be in any position to cause us trouble. Or at least, that's what I'm betting."

"You're sure about this?" Fergus asked. "The station is no doubt in chaos by now."

"So is Anchorpoint. I don't know what else we can do."

Gaius frowned. "How long will this . . . *warp* . . . take?"

"Well," Fergus said, "it took Lucian about fourteen hours to move the ship from the Nai Shairen system to Archea, and probably thirty minutes to move it from Archea to Sol. There doesn't seem to be any rhyme or reason to it."

"I just need for everyone to stand close. For such a short distance, it shouldn't take long."

The ground vibrated with a distant explosion. The four of them ducked into a narrow alley, hiding behind a trash compactor. It wasn't the most glamourous spot, but hopefully it was isolated enough for people to avoid.

"All right," Lucian said. "I need full concentration."

He kneeled against the wall, the other three gathered close. He reached for his Focus and streamed, filling the Orb of

Space-Time from the Aspects of Radiance, Binding, and Psionics.

He formed an image of his cabin aboard *Talaria*, the one he had memorized perfectly, knowing that this moment might one day come. The magic of the Orbs surrounded him and the others, the warping field building in power as time passed.

Outside his Focus, Lucian heard a few shouts, but they seemed to come from far away. With a last burst of magic, the image of the ship's cabin became real, and all four of them stood there, eyes wide.

Gaius looked around, as if in disbelief. "Incredible. . ."

"Let's get out of here," Lucian said.

As they ran to the bridge, everything seemed in order. The ship was dark and quiet. The lights powered on automatically as they went up the central corridor. But as soon as they were on the bridge, looking out into the hangar, Lucian's heart dropped.

There were at least thirty men out there, most of them armed. None of them seemed to look up at them, but that was because the forward viewport was only translucent from their side.

"Are they onto us?" Serah asked. "How could they possibly know this ship is us?"

"She knows I'm in this system," Fergus said. "She'd have to, with the nanites in my bloodstream."

"Filthy pirates," Gaius said. "If only we could open the hangar doors, we could blast them into space."

Lucian wondered if that was something he might have been able to do with the Orb of Radiance. Emma knew how to use wireless signals to access computers, or at least she had when she'd uploaded the Dark Gate's location to *Ethereal's* navigation computer.

"Is there anything you can do, Fergus?" Lucian asked.

"Remote hacking is not my expertise. Emma might have been able to, with the Orb."

"What are our options, then?" Serah asked. "We can probably take them on."

Fergus looked down at the hangar deck, seeming to consider. "Without the hangar doors opening, there's no possible way of escape. Yang won't let any ship leave the station, of that you can be sure. And of course, she has this ship under guard in case we decide to return."

"Why aren't they breaking into it?" Gaius asked.

"Likely, they've already tried. But it's no simple thing to pierce a spaceship's hull. It can be done, but they've likely determined earlier that no one was on board."

"Hey, one of them is looking at us and pointing," Lucian said.

And it wasn't just one of them. Multiple pirates were looking up, while one was scratching his head in confusion. Some started approaching, gauss rifles in hand.

"They know we're here," Serah said. Her eyes became somewhat panicked. "How do they know we're here?"

"Warp us out," Gaius said.

"It's too late for that," Lucian said.

"We've got to try something!"

"There's only one thing we *can* try," Fergus said.

"Hold on," Serah said. "You're *not* giving yourself up."

"They know I'm here. I'm close enough to be tracked now."

Pounding came from the blast door amidships at the same time that a hail request lit on the dash. Fergus's face darkened upon seeing it.

"*Stars' Blood*," he said. "That's Yang's flagship."

"Just ignore it," Gaius said.

"I'm afraid that would do more harm than good." He drew a deep breath, and hit accept. "Hello, Zheng."

"Fergus Madigan." There was a short pause. "It almost doesn't feel real, does it?"

"What do you want?"

There was a moment's hesitation, and then a light laugh. "After all these years, *that's* the first thing you want to say to me?"

Fergus remained silent.

"Are you alone, Fergus?"

"Yes."

There was a long pause. "Liar. There's someone else there. Put them on."

"Admiral Zheng Yang," Lucian said. "I'm Lucian Abrantes, the captain of *Talaria*. We're a registered mage vessel, and if you try to interfere with our coming and going, then—"

Zheng just laughed, cutting him off. "No. I'm not playing games with you, Lucian Abrantes. I know who you are. Your friend, Quentin Vasser, made sure of that."

"Why am I not surprised?"

"You must learn to pick better friends, Lucian. But since you're so dead set on giving me a hard time, allow me to give you a proposition. You are at my complete mercy. We could spill a lot of blood over this, but I assure you, I have tens of thousands of loyal subjects who would die just for the chance of giving me Fergus. I would like to avoid that."

"What do you want, then?"

"Do I really have to spell it out for you? Give me Fergus. If you do so, I'll let you go. But if you insist on being stubborn, I'll order my men to laser a hole in your hull. That entire process will only take fifteen minutes."

"You'll have to kill us all," Serah said.

"No," Fergus said. "She won't." Everyone turned to look at him as he muted the mic. "I have to go. No need to spill any blood on my account."

"You don't have to do this, Fergus," Lucian said.

"Yes, I do. It's only until my contract is complete."

"You had two years left, if I remember right."

"You guys will have to continue without me."

"Fergus, you can't," Serah said.

"Do you think I have a choice? I would have gone to the end. Whatever the end was, even if it was down there on Hephaestus. But there's no way we can get the ship out of here before her men break through. Unless Lucian can use the Orb of Space-Time right now."

"I can't." He reached for it, just to be sure, but couldn't find a connection. "It'll be a day or two before it's ready. It's hard to know for sure."

"Your skill set will be missed," Gaius said. "According to everything you've told me, it makes the most sense for you to go."

Fergus nodded, as if that decided it. "I can't put her off any longer. Let me talk."

He unmuted the mic. "All right, Zheng. I'll come out. I only have one ask, besides allowing everyone else on board this ship to go free."

"You don't have the power for an ask. But I will entertain you. If only because it entertains me."

"There is a squadron of League Blackguards on Hephaestus Station. They'll want to get their hands on me almost as much as you. You should be aware that getting involved with us will make you a target of the League."

Zheng just laughed. "As if I'm not already. The Blackguards, though . . . what did you do to kick *that* hornet's nest?"

"It would take too long to explain. Do I have your word that you'll let them leave?"

"Of course. I'm a crafty, manipulative, and self-interested pirate empress. You can count on me to keep my word."

"Be serious."

"Your friends can go. However, they must burn as hard as they can for the nearest gate. Which is . . . Archea, last I checked."

Lucian couldn't allow that to happen. "Admiral Yang?"

"Yes, Captain Abrantes? What can I, Zheng Yang, the Terror of the Stars, do for you?"

Lucian ignored the irony in her tone. "We can't leave Hephaestus. I won't say the reason, but it's of vital importance that we be allowed to stay."

"And why is that?"

"We're on a mission from the Volsung Academy to find something on the surface of Hephaestus that can help with the war against the Swarmers."

"A weapon?"

Lucian was in too deep now. "Sort of. Something left behind by the Builders that only a mage can use." He paused. "Actually, that only *I* can use."

There was a long pause after this. At last, she spoke again. "Well, you are a very foolish man, Captain Abrantes."

"What do you mean, *foolish*?" Serah asked.

"You could have easily just escaped my net, and as soon as we lost signal on your ship, turned right back around to search on Hephaestus to your heart's content. But now I'm curious about what you're looking for. Most curious."

"So . . . you're not letting us leave?"

"Oh, no. It's been years, but there's such a fine restaurant here in the Upper Torus. Perhaps it's still around. I would have dinner with you, Fergus, and whoever else is with you."

"Dinner?" Fergus asked. "Zheng, this is completely unnecessary—"

"Quiet, Fergus. That's an order." Much to Lucian's surprise, Fergus went quiet. "I will hear no arguments. That would be rude. I will hear everything about this weapon. It's been too long since I've had a mage in my employ."

"Zheng..." Fergus protested.

"My men will take you there. Talk soon."

With that, she cut out.

Serah sighed. "Well, we're screwed now."

21

IT WAS ten minutes before Lucian heard a knocking on the blast door. When he answered, a short, bald man with a pockmarked face stood there, flashing a yellow smile while giving a gracious bow. Several scraggly men with particle impact rifles stood behind him, their faces hard as stone.

"Altan Gan Baatar, at your service," he said. "First Quartermaster of Admiral Yang's Golden Armada."

"Hello, Altan," Fergus said, somewhat distastefully. "Got that promotion you were after, did you?"

The man's smile widened, his canines seeming longer than typical. "I've served my master well." He straightened his back. "Well, shall we?"

There was nothing left but to follow him down the boarding ramp and into the hangar. Fergus went first, as if resolving to meet his fate head-on, whatever that may have been. Serah fell in on Lucian's side, while Gaius brought up the rear. The heavily armed pirates formed a protective shell around them, designed to keep them from changing their minds.

"Awfully brave of them," Serah muttered.

If the pirates heard her, they gave no sign.

They headed into the Lower Torus. If Zheng wanted them to go to the Upper Torus, Lucian wondered just where this Altan was leading them. But he seemed to know where he was going. Upon entering the streets above the Lower Torus's Undercity, Lucian saw heavily armed pirates filled the streets. They were doing an effective job of keeping the peace. He would have expected half the buildings to be burning, with each man carrying as much loot as he could. That was certainly a pirate's reputation in stories and media, but perhaps the reality was different. Or maybe Zheng had ordered them to stand down, and the pirates feared her enough to obey.

Whatever the case, it seemed this was a force to be reckoned with.

It took about ten minutes to cross the Lower Torus, to a shuttle that was supposed to be taking them to the Middle Torus. However, there was no interstation shuttle out there, but another ship entirely, about the same size as *Talaria*. The last thing Lucian wanted was to get on that ship, but he had little choice in the matter. Altan boarded first, followed by Fergus, and then the rest of them, including the four pirates who had been tailing Altan from the beginning.

As soon as they were on board, they were blasting away with surprising speed. Lucian almost tripped from the sudden shift in trajectory, along with Serah and Gaius. Fergus was the only one who easily kept his feet, along with the rest of the pirates.

"Still got your space feet, I see," Altan said, approvingly. "Aye, the pirate's blood hasn't left you yet. Mark my words."

"It was never in me to begin with," Fergus said.

"Oh? You were the most rotten villain I ever did see. A cold-blooded killer. Aye, you made the rest of us look like suckling babes."

"I did what I was contracted to do."

"That, and more. You're returning at an auspicious time, my friend. Admiral Yang has grand plans for the galaxy. Aye. That she does. The stars will know and fear her name, from Terminus to Sulisto. And beyond, too, I would wager."

Fergus let the conversation lapse as the vessel connected to an airlock on the Upper Torus. The door slid open, revealing a pristinely white lobby with curving walls. A central fountain was filled with dancing, silvery water, surrounded by modern sculptures. They walked across the lobby, a large archway on the other end leading into a garden, filled with colorful flowers in bloom, trees with wide, welcoming boughs, and even a trickling stream. It reminded Lucian very much of the Almaty's estate on L5, though much smaller in scale.

Above, Lucian could see multiple tiers of shops and restaurants, and above those, what had to be living spaces for Carthago Corporation's ultra-wealthy. Of those ultra-wealthy, there was no sign, though there were ragtag men and women with rifles wandering the upper corridors, along with some admiring the gardens. None cast Lucian or his group more than a cursory glance.

At last, they entered a restaurant with a stunning view of the planet outside every time the spinning Upper Torus made its round. All fifty or so of its tables were empty. All but one, where a beautiful woman, perhaps in her late thirties or early forties, was sitting, watching them approach with a barely concealed smile. She had raven-black hair that fell straight to her shoulders, sharp features, and light brown almond eyes that had an almost hypnotic quality. They were dangerous eyes, that much Lucian could see. Geometric tattoos covered her arms and the left side of her neck, while multiple hoops pierced each of her ears, along with a nose ring beset with jewels. On her either side sat two handsome men, both of whom sat rather close to Zheng. Lucian remembered Fergus telling him that Zheng was known for keeping multiple husbands. Perhaps that remained true.

"Fergus," she said, pleasantly. "My, how the years have aged you like fine wine."

The two men didn't seem to mind the comment. It was as if they had been trained to be silent when their wife was speaking.

"Zheng. You seem the same as ever."

"And how is that?"

"Beautiful, and quite pleased with yourself. As if you're the only one who understands a joke no one else seems to get."

She smiled broadly. "Well, I try to stay young. I'm glad the longevity treatments seem to be working. And why wouldn't I be pleased? Hephaestus Station is mine, and I'm glad you're with me to celebrate. It's almost like old times." Her smile faltered as her face darkened somewhat. "Although, I should know trying to recapture old times is a fool's errand."

"You're right in that."

Zheng gestured toward the table. "Please, sit. Don't be shy." She looked to Lucian as everyone took up their seats. "Lucian Abrantes, I presume. Surprising, that you would be the captain when there is one older with you. But you walk with a heaviness that tells me you earned the seat."

"I'm no one special," Lucian said.

"Maybe. Maybe not." Her eyes went to Serah next. "Who is this lovely lady?"

"Serah Ocano."

"Your accent. I can't quite place it. I've been to almost every world in the League, and many beyond. It is . . . a sweet voice."

"I'm from Psyche." Her eyes narrowed as she grabbed Lucian's arm. "Are you hitting on me? I have a man. And it looks like you already have two."

Zheng smirked. "Psyche. Well, that explains why I don't

recognize your manner of speech. You'll have to show me your world sometime. I would love to see it. If it produces a people half as spirited as you, it would be my dying wish." Zheng looked at Gaius. "Which leaves you. The only one who looks like a mage on the surface. You have that uppity, high horse look about you. Fergus was like that when we met. Weren't you, Fergus?"

Fergus ignored her question. "Zheng, let's cut to the chase. What are you doing here? Did you seriously just order your entire fleet to take Hephaestus on the chance to capture me?"

She chuckled. "No. Capturing you was a happy accident. My designs on Hephaestus are more mundane, I'm afraid, though I like the idea of pillaging and burning my way across the galaxy to chase the one who got away."

These words seemed to give Fergus pause, but only for a moment. "Be serious. Why Hephaestus?"

"Why not?"

"Don't be coy. More is at stake than you know."

"Oh, I'm well aware of that. Hephaestus, as you know, is the League's main industrial center outside the Solar System and the First Worlds. I have long coveted its mineral wealth. And soon, Carthago will sign a contract with *me*, after we've done a bit of rearranging of the management. This world's shipyards are also famed, as you know. For years, my men have had to make do with the limited resources of Brennus. But with *this* planet, and enough time, the Golden Armada will be powerful enough to make the League bend to its will."

At this moment, a nervous, stiff-necked server came by, depositing several plates of bread and soft butter. He bowed, then went on his way. Another two came by to top off everyone's wine.

"There won't *be* a League soon," Fergus said. "By the time they finish your ships, Earth will be a wasteland."

"That, I very much doubt. My spies have seen the Jovian

shipyards. You wouldn't believe how many capital ships they have in reserve. What's gathered at Alpha Centauri isn't even half of it." She turned to each of her husbands. "Dears, I'll catch up with you later. Why don't you see if there's anything interesting to do?"

The husbands shared a look, but did not argue. Each kissed her on either cheek and bowed graciously before leaving.

"You have them well-trained," Serah said, somewhat approvingly. "Any tips?"

Lucian lightly stepped on her foot as she smirked.

"Well, men are simple, if you know what they want. Then again, the same could be said of anyone."

Lucian didn't like the way she was looking at Serah when she said that. He redoubled his effort to hold his Focus. He needed to be settled when dealing with this woman. Everything was calculated to unbalance him.

"Let's get back on track. If the League has more ships, why aren't they deploying them?"

"They will. Soon. The reserves are likely being held in case Sharo Khalin makes his own play. A wise move on the part of the Hegemon. The man isn't as stupid as he sounds."

Especially, Lucian thought, when he was being influenced by the most conniving mage in the galaxy.

"You really think the League can stop the Swarmers on their own?"

"I do. Especially in conjunction with the firepower of Starbase Centauri. Its stockpile of atomics reaches into the tens of thousands. And likely more, since those numbers are from the close of the last Swarmer War."

Fergus's eyes narrowed. "I know what you're up to."

Zheng smiled sweetly. "And what's that?"

"You're betting the Swarmers will invade Alpha Centauri before they come here. And you're betting that the League will win that battle. After which, you will swoop in and destroy whoever is left."

"Very good. You haven't lost any of your sharpness."

"That's crazy," Lucian said. "You need to be working with the League to stop the Swarmers, not shooting at each other. You're only guaranteeing humanity's extinction."

"The same League that wants *you* dead?"

"The situation is complicated."

"I imagine so. Still, I'm more interested in hearing about this weapon you mentioned earlier."

Her eyes locked onto his, demanding to know the answer. If he didn't have his magic, or the ability to dampen his emotions by locking onto this Focus, he would have been far more afraid than he was now.

"It's not for you to use, Admiral Yang."

"Please, call me Zheng."

Serah frowned. "You flirt with anything with two legs, don't you?"

"What? Jealous?"

"Hardly."

"What can I say? I like beautiful things."

"I'm no *thing*," Lucian said.

Zheng chuckled. "Now, this weapon. I must know everything about it."

Fergus looked to Lucian, as if to ask for permission to explain. Lucian nodded.

"It's an artifact of great power from the time of the Builders. There are eight of its kind in the Worlds, of which Lucian has already gathered four. We need all eight to stop the Swarmers."

"Why eight? What do these artifacts do?"

"They amplify the magic of a mage," Lucian said. "And I can combine their magic for even more powerful effects. All of them together will be enough to stop the Swarmers. Even to heal magic itself."

"Heal magic itself." Zheng chuckled. "And what does *that* mean?"

"Mages will no longer fray."

"That's madness."

"It's the truth," Serah said. "If you've seen half of what we've seen, you'd believe it, too."

"Then convince me. It sounds like a fantasy to me."

Convincing her meant telling her the entire story. That wasn't something Lucian wanted to do in the slightest.

"We need to go down to the surface of Hephaestus, Admiral Yang."

"Zheng. You're making me feel old."

Lucian ignored that comment as an army of servers brought the food. Half of the dishes were things he didn't even recognize, but certainly richer than anything he'd ever eaten. There was some sort of stuffed meat covered in gravy and herbs, along with butter-laden trays of escargot, raw iced oysters, a colorful salad, a thick soup, fish slathered in a thick, green sauce, and much more. It was far more food than five people could ever hope to eat.

Zheng filled her plate, eating with delicacy and relish. If no one else joined in, she didn't seem to notice.

"I've asked nothing of you, Zheng," Fergus said. "Lucian is right. Gathering the Eight Orbs is the only way we can save humanity. They will need uninterrupted time to search the surface. With time, they'll find what they're looking for. Of course, I will remain to complete my contract."

"That goes without saying. As if I'd ever let you slip through my fingers again." Her eyes refocused on Lucian. "The question is, do I believe you? You've told me almost nothing. It's almost insulting."

Lucian wanted to argue his case further, but that would just make him look desperate. He had to trust her to come to the right conclusion on her own.

"I don't trust you, Lucian Abrantes. I can usually see into a man's eyes and know what he wants. But I don't know what you want. And that makes you dangerous."

"I want to find the Orb of Thermalism."

"You say you do. And yet, I remain unconvinced. You have the same look in your eyes as this one here." She nodded toward Gaius. "Those eyes are . . . dead. Unfeeling. Lacking soul."

"I've become what I must, Zheng. You're right in that I don't want the Orb. Not really. I would have someone else claim it before me. But I'm the only one who can be trusted with it. There are other mages in the Worlds who would use it to empower themselves. I simply want what is best for humanity."

Zheng smiled. "And who are you to judge your own heart, Lucian?"

It wasn't a question he'd expected. And he didn't know how to answer it.

"There's always doubt. All I'm saying, of everyone possible, I'm the Worlds' best shot."

"Dear God, you think that'll convince me?"

"I *can* convince you. It wouldn't be pretty, though."

"Is that a threat?"

"No. I just don't think you get it."

For the first time, her small, pithy smile evaporated and she gazed at Lucian almost murderously. Fergus was staring at him in wide-eyed shock. Certainly, she'd killed people before, and quite brutally, for far lesser infractions.

"I'm the Chosen of the Manifold. It's my fate to gather the Orbs. In fact, I'm the only one who can do it. And you will not stand in my way."

"What madness is this? I stand in the way of whoever I

wish. I will not be spoken to in this manner. You know I could have you killed, right?"

"Would I say such things if I truly believed that? This is the truth. If you choose to stand in my way, then soon, you will no longer stand. The Manifold will mow down anyone who tries to stop the Chosen."

It almost seemed as if the air went out of the room, but Lucian felt nothing. He just watched Zheng watching him. There was no longer any flirtation in her eyes, any sign of a joke. She seemed to be staring him down, looking for any sign of weakness, any chink in his armor. But Lucian knew, through and through, that there was none.

"You must decide," he went on. "Do you trust me, or not? If you don't trust me, then call my bluff. Have your men called in here to shoot me dead."

Lucian watched her for a reaction. To his surprise, she seemed nonplussed, waiting for him to go on.

"When I leave this room, I'm going to get on my ship. I'm going to find the Orb, and you are not going to interfere. No one can stand between the Chosen and destiny, and if you want to test your luck, then you are welcome to try. The Manifold is greater than all of us, Zheng Yang. As far as you have come, as much as you've accomplished, you are not the Chosen."

"I've heard enough." She stood, seeming to lose all appetite. "I almost wish to order you dead right now, but I would spoil my dinner. But there is something in you, I must admit. I'm not ready to kill you. Not yet."

She watched him, seeming to wait for him to make a move. In the end, though, she continued.

"Leave. Return to your ship. Do what you need to do."

"You're letting us go?" Serah asked.

Zheng positively glowered. "You question me, Serah Ocano? Count yourself lucky that I bought that codswallop. My Fergus has returned. That's what truly matters."

Fergus just stared dead ahead out the viewports, never looking more miserable.

"Come," she said to Fergus. "There is much to be done."

To Lucian's surprise, Fergus obeyed, standing with her. It wasn't as if he had much choice. He wasn't sure what would happen to him if he refused, but apparently, it was far easier to just do as she said. Lucian wanted to tell him he would get him out of that situation, but he knew that was a lie. Only one person could release Fergus from his contract, and it was guaranteed she wouldn't be amenable to the idea.

Of course, there was the nuclear option. A mind control stream would force the issue. Of course, there was no telling what would happen as soon as Lucian let *go* of the stream. Vera had never taught him to make possession brands, such as the kind that controlled the Hegemon. No doubt, it required a lot of mental energy to maintain. But nothing less than that would make for a permanent solution.

"Zheng, I must ask you to consider releasing Fergus from his contract early. Or at least permitting him to come with us."

"Go," she said, coldly. "This audience is over."

"As you wish." He nodded to Serah and Gaius. They looked at Fergus one last time, who was still staring out the wide viewports.

They left the restaurant, Altan escorting them back to their ship. As soon as they were on board, Gaius guided the ship out of the hangar and into a wide orbit around Hephaestus itself, allowing the station to fall away.

22

THE SHIP FELT QUIETER than Lucian could ever remember. It was hard not to feel despondent with just the three of them. Fergus had been with them since the rifts of Psyche, and without him, there was a stark emptiness.

It was strange how Lucian was considering even Gaius one of them, now. That was a dangerous thing. No matter what they went through, there would always be a part of him that distrusted the Psion.

It was hard for anyone to speak. They sat in the wardroom, no one really knowing what to say. Eventually, they all just went to sleep. They hadn't had a decent rest since the mage embassy, almost a full forty-eight hours before.

And when Lucian awoke, it was to the blare of the klaxons.

He and Serah ran to the bridge, where Gaius was already seating himself, blinking away sleep.

"Someone's got a lock on us. No torpedoes away yet."

Lucian and Serah strapped themselves in for action.

"We shouldn't wait around," Serah said. "Get us down to the surface."

"It would be the Blackguards, if I had to guess," Gaius said. "Looks like they left the station, but not the system." Gaius frowned as the frames of two vessels materialized on the dashboard screen. Then four. "They . . . have pirate markings."

"That bitch double-crossed us," Lucian said. "Waited for us to get off station to finish the job."

"Torpedo away," Gaius said, still utterly calm. "Hold on tight. Things might get a bit dicey."

He angled the ship down toward the planet. Gaius punched a few commands, deploying the rearward point defense cannons. With four of them on the ship's stern, the system was far more comprehensive than *Ethereal's*, but by no means foolproof.

"Scratch one," Gaius said.

"Two more on the way," Serah said. "No. Six!"

Lucian's face paled. They might shoot down three or four of them, but the odds of catching all of them were low. The LCD screen was detecting a survivability at eighteen percent. Time to impact was thirty seconds.

"Lucian?" Serah asked, tremulously.

He couldn't get suited up fast enough to directly stop the missiles. They were too close to the planet's surface, anyway, which was already pulling them into its fiery embrace.

"Escape pod," he said, simply.

"You know how much this ship is *worth*?" Gaius protested. "Almost four million creds!"

"Come on, go! No arguing."

Gaius cursed, and the three of them abandoned the bridge, heading for the pod amidships. There was no time to grab any personal items. Within seconds, the place they were standing would probably no longer exist. He would only have the clothes on his back, his shockspear, and the emergency supplies and envirosuits already stocked in the pod itself.

They rushed into the tiny pod, strapping themselves in. No sooner was the action done, Lucian slapped the eject button, blasting them away with unreal force. Out the tiny porthole, just three seconds later, the ship had already gained some distance.

Much to Lucian's surprise, a stream of PDC fire shot down the incoming torps, causing them to momentarily light up like fireworks. A wave of exploding metal shot outward. A particularly hefty piece scraped the escape pod, causing it to spin wildly. The porthole, now facing the planet, showed the red surface below them, rotating in a sickening manner. Lucian felt his vision receding, the blood unable to reach his brain.

He reached for the Orb of Psionics, pushing *against* the force of the spin, which slowed it somewhat. He pushed again, until they were merely heading straight down toward their deaths, rather than spinning toward it as before.

He tried to hold back his nausea, though that was difficult. Already, the pod was shaking from entering Hephaestus's thick atmosphere.

Lucian ground his teeth as the exterior of the pod became a fireball falling from the heavens. Side panels deployed, somewhat slowing their descent. They broke through the layer of thick, gray clouds, revealing a red, rocky landscape filled with canyons, buttes, mountains, and the odd crater filled with lava. It looked like Hell itself.

The warning alert kept beeping, and thankfully ended with the deploying of a wide parachute that seemed to yank them into the air. They drifted down lazily, at times thermal columns pushing them higher. The wind blasted around the pod, causing them to sway as they sunk lower and lower.

Right over a wide volcano of bubbling lava.

"Lucian?" Serah asked.

He reached with his Focus, tethering the outside of the pod

to a distant butte beyond the lake, drawing ether deeply from the Manifold. The tether materialized before the pod, strengthening in a long, shimmering line of blue. The pod was pulled down, as if it were a gondola, over the surface of the lava, touching down lightly on the planet's dusty, infernal surface.

Lucian let go of the stream. "Everyone all right?"

"There's no time," Gaius said. "If they detect our pod, they'll find us."

"They can't track something this small," Serah said.

"Did you see the ship *actually* get hit? If it survived, it will go down somewhere nearby. They can find *that* easily enough, and guess we're close to it."

"Duly noted. I didn't hear it go down, yet . . ."

She unstrapped herself, rubbing a bruise on her forehead that Lucian was just now noticing.

"You okay?"

"Yeah," she said, standing. "Looks worse than it actually is."

Gaius and Lucian followed her example, slipping into their prepared suits. Fergus's sat empty. Gaius had the foresight to loot the extra coolant gel. It was something they would surely need outside.

Lucian tapped on the pod's touchscreen, which was asking for confirmation to send out an emergency broadcast. He denied the request.

"Rotting hell," Serah said, looking at the screen beside him. "71 degrees Celsius out there! That'll cook us."

"Our suits are liquid-cooled," Gaius said. "We can't be outside them for long, and when we are, we must always wear at least a rebreather. I'd only recommend stepping out for quick evacuation procedures."

"Evacuation procedures?" Serah asked.

"Number one and number two," Lucian said.

"This is not the time," Gaius said. "Are we all suited up?"

Everyone was in their suits, with their emergency packs on, and shockspears holstered on the suits' exteriors.

"Let's move," Lucian said.

"Move *where*?" Serah asked.

"We're about to find out."

Lucian pressed the door open. A wave of dry air rushed inside, carrying with it dust and smoke. Lucian stepped out into the heavy gravity, crunching across a cracked flatland that extended in all directions, broken only by some low, yellowish hills in the distance that had a poisonous appearance. The sky was more gray than blue, and a volcano rose toward the north, complete with belching smoke and rivulets of lava running down its side, almost lost to the haze.

"Where to?" Serah asked, her voice entering his helmet's earpiece.

Lucian closed his eyes. He was here now, on the surface. They had no ship to explore with, just their suits, supplies, and wits. It was as good as it was going to get.

He reached for the Orb of Space-Time, not sure how he would begin seeking the Orb of Thermalism. Arian had said it was the key to finding the rest. He expanded his Focus outward, something easy to do with the Orb. Distances seemed to matter little to it, which made sense if it could transport people and even entire spaceships across star systems.

And he felt a power emanating from the east, beyond those yellow hills in the distance.

"Let's head east," Lucian said. "We'll see what we can see from there."

"Is the Orb out that way?" Gaius asked.

"Something is. I'm not sure how far, but I know it's that way."

"It'll have to do."

The three of them headed away from the pod at a brisk walk, leaving its wreckage far behind.

WITH THEIR LIVES on the line, there were no holds barred for Lucian. It was them against however many ships Zheng Yang sent.

As soon as he reached the top of the rise, Lucian tethered Gaius and Serah ahead of him toward a distant rock, following them shortly after.

He kept his Focus strong and sure, cycling tethers to get them across an incredible stretch of terrain. Lucian had progressed much since his days on Psyche, and here, he could stream as much as he wanted. There was no Sorceress-Queen to detect his heavy streaming.

Hours passed like this, with no sign of pursuit from behind. They passed over canyons, rivers of lava, cracked badlands that would have been utterly impassable. They shot up and down mountains, across valleys, and even down a massive cliff that had to be five kilometers high.

And then, they found themselves before a horribly flat surface, with nothing obvious to tether, and night was cloaking the land.

"We'll stop here," he said. "Gaius, set the tent up."

This time, Gaius didn't bother to tell him to address him as "Psion." Maybe now that he had seen him fully display his powers, he was willing to be a bit more meek. Lucian could only hope.

Within minutes, they were inside the tent. Before Lucian ducked in, he took a temperature reading outside. He was shocked to see that it was 76 degrees, despite the fact it had been dark for over an hour. These lower flatlands held heat easily.

The liquid-cooled tent, complete with a rattling air recycler, allowed them to at least take off their helmets. Even so, the temperature was a bit too warm for comfort.

They ate some ready-made-meals directly from their packages. Lucian tried not to taste them, something Serah didn't seem to be successful at, from the way she was gagging.

"I'll be the first one to say it," once she'd forced herself to finish. "Hephaestus is probably my least favorite planet."

"It is truly uninhabitable," Gaius said. "If the heat doesn't kill you, the three percent atmospheric composition of carbon dioxide will."

"That's a lovely motto."

"Was that a joke, Gaius?" Lucian asked. "Didn't think you had it in you."

"We have a long day tomorrow. We must have crossed a hundred kilometers today. Hopefully, enough for that pirate scum to think us dead." He stifled a yawn. "Well, goodnight."

Gaius rolled over on the tent's side and immediately fell asleep.

"He's . . . not totally annoying anymore," Serah said, as if the fact surprised her.

"He has his uses."

"So, any closer to the Orb? I want off this planet."

Lucian reached out, feeling for the Orb again. It wasn't discernibly closer, which wasn't surprising. Hephaestus had a diameter of about fourteen thousand kilometers, so even if they had crossed a hundred kilometers today, then that was just a drop in the bucket.

"Well, I don't think we've moved the dial much today," he said. "We'll cover a lot more ground tomorrow."

At that moment, they heard the streak of spacecraft passing overhead. The noise faded into the distance.

"Well, I guess we know they're still on the hunt," Serah said.

"With the heat outside, they'll never pick us up here," Lucian said. "I doubt they can find us unless they have a hard visual."

"Yeah, I figured as much." She yawned. "Well, I think the Psion has the right idea, for once. I'm pretty beat."

Lucian was too. As soon as he closed his eyes and set his nightly Psionic ward, he fell asleep.

23

AS SOON AS they had eaten breakfast, they dressed in their envirosuits and broke down the tent. Within minutes, they were off again.

Lucian considered the flat expanse before them. They had to head off to the northeast, if Lucian's readings with the Orb of Space-Time were any sign. Creating a wider anchor point on the flat surface of the desert would take far more ether. With luck, though, heading to each horizon might reveal some landmarks that were easier to tether, making the process easier.

The sky above was empty of passing ships, and the temperature had already crawled to 78 degrees. Lucian wouldn't have been surprised if some places on the planet were hot enough to boil water. The waves of heat undulating over the flatlands were so intense that it was impossible to see the far horizon.

That was going to be a problem for tethering, but thankfully, the Orb of Radiance would allow him to cut through the refraction.

"What's the plan?" Gaius asked.

"We've still got to get across," Lucian said. "No way around that. A sight ward will cut right through that haze, no problem. I can stream someone at least a kilometer with no issues."

Serah sighed. "If there's really no other way . . ."

He reached out, creating a wide anchor point on the ground in the distance.

"When I tether you, jump as high as you can," Lucian said. "Otherwise, you'll be dragging your feet on the ground."

Gaius was the first to shoot off, completing the tether in a little over a minute. Lucian switched the anchor point to Serah, and then himself.

When he looked back, the eddying waves of heat almost completely obscured the high cliff from view.

"I'm starting to feel the heat through my suit," Serah said.

Lucian felt that himself. Sweat was already running down his forehead, and there was nothing he could do to wipe it off.

"We better hope we can get to higher ground quickly," Gaius said. "According to my map, there's about two hundred kilometers of this. That means you'll have to tether us two hundred times before the sun goes down."

Lucian knew that wasn't going to fly. "Assuming it takes five minutes to move all three of us a kilometer, with no breaks at all, that would take . . . how long?"

"About sixteen hours," Gaius said. "Do eight hours today, and the rest tomorrow."

"Can the suits stand up to this heat?" Lucian asked. "It'll only get worse as the day drags on."

"They should've called *this* place the Burning Sands," Serah said.

"Well, we can always raise a Thermal shield," Gaius said.

"And by *we*," Serah said, "you mean *me*."

"It will be necessary to cool the suits. Unless you want the cooling system to be overwhelmed?"

Serah remained silent.

"We just need to make it to evening," Lucian said. "After that, we can set up the tent and cool off. We have enough water in our suits to last until then."

"No food, though," Serah said.

"Double rations for dinner," Gaius said. "We're wasting time."

As much as Lucian wanted to disagree with Gaius, he was right. Without waiting to see if he was ready, Lucian tethered him into the distance. The look of shock on his face just before he shot off was worth it.

"Nice one," Serah said.

They continued on through the morning, as the sun brightened and the temperature inched up. By high noon, it was over 85 degrees. Serah set a strong thermal to cool them off during their brief breaks. Lucian wasn't sure how much of an effect it had. Each of them only had a few seconds to stay within it, and his face was sweating profusely. Not being able to wipe the sweat dripping from his eyebrows was almost as maddening as the heat.

But in the middle of the afternoon, a high spire of rock became visible, rising above the miasma of heat. He spied a ledge that looked large enough to hold the three of them and sent Gaius up first. When he reached the ledge, he raised a single hand to denote its safety. Lucian sent Serah up after him, and by the time he joined them himself, they stood high off the ground, where the temperature was ten degrees cooler. Their suits cooled quickly, providing much needed relief.

They took a break, going to the spire's other side to rest in the shade and get a view of the distance. Several more spires rose in that direction, similar to the one they were standing on.

"Strange," Gaius said, touching the red stone with a gloved hand.

"What?" Serah asked. "These look a lot like some mountains on Psyche. Especially in the Westlands."

"Are there ruins in those mountains, too?"

"Yes, many. The Old Ones, we called them. But I suppose that's just another name for the Ancients."

"This was a city, once, hundreds of thousands of years ago. I imagine this entire valley was. If we chipped away at enough of this rock, we'd see the ruins."

"Whatever the case, looks like we have a shortcut, now," Lucian said.

"You have no appreciation for the past, Talent Lucian. This is history before our very eyes! How long have these edifices remained buried, gathering dust?"

Serah rolled her eyes. "Just say *buildings* like a normal person."

"We're not here to do archeology," Lucian said. "We have a long way to go."

Gaius seemed not to notice. "I wonder if this world was always like this? It's quite possible it wasn't always so geologically active. Perhaps the constant release of gases by tectonic activity has created a runaway greenhouse effect."

"I thought volcanic ash was supposed to produce global cooling," Lucian said.

"In the near-term, yes. But over the long-term, it would have turned this world into a hothouse. It would have killed whoever lived here as surely as the Swarmers."

"I assume the Swarmers got to them first," Lucian said, focusing on the next spire. "Looks like there's a decent ledge that way. I'll stream you over first, Gaius."

They continued their way across the valley, their speed greatly increased by the advent of the rock spires. After Lucian's comments, it was easy to notice just how artificial they looked. The Psion's suspicions were proven true when Lucian spied dull metal peeking through a crevice in one of the rock structures.

By this point, the sun was westering, casting the entire desert red as blood. Lucian was beginning to lose hold of his Focus. Even he had his limits, though he'd had more practice with Binding than any other Aspect.

So, he streamed the three of them one last time toward a final spire, at least two hundred meters above the desert floor. This one had a little alcove of sandstone that would provide them some shelter from passing ships.

They set up the tent and spent another night, this time, high above the hot sands. There were no ships passing overhead, for which Lucian was thankful. Maybe they had come far enough now for the pirates to give up the chase.

The next day, they no longer had the benefit of the spires. From their updated position on Gaius's slate, they had fifty more kilometers to go until they reached the end of the valley.

"*Please* tell me there's a lake or something on the other side," Serah said.

"Well, there *is* a lake," Gaius said. "You might not like it, though."

"Why not?"

Lucian shot him off into the distance before he could answer.

"You enjoy doing that, don't you?"

"It's a bit satisfying. Not going to lie."

"You're truly evil sometimes."

He shot Serah off toward the horizon, a bit more gently, before following himself a couple of minutes later.

Today didn't seem to be as hot, though on Hephaestus, temperature seemed to be a relative thing. The desert still baked under the heat of the sun. They made quick progress, though, so by high noon, a line of mountains could be discerned in the distance. As Lucian tethered everyone closer to them, it became apparent they were not merely mountains. Many were cone-shaped, with smoke rising from them.

Reaching for the Orb of Radiance, Lucian sharpened his vision, bringing the details in sharp relief. There was no evidence of any lava, but with his enhanced vision, he found the perfect place to tether them to.

Over the next hour, he pulled them closer, into the blasted foothills before the high brown peaks. And then he streamed everyone up the mountainside. By the onset of evening, they had made it to the top.

Lucian immediately saw what Gaius meant. A lake, or perhaps even a small sea, of bubbling lava was in a crater. The mountains they stood on were the outermost ring of that lake. There were many blackened islands of solidified igneous rock, in between which lava flowed. A great, dark haze clung to the surface, though up here in the mountains, it was cooler, allowing Serah to release her Thermal ward.

"Don't tell me we're going down there," Serah said.

Lucian reached for the Orb of Space-Time, closing his eyes and seeking the source of the Orb of Thermalism. He faced northeast.

"We're closer. Still a long way to go, though."

Serah sighed. "Not what I wanted to hear. I assume we're going to skirt the rim of this crater?"

"That's the idea. Just avoid the smoke and lava bits and we should be golden."

"And what happens if one of those things goes off?"

"We'll cross that bridge when we get there. For now, it's time to hunker down for the night. It's been a long day."

No one argued, and they began setting up the tent in a cleft that would afford them some shelter. Lucian didn't think the pirates would hunt this far. They must have done nearly three hundred kilometers by now across the surface of Hephaestus.

Once inside, they took an inventory of their supplies. Water was the main issue. There wasn't much of it, and the water reclamation systems built into their suits and tents didn't recycle everything perfectly.

"I estimate we have about two weeks of water," Gaius said. "Hopefully we find the Orb before then, or we'll be forced off planet."

"That won't happen," Lucian said.

Serah looked as if she was about to say something, but thought better of it. Lucian knew her well enough to know what she was going to say. What if he was wrong? What if they had to evacuate the planet? Something in his face probably told her not to ask.

"There has to be surface water somewhere on the planet," Lucian said.

"It's all underground," Gaius said. "My Atomicism is . . . poor. An elemental sensing ward could probably point us in the right direction."

"I know nothing about Atomicism," Lucian said. "I can try some time, I guess."

"You guess?" Gaius asked, chuckling darkly. "Atomicism is *not* an Aspect you mess with unless you've had a lot of training."

"I *can* use it. With the Orb of Space-Time, it won't fray me. It's just a matter of experimentation."

"One thing at a time," Serah said. "We're still good on the water, so maybe we can just stretch what we have."

"Food will last us a good while," Gaius said. "The meal packets might not taste good, but they are calorically dense with all the micronutrients we need. I estimate about a month's supply."

They gathered around the map on Gaius's slate. The GPS was placing them somewhere on the fortieth parallel, at the beginning of a crater that was to the southwest of a massive salt flat.

"That's going to be hell to cross," Lucian said. "It'll take about three days just to wrap around this crater. Those flats must go on for half a thousand kilometers."

"It won't be easy," Gaius said. "But you seem to be sure the Orb is in that direction."

"I know it is."

"Then that's our path."

24

THREE DAYS PASSED as they skirted the rim of the crater. By now, nonstop streaming was second nature to Lucian, as simple as breathing. His mind seemed to separate from reality itself, completely focused on the task at hand. He barely noticed the columns of smoke rising from volcanoes, the rivers of lava sliding down to join the lake of fire.

One day, he was streaming them over a particularly large river of lava, at least a kilometer wide, with a single island of rock rising from the center. Without hesitation, he shot Gaius to the top of that island, followed by Serah. Though he could see the fear on their faces, he felt none himself.

He was sure of his power, his abilities. The power of the Orbs was becoming a part of him.

Yes, a voice intoned within his mind. *You grow into them well.*

The Ancient One was the only thing that could have broken his focus. He pushed the voice aside, concentrating on getting Gaius to the other side.

Soon, we will be one. The Ruby of Starsea calls to you. Just as it

241

calls to me. When you hold a majority of the Seven, that's where you will end, and I will begin.

Lucian wrapped his Focus in a powerful Psionic ward. He could still hear whispers of that fell voice, but at least the words were no longer clear. It was a temporary reprieve, and better than listening to the poisonous words, the words that were surely lies.

But he couldn't resist lowering the ward to get his own word in.

The Manifold has plans, and I will fulfill them.

Yes. You begin to understand that this is larger than us. Things are in motion since the birth of Shadow and Light, now and into the future. Your strange journey has only begun, Lucian Abrantes, Chosen of the Manifold.

There was something in that voice that was different. It no longer seemed to taunt him, but to . . . *respect* him. It was a strange thought, but deeply holding his Focus, that observation seemed to make sense. The Chosen would know the way. That was all Lucian needed to recognize. It was the only truth that mattered.

Holding his Orbs, streaming their power, was a higher truth than he had ever known. It . . . separated him from the here and now, and that was a welcome feeling. He barely spoke, finding that there was no need.

And it was like this that they finally circumvented the large lake. Before them stretched what appeared to be a white crystal sea, what must have once been the bottom of an ancient ocean. His suit's visor automatically tinted itself due to the intense glare.

"This looks bleak," Serah said.

Unfazed, Lucian continued to tether them ahead. He could feel the Orb of Thermalism now, seemingly so much closer than before. Or perhaps after so much streaming, he was simply more attuned to the Ethereal Background than he had ever been. The Ether. That was what the Ancients had called it . . .

Where had *that* thought come from? He knew it to be from the Ancient One, and yet, the realization didn't concern him. So what if some of the Ancient One's thoughts were as familiar as his own? What was the harm, as long as *he* remained in control?

But something told him things might really start changing upon receiving the Orb of Thermalism. Did it *really* matter if he held a majority of the Seven? He had the Orb of Space-Time, something the Second Immortal had himself never touched. Might that protect him?

There was no way to know for sure. All he knew was that they had to continue interminably forward toward the goal.

———

FIVE DAYS PASSED with no change in scenery. The only difference was that they were closer. Lucian felt the Orb beating within his Focus like a phantom heart. It belonged there, only it hadn't come home yet.

"The hell is that?" Serah asked.

Breaking the monotony of the salt flats was a distant rock, though it was hard to tell through the undulating waves of heat.

Lucian let go of the Orb of Binding and reached for the Orb of Radiance to cut through the shimmering mirage. The image focused until what he saw somewhat resembled a spider. It was facing away from them, with ten long, sharp legs supporting a bulky abdomen. Lucian also spied a tiny head with two long, serrated pincers. But this was no typical arachnid. Its exterior was rocky as it grazed in the salt, apparently taking it in as sustenance.

"Looks like some sort of animal," Lucian said. "A strange one at that."

At his voice, the rock spider's form went rigid. It raised its head, turning it sideways toward them. Lucian took a single step forward, and instantly the spider scuttled toward them. Lucian bound it with a controlled tether. It took far more magic than he expected for the tether to gain enough strength to throw the spider skyward. Its legs scuttled at the air frantically before it landed hard on the ground, collapsing into a pile of rock just ten meters in front of them. There was no evidence of blood or organs within.

"What *is* it?" Serah asked.

"It must have been feeding on that salt," Gaius said.

Lucian scanned his surroundings. More shapes were materializing in the distance. Four, by his count.

"We've got more. Better keep moving."

Lucian kept streaming them in the Orb's direction, across the flatlands. More of the lithoid spiders appeared, until there were at least twenty, all converging on them with surprising speed. It was only a matter of time until there were so many that Lucian couldn't out-tether them.

Two spiders were alarmingly close. There would not be enough time to escape them. Gaius blasted one of them away with a kinetic wave. It flew, while Serah slowed the other down with a gravity disc, causing the sharp points of its legs to sink into the salty surface. Lucian finished it with a shattering stream, the combined Psionic and Binding Magic fragmenting the beast from the inside out.

He created just enough space to get them to the next horizon, leaping from the ground seconds before one of those spiders reached him. Once he landed, he got some reprieve, but already, more of the monsters were materializing from seemingly nowhere.

"Where . . . are they coming from?" Serah said, gasping for breath.

"The salt," Gaius said. "They must be buried within in."

As soon as Gaius said that, two spiders shimmied from beneath the surface and scurried in their direction.

"There's *so many*," Serah said. "How can we ever fight them off?"

Lucian deepened his connection to both the Orbs of Binding and Psionics, infusing in his Focus an incredible amount of ether. He concentrated on each spider in tandem, starting with the nearest and going toward the farthest. A few seconds of concentrated energy from his dualstream was enough to shatter each monster to rocky bits.

"Focus on the ones behind us," he said. "I'll take care of these."

And he did. Violet and blue energy raced out of his fingertips, showing no signs of slowing. The Orbs were fathomless fountains from which he could draw endlessly. One by one, the spiders were obliterated, and the Orbs' power only grew in intensity. It seemed that with each kill, the Orbs sung, drawing more ether, creating more magic, allowing for more death and destruction.

Soon, the spiders were more or less exploding instantaneously, and more than that, the dualstream branched on its own, finding new targets, like chain lightning.

Such was his concentration that when Serah called out to him, it felt as if it were from another dimension.

"Lucian! A little help over here!"

Rather than turn and break his concentration, by instinct, he reached for the Orb of Radiance, adding it to the dualstream. He nearly screamed as the outflow of magic more than doubled. For the first time in his life, Lucian had created a tristream, the effects of which he couldn't begin to guess. The properties seemed to be mostly the same, except for the fact that the Radiant Magic allowed him to *shape* the outflow of his shattering streams. Rather than a lightning-like blue and violet tether, he was now shooting sharp lasers from his hands. Anything those lasers touched was instantly vaporized.

His Focus could hardly control it. He was blind to everything, the Shadow Realm fading. There was only the Ether, green, blue, and violet lines racing along his hands, lines which were redirected and shot at an endless horde of creatures. Somehow, the Orb of Radiance also gave him awareness and vision of *anything* nearby, even if he wasn't directly looking at it.

He turned by instinct, firing, only very dimly aware of Gaius and Serah cowering near him. The White Psion had streamed a Psionic shield over them to keep the shards of falling rock from tearing them to pieces. That shield was like a candle against the sun, and Lucian *was* that sun, going supernova.

Yes, the Ancient One said. *Such power. It is but a taste of your future.* Our *future!*

With a final cry, Lucian drew in all the ether swirling around him, until he had created a void for kilometers around. Green, violet, and blue light shot from his body, a form glowing with resplendence. Every single one of those sharp, deadly lights found a mark, the exact amount needed to destroy each lithoid spider, of which there were at least a hundred left.

Lucian collapsed, at last letting go of his Focus as a storm of falling rock pelted Gaius's shield. He heard Serah speaking, though he couldn't make out anything over the din. How long that deadly rain fell, he couldn't say. All he knew was that, when he finally opened his eyes, they were greeted to a desolation of rocky debris, some in the shape of spindly legs, others in the shape of heads and pincers, stretched for at least a hundred meters in every direction. They occupied a small crater that had been kept clear, while the rubble piled above them went as high as two meters.

How *many* had he killed? Even he didn't know the Orbs held such power. A *tristream.* How could anyone stand up to that? What *were* those things he'd created? He remembered Xara and her death lightning. Had he done the same thing?

No. Somehow, he knew that whatever he had done was different. And deadlier, if that was even imaginable. Where had the knowledge come from? He had a feeling that he wouldn't like the answer, if he dared to think about it too much.

Finally, he stood on shaky legs, Serah and Gaius looking as if they didn't recognize him. He didn't blame them. He didn't know *himself*.

"What *was* that?" Serah asked.

Lucian shook his head. "I don't know. Something that seems like it should be impossible."

"A tristream," Gaius said. "Impossible for almost any mage to perform, except the most powerful of the powerful. It requires not only an unimaginable amount of ether, nine times more than an ordinary single stream. It also requires a Focus of unusual strength. Only a few mages in the history of the Worlds have done such a thing. The Old Masters. Ansaldra Dara. Oreys Lethon. Vera Desai. Arian. Xara Mallis. Transcend White." He paused, his face pale behind his visor. "And now . . . Lucian Abrantes."

"What did I *do*, though?" Lucian asked.

Gaius nodded. "There is a book in the Volsung library, by the aforementioned Oreys Lethon. The first volume details every dualstream in detail, in each forward and reverse configuration. The knowledge is forbidden to Novices, and can only be studied by Talents who have permission. There is also a second volume, detailing theoretical tristreams. I have studied that tome, though most of its details elude me. With a tristream, there is only one possible configuration upon combining the three chosen Aspects."

"So, you don't know?" Serah said.

"This one must be a tristream Lethon called a *shattering laser*, made from combining Binding, Psionics, and Radiance.

It's a laser that takes on the properties of a shattering stream. It will disintegrate whatever it touches. Normally, a powerful mage capable of such a thing would burn through their entire pool of ether just to produce one, and overdraw one or two times besides." Gaius's features within his faceplate were pale as he regarded Lucian. "You must have shot off no less than a hundred, all at once, besides the more conventional shattering stream you were using before. And to think you've been tethering us all day, and every day since we've gotten here . . . these Orbs are truly unlimited in their potential. I didn't believe it before. Not fully. But I do now."

"Xara mentioned death lightning," Lucian said. "The effects seem similar."

"Death lightning is a dualstream of Atomic and Dynamistic Magic, and the bane of organic matter. I don't think it would have worked against these creatures and their stone-like bodies. But against flesh, it's a terrible weapon. One feared by League soldiers during the Mage War." Gaius observed him. "Have a care, Talent Lucian. What you have used is far more dangerous than death lightning, and more difficult to control. It worked out this time, for which we can thank the stars. But even a Transcend would think twice before attempting such a stream, and only at the greatest need. Indeed, if they're even capable of it to begin with. Besides Transcend White, I can only imagine Transcends Red, Yellow, and Blue being so powerful."

"They're strong, huh?" Serah asked.

"We should get moving," Lucian said. "Only . . . I'm exhausted."

"A small reprieve would not be remiss," Gaius said. "Whatever those creatures are, I don't believe there are any more of them. Not for a while, anyway."

Gaius and Serah made to sit down, but Lucian raised a staying hand. He felt the pull of the Orb of Thermalism. He felt time pressing at him. And after this display, if any pirates were watching, then they needed to get moving. It was quite possible that light display would be visible for untold kilometers.

"We must continue on," he said.

He climbed on top of the broken stone bodies until he had a good view of the horizon. He reached for the Orb of Binding, opening himself once again to its power. It responded instantly to his need, seeming to recognize the importance of moving on. The Orbs wanted to keep going, too, to keep moving, especially when one of their brethren was so close, ready to be claimed.

Soon, his four would become five. And nothing would stop him from achieving it.

He pulled them across horizon after horizon until there was nothing left of the day. Only late into the night did they pitch their tent, despite the lack of shelter in the open flats.

That night, Lucian didn't set his Psionic ward. He no longer feared the Ancient One, Vera, or whoever else might be trying to hunt him.

It was time instead for *him* to be the hunter, for him to be the one feared.

As soon as he closed his eyes, he went into a dream.

25

HE WAS BACK at the promontory over the lake of fire, a massive volcano in the distance spewing smoke into the gray sky. The Orb was in there. He knew it.

He reached with the Orb of Binding, drawing himself toward the crest of the volcano. He landed at the rim of the crater and immediately felt heat radiating into his suit. He peered down into the wide opening, finding a bubbling reservoir of magma.

And to his surprise, a path ran down the rim's side, created from the same material as the desert spire on Psyche. The Ancients had built it to stand up even to the heat of this place.

But the crystalline path was not the only thing inside the volcano. There was something else down there. A long, snake-like creature, rising from the hellish depths, its eyes glowing like burning coals . . .

Lucian reached for his shockspear, whatever good that would do in this place. He began to stream a kinetic wave to push back the monster. But such was its size and weight that it didn't make a dent.

As its massive maw opened to receive him, Lucian could see fire in its depths. Fire that shot out to consume him.

———

HE SAT UP INSTANTLY, reaching for his Focus to control his panicked breaths. Serah and Gaius awoke too, looking over at him.

"Lucian?" Serah asked. "What's going on?"

"I saw where the Orb is," he said. "And what's guarding it."

"Guarding it?" Gaius asked. "What do you mean?"

"This massive snake, or dragon. I'm not sure which. It . . . breathed fire on me and that's when I woke up. It was inside this massive volcano . . ."

"A fire basilisk," Gaius said. "It's the life this planet is most known for. They only live in the Infernal Sea."

"How close are we to that?" Serah asked.

"Not far. A hundred kilometers, maybe."

Lucian held up a hand. "Wait."

Instantly, everyone went quiet, listening. At Serah's questioning look, Lucian nodded toward the outside.

Something was out there.

He stood and left the tent, reaching for the Orb of Radiance to see. The details of the landscape came into sharp relief, and directly in front of him floated a single drone, which went still.

Opening a Binding stream, Lucian extended his shockspear and tethered the drone toward the point, which became awash in electricity from a Dynamistic brand. Ether roared out of him to supply the three separate streams, including the Radiant stream he was using to see. When the drone contacted his spearpoint, it was instantly fried, dropping to the ground as smoke rose from its charred husk. He let go of his Binding and Dynamistic streams, leaving only the vision stream.

At that moment, Serah and Gaius joined him. Lucian

scanned the landscape for more, but they were still alone. But they wouldn't be for much longer.

"What is it?" Serah asked, looking at the broken machine.

"A drone," Gaius said. "Zheng must have them searching the planet. Or maybe the Blackguards."

"Oh."

"It almost certainly reported our position."

"Then let's get going," Lucian said.

Gaius instantly set to work collapsing the tent. Within minutes, the three of them were ready to set off.

Once again, Lucian scanned his surroundings using the Orb of Radiance, including the sky itself, in his search. So far, they were still alone.

Though it was still night, Lucian could pull them across the landscape, using the sight provided by the Orb of Radiance to set the focal points for his tethers. It required a significant amount of ether, but it was a mere stream compared to the torrent of the tristream earlier. It felt disappointing, hardly enough to satisfy his appetite for magic.

You hunger for it now, the Ancient One said. *That is good. With the Ruby of Starsea, you will slake your ever-growing thirst.*

Lucian pushed the voice from his mind. It was the last thing he needed.

Just as he was flying across the surface of the desert a roar from above announced the coming of a spaceship. He thought about cutting off the tether, but chances were, it was already too late.

As soon as he landed next to Serah and Gaius, the three of them stood, ready to fight. More ships fell in behind the first, what looked like League ripsaw fighters. Though to Lucian's eyes, enhanced with Radiant vision, he noticed several details were off, including a general shabbier appearance and less wide wingspan, and smaller fuselage. These vessels also did not have League markings, though that might be expected from the Blackguards.

Still, he knew it wasn't them.

"It's Zheng," he said.

Six fighters swooped around, racing lower over the desert straight toward their position. They fired their heavy gauss cannons, which shrieked across the desert. Lucian streamed a Binding shield as strong as any he ever knew, and as soon as it received the volley of fire, it instantly knocked him back a good fifty paces.

He streamed an anti-grav disc beneath him, enough to soften his fall into the salted ground. He rushed to stand, finding himself separated from the others. The ripsaws raced above the surface of the desert, angling around for another run.

They couldn't last out here, nor could they escape. Even the Orbs would not be enough.

Lucian tethered himself next to Serah and Gaius, and while doing so, reached for both the Orbs of Psionics and Radiance, combining their might with the Orb of Binding. With all three, he fed their magic into the Orb of Space-Time. He gathered ether as quickly as he could, never minding the consequences of drawing too much, too fast.

There was only one chance, as he saw it. He could escape this world, but that wasn't what he wanted to do. Not when he was so close to the goal.

Lucian formed an image in his mind, one still fresh in his memory. He wasn't going to warp them to Hephaestus Station, or even to Earth, probably the safest place in the galaxy he could conjure up at this moment.

If he was to attain the Orb of Thermalism before Xara Mallis, then this was his only option.

The volcano was clear in his memory, along with the promontory looking out over the lake of fire. He saw the dark gray clouds that had formed from its smoke. The scarred ground, the flames spewing from the lava's surface. It was so clear in his mind that Lucian might as well have been there himself.

He streamed with everything he had, just as a new volley of fire ripped across the desert, lights flashing.

Lucian opened his eyes to find himself, along with Serah and Gaius, to be in the place of his dreams. The volcano loomed before them, almost unreal in its scale and destruction. Smoke poured from its open top, lava bled down its sides, joining the fiery sea at its foot. They stood on an island, rising high above the infernal surface. Below them swam long, snake-like creatures, their rocky exterior glowing with molten radiance.

"Rotting hell," Serah said. "Where are we?"

Lucian closed his eyes, feeling the missing Orb thrumming in his Focus. The Orb of Space-Time sensed it. It had led him here. He almost couldn't believe it had worked.

And now, it was time to claim what was his.

"Both of you stay here. I need to go in."

They gazed up at the volcano in disbelief.

"It's *in there*?" Serah asked. "You'll roast for sure!"

Gaius remained silent, his face pale. "Are you sure, Lucian?"

"Yes. There's a fire basilisk in there. The same one that was in my dreams. I believe my test is to kill it."

Serah shook her head fiercely. "Not alone you won't. You'll need my Thermal shield so you can focus on downing it."

"I won't stay behind, either," Gaius said. "Transcend White sent me here to help you, and stars willing, I'll see it through."

Lucian looked from one to the other. Seeing their seriousness, he nodded. "There's a good chance we'll die."

"Well, at least you won't die alone," Serah said. "Besides, if we waited out here twiddling our thumbs, we'd eventually die waiting for you to come back. That's a terrible way to go, if you ask me."

Lucian couldn't argue with that. "All right. I won't stop you as long as you both know what you're getting into. Now, let's kill this basilisk bastard and get him out of my dreams."

"Sounds good to me," Serah said.

After fighting so long, and resting so little, Lucian knew he should have been exhausted. But the Orbs refused to let him stop, seeming to infuse fresh strength into him. It would be impossible to stop now.

Reaching for the Orb of Binding, he tethered the three of them to the top of the distant volcano, the Orbs singing with power and ready for battle.

LUCIAN LOOKED over the rim of the volcano. It was just as it had been in his dreams. Magma bubbled within as incredible heat rose from above. The same crystalline trail followed the interior of the cone downward, though he could not see where it ended, being lost to the haze within. Nor could he see the monster, the fire basilisk guarding the Orb of Thermalism.

"It's rotting hot down there," Serah said. "I'll get a ward up."

Indeed, Lucian's suit informed him it was ninety degrees at the top of the volcano. As soon as they were inside, it would no doubt climb to well over a hundred.

Standing here at the top, he felt a sudden onset of fatigue, despite the deep-seated need to continue. He'd streamed more in the past two weeks than he ever had in his life. A moment of doubt gave him momentary pause, but he had come this far. Stopping now when the goal was in reach was unthinkable.

He would have to prove himself, or die trying.

"We need to reach the end of that path," he said.

"You could just stream us down there," Gaius said.

"That material repels magic," Lucian said. "It's seven-sealed."

Serah nodded. "It's the same stuff Lucian used to protect himself from Vera and Xara back on Halia. If they can't affect it, we can't, either. Not unless we stream all Seven Aspects at once, in confluence."

"That's out of the question," Gaius said. "Not when we know something's down here. We need to be ready to attack at a moment's notice."

"That's the plan," Lucian said. "Serah will just concentrate on keeping her Thermal ward up, strong enough to protect the three of us. Change it to a shield for extra strength only when necessary. Gaius will just keep the basilisk distracted, not focused on Serah. If her ward collapses, all of us are toast."

"And you?" Gaius asked.

"I need to get to the Orb, wherever it is. There will probably be some sort of temple at the end of this path, if the past is any sign. The plan is to get down there, get the Orb, and warp the hell out. I'd like to avoid fighting the beast, if possible."

"You just warped us here," Serah said. "Will you have the strength to do it again? Maybe we should wait a bit. You've been pushing yourself so much . . ."

But Lucian was already looking back down into the volcano. The time was now.

"All right. Let's get this over with."

Lucian led the way down, and Serah and Gaius followed, a bit reluctantly.

———

THEY WALKED down the crystalline path under the protection of Serah's ward. After a couple of minutes, it was clear the ward wasn't cutting it. She replaced it with a shield, red heat radiating from its sides. Even under the shield, the temperature was rising all the time, and Lucian could see the strain on her features from keeping it up.

Time was of the essence. They ran, circling down the interior of the cone on the white, celestial path.

Don't you feel it? the Ancient One said. *So close. How it tantalizes! I can almost taste it in the very air. Soon, we will know its power!*

Shut up. This isn't about you.

Serah's voice entered his ear. "Don't see this basilisk fellow anywhere..."

"No complaints here," Gaius said.

"Keep alert," Lucian said.

The path beneath their feet shifted as the magma below began to churn. The walls shook, while stray bits of rock rained on the path before them. Gaius raised a Psionic shield, keeping them safe from falling debris.

"Rot it, it's hot," Serah said with a gasp. "Don't know how much longer I can keep this up."

Lucian enhanced his vision with Radiance. Through the smoke-tinged, reddish light, he could see the path wrapped around once more before reaching its end at a large, crystalline door with the Septagon engraved on its face. This low, the path was just about even with the surface of the magma below, perhaps only five meters above it.

"Nearly there," he said. "Stay strong."

They ran the rest of the way until they stood before the entrance. The door was completely shut.

Lucian reached out with the Orb of Binding, but as he suspected, he couldn't set an anchor point on it. He knew, deep down, that this door would not open for him unless he passed the trial.

"What now?" Serah asked.

The hairs rose on the back of his neck. Slowly, he turned.

At least ten meters above him, the mouth of the basilisk

hung agape. In utter silence, it had risen to catch them unaware, bearing two long, curved fangs that could pierce any of them straight through. Its body was completely black. Its stony exterior had developed to stand up to the insane temperatures of the molten liquid it inhabited. This one was so much larger than the ones outside the volcano. Lucian also knew, though he didn't understand how, that this basilisk was much larger than any other on the face of Hephaestus. It had lived here since the times of Starsea, growing little by little, until it had reached its current size, tens of meters long.

Drawn to the power of the Orb of Thermalism, it had nested here. Lucian had invaded that nest, and now he would pay the price.

The basilisk gave a bone-shattering shriek, so deafening that Lucian vibrated from head to toe. He could not think, couldn't even reach for his Focus. Serah cowered beside him, while Gaius was *fleeing* up the path from which they had come. Only Lucian remained standing, somehow extending his shockspear while facing down the creature of his nightmares.

Serah's shield collapsed, and now, the incredible heat of the volcano was pressing on him, making him woozy. He reached for Thermalism, streaming his own shield, powerful enough to provide some relief.

The basilisk struck with incredible speed, going for Serah first. Lucian hit her with a reverse tether, which worked as effectively as a punch that sent her flying, though he did what he could to blunt the attack to keep her unharmed. The basilisk's open mouth only found empty air where she once stood. Lucian re-tethered her to the rock wall, placing her up on the crystal path about twenty paces away. Gaius was already a quarter of the way up the path, with no signs of slowing down.

"Gaius, get back here and fight!" Lucian said.

The basilisk swiveled in the magma, bludgeoning Gaius

with its head. The Psion screamed as he flew toward the magma below.

Lucian tethered Gaius and pulled him toward himself; luckily, Lucian was larger than him, allowing him to remain rooted while Gaius flew toward him. Serah was already standing, re-raising her Thermal shield. Lucian had let go of his own shield, freeing his Focus for other tasks.

Lucian dropped Gaius on the path next to him. The Psion scrambled up, and was already backing away toward the rock wall, his eyes wide with fear.

"You can't run from this," Lucian said. "Stand and fight!"

"It's over," Gaius said. "It's over!"

"*Do something!*" Serah screamed. As a fresh wave of heat pummeled them, she strengthened her Thermal shield to match.

The basilisk rounded for another attack, sweeping with its long neck toward all three of them, looking to scatter them like pins. Serah streamed an anti-grav disc beneath them, allowing them to leap high into the air. While Lucian and Serah cleared the basilisk's body, Gaius didn't. Such was the force of the attack that Gaius went flying, so quickly that Lucian couldn't tether him in time before he crashed against the rock wall, hard.

As Lucian and Serah fell back on the ethereal path, Gaius tumbled down the interior of the cone, coming to a halt on a ledge just short of the lava. His neck had contorted unnaturally, and from his lack of movement, Lucian could only assume the worst.

"Gaius?" he said. "Gaius!"

The Psion was deadly close to the magma below, his suit melting and exposing his skin. Within moments, his body was afire. Serah gasped in shock. Lucian could only hope that he was already dead, and from the lack of screams coming into his headset, that seemed to be the case.

The basilisk was already coming in for another attack.

Lucian reached for all his Orbs, finding a connection to all but the Orb of Space-Time. Remembering the effectiveness of the shattering laser on the stone spiders, he collected all of his magic for a single attack designed to obliterate this monster once and for all.

But before he could unleash his stream, the basilisk was arching its neck back, a vortex of flame coalescing within its mouth. Before Lucian knew what was happening, a stream of fire was blasting out of his maw. Serah strengthened her Thermal shield, screaming with the effort, while Lucian dropped his stream and reached for Thermalism himself to add to its strength. Even with the both of them, the heat was unreal, baking through their suits and sizzling on his skin. He didn't know how long that stream of fire lasted, but it was at least half a minute.

As soon as it was gone, he let go of his shield. The basilisk ducked into the magma. Lucian began gathering more ether for a shattering laser tristream. As soon as the basilisk was above the surface, he would end it.

More and more ether gathered, so much that Lucian could barely contain it. Just when he couldn't hold it any longer, the basilisk surged upward, directly toward them with unreal speed. Lucian unleashed the laser, his fingers wreathed in blue, violet, and green energy that raced forward at the speed of light. It connected directly with the open maw of the beast, causing it to jerk back with an unholy, pained roar. Much of its length was thrown from the magma, its form crashing against the rock wall across the volcano. To Lucian's dismay, the laser did not shatter the beast, as Lucian had hoped. Only a few chips of rock fell from its exterior, flaking into the magma.

The creature swiveled its head, diving back into the magma. Only seconds after it had completely disappeared, it reemerged, rising on high, its mouth opening for another attack of fire breath.

"I can't hold through another one," Serah said.

Lucian reached for the Orb of Space-Time. They *had* to get out of here. But the Orb wasn't responding, and his other Orbs were apparently weakening, sensing his mounting fear.

Before Lucian could do anything, a column of liquid fire shot from the basilisk's mouth. There was no possibility of running or hiding. Lucian reached for Thermalism, streaming with all he had, though that was nowhere near enough. Serah was bearing the bulk of it, trying despite everything to stay alive. As fire blasted into them, her pained scream wrenched at Lucian's soul, a scream that had nothing to do with the insane heat, but Serah's attempt to counteract it. There was absolutely nothing Lucian could do to protect her.

It seemed that hell would never end, but at last, the inferno ebbed. Lucian wobbled, lightheaded and unable to focus. Instead of going back under the magma as it he had hopped, the basilisk was attacking directly, gunning right for Serah, who had gone down on her knees. Lucian streamed a basic laser with a Binding and Radiant dualstream, but this did nothing more than chip away at some of the monster's rocky exterior. If this monster could stand up to the insane temperatures of this magma day in and day out across thousands of years, what hope did Lucian's laser have, even amplified with the power of the Orbs?

The basilisk nearly succeeded in grabbing Serah with its massive jaws, but Serah suddenly became alert, streaming a gravity amplification disc of great power, her whole body shaking with the effort. The basilisk's head fell like a stone, crashing into the ethereal walkway, but not making a dent. Lucian ran forward to attack, shockspear in hand, working with the Orb of Binding to tether the basilisk's head to the surface. But the tether was repelled by the ethereal surface.

Serah weakened, and the basilisk wrenched its head free, swiping at Serah and sending her flying over the surface of the magma. Lucian tethered her, bringing her down on a large ledge on the opposite side of the crater. There she settled, lying down and apparently out for the count.

Lucian looked up at the basilisk, which was staring down at him balefully with two fiery red eyes. Lucian met its gaze. He wanted it to focus on him, not Serah. All the monster had to do was turn around and end her life, and there was nothing Lucian could do. But as long as it had Lucian in its sights, Serah would remain alive.

Lucian shot a few more lasers at the leviathan, if only to aggravate it further. It seemed to have the intended effect, as it let out a pulverizing roar that shook Lucian to the marrow of his bones.

He was down, but not out. He would make one last ditch effort at an attack, giving it everything he had. He had no choice. Serah was down. Gaius, dead. And now he stood alone against the great basilisk, knowing it was probably over. None of his magic seemed to have any effect. Binding, Psionics, Radiance. Even all three combined didn't have the requisite power.

With Serah separated from him, there was no chance of tethering her and warping out of here.

The basilisk rose on high, until it positively towered above Lucian. Lucian faced upward to meet it head on.

If he was going to die, at the end of this long, hard road, he would die with dignity, fighting to his last breath.

But then he remembered the words of the Ancient One. If he needed his help, to only call.

If there was ever a time to take him up on the offer, that time was now.

Ancient One ...

He felt a darkness stirring within him. A darkness that *was* him.

Recognize that we are one. Embrace that truth. We are the Shadow Lord.

The basilisk coiled back like a whip, seeming to move in slow motion through a rain of swirling ash.

You must give yourself to me, Chosen. I will show you magic such as you would never believe . . . magic that can save you from this disaster.

Lucian almost wanted to protest. He had tried everything. If he died here, then Xara would find this place, eventually, and harvest his four Orbs, claim the fifth, and then go on to find the final one.

His death would allow her to be the Chosen of the Manifold, to let the Ancient One rule through her when she transformed into the Third Immortal.

But wasn't that what *he* was doing?

Time seemed to slow further. The basilisk was starting to fall forward, its mouth expanding, fire coiling within.

Lucian . . . you must give me control. You must give yourself to me.

Something in Lucian recoiled against the idea.

He directed his next words at the Orbs within him. "Work, damn you. I am the Chosen of the Manifold. Work, or die!"

At that command, Lucian felt the Orb of Space-Time stirring in his Focus. In just the nick of time, it was ready to be used.

It was a chance. Perhaps the chance he needed.

Lucian shouted at the top of his lungs, a roar defiant of his pending death. A roar defiant of the Ancient One, defiant of the basilisk that had nearly bested him, defiant of his impossible mission. He reached for all four of his Orbs, and the other Aspects besides, drawing seemingly boundless ether into his Focus. He shuddered at the power pulsating within him.

Dynamism. Atomicism. Thermalism. Gravitonics. All were added to his tristream, seven-sealed, and compressed and controlled by the Orb of Space-Time, the master Orb, with which he could bend the galaxy to his will, should he survive this day.

Now, Lucian! the Ancient One implored.

The basilisk was falling, just seconds away from ending his life.

Never.

Lucian unleashed a mighty stream. Not at the basilisk, but at the air in front of him. A black, sinuous line stretched before him horizontally about ten meters, right in the basilisk's path. Lucian sensed a moment of doubt from it, but the monster's course was set and couldn't be averted. That line, black as space, expanded, rotating counter-clockwise, until a dark circle floated before him through which Lucian couldn't see. Through that rift of space-time, he could see the stars, poking out as if it were a night sky. Air roared around him, entering the vacuum.

As did the fire basilisk. Its high screech was silenced as soon as it passed through the barrier. Lucian planted his boots on the ground with a simple binding, while Gaius's dead body tumbled into the rift as well, along with the fire, smoke, and solidifying magma of the volcano. Serah, too, was flying in that direction, along with the floating tendrils of lava and flame. With the Orb of Radiance, he picked her out from the debris, even while holding open the rift. He opened a separate stream, a simple tether, that grabbed hold of her, drawing her to himself.

But even that simple action was too much added pressure. The Shadow Realm had long faded, replaced only by the Ether. All Lucian could see was an endless field of white. His Focus collapsed, cutting off all his streams.

Serah fell toward the magma. Lucian's heart lurched, and he reached out with all he had, barely tethering her again and drawing her forward.

Just as she entered his arms, a thunderous crash resounded.

The collapsing of the rift had cut the basilisk in half, and the back half of its long, snakelike form still had momentum carrying it into the ethereal path, which held strong despite its great weight. Lucian pulled Serah, leaping aside just before it could hit them. Magma burned and bubbled, long plumes of fire rising with alarming speed. The volcano was erupting.

Lucian dragged Serah, eyes closed, toward the door, even as hot magma swept over the path in their direction. Streaming only Thermalism to save them from the heat, he beat on the door.

"It's dead! I've passed the test!"

The door remained closed as the magma was inching closer, the ethereal path seemingly absorbing its heat and power, but doing nothing to stop it.

"Open, damn you!"

Lucian blasted the magma away with a kinetic push, but it was only a temporary reprieve. He kept pushing with the Orb of Psionics, but the magma was coming forward, faster than before as it rose around them. Within seconds, Thermal shield or not, they would be incinerated.

Then the door swung open.

Lucian pulled Serah through, but it wouldn't *stop* opening. Turning back, he tried to close it with a tether, but it was useless, made of the same ethereal substance as the path.

But when the magma reached the threshold, it was simply . . . stopped. It kept rising on the outside, but would not pass. Lucian watched in disbelief as the fiery liquid rose higher and higher, beyond even top of the door, leaving only a molten frame of magma repelled by an unseen force.

Safe for the moment, he laid Serah on her back. Her eyes were closed, but she was still breathing. Lucian heaved a sigh of relief. The chamber within was cool, and Lucian's suit detected a breathable atmosphere. So, he took off Serah's helmet.

"Thank God," he said, kissing her forehead.

He held her close. Even if she couldn't respond, he cried tears of happiness.

When he set her back down, gently, that was when he noticed her neck. He unzipped her envirosuit, finding his worst fears confirmed. Sickly gray skin covered her entire body. Her arms, her legs, seeming to spare only her face above her throat.

He couldn't believe his own eyes. How much had she streamed to protect him? How many times had she overdrawn? If she had streamed a whit less, they'd have been overwhelmed by the heat, unable to last long enough against the basilisk.

He gasped when her eyes opened and found his. "Lucian? Are we dead?"

She struggled to stand, but he held her down.

"Be still," he said, his throat thick. "You took a little bit of a beating."

"That bad, huh? It rotting hurts . . ."

"You'll be okay. Just rest."

"Everything burns."

"You're alive, that's what matters. We can get out of here and get you in a medical pod."

"Are we here? Did we do it?"

"Yes. We're here."

"*That's* all that matters."

"We'll get you out of here in a second. We just have to wait for the magma to go back down."

Her eyes went up to the open doorframe filled with fire. "Doesn't look like we're going anywhere for a while."

He held her face as she just smiled at him.

"Did you get the Orb?"

"No. Not yet."

"Don't wait any longer. Get what we came for. I'm not dying until I see it in your hand."

"I won't get it, then."

"Rotting *get it*, you stubborn fool. Please."

There was no arguing. He fought the tears that wanted to come, and instead turned his attention to the chamber they were in. He'd been so focused on Serah that he was just now noticing, for the first time, that the Orb of Thermalism was literally steps away behind them.

It waited on its pedestal, its circular dais with steep steps leading to its top. It shone with fiery resplendence, casting the interior of the chamber with ruby light.

He looked back at Serah, but her eyes were on the Orb, too, her entire face shining with its reflected glory. She smiled, as if at its beauty.

Lucian knew he had to claim it, even if all he wanted to do was stay by her side. He walked up the steps, feeling as if he were in a dream. When he reached for the Orb, no force repelled him.

The Orb of Thermalism is yours, Chosen, a deep, male voice intoned inside his mind. *Use it with strength and conviction. Restore it to the Heart of Creation. The Chosen will know the way.*

The spirit dissipated, and Lucian absorbed the Orb, its red lines racing toward his heart. He felt it infuse into his Focus and fill the void, and with its absorption, he felt renewed vigor, as if he had slept twelve hours straight. The light it had emitted into the surrounding chamber faded.

He ran down the steps toward Serah, fresh ether swirling within him and ready to be used. His heart nearly stopped, though, when he saw her eyes had closed again.

He kneeled beside her. "Serah?"

She didn't respond. He felt at her mottled neck and breathed a sigh of relief upon feeling a pulse. Her chest was moving too, in shallow, ragged breaths. Lucian reached for the Orb of Space-Time, hoping against hope that after the rift he'd made, there would be magic left to use it. While he himself felt restored, it didn't seem as if that applied to the Orb of Space-Time. Getting out of here would be anything but simple.

It was at that moment that Fergus's voice entered his mind.

Lucian?

Fergus? Where are you?

Outside the volcano.

What? How did you find me?

Ethereal fluctuations like you wouldn't believe. I knew it had to be you. And from my readings, you're inside the volcano. But if that's true, how are you alive? That thing is about to go off! Lava is pouring down its sides . . .

I'm stuck here for now. Gaius is gone. Serah hanging by a thread.

Did you get it?

Yeah, I've got it.

Listen. You've got to get out of there. There's a lot that's happened on the outside. The Swarmers are in the Hephaestus System. There's going to be a battle soon.

Lucian looked at the magma covering the threshold of the door, still held back by an invisible wall. Though Lucian recognized the gravity of that news, it paled in comparison to what he was dealing with now.

Serah needs medical help. I don't know if I can get her out in time.

I've got Talaria *back. We can put her in the med pod.*

I thought that thing was wrecked!

No. The pirates caught it before it fell from orbit. Not a scratch.

He felt at Serah's pulse again. Was he crazy, or was it weakening?

Stay out there. I'll be there soon. Set a beacon on the ship bright enough for me to see.

Lucian, you can't seriously be considering—

Lucian cut off the connection. It was not something he needed right now.

He stood, securing Serah's helmet on her head. He *would* save her. It wasn't over until it was over.

He stepped toward the threshold, reaching for the Orb of

Thermalism. Its power was like a punch in the gut. It swirled around him, creating a Thermal shield that, Lucian knew, could stand up to the heat of the magma itself, *plus* some. He also created a Binding shield, designed in the shape of a bubble to repel the insane pressure of the magma. And finally, a vision ward with the Orb of Radiance, to better see what he was doing out there.

Vera had once talked to him about walking through fire without being burned. Well, he was about to do just that in the literal sense, utterly confident that he could do it.

Serah's life depended on it.

He stepped outside the door frame, into a world of boundless heat and fire.

27

AS SOON AS he entered the surrounding magma, he was borne up in his Binding bubble. He clung to Serah tightly as the fires swirled around him, as he rose faster and faster with her in his arms. The pressure of the magma pressed in around them, but Lucian's shields were far from breaking in the slightest.

And then he shot out of the volcano itself, high into a blinding column of ash and smoke. There was no way to see through such a thick plume, and gravity would only pull him down again, given time. Still holding his two shields, Binding and Thermalism, he reached for the Orb of Psionics as well, drawing a large amount of ether and focusing it into a massive kinetic wave, blasting it outward in every direction.

The air was cleared around him, just long enough for him to catch sight of a bright beacon of light shining from an island down below. Lucian tethered it quickly, attaching it to the Thermal shield surrounding him and Serah. Instantly, they were pulled downward, away from the smoke column issuing from the great volcano below them.

271

Lucian slowed the tether on their approach, letting go of all his streams but the Thermal shield, which kept the surrounding air as cool as an air-conditioned room. A single, white-suited figure stood about twenty meters away, in front of the spaceship, *Talaria*.

Lucian let go of all his streams. With that action, he kneeled on one knee, still holding Serah in both arms.

Fergus approached, a worried expression on his face. He nodded toward the ship. "Let's get her into the med pod. The . . . fraying has her bad, doesn't it?"

They were wasting time. "Let's go."

He carried Serah on board *Talaria*. They headed toward the clinic, the medical pod opening with a hiss. Lucian removed Serah's helmet and envirosuit and laid her gently inside. Her eyes remained closed, though she was still breathing. The pod closed automatically as it began its diagnostic.

"I . . . must bring you back to the bridge of *Stars' Blood*. If that's all right with you."

"I'm sure you're dead if you don't."

"I am," he confirmed. "And it would serve nothing to flee, especially given Serah's state. Besides . . . there's something else you have to see."

"Something besides the Swarmers?"

"You'll see. But . . . I think you'll be pleased."

"That's cryptic as hell."

"It's for you to find out on your own." He looked down at Serah. "What happened down there?"

Lucian shook his head. "Gaius died. And Serah nearly frayed herself from head-to-toe, trying to keep the heat off us in the volcano. I don't know how many times she overdrew. Far too many . . ."

"There was nothing you could have done, Lucian. She knew what she was getting into."

Lucian couldn't bring himself to respond. But thinking back

to the determination on her face, she was committed to go to the end. Even if it meant *her* end.

Lucian was just furious that there had been no way to stop it. Without fraying, there was no way they could have stood up to the heat of the basilisk's breath.

"I can't talk about it anymore," he said. "Just get us off this rock. We'll talk later."

"Of course. I'll let you know when we've arrived."

He placed a hand on the glass panel right above Serah's face. He couldn't help but look at her frayed skin covering her entire body. By some mercy, only her face remained unchanged. She was further gone than most of the ghoulish frays who lived in the Darkrift.

It seemed wrong to think of her like that: a fray. She had always been one, of course, but she was much more than that. Not that a fray wasn't a human, but there was a point, an unknowable point, where a fray turned into something else. Something horrifying. When they'd first met, the wound had only been a small thing, a finger's length. But ever since she'd met Lucian, it had grown to consume her almost entirely.

Even as the guilt ate him up, he felt a determination such as he had never known. He *had* to find the other Orbs. To find and defeat Xara Mallis and claim what was rightfully his. And to use the Orb of Space-Time to seek out the final Orb, that of Dynamism, wherever it happened to be hiding.

It was out there, somewhere. Waiting for him to find it.

The deck shifted beneath his feet, a sign that they were finally moving. The medical pod was already working. While nothing could cure the fraying, perhaps her burns could be healed and the pain somewhat remedied.

If she had the will, she might even survive. And if anyone had will, it was Serah.

He looked up at a sudden shifting of shadow. It seemed to be going in the direction of the main cargo hold aft.

He stood, running after it. "Fergus? That you?"

There was no response. He looked among the various crates and plasteel cylinders, but there was nothing.

He had seen it on *Ethereal*, had sensed it on L5, and noticed it staring at him from that alley on Hephaestus Station. And now, it was here, of all places.

"What are you? Why are you following me?" There was no response. "Answer me!"

His only answer was the steady thrum of the fusion engine. The shadows seemed deep here, where anything could be hiding.

"Great. I'm going crazy."

Lucian turned and headed toward the bridge.

———

LUCIAN COULDN'T BRING himself to say anything to Fergus as he piloted them toward the Golden Armada, stationed in orbit near Hephaestus Station. It seemed only the capital ships were locked in orbit, the smaller vessels probably being docked on the station itself to conserve fuel. Even so, it was an impressive sight, at least a hundred battleships, cruisers, and carriers all facing the same direction, orbiting the fiery world in lockstep.

Talaria wove in and around the massive ships, which had a rougher appearance than the slick League vessels orbiting Chiron in Alpha Centauri. The Pirates' fleet was dingy and faded, as if they had made do with decades-old equipment. Some had the look of older Calamity class dreadnoughts from as far back as the Mage War, containing even orbital rings for their crew to produce gravity by centrifugal force. Pirates were known for retrofitting old tech and making it work for the times, and as a rule, they were the most handy spacers to sail the stars.

But the ship Fergus was piloting toward was anything but

dated. It practically gleamed under the light of Hephaestus's red-orange sun, a carrier with a wide base that had room to house hundreds of fighters and bombers. Toward the back of that carrier rose a high tower, at the base of which opened a hangar, large enough to accommodate ships many times *Talaria's* size.

Fergus edged *Talaria* into the carrier, where it was just one among about a dozen.

Lucian felt nothing as they touched down. No fear, no expectation, and not even anger at Zheng Yang for what she had done. All he cared about was Serah. What if she woke up while he was gone? What if she spent her last moments alone?

He shook off the thought. It was too horrible to think about. He had to believe she would be okay. That was what she would want.

He hesitated before the blast door, and Fergus looked at him with concern.

"She's safest here for now," he said. "I'm sure we can talk Zheng into finding her something better."

"Don't even mention Serah."

"I . . . understand. She'll be here when we get back. I promise."

Lucian knew Fergus couldn't promise that. He was just trying to make him feel better. He wished he would just stop.

Lucian was the one to open the blast door. At the bottom of the boarding ramp, First Quartermaster Altan Gan Baatar was waiting, a solemn expression on his oily, pockmarked face. Several other pirates waited, including, Lucian noticed, the dark-haired woman who had overheard their conversation all those months ago at the bar on Archea Station. She cracked a smirk as they walked down the boarding ramp, but something about Lucian's expression made her wipe the smile off her face.

"Take us straight to Admiral Yang," Fergus said.

"At once, sire," Altan said. "You made quick work of finding him."

"When they say I'm the best Radiant in the Worlds, that's not idle talk."

Altan went quiet at that. Apparently, he didn't like being reminded of Fergus's abilities. The only thing standing between Fergus and escape were the killer nanites in his blood. Nanites that would turn on him the instant Zheng judged he was working against her.

They were already being whisked toward an elevator. Lucian, Fergus, and the pirates rode up in silence to the bridge level at the top of the control tower.

When they stepped out, it revealed a spacious area filled with a couple of dozen technicians working at their consoles. A central walkway led to the wide viewpoints in front, where Zheng stood waiting, hands behind her back. Her expression was expectant, a small smile on her lips that seemed almost cute, as if she were a child caught red-handed with her hand in a jar of sweets.

No, Lucian would not forgive her. No matter what she said, no matter the situation.

But nothing prepared him for who stood beside her. There was another woman, of late middle age, facing out the viewports toward the planet below. Lucian felt the hairs on his arms rise. He could not stop staring as they came to a stop just a few paces away. It couldn't be. His eyes refused to believe it.

The woman's hair was shoulder-length and brown, and she wore the golden uniform of Zheng Yang's armada. She was about the right height, the right build. The right head shape, even. Even as she began to turn, and he saw the side profile of her face, thinner than he remembered, but with glasses and pockmarked with tiny moles, he knew his instinct to be the truth.

When she faced him in full, tears were in her brown eyes.

"Lucian," she said, her voice choked up.

He couldn't think, and he couldn't speak. She was *dead*. Transcend White had told him that. Killed by the Swarmers in the Alpha Centauri System over two years ago.

And yet, here she stood in the flesh, as real as anything.

Against all odds, his mother was alive. And apparently, she was a captain in Zheng Yang's Golden Armada.

28

LUCIAN STOOD RIGID WITH DISBELIEF, even as his mother came toward him and hugged him tight. Lucian felt shocked to his core. It was her all right. Here, on the bridge of Zheng Yang's flagship. What in the Worlds was going on? What was this?

But then, his mind caught up to reality. He hugged her back and felt a gasp escape him. He pulled back, looked at her face, saw her smiling.

"This isn't real," he said. "Is it really you?"

"Yes, son. It's me. I have a lot to tell you, but there'll be time for that later."

Lucian nodded, remembering where he was. He backed away from his mother, and instead looked at Zheng, who still wore that satisfied smirk she seemed to always have. Despite the situation, he had to be on his guard.

The Pirate Admiral regarded him. "I believe I owe you an apology. Had I known you were the son of Mira Abrantes, I would have given you all of my resources."

Lucian had been prepared for anything coming up here, up to fighting Zheng herself, or possibly Psionically forcing her to release Fergus from his contract. He was tired of being pushed around and used.

For the moment, though, he had to wait and see. His mother changed the equation entirely.

And it seemed Admiral Yang knew that.

"Obviously, your mother survived the battle of Alpha Centauri over two years ago. For most of that time, she's been working with me in the Golden Armada, where she has more than proven her abilities. I'll let the two of you catch up soon."

"You tried to kill me," Lucian said. "Did you tell my mother that?"

"An unfortunate misunderstanding," Zheng said. "All the facts have come to light in the last few hours. I pray patience on your part. I would beg a moment of your time to explain myself. It's the only way we can get out of this mess."

"Why should I give you a chance? Everything has been made abundantly clear, in my view."

Lucian felt the tension mounting, and his mother's eyes going wide. She said nothing, though. It was hard to tell just what she was thinking, who she was loyal to. Zheng Yang, who had likely saved her life by taking her into her fleet. Or her estranged son, who she'd thought dead or training on a faraway planet.

His mother broke the silence. "Let's talk it out first. No need to be making a mess when we can make peace."

"A mess has already been made," Lucian said. "Admiral Yang betrayed us, guaranteeing us safe passage out of the Hephaestus System. Then, she attacked."

"That wasn't me," Zheng said. "That was what I was hoping to explain."

It wasn't *her*? "You're lying. Gaius himself said it was you. Those ships were not League make."

"I agree they were not. But the Blackguards don't use ships of League make. It would tie them to their government. For space operations, they often disguise themselves as pirates. It's the perfect cover."

"How can I believe you?"

"Because, Lucian, I have nothing to gain from killing you. But it would seem the Hegemon does. And if so, that would make us allies, not enemies."

Could it be true? He looked from Fergus to his mother, even to Altan. All were watching him seriously, and he knew they weren't lying.

He had been played one too many times. He wouldn't leave anything up to chance.

So, he reached for the Orb of Psionics, creating a psychic stream that would reveal the truth once and for all. He reached for Zheng's mind, not waiting for permission, nor even bothering to hide his magic. He wrapped her head in an aura of violet energy, as everyone on the bridge gasped at the display of power, his mother most of all.

Instantly, Lucian found himself the target of many weapons, only stayed by Zheng raising a hand. "Don't shoot. Let him see I'm not lying."

Lucian read her mind then. It took little parsing, sifting through thoughts and memories, to realize that Zheng wasn't lying. It *had* been the Blackguards, and apparently, so had the attack on the surface. He let go of his stream.

"We detected their vessel burning hard for the Astravan Gate," she said. "I already sent my fastest ships to catch them. In just hours, they will blow them to dust."

"It's true," Fergus said.

Lucian watched him, not even sure of *his* loyalties. He'd allowed himself to be brought here to save his friend and go after Xara Mallis. Now, he wasn't sure *what* was right. And there was Serah, too, who might need more advanced medical attention than what *Talaria's* pod could provide.

As much as he hated it, his hand was being forced.

"Tell me about these Swarmers," he said.

"It's the Kasturi Swarmer fleet," Zheng said. "They've split into two forces, the smaller one coming here, and the rest heading for the League fleet in Alpha Centauri."

"It's not small, though," Altan said in his gravelly voice. "It be bigger than what we've got, and we've got near a thousand ships. Aye, that we do."

"This is a fight we must win," Zheng said. "Fergus told me you have found this Orb of Thermalism. I was wondering if we might put it to use."

Was she serious? "What do you want me to do? It's not as simple as me using my magic to destroy entire ships, especially if there are over a thousand of them. The only way we can stop the Swarmers is by getting the rest of the Orbs. There are three left, and Xara Mallis holds two of them."

"Xara Mallis is dead," Zheng said.

"She's alive," Lucian said. "She has two of the Orbs, and there is one more that hasn't been claimed yet. So I either need to go after Xara to get the two she has, or get that other Orb. Fighting the Swarmers is pointless, because they'll just keep coming. They can't be stopped until I find all the Orbs."

"Why does it matter?" Zheng asked. "Why do they care about these weapons?"

"I'm done talking," Lucian said. "You've turned my mother and friend against me. What else are you going to take?"

"Lucian, you're exhausted. If it's rest you need . . ."

"Serah is going to die, and it seems no one cares but me!"

"Does she require medical assistance? My doctors are as good as any you would find in the League. Perhaps even better."

The last thing Lucian wanted was for *any* person who worked for Zheng Yang poking around Serah's body. "No, there's nothing your doctors can do."

"Son," his mother said. "We'll figure this out, okay? I can't pretend to know what you're talking about, but what I can tell you is no one here's trying to get you. I won't let them."

"Do you know how many times I've been backstabbed? I'm not going to let it happen again. Either you're with me, or you're not. Getting the Orbs is the only way to stop the Swarmers. If you try to fight them, you're just going to lose lives and ships. And they'll just keep coming. And coming. There'll be no end to them. They destroyed the Builders over a million years ago, and they'll destroy us even easier."

He looked around at everyone, all of them looking at him as if he were a crazy person. None of them believed him. The Worlds were coming to an end, and they actually believed they could stop the *Alkasen* from wiping out humanity?

"What do you want me to do, Lucian?" Zheng asked. "Fergus trusts you, and that's enough for me."

"I don't understand why we're pretending you care. All you want is power."

"Listen," Zheng said. "I've been tolerant, but this is getting ridiculous. Do you need a nap or something?"

"I can't do what you're asking. I can't just magically shoot down ships with my hands, if that's what you're wanting."

"That's all I needed to know. Take some time to wash up and rest. And of course, you and your mother can catch up. I imagine you have a lot to say to each other. And of course, I'll send my doctors to your ship."

"Don't. No one steps on my ship without my approval."

Zheng raised her hands placatingly. "Fine."

"Come on," his mother said.

She grabbed him by the arm, leading him toward the elevator. Fergus, Lucian noted, stayed behind. Where were the man's loyalties at? Had Zheng somehow gotten into his head? What happened to all that talk about her being the definition of pure evil?

Physically, Lucian knew he could destroy whoever he

wished. But whenever that person had people he cared about in their employ and care, things got complicated. And confusing.

Even if his mother was alive, the circumstances deflated a lot of that happiness.

Lucian supposed he would learn the full truth soon enough.

———

WHEN THEY BOARDED *TALARIA*, Lucian simply didn't know how to feel anymore, so he felt nothing. Gaius had died, Serah was *almost* dead, Fergus's loyalties were questionable, he'd gotten a new Orb, and his mother was still alive, over two years after he had accepted her death. All this had happened in a few hours.

So, when he took up a seat in the ship's small wardroom, he couldn't do anything but break down and cry. Despite his exhaustion and his general state of filth, his mother held him as if he were still a child. That was all he had wanted for the past two years, but now that he had it, it wasn't helping in the way he had hoped.

"It's all right," she said, holding him tight. "I'm here."

After a while, he broke away. "I can't do this anymore. It's all too much."

"You need to rest, Lucian. You're tired, dirty, and hungry, too. I'll make you something to eat. Go take a shower, come back here, and get some warm food in you. Then go to sleep. When you wake up, I'll be here."

"I'm afraid you won't be."

"I will. Battle orders don't get carried out for another day or two. So unless you sleep that long, I'll still be here."

"What about Zheng? What if she has new orders for you or something?"

"She won't, and if she did, I'd give her a piece of my mind.

Not something I'd usually do, but you're my son. I won't let anything get in between that, even if I owe the Golden Armada my life."

"Okay. I want to know what happened to you first."

"Shower, food, sleep. I won't say a word until you do all three."

Lucian was about to argue until he realized just how pointless that was. He was the Chosen of the Manifold, but she was his mother.

He went to check on Serah, the window of the med pod no longer tinted. She looked almost peaceful lying on her back, eyes closed. He placed a hand on the pane, hoping that she might open her eyes. But she remained still.

He showered, and when he went back to the table in a fresh change of clothes, he found a warm meal waiting for him, along with a cup of herbal tea. He ate the food and drained the cup, his mother just watching him and smiling, as if content to do just that.

She took his tray and empty mug. "Go to sleep, son."

He headed to bed, a bed that seemed empty without Serah. Such was his exhaustion that he fell asleep as soon as his head hit the pillow.

29

LUCIAN SWAM through dreams and nightmares. Gaius stared at him accusingly, blaming Lucian for his death. The basilisk leered at him from the flames of the volcano. Lucian ran across the scarred surface of Hephaestus, but it seemed that no matter how far or fast he ran, he could not escape a nameless fear.

And deep in the recesses of his mind, a voice whispered.

Four Orbs, and the Lost Aspect, the Ancient One said. *No longer can you guard your mind from me. Soon, we will be one . . .*

Lucian ran faster, what little good that did him. The horizon seemed to stretch into the distance, into infinity.

Running is futile. The Joining is inevitable . . . just as I am inevitable . . .

Lucian reached with the Orb of Binding, to escape to the far horizon. But the Orb did not obey him.

Your path is set, Chosen. Never forget who the Orbs truly serve.

I'm the Chosen of the Manifold. They are mine.

Only on the promise that you complete the Joining.

At that moment, Lucian felt himself pulled forward by an unseen force. He gasped, stumbling to the ground.

Four lights spilled out of him. Blue, red, green, and violet. He did not have to ask what they were.

But one remained to him. He felt it being pulled at, but he assumed his Focus and held on to the Orb of Space-Time.

Ah, the Ancient One said. *That one will be mine, too. Soon enough.*

It was never yours. It will never be yours.

We shall see. You may have my four Orbs and the Lost Aspect. But already, my Psion of Darkness is working. You are already too late . . .

What are you talking about?

You will learn. Your path is set, Chosen. As is hers. Don't fail me.

The Orbs shot back into Lucian's body, and the shock of it rocked him from his dream.

———

LUCIAN SPRUNG UP IN BED, only barely holding back the scream that wanted to escape his lips. He reached out to find Serah, only to find she wasn't there, meaning she was still unconscious. He reached for his Focus, for his Orbs to make sure they were still there. He felt them resonating within him, a reassurance that the dream hadn't been real.

Deep down, Lucian knew an aspect of it *was* real, though. The Orbs, at least the original Seven, had some sort of connection to the Ancient One. A connection that would force him to join with him, should he gather all Seven into his Focus.

But there was a kink in the Ancient One's plan, a gap in his armor. He hadn't counted on the Orb of Space-Time. That one belonged to Lucian, entrusted to him fully by Arian himself. Perhaps there was a way to use it to "cleanse" the other Orbs of the Ancient One's hold.

The First Immortal, the Shadow Lord, had held all the Orbs, including that of Space-Time. But somehow, he lost his hold on that one while retaining some nominal control of the rest. That proved the Orb of Space-Time worked differently. Khairu had mentioned that the Old Masters of the Volsung Academy had theorized the existence of a Lost Aspect, though Arian surely knew what it was, and simply kept that information to himself. And Space-Time's depiction on the wall reliefs of the Starsea Sanctum, occupying the epicenter, told Lucian that it was the Focus of the others. That it somehow controlled them.

Even as he held it now, he was immune to the effects of the fraying. Magic didn't work properly without Space-Time to hold it all together.

Lucian needed to learn more, but he didn't know who to learn *from*. The only person who had made a study of it, Vera, would certainly not help him, nor would Xara.

The Psion of Darkness. Who was the Ancient One referring to? Was it Vera or Xara, or someone else entirely? Xara supposed herself to be the Chosen, so it could be none other than her.

Lucian pushed these thoughts from his mind. He couldn't answer them.

Checking his slate, he'd been asleep for a full ten hours. He got up and dressed in his Talent robes. If he had to meet with Zheng today, it would do well to remind her of what he was.

He found his mother drinking coffee in the wardroom. She smiled, pouring him a cup and pushing it across the table as he sat.

"All better?" she asked.

Lucian tried to push the thought of the dream from his mind. "I'm rested, at least."

Now having some of his faculties, Lucian looked at his mother's face. He noticed new lines, a gaunter appearance that had been absent before. Though she smiled, there was a tiredness to her eyes that was deeper than the last time he saw her.

It seemed she was looking him over, too. "I hardly recognize you. You left a boy, but now you're a man. You look ten years older. You've . . . been through things. That much I can see."

"That about sums it up."

"Well, which of us is going first?"

"You. Transcend White told me herself that you had died."

"Transcend White?"

"She's the leader of the Volsung Academy. The League even gave me a stipend for your funeral."

"How much?"

"2.5 creds."

She laughed. "Cheap bastards. Well, the pirates are paying me a lot better, at least. Not that my newfound riches matter a single whit. They keep me busy. That's good, though. Keeps my mind off things."

"So, what happened?"

His mother leaned back in her seat. "It's a long story. For however long mine is, I'm sure yours is twice as long, if not more."

"Tell me."

So, she told him over the next few hours exactly what had happened. Almost three years ago, the Swarmers had come down so fast and hard on Starbase Centauri that the fleet barely had time to prepare. She hadn't even boarded her own ship, instead doing training exercises on the carrier, *Refuge*. She'd been one of the few close enough to the escape pods to get out before the ship was completely torn asunder.

Her communications equipment had been knocked out, so she'd survived about a week floating in the cold vacuum of space, presumed dead. A week later, pirates scavenging the wreckage came upon her pod after detecting her thermal signature. She was imprisoned, taken on board their brig.

Later, the ship had been attacked by a League vessel. The brig got a couple torpedo shots off, destroying the League vessel, but not before railgun fire went straight through the ship's bridge, venting the compartment and killing both the ship's captain and navigator. Once the pirates had repaired the breaches, and having no other choice, they put his mother in the pilot's seat, as she was the only one who could fly.

Under these conditions, and other trials she pretty much glossed over, she piloted the ship the rest of the way to Brennus. But upon hearing her story, Zheng Yang made her a captain of the Golden Armada, a title which no one contested. Zheng put her in charge of one of her own destroyer squadrons dedicated to fleet point defense, which had been his mother's specialty during her time with the League.

Mira Abrantes had spent most of the last two years fighting for the Golden Armada, with no real plans of going back home, since she was considered dead by the League, and the working conditions with Yang's fleet were much more humane. However horribly people were treated outside her fleet, she treated those within it to a fair share of the spoils.

Lucian could only listen in shock and disbelief. His mother had always complained about life in the League fleet, but he would have never imagined her being a turncoat. Then again, it wasn't as if she'd really had a choice in the matter.

"So, that's the long and short of it," she said. "Sometimes, I can't believe it myself."

"Are you happy?"

She shrugged. "You know me. Nothing affects me much. Admiral Yang treats me well, so I can't complain. Can't say the same about my old C.O. And ever since that blowhard Richard Palmer got to be Hegemon, things just got worse."

"I have a few things to say about him."

"Oh? What's that?"

"We'll get there."

As they ate lunch, Lucian started his own story. He knew it was going to take hours upon hours, but he didn't want to leave anything out. He lost count of the times where she either gaped, or her eyes went so wide it was a wonder they didn't pop out of her head. She asked all the right questions, and Lucian had to give her a basic understanding of the Orbs and the mechanics of magic, but she seemed to get the gist of things easily enough.

By the time he was done, they'd gone through two pots of coffee. She just watched him incredulously.

"So, this Serah girl," she said. "You love her?"

Lucian couldn't help but laugh. "After everything I've told you about how the human race will go extinct if I don't find all the Orbs, *that's* your first question?"

"I'm your mother. I care about you more than all the stars in the galaxy. She seems like a plucky one. I always imagined you with someone calmer. Someone older, who could rein you in." She considered him for a moment. "You've changed, though. Now, you are the older one. You're the one who takes care of your partner, not the other way around."

"We take care of each other."

"Are you happy with her? What about this Emma girl?"

"She's a friend. I had feelings for her before, but we've moved on."

"All right. Well, things can be complicated, I get that. You know, before I married your father, there was another guy I was crazy about. Complete opposite of him. Bookish, had all these old poems memorized. He wasn't adventurous at all. Not like your father, but he was a handsome one. And he treated me well."

"What made you choose Dad, then?"

She smiled in memory. "Well, I just loved your dad when it came down to it. That's the hard truth. It was harder to love him, but I don't regret it for a moment. That's how I got you." She looked at him seriously. "You don't choose who you love. Everything can make sense in your head, but if your heart isn't in it, it's not worth a damn."

"Why are you telling me all this?"

"I don't know. You probably don't need my advice anymore. You probably know as much as me. Which isn't much."

"Well, I love her. No question about that. She's the light of my life."

"Glad to hear it. Love makes everything worth it. You can get through anything if you have love. And you've been through some shit, to put it mildly." She looked at him seriously. "So, this Serah is the real deal. When can I meet her?"

Lucian's face fell. "Soon, I hope."

"Well, is there any way to cure her?"

"Only by finding the Orbs."

"I can see why you said all that to Admiral Yang. I have to say, that took guts, kid. You know what she's done to people for saying much less?"

"I heard some from Fergus. Murder, to say the least."

"Yeah. That *is* the least. You're strong, Lucian. Not everyone is. Zheng respects strength. One might say it's the only thing she respects. While she didn't outright try to kill you, she left one thing out. She knew those Blackguards were after you, and she didn't say a thing. She meant you to die after you left Hephaestus Station, by omission. You shouldn't trust a word she says, despite whatever *I* say up there just to save my neck."

"Trust me, I don't. She just has my people. Fergus was forced to work with her because of the nanites in his blood. Serah's out of commission, and you work for her. She can always use my friends and family against me."

"That's true. Well, if she had a mind to get you out of the way before, she most likely doesn't anymore. She needs you."

"I already told her I won't help. I don't know what she's trying to accomplish here, but it's not going to work."

"You haven't figured out what she wants yet?"

"Power?"

"She wants to bring the League to its knees, Lucian. She wants to assume control of the entire government, and that includes the mages and the navy. Nothing less will satisfy her."

"Is this really the time? Even if she wants that, she has to see that the Swarmers will just kill her off too, in the end."

"You don't know her ambition. On Brennus, no one challenges her. Everyone who has ever tried has not only died, but died horribly." She lowered her voice, even though they were the only ones there. The fear in her eyes told Lucian everything he needed to know. "You think *I* want to work for her? Do you think I could escape, even if I wanted?"

"Come with us, then. I got what I wanted out of Hephaestus, and I don't care if I ever see it again."

"It's . . . not that easy, son."

"Nothing ever is. I will ask her once, politely, to release you and Fergus from your contracts. If she says *no*, then there'll be hell to pay."

For a moment, it almost looked as if she was about to laugh. And then, her expression became fearful. "Lucian, you can't mean that. She'll never agree. As you said earlier, she holds all the cards. We would never escape. And if Fergus is under contract, like you said, with no way out . . ."

"I have something she doesn't know about," he said. "The Orb of Space-Time. We don't *need* a ship."

"Okay, even so . . . she would never agree to let Fergus go, let alone me. I might not be killed the instant I run away, but he will be."

"I can convince her."

"How?"

"With the Orb of Psionics, I can force the issue. I just need her to physically release Fergus from the contract, and then we're good to go."

"You make it sound easy . . ."

"It won't be. Nothing ever is. But I'm not going to let her have you, or him."

"Son, that's crazy talk."

"It wouldn't be the craziest thing I've done. You said it yourself, Mom. You don't want to work with her. Fergus doesn't, either. As long as I can gather everyone together in the same spot, we can all go back to Earth. Or just about anywhere I've visited, really. From there, we can figure out what to do next."

"What about Xara Mallis?"

"I don't know what her next move is. And until I figure it out, there isn't much I can do. I can try to go after the Orb of Dynamism. We'll figure it all out later. We just need everyone out of here before everything blows up."

His mother looked down at the table, seeming to go deep into thought. "I can't believe we're seriously considering this . . ."

"*We're*? So you're coming around to the idea?"

"Well, after everything you've told me, we're all dead in the end anyway, right? Might as well go out with a bang."

"We're not going out with a bang. You just have to trust me."

"So, how does this Orb of Psionics thing work? You can just make *anyone* change their mind about something?"

"It requires a lot of power, and someone with a strong mind will be harder to break."

"That describes Yang."

Thought control was something Lucian tried to steer clear of, because of the moral dubiousness of the proposition. However, if there was *anyone* who deserved to have their mind tampered with, it was Zheng. Whatever her excuses, she'd tried to have him, Serah, and Gaius killed.

That could never be forgiven.

"As soon as she's released both you and Fergus, we're heading back here. We'll have to get Serah out of her pod, and then we can warp back to Earth. Either that, or I could create a gate, sort of like what I did with the basilisk. Except this gate would go somewhere, not space."

"And we'd just . . . walk through?"

Lucian nodded. "There's no way we can outrun her fleet with this ship. All I need is time to gather my magic. At least with the gate, it seemed to work a lot faster. It just required me to stream every Aspect of Magic. Difficult, but doable."

"I'll take your word for it, son. So, what do you need *me* to do?"

"Just give me access to Zheng. Ideally, we can get a private meeting with just her and Fergus."

"And you're certain of his loyalties? You said he and Zheng were lovers once."

"I'm certain. With the things he said about her, it's hard to imagine he still has feelings."

"You might be surprised. Remember what I said about love?"

"He doesn't love her, Mom. No way."

"Just be careful. Things could play out far differently than you expect."

"Well, even if that's the case, which it *won't* be, I can still get you back, at least. We would just need to return to the ship for Serah. And then . . ."

"The great escape. You're thinking Earth, then?"

Lucian nodded. "From there, we can get anywhere we need to go. For now, it's the safest place."

"And what about after? How long do you think I can live there before the Blackguards find me and use me against you?"

It was a good point, and something Lucian hadn't considered. Earth would be the hub of all League activities, and there was no way she could stay off the grid there for long.

"You can come with us," he said, finally. "We need a pilot, anyway."

"Seriously?"

"Yeah. After what happened with Gaius, we don't have one anymore. And you're the best one I know."

"Well, it *is* an idea. But we wouldn't have a ship."

"Ships come and go, in my experience," Lucian said.

"You're talking about something that costs quarter of a million creds, minimum. At least something that will crew as much as what you have here would cost half a million, plus."

"Well, we're not getting out of here with this ship, that's for sure. We'll find something, I'm sure. I've got my ways."

"There's Ravis, too."

Lucian scoffed. "He wouldn't give me a sub-cred more than your funeral expenses. What makes you think he'd give us an entire *ship*?"

"Because I'm his sister, and he owes me. You know most of the story now, but he made off with the family fortune. He can justify it however he wants, but I know there's some small kernel of guilt in him. He has something we can use, I'm sure of it." She looked at him seriously. "So, can you get us to Halia?"

"Yeah, I can. Just . . . are you sure?"

"You want a ship? That's how you get a ship. Unless you plan to work for the next hundred years to afford one."

Lucian most certainly didn't have time for that. "Okay. So, rescue Fergus. Get Zheng to release the contract. Get back to the ship and open a gate to Halia for Ravis's estate. Anything I'm missing?"

"That should be it. Is all that *really* doable?"

"Someone needs to put Zheng in her place. It has to be me."

His mother watched him, her eyes filled with respect. For the first time, Lucian knew she saw him as another adult, something he had always fought for in his old life.

No, not just an adult. Someone worthy of being followed.

"I'm behind you. If you need anything, just say the word. Only one thing."

"What's that?"

"Something you haven't really mentioned. I understand you want to go after the Orbs, that they are the only way to save the galaxy or something."

"Yeah, that's right."

"Well, what about this system? If we just leave, if we don't help Zheng, then tens of thousands stand to die." She looked at him critically. "You think you have the stomach for that?"

"I don't think I could save them, even if I tried."

"What if there's a chance?"

Lucian had to admit, it placed some responsibility on him. "I don't know. Why do you have to make things morally complicated?"

"I'm not pushing you either way."

Lucian stood. "I'm going to check on Serah. And I need to talk to Fergus, too."

"If you plan on calling him, all incoming signals are being monitored."

"No, I plan to use a Psionic link."

"Oh." She laughed. "I keep forgetting what you are. Seems like yesterday when I came home on leave, and you were this angsty teenager who was so *mad* at everything."

"I wasn't a teenager."

"Well, you sure acted like one."

Lucian couldn't help but smile. "Well, I had a good reason to."

"Go check on your girl. We've been yakking long enough."

Lucian left her there and headed to the clinic.

30

LUCIAN LOOKED through the window of the medical pod to see Serah still unconscious. It sickened him to see that, knowing that her eyes might never open again. He placed a hand on the pane, willing her to hang on just a little longer.

He sat in the jumpseat next to the pod, closed his eyes, and assumed his Focus. He reached out for Fergus, finding him easily.

Fergus. You ready to bust out of here?

It only took a moment for him to respond. *Lucian, I was wondering when I'd hear from you. But I'm afraid that won't be so simple. There's a lot going on . . .*

Here's the plan. I'm going to use the Orb of Psionics to force Zheng to release you from your contract. Doing it that way, I can be sure she disengages the nanites as well.

That's fine, Lucian, but have you not looked out of a viewport lately?

No. Why?

We're not outside Hephaestus Station anymore. We're about to be in the middle of a battle. I'm surprised Captain Abrantes is still down there.

Listen, Fergus. We need to gather everyone here on Talaria as soon as possible so I can warp everyone to Halia. My mom thinks she can talk my uncle into giving us a ship.

She thinks, or she knows? That's a pretty big risk...

Well, I don't have a better idea. If he doesn't want to, we can figure out something else. We don't have much time, so what else can we do?

Look, more's at stake than you realize here. If anything about this battle goes wrong, many people are going to die. Not just pirates, Lucian. Tens of thousands could die on Hephaestus Station alone, not to mention what would happen to Anchorpoint and much of the Mid-Worlds. If the Swarmers take over this system, it would be like a domino falling. The rest of the League would follow suit, hastening the collapse by months. Perhaps even years.

As much as Lucian hated to admit it, there was something to Fergus's point. Hephaestus contained most of the industrial capacity of the League outside of the First Worlds, not to mention hundreds of thousands of lives in the system itself. Maybe Zheng Yang controlling it wasn't ideal, but it was better than the Swarmers outright destroying it, or worse, using its industrial capacity to their own ends.

Fergus continued. *I know what you want is to go after the Orbs, and to hell with everything else. I get that. But if we allow Hephaestus to fall, there probably won't be much humanity left to defend. We need to stop them here.*

How sure are you about this?

One hundred percent. Zheng Yang will get her comeuppance someday. It's just not going to be now. I know you think you can change her mind with the Orb of Psionics, and I have no doubt that you can. But Zheng is strong-willed, and by the time you break her, her mind would be too frazzled to command the fleet. That would spell disaster. To leave now would certainly consign thousands upon thousands to death.

Lucian clenched his teeth. With just a few words, all his plans had gone up in smoke. Fergus was right, and there was no way around it.

What about you, then?

We can figure out what to do, assuming we survive the battle. With what we're up against, even with your help, victory is far from assured. But give her a victory, and perhaps she might be more amenable to releasing me early. If not, a year is not a long time.

We need you though, Fergus.

You found the Orb of Thermalism without me. I know how to handle Zheng. Having some sort of rein on her might be a good thing. I can advise her and control her worst proclivities. It's not what I want, but it's my part to play. At least, it is for now. I won't risk losing everything just because I don't want to accept my fate.

Lucian found he had no counter to that. *I can't fault you for saying that, I guess. If I can release you, I will.*

And I support that. But do not burn down the house trying. If you must go, then leave me here. You, Serah, and your mother can get out of here. Wherever you go, you can get access to a ship to find the Orb of Dynamism. Or maybe you can somehow get back to Talaria and warp it out, which cuts out the need for your uncle. Either way, I assume the Orb of Dynamism is next on your list?

Yeah. Either that or hunt for Xara.

Lucian remembered what his mother had suggested. Some of Fergus's old feelings for Zheng might confuse things. So, he had to be sure.

Are you sure being so close to her isn't . . . hurting your judgment?

There was a moment of hesitation. *Not at all. While I'll admit that being near her has somewhat unbalanced me, I've grown, and it's nothing I can't handle. Do what you must, Lucian. Decide amongst yourselves. But from me to you, I think you need to do whatever you can to help us out. It could be the difference between humanity falling, or not.*

You've . . . given me a lot to think about.

Don't take too long to think about it. I have to go. Good luck, Lucian. Whatever you decide. But if you decide to help, come to the bridge of Stars' Blood.

I don't trust Zheng. You know that.

I don't, either. But I'm afraid we don't have a choice. There was a moment's pause. *Farewell, Lucian.*

Lucian felt the connection sever. From Fergus's tone, it seemed as if he thought there was no chance Lucian would go up to the bridge. Lucian had to say Fergus was probably right in that.

Lucian looked down into the medical pod, and was surprised to see Serah's eyes opening. She gave a weak smile. He looked at the pod screen, seeing that whatever operation it had performed was complete.

He opened the door, leaned down, and cupped her face in his hands. To his surprise, she moved, sitting up and wrapping her frayed, mottled arms around him, hugging him with surprising strength.

"Hey, take it easy."

"I . . . feel fine, actually. I just might not look it."

"You're alive."

"Of course I am. It'll take more than a lava snake to kill me." She blinked and looked around the clinic. "Are we . . . on *Talaria?*"

"Yeah. Apparently, the pirates rescued it before it crashed."

"Then how are we here? We're not prisoners, are we?"

"It's a long story. I'll explain later."

How long was I out?"

"About a full day. Maybe a bit more. *Talaria* is docked on Yang's flagship."

"Rotting hell. I'm out for a day and everything goes to shit. What did I miss?"

Lucian didn't even know where to begin, so he started with the most shocking news. "My . . . mom is alive, for one."

Her eyes widened. "What?"

So, Lucian told her a much shorter version of the story his mother had told him. Short, because they didn't have much time.

"And she's on board?"

"Yeah. You'll meet her soon."

She looked down at her skin, horrified. "She can't see me like this!"

"It'll be fine. I mean, I already told her that bit, so she'll be expecting it."

"Cat's out of the bag, then. Lucian. I'm not ready to meet your mother! That's a big deal. I need to shower, try to remember my manners, which I lost somewhere on the way . . ."

"Well, sorry to say, but we don't have time for all that. We're about to be in a huge battle with the Swarmers in about . . ." He checked his slate. "An hour and a half now."

"Seriously?"

"Yep. Let me bring my mom in here. We should talk about it together."

"Wait! I'm barely clothed!"

She scrambled out of the pod, grabbing some Talent's robes that had been set aside for her.

"Do you really feel okay?" he asked.

"I'm not hurting. With fraying wounds, the pain comes and goes. And right now, it's gone." She looked up at him somewhat vulnerably. "Do I look all right? My hair's probably a mess . . ."

"Beautiful as always."

A smile tugged at her lips. "Well, I guess I should just take the compliment."

She checked to make sure her clothing was covering every part of her body except her face, though there was nothing she could do to hide the wounds marring her hands. She strapped her shockspear to the robe's side. With that action, she let out a small breath.

"All right. Ready as I'll ever be."

"You'll be fine. Don't worry. I'm proud to show you off."

"If you say so."

"Come on. Let's not keep her waiting."

He took her by the hand and led her out toward the wardroom.

———

LUCIAN FELT a little nervous as he and Serah approached his mother, who was sitting and enjoying a dark cup of coffee. He wasn't nervous about how she might react to Serah. He was worried about how Serah would handle the situation.

It would be fine. He had to tell himself that.

His mother turned at their approach, her eyes widening slightly upon seeing them together.

"Mom, this is Serah. My girlfriend."

"Err . . . hi," Serah said, her cheeks coloring slightly.

"Well," his mother said, looking her up and down, "he wasn't lying. You're a pretty one. How are you feeling, hon? Don't be shy."

"I'm not shy," Serah said. "Usually. I'm feeling all right, for now."

"We don't have time for shyness, anyway," Lucian said. "There's a lot we need to cover."

"What's going on?" his mother asked.

Lucian explained everything Fergus had told him, also catching Serah up on everything in the meantime.

His mother was the first to speak. "So basically, we have an hour to decide whether we can trust Zheng farther than we can throw her."

"Well, Lucian can throw her pretty far with his magic, Mrs. Abrantes. If it comes to that."

"Relax, honey. Just call me Mira."

The red of her cheeks deepened at the suggestion. "Of course, Mrs. Abran . . . I mean, Mira. Sorry. On Psyche, things are a lot less casual with these kinds of things. My mom died when I was young, so I guess I don't know how to act around you."

Lucian thought back to her father, Elder Ytrib, and his wife, Elder Gia. That must have been her stepmother. He had difficulty remembering their faces after so long, but Elder Gia did not look like Serah much at all.

"I'll just say this," Mira said. "You seem more wholesome than the girls Lucian used to hang around with. I got some stories to tell you."

Lucian almost choked. "We don't need to get into that . . ."

"I remember that one girl. What was her name, Lo? Oh boy, was *she* trouble—"

"New subject," Lucian said. "We have to decide what to do here."

"I'm interested in hearing about this . . . *Lo*," Serah said, her tone somewhat edgy.

"Maybe later," Mira said. "What's your plan, Lucian?"

"You're acting like I *have* one. Has Zheng reached out to you at all?"

"Nope. You'd think she would, if we're literally an hour away from a battle."

At that moment, the ship suddenly jolted, throwing them out of their seats. Lucian rolled across the deck, catching Serah in his arms. His mother clung to the table for dear life before the ship steadied itself.

"Well, looks like it's decision time," Mira said.

They both looked at Lucian, waiting for him to make the call. All he could think of was Fergus's words. Was Fergus being influenced by Zheng, or was Lucian truly needed to save the fleet and all the lives in this star system?

In the end, he decided he had to make the harder choice. "Let's get up there."

Mira nodded approvingly. "I'm right behind you, son."

"All right," Serah said. "Let's do it."

31

AS THEY RAN off the ship toward the central elevator that would lead them to the command deck and the bridge of *Stars' Blood*, Lucian reached out for Fergus.

We're coming up.

Glad to hear it. Hurry!

They shot up the elevator. As soon as the doors opened, they ran down the length of the bridge, where Fergus, Altan, and Zheng Yang stood side-by-side, surveying the battlefield before them. Lucian gasped at the sight. Spread out before them were hundreds of pirate vessels, all arrayed facing out into the system, ranging from long capital destroyers, smaller cruisers on the flanks, with swarms of destroyers, fighters, and bombers well beyond the range of the larger vessels.

Opposing them on the other side, much to Lucian's surprise, were only five enormous ships. And they hardly *looked* like ships, at that. They were huge hunks of rocks, ovoid and riddled with cracks that glowed blue. That light looked very much like a reverse Binding field, designed to hold the ship intact. Those ships, though, dwarfed everything on the field of battle, even *Stars' Blood* itself.

For now, both sides faced off, seeming to get the measure of one another. From the drawn faces of the pirates staring out the wide bridge viewport, it was clear no one had ever seen anything like it.

"Death comes," Zheng Yang said.

Fergus cleared his throat before answering. "For us, or for them?"

"That will soon be decided." She turned to Altan next to her. "Are we in range?"

"Aye, Admiral."

"Begin the bombardment."

Altan raised his slate, about the length of his hand, to his mouth. "Golden Pirates! Unleash hell."

At that moment, bright blue flashes of lightning extended from the Pirates' capital ships, all focused on the leftmost Swarmer carrier. The lightning smote upon the rocky hull, the energy seeming to be absorbed by the blue-glowing cracks binding the vessel together.

"Tachyon lances," Mira said. "Nothing can stand up to their fire for long."

"Recharge," Zheng said. "And fire at will."

After another thirty seconds, another volley of lances flashed outward, but this time, the fire wasn't as concentrated. Again, the rocky hull of the Swarmer carrier absorbed the impact, blue lightning now racing along the ship's outer shell.

And that shell disintegrated.

"Scratch one," Altan said, a pleased smile on his face.

They watched as the shell came apart like a cracked egg. But between those cracks, the blue light only intensified, holding the vessel together, at least somewhat.

"What in hell's name is that?" Altan asked.

"I'm afraid we are celebrating too early," Fergus said.

His words were like a prophecy. At that moment, hundreds of ships poured out from the cracks like swarms of locusts, a plague of vessels with the same rocky exterior as their mothership, shining with blue and white iridescence. They teemed as if of one mind, spitting concentrated lines of green lasers upon the front row of Pirate vessels already advancing to meet them. A few, and then a couple of dozen, instantly lit up in balls of flame, with only a few countering shots offered. One Swarmer vessel may have gone down, Lucian couldn't tell.

Zheng's face reddened, apoplectic. "*Where* are my destroyers?"

By now, the other Swarmer carriers were opening up as well, and between the bluish cracks came hundreds upon hundreds of Swarmer fighters, joining their firepower in wave upon wave. The battle became a chaos of green flashing lights, along with the answering white streams of kinetic railgun fire from the pirate vessels. As ships bristled around each other, hundreds of men were dying.

"Concentrate all battleship fire on those carriers," Zheng said, tensely. "Everyone else, deal with the fighters."

From the way things were going, it seemed Lucian had a front row seat to the end of Zheng Yang and the Golden Armada. But relentlessly, the Pirates fought on, somehow surviving against the onslaught. And all the while, Yang never called off the barrage of her tachyon lances. The original ship that had been fired upon received the brunt of these attacks, flash after blue flash of lances, extending kilometers from the capital ships, striking the egg-like carrier again and again. With each flash, it seemed it brightened even more, until it was white-hot.

"Break, damn you!" Zheng nearly screamed.

At that moment, the carrier shattered into a million pieces, exploding outward like a frag grenade. Pirate and Swarmer vessel alike were pelted with that barrage, and at least a couple of dozen explosions lit the darkness of space, including one from a larger Pirate cruiser that had to have been manned by at least five hundred souls. The ship veered off course, heading directly down toward the fiery surface of Hephaestus below the plane of battle.

"Next one," Zheng breathed. "Where is the relief force?"

"Still ten minutes out, Admiral," Altan said.

"Tell them to burn harder!"

At that moment, some of the debris from the broken carrier slammed into *Stars' Blood*. Most of it was deflected by the sudden flash of the electromagnetic shield, but several pieces slipped through, hitting at high impact near the bow, their momentum causing them to scrape along the upper surface of the ship. The deck rumbled beneath Lucian's feet.

"Multiple breaches," reported one of the female engineers, from a nearby console. "Fires in quadrants A and D."

Zheng cracked her neck. "Nothing critical. Vent them fully. Batten the hatches."

Lucian didn't want to ask how many lives would be lost because of that order.

"Hatches closed," the engineer said. "Quadrants A and D totally vented."

"Concentrate capital fire on the planetward carrier."

"At once, Admiral," Altan said.

New lances concentrated on the new target. Lucian noted that the number of green lasers had lessened somewhat, as if a good number of the Swarmer vessels were knocked completely out of commission.

"Just like the First and Second Swarmer Wars," Zheng said. "The carrier contains the mind of their dependent fleet. Knock out the carriers, and we can turn the tide."

"Looks like *we* might get knocked out first," Serah said.

Zheng turned on Serah, but instead of lambasting her,

focused on Lucian, realizing he was there. "*You*. How long have you just been standing there?"

"I don't know. Ten minutes, maybe?"

"And you have said *nothing*? I need you to blast these ships with your magic. You have this Orb, yes?"

"I do."

"Well, use it, damn you! Or would you have all of us die here and have the blood of this entire star system on your hands?"

"Well, you named this ship *Stars' Blood*."

"If you were anyone else right now, you'd have died long ago. *Horribly*. You know that, right?"

Lucian stepped forward, brushing past Zheng, Fergus, and Altan to get a good view of the action. Before his eyes, another Pirate cruiser went down under a hail of green lasers. The tachyon lances were having little to no effect on the second Swarmer carrier. There appeared to be some shield around it, Binding in nature. It would take some time yet before its defenses were overwhelmed. And if enough battleships armed with the heavy lances went down, there would be no hope of destroying it at all.

"I think you've bitten off more than you can chew. And you expect *me* to bail you out?"

"Yes! Don't you want to save the galaxy or something?"

"Well, yes. But that doesn't mean saving you from your mistakes."

Zheng screamed, raising a handgun in his direction. It was an action as pointless as it was pathetic. Lucian raised a Binding shield large enough to cover himself and his friends.

Zheng, seeing the display, lowered the gun. "What do you want, then? That's what this is about, isn't it? You're extorting me."

"Glad you've figured that bit out. As a pirate who extorts people for a living, I thought you'd be quicker on the uptake."

"Let me strike him down, Admiral," Altan said with a growl. "This insolence cannot stand!"

Lucian smiled. "Nor will you, Altan, unless I save you and your doomed fleet."

The man cursed and spat on the deck. "Cocky little runt, aren't you?"

"I'll ask you again," Zheng said. "What do you want?"

"Three things. Release Fergus from his contract. My mother as well." He thought for a moment. "And let me take *Talaria* and don't interfere with our escape."

She laughed. "You'll never get out of here with it alive."

"I hope that wasn't a threat, Admiral."

"It wasn't. You'll never outrun the Swarmers. They are faster than before. Stronger."

"Let me worry about that myself. Those are my terms. I don't think I'm being unreasonable."

"We can talk about that when you've done your part."

"I wasn't born yesterday. Do all three things, and do them now."

As soon as Lucian finished saying that, the flagship rocked again. A squadron of Swarmer bombers had broken through the main line for an attack run, raining heavy green lasers from above. Most were shot down by the ship's auto-tracking cannons, but it was a reminder that time was of the essence.

"Fine," Zheng spat, her eyes murderous. "Captain Mira Abrantes. I relieve you from all duties and rank in my fleet, to go wherever you will in the Worlds." She opened her own slate, showing something to Fergus. "And this is your contract, Fergus Madigan. It's tied to the nanites Vassar injected into you, as you can see here. As soon as I absolve it, you will be free."

Fergus looked at the contract, his eyes wide and unbelieving. This was all happening far faster than he had expected.

She held her hand over the screen for a second, as if second-guessing herself. She turned her face to the battle, in the vain hope that the action might prove unnecessary. But that notion was dashed as soon as one of their battleships lit up in magnificent explosions as at least a hundred Swarmer bombers broke through the disintegrating Pirate lines.

She thumbed the screen. "You're a free man, Fergus."

He nodded, closing his eyes in relief.

"Now," Zheng said, turning back to Lucian. "It's time for you to do your part."

Lucian watched the battle before him. He realized, if he so wished, he could gather his friends and warp them away. He could feign attacking the fleet before him as he gathered the requisite ether. Zheng wouldn't know the difference. By the time she figured out what was happening, it would be too late for her.

He didn't do so for three reasons. They would need a ship at the end of it all. His honor wouldn't let him, and it was more than the Pirates' lives at stake. If Zheng Yang, the Terror of the Stars, could hold herself to a deal, then Lucian Abrantes, the Chosen of the Manifold, could as well.

"I promise nothing, but I'll give it my best shot. Just keep in mind that I can't lose visual of my target at any time, or the magic will fail."

"*Stars' Blood* won't flee," Zheng said. "On that, you have my word."

Lucian nodded. He closed his eyes and reached for his Focus. The truth was, he wasn't sure his magic would be powerful enough to destroy an entire *starship*.

He supposed in a moment, he would figure out the truth.

32

LUCIAN DIDN'T KNOW the first thing about what to do. It was hard to tell the distance from the bridge of the flagship to the closest *Alkasen* carrier, but he'd never streamed so far, except for Psionic links.

But he had no choice but to try. And he had no choice but to delve the Manifold itself to complete the action.

He reached for all four of his Orbs, opening himself to them fully. Instantly, a flood of ether entered his Focus, ether which he gathered in a focal point just on the other side of the viewports looking out on the destruction. The Shadow Realm faded away, replaced by the Ether itself, a maelstrom of vibrant, rainbow hues, too dazzling to behold. To think this entire reality pulsed beneath the fabric of existence was almost too much to contemplate.

He shut out the vast sensory input, holding instead to his Focus, allowing it to channel the Manifold streams entering it. Magic gathered toward the focal point. He drew deeply from his Orbs, and less deeply of the Aspects that did not have an Orb. He used the Orb of Space-Time to compress the magic further. Magic rushed through him. If he let go, even for a moment, he knew his death, and along with the death of everyone aboard this ship, would be instantaneous.

Outside the viewport, a tiny crystal of light shone with unreal resplendence. All hands on the bridge covered their eyes as the point of light compressed even further, shining ever more brightly, like a miniature star.

"What are you doing?" Zheng asked, fear creeping into her voice.

Lucian ignored her. He strengthened his Focus, went deeper into the Manifold, became completely separated from the Shadow Realm. Here, there was only the Ether, trailing light absorbing into this spark of devastation.

He needed to draw more.

He opened another stream, a Binding tether designed to connect that crystal to the most distant of the Swarmer carriers. But such was the incredible mass locked within the tiny grain he'd created that it wouldn't budge even a nanometer. He needed to get the crystal into one of those carriers. But he couldn't stream it anywhere he couldn't physically see, and he wasn't sure it would be strong enough to destroy the ship itself from the outside.

Of course, if it was strong enough to destroy the Swarmer carrier from the outside, it was also strong enough to destroy the ship he now stood on.

Lucian knew the danger, but he couldn't stop building the crystal. To do so would be everyone's deaths.

He dipped out of the Light Realm long enough to be cognizant of what was happening in the Shadow Realm, his reality. Here, he could not hold the stream, and the longer he stayed here, the more the stream would be in danger of slipping from his grasp. He looked around to see nearly everyone cowering away from him, all except Fergus, Serah, and his mother, who watched with widened eyes. A rainbow tapestry of light was swirling around him, entering his body, only to be streamed outward from his hands toward the light crystal still growing in front of the ship. It wobbled, as if growing unsteady.

"Retreat," Lucian managed. "Do it now before it's too late."

That was all he had time to say. Just before he dipped back into the Light Realm, he had time to see that some Swarmer vessels, which had gone too close to the crystal, were being *absorbed* by it.

As time wore on, he saw additional shadows added to the crystal, getting absorbed as well. Small ones at first, and then larger ones could not escape its pull.

Ships, he realized. And the crystal was getting smaller, denser, and heavier all the time. The light it emitted was blinding.

Lucian realized that if he didn't stop it, and soon, he might make that point of light powerful enough to collapse into a black hole. Could such a thing be possible? Already, its gravitational pull was affecting the vessels around it.

And if Zheng Yang didn't retreat, it would be too late for all of them.

Lucian was nothing more than a conduit for magic. He couldn't stop feeding it, nor could he let go for an instant. As soon as he did, the resulting gravity wave would be enough to not only pulverize every ship in the Swarmer fleet, but the Golden Armada as well. It would be enough to destroy *Hephaestus Station*, sending it careening toward the planet below, assuming it was still on the same side of the planet as them. While it wouldn't destroy the planet itself, it would scar the surface far more than it already was.

You see it now, the Ancient One said. *Did I not tell you the power you would wield? You no longer recognize yourself. That is because you are no longer yourself. The Joining draws nigh . . .*

Leave me alone.

The Jewels of Starsea will not be denied. Do you really think you can resist them? Their power, their allure? Greater beings than you have fallen under their influence.

They don't sound so great to me.

Fool. Even now, you can't control what you've wrought! How will you escape the gravitational rip when you release the stream? You and your friends will be torn asunder.

Lucian continued feeding the stream, trying to push the voice out of his mind. Even so, the power of the gravity field was growing stronger, pulling more and more ships into its wake.

He screamed as he felt ether burning through him. He didn't know if it was possible for his own Focus to burn out from such power, but he was streaming all Seven Aspects at once, an action only possible because he was also streaming from the Orb of Space-Time. What would happen once that Orb decided it would no longer cooperate?

But it was behaving much differently than when he'd only had three Orbs. As Arian had said, the addition of another Orb had only strengthened it. Where would this power end? What could Lucian do with it, now that it was gathered? The only thing he couldn't do, he realized, was to stop it.

He ducked out of the Light Realm, finding that the Golden Armada was in full retreat. Several Swarmer fighters were getting pulled into the maelstrom, and its influence seemed to extend the longer things went on.

Zheng was screaming, and from the rawness of her voice, she had been for a while. "Stop! You're going to kill us all!"

There was no time. Lucian had to figure out how to finish this. But it had grown so large that there was no way *to* stop it, unless he were to physically remove himself from the situation.

So that was what he would have to do: remove himself from the situation.

That was when he felt the force pulling *him* forward. And that same force that was pulling him was also pulling the rest of the fleet.

With the last of his strength, he cut off the stream entirely, immediately redirecting the torrent of ether within him to create a rift. Only this time, the rift was so much larger, big enough for *Stars' Blood* to pass through with careful maneuvering. Already, a great many of Zheng's ships were pouring into it, drawn by the gravity of the seed crystal, which was pulsing with barely restrained power. Lucian didn't know how long it could last before the density was simply too great, and it exploded outward, destroying everything in its path.

The other side of that rift opened to the first place that had popped in Lucian's head; the planet Chiron in the Alpha Centauri System. There was no time to change the destination. The image manifested into reality. They had to escape there, or escape nowhere at all. Every second that passed, the compression of the crystal would lose strength. Lucian didn't know *when* it would blow, but he didn't want to stick around to find out.

"What the hell *is* that thing?" Altan breathed.

"Our only chance," Lucian said. "The crystal I created is going to blow up at any time, taking out anything within hundreds of kilometers. The only way out is into that rift. Order all your ships in."

His mother watched him with a terrified expression, while Fergus and Serah stared open-mouthed at the rift, through which lay a starfield markedly different than what surrounded it. A pearlescent line surrounded the elliptical plane, holding the rift in place.

To Lucian's surprise, Zheng did not question him as she raised her slate to her mouth. "Vessels of the Golden Armada. Burn ahead full to the rift that's just opened. If you don't, you will die. I'm going in first to prove that it's safe. That light you see is going to blow up, and any ship that's too close to it will meet its end. Again, burn ahead full to the rift!" She nodded to the female officer to her right. "Navigator Gardner? Full speed ahead."

"Aye, Admiral."

At that moment, Lucian felt himself pushed back as the ship raced forward. Many other ships rushed for the open rift, though some, Lucian saw, were hesitating. Others still were drawn toward the gravity of the crystal, unable to escape. The crystal, floating several kilometers away from the rift, pulsed and oscillated quickly at first, but then more slowly, like a spinning top losing its momentum.

As soon as that momentum was lost, the entire thing would collapse, unleashing a massive explosion.

"I don't know what you did," Zheng said, as she watched dozens upon dozens of ships disappear into the rift, "but it's going to cost me half my fleet."

"Better than all of it, Admiral," Lucian said.

To this, she made no reply.

Ahead of them, a flotilla of heavy battleships and light cruisers slid across the plane, though there were still many behind them. Most were advancing quickly, leaving *Stars' Blood* well behind. It was hard to say, but at least two to three hundreds ships of varying sizes and classes had made their escape.

By now, Lucian could sense the seed crystal's compression weakening. The ovoid Swarmer vessels were still in position, their fighters and bombers taking easy shots at the fleeing ships. Several smaller Pirate destroyers disintegrated under a brutal barrage of green lasers, keeling into each other and going up in balls of fire and debris. Half a dozen Pirate fighters were torn to shreds by pursuing Swarmer vessels. The tachyon lances of the Pirate battleships were useless at close range, and the railgun fire was too inaccurate to score anything more than a few lucky hits.

"Death," Altan said. "So much death . . ."

Stars' Blood shuddered as a line of Swarmer bombers flew over the crest of the rift, making an attack run over its kilometer long surface. Fires lit from the impact of green lasers, the shielding doing almost nothing to avert disaster. A couple of lasers found their mark on the base of the tower, causing the deck to heave beneath Lucian's feet. He flew into the air with such force that he was certain that the base had become separated from the rest of the vessel. But once he landed on his back, things were steady enough for him to stand.

Everyone else seemed to be okay, nothing more than bruises at first glance. A look out of the viewport revealed no more Swarmer vessels between the flagship and its destination.

Just as *Stars' Blood's* bow teetered into the rift, a blinding flash of light made everyone throw their hands over their eyes. The seed crystal had come loose, unleashing untold devastation at the speed of light, wiping out anything and everything in each direction. The only thing that kept *Stars' Blood* safe, along with any other ship fortunate enough to be in its shelter, was the plane of the rift itself. There was a thunderous shaking throughout the hull. Lucian lost his feet again, almost losing his Focus and causing the rift to collapse. But he held strong, knowing it was their only chance of survival.

When his Focus finally collapsed, he crawled up from the deck, remaining conscious long enough to see a spread of Pirate vessels before him. They were battered, beaten, but mostly intact. Already, the ships were arranging themselves, pointing their bows toward Chiron, just large enough to be covered by one hand in the distance.

Lucian was confident that the Swarmer carriers left behind had been destroyed. Against all odds, they had made it through the rift to safety.

If this star system, where the Hegemon was, could be considered safety.

33

THERE WAS a moment of shocked silence from all on the deck. Zheng blinked in surprise, hardly able to believe the sight before her.

"Chiron," she said. "So close to the heart of the League." She turned to Altan. "Prepare the fleet for battle."

"Battle? Are you crazy? You'll never win!"

She turned on him furiously. "What do you think *they'll* do as soon as they detect us? We have no choice but to fight."

Altan was scanning the LADAR screen furiously. "League fleet is moving, Admiral. Incoming hail request from the *LCS Volga*."

"Answer."

Altan punched the screen, accepting the incoming voice call.

"*Volga*," Yang said, cool as can be. "To what do I owe this pleasure?"

"This is Admiral Thoran of the First League Fleet. Identify yourself at once or face immediate destruction!"

"Admiral Thoran," Zheng said, with breezy confidence,

"this is Zheng Yang, Admiral of the Golden Armada, Terror of the Stars, Dread Pirate Extraordinaire, the Bane of Archea, et cetera, et cetera. Be advised that we have just entered a space-time anomaly, which is how we've found ourselves so suddenly in your system."

"You expect me to believe that? How did you manage to get this close without us spotting you?"

"This is Talent Lucian Abrantes," Lucian said, butting in. "She's telling the truth."

"Lucian Abrantes?" Admiral Thoran asked. There was a long moment of hesitation. "You're a wanted man. We've been told you have access to unlawful stealth technology, which you must hand over to the proper authorities."

"Oh, come off it," Zheng said. "We have no interest in killing you. I'm only preparing my fleet in case you try something stupid. In fact, you should be *thanking* us. You should be getting the news within hours."

"*What* news?"

"Why, our defeat of the Swarmer fleet attacking the Hephaestus System, of course. Despite being outnumbered and outgunned, I brilliantly led the Golden Armada to victory against a superior force."

Lucian got the implication. If she had won the battle at long odds, she could do so again. Never mind the fact she would have gotten nowhere without him.

There was a long moment of silence after this, so long that Lucian thought Admiral Thoran had cut off the transmission. But after a minute, his voice returned.

"This . . . will be verified. In the meantime, I've received direct orders from the Hegemon himself. Lucian Abrantes, you are ordered to report to the bridge of *Volga*."

"Like hell I'm doing that. He can come to *me*."

"You can do it in order to secure a temporary truce. Otherwise, we will fire upon you. Our preliminary scans reveal you to have less than half of our numbers, and many damaged vessels."

"Yeah, because we were in a battle with the Swarmers. You really mean to tell me you're going to kill a potential ally?"

"These are the orders from the Hegemon."

Lucian sighed. It looked as if there was no choice. He would have to face the Hegemon, and through him, Vera herself.

"Fine. I'll talk."

"A transport is already on the way. Please send your docking code to *L.S. Chengdu*."

With that, Admiral Thoran cut out.

"What does the Hegemon want with you?" Zheng asked. "We can't win an all-out battle with the League, especially with support from Starbase Centauri."

"It won't come to that. All he wants is me."

"He's going to kill you before you even get close," Serah said. "Vera won't risk him going face-to-face with you."

"Vera?" Zheng asked.

Lucian ignored her. "We have to get him before he gets us. Attack on our *own* terms."

"Attack?" Zheng asked. "All that earlier was a bluff, and damn it, that's all I have! I won't waste my fleet uselessly."

"You won't have to. The Hegemon isn't far. I should be able to warp Serah, Fergus, and myself on board. Between the three of us, I'm sure we can handle him."

"*Handle* him?" Zheng asked. "You mean assassinate him?"

"We need to get moving now. Just keep them busy, okay? We'll be done before they figure out what's going on."

"I won't let you risk my crew in this way," Zheng said. "You're getting on that ship!"

"Make me."

Before Zheng could say anything more, Lucian reached for the Orb of Space-Time. Having recently been used, it was difficult to grasp, but with the addition of one more Orb, that of Thermalism, the issue could be forced.

So, Lucian used it, streaming magic from the four Orbs into it. The bridge of *Stars' Blood* wavered before him, even as he fought to remember the lounge aboard *Volga*. Its reality was manifesting far more quickly than he would have guessed. It was amazing how one extra Orb aided the Orb of Space-Time's functionality.

Serah ran to him, just in time to enter the warp, though Fergus was not as quick. Lucian pushed his mother away with a small kinetic wave, just enough so that she wouldn't be risked in this dangerous gamble.

In the next moment, Lucian and Serah were standing in the Hegemon's lounge on *Volga*.

————

LUCIAN LOOKED AROUND to find the space completely empty. Empty glasses covered the tables, along with half-eaten trays of hors d'oeuvre and discarded cigars. There had been a party here not ten minutes ago, and no one was bothering to clean up.

"They must've heard we were coming," Serah said, popping a puff pastry in her mouth. "Hmm. Not bad."

"I don't blame them. Where is the Hegemon taken in an emergency?"

"It's *not* the Hegemon, though," Serah said. "It's Vera. Where would *she* be?"

The answer was obvious. "Right in the thick of it. I imagine right next to wherever this Admiral Thoran is."

"The bridge, then. So, it's us against an entire army, then? I don't want to kill dozens of boys who probably had no say in being here."

Lucian didn't like the sound of that, either. "Just remember, a lot of these guys are hardened killers. They will not hesitate to fire upon us to protect their lives."

"What do we do once we find him, anyway?"

"Simple. We get Vera out of his head, one way or another."

"I thought Transcend White said that would kill him."

"Well, maybe I just don't know what the hell I'm doing. But I want these Blackguards to stop chasing me around, and that doesn't happen until Vera is ousted. Maybe I can succeed where she couldn't."

At that moment, the elevator doors dinged. There was no time to hide, so thinking quickly, Lucian reached for the Orb of Radiance, streaming a light reflection stream Fergus had shown him during one of their many training bouts. With any luck, it would make them completely invisible.

The doors opened, and Lucian stared out at a red-armored Ranger sergeant, along with four blue-armored privates. All four had their visors down and coilguns in both hands, ready to fire.

They only stared and did nothing.

"Looks clear, Sergeant," one of the privates said.

"Nah. Thermal sensors went off. There's someone in here, skulking about. I just wonder how he got past security."

"*Your* security, Sarge."

"Shut it, Wardley. You and Garcia take point. Fan out, head for the kitchens. That's probably where we'll nab him."

"Damn," Wardley said, looking at the food. "The fat cats wasted all this grub…"

"I'll waste *you* if you don't get moving. You're an embarrassment to the League Rangers."

The two privates went wide, breezing past Lucian and Serah easily. Lucian stayed put. Any movement would cause the ward to recalibrate, creating a mirage-like effect that would easily get them caught. Lucian also reached for Thermalism, creating a small reverse stream that cooled the heat radiating from their bodies. If the Rangers did a thermal scan, they would be safe from detection.

The next two privates came forward, passing within a meter of them both. One of them paused for a moment, seeming to sense something, but ended up grunting and moving on toward the kitchen. The sergeant came last of all, clinking in his power armor and coming to a stop not three meters in front of them. Lucian readied himself to reach for Psionics.

As soon as the grunts were in the kitchen, the sergeant raised his visor, revealing a pockmarked man of middle-age with a brown walrus mustache. He looked over at a nearby tray of finger sandwiches, checked the kitchen door, and reached down with his armored glove, allowing the fingers to retract to pop the food into his mouth. He smacked loudly, his mouth wide open. Serah's face twisted with disgust.

Now, with a clear view of his face, Lucian had had enough. He reached for the Orb of Psionics and Binding, creating an overwhelming psychic stream that instantly knocked the man out before them as effectively as a blunt object right to the skull.

"Elevator," he said, quietly.

He and Serah ran, getting inside just in time. He pressed the button for the bridge.

One of the blue soldiers reappeared in the kitchen doorway. "Stop right there!"

But already, the doors were closing, and the elevator was shooting upward.

"Nice," Serah said.

"We're just getting started."

The doors opened, revealing a wide open bridge filled with at least thirty people, a mixture of technicians, engineers, and blue-uniformed fleet officers, all with their backs facing them, intent upon the fleet of Pirate vessels before them. The larger capital ships and *Stars' Blood* were visible against the backdrop of stars.

To Lucian's surprise, no one even turned at their entrance. Apparently, someone entering the bridge was an item not worthy of attention. And why would it be? Anyone who was here was someone who clearly had access.

It was almost too easy. When Lucian spotted the Hegemon facing away from them, easy to pick out from the blaze of wild, orange hair, he yanked him toward the elevator with a tether. The action was the equivalent of kicking an anthill, but by the time the officers reacted, raising guns and shouting orders, the elevator doors were closing, with Lucian flashing them a smile.

"Get your grubby paws off of me!" Palmer squealed.

"Come on, Vera. Make your appearance."

"Vera? Who in the ever-loving—" At that moment, his eyes went glassy and violet as his shoulders relaxed. "Ah. What is it you want with me, Lucian?"

"We're going on a trip," he said. "Shouldn't take long."

He reached for the Orb of Space-Time, finding plenty of juice for another warp. He formed an image of the bridge of *Stars' Blood*, and within moments, they were back on its deck, the possessed Hegemon in hand.

Everyone turned instantly upon their entrance, their eyes wide and faces shocked. Even Zheng was speechless, but she recovered quickly.

"Richard Palmer," she said. "Welcome aboard *Stars' Blood*. Now, would you be a dear and tell your ships to stand down?"

"Give me access to your control panel, and it shall be done."

"Don't give him access to anything," Lucian said. "He's being possessed by Vera Desai, the most dangerous mage in the galaxy." He cleared his throat. "Besides me, of course."

"Vera Desai?" Zheng asked. "Is that who you mentioned earlier? What am I supposed to do with him?"

"Just stand back and leave it to the professionals."

Palmer's beady eyes looked up at Lucian. "You try to oust me, Lucian, and you will bring about the deaths of millions. Do you *really* believe this oaf is capable of leading the League on his own? He needs a strong and capable hand to guide him, or all is lost."

"I might've agreed, if you hadn't made him send the Blackguards after me. Now, letting you possess him is far too dangerous. And I'd be stupid to allow it."

"You will kill him if you try. And for his death, the League will hunt you far harder than the Blackguards ever could have."

"The League has bigger problems on its plate right now. We're far past the point of talk. That's something you should've realized in your endless mechanizations. The only thing that I *don't* understand is how you can possess him when he isn't a mage."

"There are so many things you don't understand," she said, through the Hegemon. "Knowledge lost since the time of Starsea itself. Similarly, you don't understand what will happen if you dare attack me."

"It's too late for that, Vera. You are my enemy, and anything you want is the opposite of what I want."

"Then I won't plead my case. Fight me. If you dare."

Lucian wasted no time, opening himself up to the Orb of Psionics and reaching out for the Hegemon's mind. But as soon as he did so, the Hegemon glared and raised his hand, from which issued a stream of lightning.

Lucian hardly had time to raise a Dynamistic shield, only making it strong enough to somewhat eat the impact. The rest of the electric attack sizzled against him, pushing him back with sudden force.

"What the hell?" Serah shouted.

Lucian recovered, strengthening his shield in preparation for another attack, but already, just about every pirate on board was gunning the Hegemon down. He went down on his knees in a pool of his own blood, struggling for a moment on the deck before going still.

It had all happened so fast that Lucian could hardly believe it. He refused to believe that Richard Palmer was actually a mage. That meant that Vera had somehow transferred her power, or at least some of it, to him, gambling that the shock of the attack would be enough to end him.

He remembered her words clearly, spoken through him: *There are so many things you don't understand . . .*

Whatever the case, the fact of the matter was that Vera's prophecy had come to pass. The Hegemon was dead. If not by his hand directly, then through his actions.

"Well, Lucian," Zheng said. "I think you have some explaining to do."

"RICHARD PALMER WAS BEING CONTROLLED by Vera Desai, who basically wants to take over the Worlds. She's Xara Mallis's . . . teacher, you might say."

"Xara Mallis?" Zheng frowned. "What does *she* have to do with this?"

"She's alive. She hasn't revealed herself yet, but she probably will soon."

"Who *cares* about all this?" Serah said. "They saw us disappear with the Hegemon. They're going to find out what happened soon enough."

Altan growled. "No one will breathe a word standing here on this deck. Not a soul."

Heads nodded all around. Despite Altan's words, Lucian didn't believe it. There were about twenty people on this bridge who witnessed the event, and even if no one said anything, the Pirates would be blamed.

"It'll be war with the League," Zheng said, somewhat regretfully. "I knew it would come to that someday, but if we get the first shots off while their fleet is in disarray, we might have the chance to scrape out a victory."

"War with the League?" Lucian asked. "Are you insane? We need to be pointing every gun at the Swarmers, *not* each other!"

"Unless you can get us out of here, that's what's going to happen. Getting back to Hephaestus at this point would be nice, too. Really, Lucian, are you so naïve? What do you *think* the League will do when they realize the Hegemon is gone?"

"Then run."

"What do you think they'll conclude if I order these ships to go full burn toward the Astravan Gate?"

"They'll fire everything they have on us," Fergus said.

Zheng shook her head almost sadly. "A pity. This Vera was right. Your actions have killed him, and now you've gotten us into some really deep shit. You've forced my hand long before I was ready."

"They outnumber us three to one," Altan said. "It won't be an easy fight, even against League dogs."

"Battle stations, all," Zheng said. She looked hard at Lucian, as if wondering what to do with him. If he were not as powerful as he was, he knew that she'd order him killed. She settled instead for waving him away.

"Take your ship and go. Unless you mean to turn your magic on the League itself, along with your mage allies?"

Mira wasted no time. "Lucian, Serah. Come on, let's go. You too, Fergus."

She led them to the elevator, and Lucian expected a shot in the back at any moment. He raised a Binding shield, just in case, but no one made a move to attack.

They were free, at least for now.

———

THEY WERE RUNNING JUST as the alarms sounded. Beleaguered pirates ran to their battle stations just after they'd thought the battle over.

"I don't trust that she'd let us off so easy. She expects us to go to *Talaria*, so we have to go somewhere else."

"Where?" Serah asked.

"*My* ship. In the confusion, we'll be out and away before she realizes what's happening," Mira said.

"And when she *does* realize?" Fergus asked.

"Well, let's just hope that she doesn't."

Serah sighed. "*That's* reassuring."

Mira led them to a wide hangar far away from the tower that contained the bridge. They were just one among dozens of pilots jumping into their vessels, many of which were scarred from the recent battle. Mira's vessel stood alone, what looked like a larger version of a ripsaw fighter, jerry-rigged from multiple parts. Though larger than the typical one-man craft, it would be a tight fit for four people.

"That thing doesn't look fit for flying," Fergus said.

"Well, it's all we've got. Unfortunately, it's not meant for travel in deep space."

"So, how are we supposed to escape?" Fergus asked.

"I've got a plan."

Lucian just had to trust her. He climbed the ladder into the ship, which was nothing more than four seats, each with a control panel in front.

"Don't touch anything," Mira said. "We'll be out of here in a jiff."

The deck rocked below the bomber, causing it to skid a bit to the side. With a grimace, Mira powered on the engines and joined the line of ships already shooting off into the black of space.

The radio crackled to life. "Bomber forty-two," came a deep, male voice. "You are not cleared for takeoff. Power off your engines and await further orders."

"Roger that, Control."

Mira made no move to power off her engines, continuing to follow the line of bombers.

"Bomber forty-two, this is your final warning. Power off immediately, or face annihilation."

She shut the radio off. "Almost out of here."

Although a couple dozen bombers had yet to take off, the hangar doors were already closing. The front bomber in the line squealed to a stop, causing the rest behind it to follow suit.

"Looks like they're onto us," Fergus said.

Mira swerved to the side and powered the engines on full. Lucian was pushed back into his seat as the ship roared ahead, right for the narrowing crack in the hangar doors. Serah screamed, either in terror or excitement, or perhaps both.

They weren't going to make it. At the last moment, Mira turned the ship sideways, barely squeezing through the opening and breaking free of *Stars' Blood*.

"That was the easy part," she said.

"Mrs. Abrantes, you might be crazier than your son."

"We're just getting started."

She weaved through the squadron of bombers, heading straight into the thick of battle ahead. Already, the League fighters were going after the Pirate bombers heading for an attack run on a nearby League battleship, *Estonia*.

But Mira didn't follow them. She went off on her own course, heading under the wider League fleet, keeping a fair distance away from the battle.

"We just need to get close enough to the planet," she said. "If we can get into the atmosphere, we'll be safe."

"If we can get past the fleet."

The ship jerked suddenly, avoiding a stream of white-hot railgun fire. She swerved again, avoiding another stream of fire.

"Shit," she said. "This might've been a bad idea . . ."

"Are we seriously going to die?" Serah asked.

Not if Lucian could help it. He reached for the Orb of Space-Time, setting an anchor point in the distance, just beyond the last of the League battleships, while he formed a gate right in front of them. Instantly, the ship skipped ahead, tantalizingly close to Chiron's atmosphere.

"I can never get used to that, son," she said. "That magic is something else!"

"Torpedoes!" Fergus said. "Thirty seconds to contact."

"Warp us again, son."

Lucian was more than happy to oblige, but this time it took far more effort. Still, he moved the ship several kilometers away at a point into the distance, far enough away for the torpedoes to lose the scent.

"Prepare for atmosphere entry," she said. "Geez, looks like all ocean down there!"

"We have no choice," Fergus said. "Go!"

Within the next few minutes, the ship shook from entering Chiron's atmosphere.

Lucian could tell this bomber was never meant for atmospheric operations. It dropped like a rock, but Mira did everything she could to slow its descent.

They broke the white cloud layer to find themselves above an endless expanse of ocean. Only a single island broke the monotony. It was toward this island that Mira flew.

"You're the best pilot in the universe if you can make that," Serah said.

"Watch and learn," Mira said, cracking a smile.

Lucian had never seen this side of his mother before. It took some getting used to.

Soon, they were racing over the surface of the water, the entire ship shaking around them. The island in the distance was fast approaching.

"This might get bumpy," she said. "Hold on!"

As they glanced off the top of the water multiple times, Serah's screams ripped through the cockpit. The ship slowed precipitously, dancing along the water as massive waves flew into the air and crashed down on top of them. The ship bobbed for a moment on the waves, floating.

"That was some landing," Fergus said. "Everyone all right?"

"Still alive," Serah said.

"Same," Lucian said.

Mira was already unstrapping herself. "Told you. Easy peasy." She looked through the forward windshield. "I meant to get us a bit closer to that island, though. That'll be a swim"

"That's no problem," Lucian said. "Everyone, on top. I'll tether you over."

They did as he said, his mother opening the cockpit to the open air. A warm, humid breeze descended into the cockpit, sweltering with its heat. Lucian unstrapped himself and stood, heading for the nose of the craft, where his mother stood. Fergus and Serah stood behind.

Mira looked out at the island, a low green mountain covered with trees. "You can get us over there, son?"

"Want to go first?"

"Well, one of us has to. From what I remember, this planet doesn't have any major predators. Hopefully, what I learned in school isn't failing me there."

"Nothing more advanced than bugs on this planet," Fergus confirmed. "Though you have to watch out for the sky-locust swarms, but I doubt they would be anywhere out here."

"That doesn't sound pleasant at all." She nodded. "All right. Are you going to disappear me over there or something?"

"Something a little simpler," he said. "Ready?"

"Not really, but let her rip."

Lucian used the Orb of Radiance to enhance his vision, allowing him to set an anchor point on a distant tree. He tethered his mother, who, with a shout, flew across the blue surf toward the island.

"Looks like she's having fun," Serah said.

He slowed the stream just before she landed. She fell into the sand, quickly standing to look back at them.

Lucian tethered the other two over. Serah was so practiced that she was practically flying. Once all was done, he tethered himself last of all, joining the rest on the sand.

"I've seen some crazy shit," Mira said, "but magic by far has to be the craziest."

"What now?" Serah asked.

"Well," Fergus said, "it would appear we're in the middle of nowhere."

"You don't say?"

Lucian headed off into the trees, lightheaded from all the streaming. At last, the power of the Orbs was receding. He needed to rest.

"Hey," Serah called. "You okay?"

Lucian made it to the base of a tree with wide boughs and long, hanging tendrils of green. He closed his eyes, unable to focus. Even as the others ran toward him, all he saw before he faded was the lapping of the blue waves on the white sand.

35

HE STOOD in a grand chamber filled with many columns, rising high to a sandstone ceiling. Upon an altar shone a yellow Orb, what Lucian knew to be the Orb of Dynamism.

It was the same vision he'd had while reaching out to Ansaldra's prophecy all those months ago. It was ephemeral, though, fading to black before reappearing.

The Orb of Space-Time would show the way. The Chosen would know the way.

Of course. Could it be so easy?

Lucian reached out for the Orb of Psionics, connecting its magic to the Orb of Space-Time, treating it as if it were Ansaldra's prophecy. As soon as he did so, the image of the columned chamber returned.

So, *this* was what Arian had meant about the Orb being used to find the rest. It didn't merely feel out their locations. He could literally *travel* to them immediately, using the visions supplied by the Orb of Space-Time. The visions worked as well as memories, forming anchors toward which the Orb of Space-

Time could convey him. Just as it had with the Orb of Thermalism. How had he not seen it before?

"Lucian?"

He blinked himself awake. The sun was setting now in the west, casting the ocean red as blood. How long had he been out?

"We've got trouble," Fergus said. "The bomber's sunk by now, but now there are Pirate vessels flying above us."

Pirate vessels. Did that mean Zheng Yang had actually *won* her battle? Such a thing seemed inconceivable, but perhaps the League had panicked at the disappearance of the Hegemon.

Lucian stood facing out to sea. There was no way off this island, nothing but the Orb of Space-Time he held.

And he meant to use it to go to his next target immediately: the Orb of Dynamism.

"I've figured out how to use the Orb of Space-Time properly," he said. "To find the other Orbs, I mean."

"What are you talking about?" Serah asked. "I thought you already *knew* how to use it."

"Not like I do now. I can take us directly to the Orb of Dynamism. Right now."

They looked at him as if he were crazy. Lucian didn't blame them.

"Seriously?" Fergus asked.

"It works like Ansaldra's prophecy," Lucian said. "Remember how I got those visions of the Orbs when I reached out with Psionic Magic? Well, it seems Arian's prophecy wasn't just that data stick I got from him. It's somehow stored in the Orb of Space-Time itself. His prophecy is a revelation from the Light Realm, and he must have discovered it by connecting to the Orb of Space-Time himself. Only, *he* wasn't the Chosen, and he didn't have any other Orbs. So he couldn't use it."

All of them were silent as they thought of the implications. His mother just looked confused and worried.

"Son, you've done enough for one day."

But Lucian couldn't accept that as an answer, especially if Pirate vessels were plying the sky. "We've got to get moving. Who knows how long we'll last out here, and it's going to take some time to gather the ether to make that distance. It would be much farther than I've ever been. That much I can sense."

Mira still looked worried, but she didn't contradict him. That was how Lucian knew that things had changed between them.

"If you're sure," she said. "We'll keep watch."

"Where is this place you're seeing?" Fergus asked.

"It looks like some sort of temple, similar to the others. Looks like it's made of sandstone, though I can't be sure."

"Well, that doesn't tell us much."

"It's where we have to go. After that, we'll only have two more Orbs to find. The ones Xara has. I'm not sure if I'll be able to travel to them directly, but it might be possible."

"This is happening too fast," Serah said. "We *literally* just got the Orb of Thermalism a couple of days ago! What if there's another irate beastie guarding this one?"

"We'll deal with that when we get there. This is the way out. I'm taking it."

"All right," Fergus said. "If that's what you think is right, then I'm ready."

"We'll keep watch," Mira said.

Lucian nodded his thanks. He wasn't sure where to perform the warp, so he just found a relatively flat rock and sat down on it. Another ship screamed overhead, but hidden as they were in the trees, it wouldn't find them. Lucian wasn't even entirely sure if the ships were looking for them.

He sat on the rock and closed his eyes. He hesitated a moment, feeling a moment of doubt. What if this *didn't* work? It was a ridiculous thought. It had worked with the Orb of Thermalism. How much more would it work if he actually knew what he was doing now?

Hesitating wouldn't make things any easier. He reached for the Orb of Psionics, and streamed into the Orb of Space-Time, pulling on it as if it were a mind to be read. Instantly, the image of the temple returned, so real that it was as if he were there.

Magic poured through him, coalescing into the image, roaring out of him in a torrent. A gate formed before him, and through it, he could see the interior of the columned space.

Then, he stepped into the image, as if stepping into a picture. The others followed.

He realized the Orb of Space-Time could be used in different ways. The first way was warping, instantly teleporting him and whatever was around him to the target location. The second was this, creating a space-time rift and stepping through it at his own leisure, a rift that would disappear as soon as he let go of the stream. Each had its own uses, but warping seeming to be better for quick operations over short distances, while rifts seemed to be more effective with long distances. That was not how he had been using the warps, though, at least in the beginning, which might explain why the action had taken so long to perform. He was learning as he went, possibly the only being to use Space-Time Magic since the creation of the Gates millions of years ago.

When he turned to look back, he saw the island beach shining under starlight. Fergus and Serah stepped through, along with Mira, who looked at the new environment with wide eyes.

Lucian let go of the stream, and instantly, the rift winked out of existence.

He turned to look around the wide open space, a forest of columns, each of which gave off an ethereal, yellow glow. There were no doors or windows, only this seemingly endless expanse of pillars. The air smelled cool and damp, of earth and buried things.

"What *is* this place?" Mira asked.

Lucian reached out with the Orb of Space-Time, feeling a pull from directly ahead of him, where the light was brighter. "Where the Orb of Dynamism is."

They followed him along the path between the pillars. Looking left and right, it seemed there were more, hundreds upon hundreds more, as far as the eye could see.

He stopped short between two pillars when a fence of electric light bridged them, blocking his passage. His face was just centimeters from being electrocuted.

Instantly, streams of lightning crisscrossed various pillars, forming a maze of electricity. There were only two available paths now between the pillars. Lucian had to choose between two of them.

"Which way?" Fergus asked.

"Neither is what we want," Lucian said. "This seems to be my test. But this maze is so large that we'd drop dead before we ever found the end of it."

"Could you stream a shield?" Serah asked.

Lucian reached out to the lightning before him, getting a sense of the electricity's strength. He shook his head. "No mage in the world is powerful enough to counter that. It's powered by the Orb of Dynamism itself."

"What do we do, then?" Mira asked.

"We cheat. Get close to me."

Using the Orb of Space-Time, he warped everyone immediately on the other side of the barrier, completely bypassing the obstacle. The action was instant, and barely used any ether.

"I have to say," Fergus said. "That was pretty nice."

They walked ahead again, only to be blocked. Lucian warped them again, bypassing the electric barrier. More barriers emerged, trying to block their path, but whoever had created this maze had not counted on the Orb of Space-Time.

After an hour had passed, the air itself was brighter, shining with the radiance of the Orb. It couldn't be far now.

Another hour, and it was so bright that it was almost impossible for Lucian to keep his eyes open. Fergus streamed a Radiant ward to dim the light, allowing them to continue on.

With four primary Orbs, and another so close, the Orb of Space-Time was in no danger of petering out. A few more warps, and they stood before a wide set of steep stairs, leading up to the pedestal, upon which stood a shining nova of yellow light.

The Orb of Dynamism.

"Stay here," Lucian said.

He ascended the steps, and feeling as if he were in a dream, he reached out for the Orb.

Only to be repelled by an unseen force.

Unworthy, a female voice whispered.

The maze is impossible, Lucian said. *No one could finish it in a lifetime.*

That is the point. The Ascendant Beings prophesied that only the Chosen of the Manifold can have my Orb. Thus, I have made it impossible to test their foolishness.

Lucian didn't have time to play games. He shrugged his shoulders, and created a gate on the outside of the barrier, small enough for his hand to slip through, and another on the inside. To his surprise, it worked. He reached his hand in, grabbed the Orb, and pulled it back out.

I guess I'm the Chosen.

There was no response from the Oracle as he absorbed the Orb without sentimentality. It was just another step on his path, and he would not shy away from it. Within moments, it was absorbed, having fully joined the others.

At its absorption, the blinding light faded, and all the electricity dissipated from between the columns, throwing the chamber of pillars into darkness. From far away came a resounding echo, a sound Lucian could not exactly place.

He streamed a light sphere and went down to join the others.

36

BUT WHEN HE reached the stone floor below, he stood alone. The others were nowhere in sight.

"Guys?" he called. "Where are you?"

The cold air shifted toward his right. He turned, but saw nothing that could have caused it.

Then, the hairs stood on the back of his neck.

The shadow was back. And this time, he would confront it.

"Show yourself! Why are you following me? Who are you?" He turned around madly, looking for the source. "Answer me! What did you do to my friends?"

A low cackle sounded from the darkness of the columns. A cackle Lucian recognized immediately. He had heard it during his vision on Psyche after he had taken control of the wyverns.

"Where you end, Chosen, I begin."

Even with the Orb of Radiance, Lucian could barely see the shadowy shape shifting before him. It hung between two pillars, oscillating in the darkness.

Lucian cast a stream of light in that direction, but it did

nothing to illumine the Shadow's source. The Shadow had slunk off.

"You can't stop me, Chosen. The Joining draws nigh. Five Orbs of the Seven you now hold. And another lost to time. The time has come to meet your fate!"

The Shadow charged forward. Lucian released a blinding pillar of light from the Orb of Radiance, hitting the Shadow directly in its center. But the Shadow merely disappeared, reappearing elsewhere.

"Accept me," came the voice, from behind this time. Lucian whirled around, but saw nothing. "Accept me, and this suffering ends."

"Never."

Lucian created a light sphere, brighter than any he had ever made. This Shadow could not hide from him. But there were so many pillars that it was impossible to dispel every shadow where it could be lurking.

Lucian's chest heaved. "What do you want from me? Who are you?"

"Don't you know? I've told you this before. With each Orb you gather, I become stronger. And when you've gathered them all, I will no longer be this entity of shadow. I will become whole. Just as you are whole."

The Shadow eddied in the darkness of a pillar, forming the shape of a man. The man had no features, nothing but an elongated smile and baleful, red eyes. Those eyes peered into Lucian's soul, chilling him to the bone. It seemed somehow familiar, which only lent to its eeriness.

Lucian raised a hand, emitting a green laser, but the Shadow did the exact same thing, a mirror reflection. The lasers met in the middle, forming an orb of white-hot energy that grew in power before Lucian cut off the stream.

As did the Shadow.

Lucian grimaced, then shot off a kinetic wave, but so did the

Shadow. Even as he knocked the Shadow back, he himself was thrown through the air, and only a quick tether saved him from breaking his back on the pillar behind him.

Lucian floated to the ground, gathering magic from the Orb of Thermalism, concentrating it with Radiance and Binding. With a roar, he released a column of liquid-hot fire, fire that melted the surrounding pillars. Again, the Shadow did the same thing, and where the two columns of heat and flame met, lava dripped down and sizzled on the floor.

Lucian cut off the stream, and the column of fiery lava dissipated. "Why are you copying me?"

"Copying you? I *am* you, Lucian. As you are me. How many times must I tell you before you believe it? You are my Chosen, just as you will choose me. It is destiny, the Manifold's will."

"I don't know what you're talking about."

"No? Well, you must get to the end of your path first. All will be made clear. In time."

Lucian made to attack again, but the Shadow faded, and Lucian felt that he was truly alone. Somehow, he was now standing before the empty pedestal that had once held the Orb of Dynamism.

He heard voices behind him, and saw Serah, Fergus, and his mother waiting at the bottom of the stairs.

"Lucian!" Serah said. "Hey, you hear us?"

He looked into the distance, at the destruction wrought by his magic . . . only to find that the pillars were whole. Had he imagined that whole thing? Was he going mad?

"What just happened?" he asked.

"We saw you nab it," Fergus said. "Then you just stood there a few minutes. Were you having a vision?"

"Something like that." He suppressed a shudder. He saw something moving toward the right, but when he turned, nothing was there. Whatever had happened, it wasn't just his imagination or madness. The Shadow Lord was real. The Ancient One.

"He's . . . coming for me."

"Who is, Lucian?" Sarah asked.

"The Ancient One. I . . . can feel him. I see him sometimes. I said nothing about it before, because it scared the shit out of me. But just now, I saw him clearly. I could hear his voice talking to me, as real as any of your voices. He was just in my head at first. Then, once I got the Orb of Space-Time and Radiance, I started seeing things move in the shadows. But when I looked, nothing was there. It happened again on board *Talaria* after getting the Orb of Thermalism. And it happened just now. Only this time . . . he's almost real."

"Lucian . . ." Serah said.

"Don't tell me it's nothing. Don't tell me it's my imagination. He . . . said I would become him. That there's nothing I can do to stop it."

They all just looked at him. He knew he had to sound crazy. And who knew? Maybe he was.

"There was this sound we heard earlier," Mira said. "I wasn't the only one. Maybe we should go see what it is."

"I heard it, too," Fergus said. "Sounded like a door opening, or something. Should we go see? Or maybe use the Orb of Space-Time to go after the last two Orbs?"

Lucian shook his head. "I . . . need a break. All this is too much. I need answers. I need to find out if I can stop this . . . Joining. It will do no good to find the final two Orbs, only to have everything undone if I become a different person. The Shadow Lord is real. I can't allow him to get any stronger. At least, not until I have a plan to stop him."

Fergus looked at him pityingly. "I don't know what to say, really. There's Transcend White. She might know something. Something tells me it'll be hard to talk to her, given everything that's happened between the Pirates and the League."

Everyone stood for a moment, thinking.

"It's not all hopeless, is it?" Serah asked.

"Wait," Fergus said. "I have an idea. I don't know how viable it is . . ."

"What?" Lucian asked.

"The Mako Academy is far, but its masters are long-reputed to be the most accomplished of mages. They don't interact with the outside world, instead devoting themselves entirely to the study of the Manifold. It is said they don't often speak, but perhaps they have answers. Travelers often go there, for meditation or study, for finding direction. They stay at their monastery in the high cloud forests."

"You think those old guys know something?" Serah asked.

"If they don't, no one does."

"I can't exactly use a gate to get us there," Lucian said. "I've never been to Mako, nor anywhere remotely close to it. Volsung would be the closest place I've been."

"Mako is a spinward Border World, seven Gates from Volsung, if I remember right," Fergus said. "That would be a long journey."

"Especially without a ship," Mira said. "Maybe we can warp back on board *Talaria*. Perform the heist of the millennium."

"Even so," Fergus said. "From Volsung and using *Talaria*, my guess is we're looking at a three months' journey, minimum. Maybe two with a perfect orbital configuration of Gates, which isn't likely."

"Do we have that long?" Serah asked.

"Maybe, maybe not," Lucian said. "The Swarmers losing at Hephaestus should slow them down, or at least give them pause. Whether it's enough of a pause, who can say?"

"Well, I'm for it," Mira said. "We need answers, and this seems like a good way to get them."

All of them watched Lucian for the final decision. It was not an easy decision to make, but in the end, it was necessary.

"I think it's the right call. Better to delay the mission a few months to be more sure of things. Because if I keep going like I am now and get all the Orbs, then I don't think I can stop the transformation. If these Mako mages have learned a lot about the Manifold, then maybe they know a way to protect me. Maybe they can help me find the Heart of Creation." He thought for a moment. "And maybe they can remove this brand Vera has on me, once and for all. Transcend White mentioned they might succeed where she failed."

"It's decided," Fergus said. "But maybe we should get out of here first. We might learn about where we are. For all we know, this *could* be Mako, or at least a planet close to it. The Manifold does funny things sometimes. All of us should know that by now."

"That's a good point. Now, where is this door supposed to be?"

Mira pointed. "Pretty sure I heard something coming from that way." She looked at Lucian worriedly, then hugged him. "It'll be all right, son. We'll figure this thing out. You'll see."

He closed his eyes, hoping that was true.

Together, they walked away from the central dais, down an aisle of columns toward the exit. Lucian had never felt less certain of the future. But no matter his feelings, he had to pursue that future. Not only for himself, but for humanity.

If he didn't, no one would.

EPILOGUE

WAYFINDER FELL into orbit above the violet-shrouded world of Psyche. Vera and Xara had made record time; a journey of only three months.

But with everything that still had to happen, Vera could not be satisfied. Out the forward viewports, she watched the thick, turbulent clouds below, with her Psion standing beside her. Vera held her abdomen, where Lucian had given her the wound that had nearly ended her life. The ache was dull now, but the pain was still there. Vera had the feeling it would remain for the rest of her life.

Perhaps it was better that way. As with all things, it was a matter of perspective. She could be bitter over this wound, what Lucian had inflicted on her in blind ignorance. Or, she could let it serve as a reminder of what would happen if she underestimated him again. The young mage was like a bull, raging with anger and power, caring nothing for the plans she had laid. But even the strongest of bulls tired eventually. She could have never predicted the Lost Aspect would be so powerful. An Aspect that apparently controlled space and time itself, and perhaps other dimensions inconceivable to the human mind.

That power was wasted on Lucian. He would fail. He *had* to fail. He would grow tired, or make a mistake. And that was when she and Xara would strike. How prideful he had been, daring to risk even the Hegemon's life. Well, that was not what *truly* had happened, but the Worlds wouldn't see it that way. It was an opening, an opportunity for Vera to enact her final plan.

After everything, Vera had faith in her prophecy. Xara was the true Chosen of the Manifold, and Lucian a mere pretender. Leaving the Orb of Thermalism for him to find was a sacrifice, but a necessary one. And it was likely that after Hephaestus, he would go after the Orb of Dynamism, to face Xara on a more sure footing. For all Vera knew, he had already found it.

She and Xara had talked it over, and they had only one option that made sense. With the Swarmers on the rise, the Golden Pirates stirring, and even rumblings of Sharo Khalin's coming crusade, they could no longer stand alone against the galaxy.

They, too, would need an army. And Psyche was where they would find it.

While Ansaldra Dara would never follow Vera, she *would* follow Xara. Perhaps even that old fool Jagar could be brought around, assuming he hadn't gotten himself killed.

"What do you think, Master?" Xara asked, breaking Vera from her reverie.

The silence continued until Vera had her thoughts in order. What she had to say wouldn't be easy, but it had to be said.

"Do you remember before you followed me from Volsung? How even you didn't believe my prophecy?"

Xara's eyes became reminiscent. "That was . . . long ago. I believe fully, now. If I didn't, would have I let billions die in my name?"

"Your belief is not in question. Your oath of fealty was seven-sealed, so you cannot go against it. Not until I release you."

"Why mention the oath, Master?"

"Because the time has come for me to release you from it. I have nothing more to teach you, my Psion."

Xara looked at her, stunned. "Master?"

Vera gave a small smile. "Yes, I've often preached the importance of power, to never let it go. So you must be flabbergasted that I would give up mine so willingly. After all, if you've secretly dreamed of destroying me these long years, you will no doubt strike me dead now. Even I couldn't withstand the power of the Orbs wielded by you."

"I . . . don't understand."

"No? Well, perhaps then this will be my last lesson. There is something more important than power. It is the fate of the human race. We two are the only ones left who can save it. What's worth saving, anyway. I have taught you everything I know, and it is time for me to pass the torch. You have served me well, and thereby, humanity. For I am, above all, a servant of humanity, though it may not look it on the surface. But it is time for the next step. There is another who can teach you, one far more powerful than me."

"Who can be more powerful than you? You can't mean . . ."

She trailed off, and Vera's lack of answer was answer enough.

"Are you afraid, my Psion? Or are you ready to embrace your destiny?"

Xara's face hardened. "I fear nothing. I'm ready."

Vera closed her eyes. It was hard to say the next words. Harder than anything she had done in recent memory. But she willed herself to say them, all the same.

"Xara Mallis, I release you from your oath."

At these words, a slight shimmer of magic surrounded Xara,

barely perceptible. Over the next few seconds, that shimmer faded to nothing.

"It's done," Xara said. "I can feel it."

"As in the days of the Mage War, it is time for you to take the lead. It is time for you to swear your allegiance to a new master. One that has chosen you for your sacred role."

At this point, Vera stepped out of the way, and Xara gasped.

Beyond the doorway leading into the corridor, a Shadow lurked. A Shadow that seemed, to Vera, to be smiling, though there was no discernible face.

Xara at last found her voice. "Are you . . .?"

"Kneel, Xara Mallis," the Shadow whispered, its voice like the rattle of dead leaves.

Xara kneeled, eyes still wide.

Vera watched the Shadow approach, passing over the deck like a dark cloud. Despite her own fortitude, she had to force herself to look. Her wound seemed to throb as it brushed past her. When it reached Xara, she shuddered at its cold embrace. Its dark presence oscillated before her.

"I choose you, Xara Mallis," the Shadow rasped. "You are the instrument to enact my will upon the Worlds. Do you submit yourself to me?"

Xara looked up, her eyes no longer fearful, but intense. "Yes, Ancient One."

Seven colors swirled around Xara: violet, gray, red, orange, yellow, green, and blue, a rainbow tapestry.

"Then it is done. The Joining shall soon come to pass. When it is complete, you will wield power untold. And with that power, you will save your race from certain doom."

"What about Lucian?"

"He will be dealt with. Do you not have faith in me?"

"I believe in you utterly, Ancient One."

"Then rise, my Psion," the Shadow whispered.

Xara rose. The magic surrounding her did not dissipate, as

Vera had expected. In fact, that multicolored power seemed to shift, connecting Xara to Vera herself.

Through that linking, Vera could sense something in her former Psion shifting. Something that made Vera go cold. She reached for her Focus, but there was no magic to be found.

"Xara. Why are you blocking me?"

The Shadow vibrated. "Lucian is strong, a greater threat than even you know, Vera Desai. Against him, your plans have failed thrice. You failed to turn him on Halia. You failed to destroy him on Nai Elyn. And finally, he drove you from the Hegemon himself. And now, he has every Orb, save what Xara holds now. Your service to me has come to an end. My new Psion will need every bit of power to survive the coming storm."

Vera licked her lips. Always, she had seen the next move, but she hadn't seen this. When had she become so blind?

"And she shall have my power. I offer my counsel and my magic. As I always have."

"You have already shown the value of your counsel. We require . . . more. There is a magic from the days of Starsea, forgotten in this backward age. A magic that can only be used by the most powerful of mages. I have shared this knowledge with Xara, to use as she wills."

"You hid this from me?"

Vera's attention shifted to Xara, whose gaze was somehow . . . *hungry*.

"I see," Vera said. "Ancient One, you have used me to my fullest extent. And now, you wish to dispose of me."

"You have guessed correctly. You said it yourself. It is time to pass the torch. But not merely your ascendancy. You must pass on your knowledge, your power, and even your very Focus. But for that to happen, you must die as Xara wields this magic in my name."

Vera, despite her utter calm, could not reach her ether, and she was far too weak physically to resist. She knew in that moment, far more than any other time in her life, she was to die. *Truly* die.

She faced Xara, her head held high. "You can have my power, either directly to wield yourself, or indirectly in my person. The choice is yours."

Xara's face was as hard as stone. Through this tether, which Vera was powerless to remove, her former Psion could *feel* her Focus, could sense its potential. She could imagine what it would be like to join its power to her own indefinitely.

It would take every ounce of willpower Xara had to resist it. Assuming she even *wanted* to resist it. Already, Vera knew which way the scales would tip. She had taught Xara to seek power, to enact her will on others, at almost every cost.

"The Manifold wills it," Xara said. "You've lived a long life. A full life. But my need is great, as is humanity's."

"Then I will not beg. Do what you must do."

Without sentimentality, Xara drove her spear right into her former master's old wound.

Rather than grasp at her Focus, that numbing crutch, Vera allowed herself to feel the pain. For so long, she had forced herself to feel nothing, to become the person she had become, all in preparation for this moment. It was not how she had imagined it. She had always guessed she would enter death with her deeds unsung, but she never envisioned a death so inglorious. A betrayal from the woman toward whom she had dedicated her life.

Without her Focus to mollify her, all she felt was regret. But before that regret could crystallize into further awareness, Vera went blind with horrible, wrenching pain as Xara twisted the spear cruelly, ushering in a new wave of agony.

But the physical pain was nothing compared to what came next. As Vera fell to her knees, the seven-sealed tether absorbed multicolored streams of light from her sternum. Everything that was hers, everything she had cultivated over the decades, left in a frenzied rush, as if it had never been. Her power, her magic, even her thoughts and memories. All of it left Vera and entered Xara, whose body radiated with ethereal brilliance like some angelic being.

Vera maintained awareness, but nothing more than that. There was only the pain, and then, eternal darkness.

———

XARA WITHDREW HER SHOCKSPEAR, panting for breath. Her body was afire with potential magic. The magic that had once been Vera's now thrummed in her own Focus. It was the same feeling as absorbing an Orb, except . . . *more* exultant, if such a thing were possible.

It would have to be enough to command the mages of Psyche, to bend Ansaldra to her will, to lead them to the stars and victory.

Even as she felt her old master's power, she felt nothing for the years they had spent together, most of that in hiding. It was merely an act undertaken for the sake of the future. Vera understood that as well as Xara, and she had faced her death bravely. It was all Xara could ask.

When Xara glanced around the bridge, the Shadow was gone. Her mind swirled with thoughts and ideas that weren't her own, thoughts so overwhelming that it would take days of meditation to sort them out and form connections.

But all that would come later. For now, there were more pressing concerns.

"Alistair?" she called.

The clanking of Alistair's metallic steps resounded from the corridor. When the droid stood in the doorway, he regarded Vera's dead body with his red, emotionless eyes.

"There's been an unfortunate accident, Alistair. Would you see this cleaned up?"

Though the droid had no feelings, it seemed to be calculating a new balance. One that estimated Xara to be his new master.

"Of course. And the body?"

"Space it. Once that's done, set course for the ruins of the Golden Palace."

THE END OF BOOK SIX

THE STARSEA CYCLE CONTINUES IN BOOK SEVEN

THE PSION OF DARKNESS

ABOUT THE AUTHOR

Kyle West is the author of a growing number of "science fantasy" series: *The Starsea Cycle, The Wasteland Chronicles,* and *The Xenoworld Saga.*

His goal is to write as many entertaining books as possible, with interesting worlds and characters that hopefully give his readers a break from the mundane.

He lives with his lovely family in the Atlanta area.

twitter.com/kylewestwriter

facebook.com/kylewestwriter

ALSO BY KYLE WEST

<u>The Starsea Cycle</u>

The Mages of Starsea

The Orb of Binding

The Rifts of Psyche

The Chosen of the Manifold

The Prophecy of the Seven

The Fires of Hephaestus

The Psion of Darkness

<u>The Wasteland Chronicles</u>

Apocalypse

Origins

Evolution

Revelation

Darkness

Extinction

Xenofall

Lost Angel (Prequel)

<u>The Xenoworld Saga</u>

Prophecy

Bastion

Beacon

Sanctum

Kingdom

Dissolution

Aberration